In praise of
NANCY HOLDER

"Take an unfettered imagination, add an enviable skill
at characterization, mix with a prose style
as clear and smooth as polished crystal,
and you have the fiction of Nancy Holder."
F. Paul Wilson

"Nancy Holder . . . consistently provides her readers
with genuine wit, emotion, and real people
in stories that always deliver what they promise.
It's as simple as this: there is no one better."
Charles M. Grant, World Fantasy and Nebula Award-winner

"Nancy Holder's writing is fresh and fun, immensely
entertaining. She packs her tales with action and
fascinating characters about whom the reader must
learn more. A talented writer not to be missed!"
Yvonne Navarro, author of *Final Impact*, *Species I* and *Species II*

"Nancy Holder's stories . . . are invariably
beautifully written and quirky."
Locus

Other Books by
Nancy Holder

GAMBLER'S STAR BOOK ONE: THE SIX FAMILIES

GAMBLER'S STAR

BOOK TWO:
LEGACIES AND LIES

NANCY HOLDER

AVON · EOS

AVON BOOKS, INC.
1350 Avenue of the Americas
New York, New York 10019

Copyright © 1999 by Nancy Holder
Library of Congress Catalog Card Number: 98-93648
ISBN: 0-380-79313-X
www.avonbooks.com/eos

First Avon Eos Printing: April 1999

AVON EOS TRADEMARK REG. U.S. PAT. OFF. AND IN OTHER COUNTRIES, MARCA REGISTRADA, HECHO EN U.S.A.

Printed in the U.S.A.

WCD   10   9   8   7   6   5   4   3   2   1

In memory of my father,
Kenneth Paul Jones, M.D.
who always woke me up for the launches,
and for Brenda Van De Ven,
who gave me the stars.

ACKNOWLEDGMENTS

Writing a book is hard work, and I'm grateful to everybody who made this one easier.

My thanks first and foremost to Stephen S. Power, my first editor on the *Gambler's Star* trilogy, who founded Moonbase Vegas and gave me my spaceship. And with profound gratitude to my new editor, Diana Gill, for a creative and harmonious partnership which I hope will last until at least 2010.

Many thanks to my agent, Howard Morhaim, who is the best agent on Earth, and to his assistant, Lindsey Sagnette, who is always looking out for me.

Christopher Golden is a true friend indeed, and never was that more apparent than when I was approaching splashdown. If you hadn't sailed out on the *U.S.S. Buffalo Bill*, I probably would have drowned. Thank you, Chris.

Without the friendship of Stinne Lighthart, Karen Hackett, Linda Wilcox, and Barbara Nierman, this would have been a very lonely journey.

Kisses on the cheeks of the Baby-sitter Battalion: Ida ''Idy'' Khabazian, April Koljonen, Lara Koljonen, Bekah ''Bah'' Simpson, and Julie Simpson.

And finally, thanks to my husband, Wayne, for his unfailing support and belief in me and in my work, and thank you, Belle, for lighting up my life.

PROLOGUE

From the Captain's Log of Gambler's Star:
I include this in the record:

MEMO: TO MR. HUNTER CASTLE, CLASSIFIED A-1
SUBJ: HISTORY OF CASINO FAMILIES

A brief summation:

By the end of the 1900s, the mob Families had divided the
world (that is to say, Earthside) into various territories, but
the general feeling was that there was not enough "action"
to sustain the standard of living enjoyed by most top gangsters. A series of covert turf wars occurred, but basically,
all that happened was that the same pies got cut and recut
in varying portions.

Don Giovanni Caputo was the first Godfather to propose
territorial expansion on the Moon, which he did in 2013 at
a large gathering of the Caputo Family. His Family ex-
pressed interest, but no real action was taken in that direction.

Then, in 2022, as you know, the Quantum Instability
Effect was discovered by the posthumously named Ka-
boomtown Rats, the group of scientists who died in the first
QI explosion, which took out whole city blocks surrounding their laboratory.

Within five years, Quantum Instability bombs, each
about the size of a car, were plentiful and cheap. They were

shrunk down and then referred to as Quantum Instability Circuits, or QICs. The resultant Quantum Instability Wars of the 2030s took out half the population of Earth and destroyed almost all the vegetation.

Working together, the major nations of Earth achieved a successful countermeasure to the QICs. The Quantum Stability Field was created. So-called Feynman Fields were raised over cities and villages, townships and rural encampments, and the fields activated. The QICs were rendered useless.

As a result, a postwar world government—the Conglomerated Nations of Earth—was born. Rebuilding, reseeding, and repopulating began. As did the various illegal activities of the mob Families.

About the same time, the right-wing religious organization known as the League of Decency sprang up. According to them, the Wars were a direct result of God's punishment on a world steeped in sin. Only when sin was eradicated from the Earth would peace truly descend upon the world.

The League mushroomed in size and political muscle, until even the president of the Conglomerated Nations was forced to pay them homage. Don Giovanni, still in power, exploited the mob Families' fear of the League to renew his pressure on his Family to go to the Moon. At the same time, it was widely believed that Don Giovanni was conniving with the League of Decency to criminalize Earthside gambling. Some even accused him of creating the League himself.

Then, in 2042, a much-anticipated wrestling match was held in Earthside Las Vegas at the Gotti Memorial Coliseum, located in the heart of the Vegas strip. The primary combatants were the now-legendary Archangel and Doom Lord.

The super arena was sold out, and betting was more frenzied than the food riots had been. Massive distrust arose as to the ability of all the bookmakers to keep track of the betting, and a team of neuralinguists and AI experts and an elite team of crack bookmakers worked around the clock to produce a computerized system that rivaled the International Integrated Stock Exchange. Known as the Betting

Board, it was officially accepted as the medium through which all bets would be processed.

Although Archangel was heavily favored, he lost the match when Doom Lord actually bit off his ear. This caused a riot, during which Don Giovanni Caputo and his young granddaughter were covertly executed, mob style.

Then the entire place exploded, along with the entire Las Vegas strip. Despite the presence of the protective Feynman Field, which should have rendered any kind of Quantum Instability device useless, a Quantum Instability Circuit had been detonated. In less than a second, every man, woman, and casino within a twenty-mile radius of the Gotti Memorial Coliseum were destroyed. Several mob Families were completely wiped out. So was most of the cabinet of the Conglomerated Nations. It would have been worse if Las Vegas had not been encased inside a protective dome to prevent the poisoned atmosphere from killing everybody. The blast was successfully contained inside.

About six months later, the Conglomerated Nations assured everyone that they had detected the nature of the QIC that had been used; that they could reveal nothing about it except that it had been much smaller than the earlier version; and retrofitted all the Feynman Fields to prevent a repeat occurrence. But rumors also spread that the Conglomerated Nations themselves had set the QIC off to hasten the criminalization of gambling and the destruction of Las Vegas, in order to please the League of Decency. Stories were circulated about hit lists of casinos. Of other crime dons slated for execution.

At Don Giovanni's funeral, Giancarlo Caputo, the new Godfather, had begged the Family not to take up the gauntlet flung at them by the League and coopted government officials. Fighting back was foolish and useless. He urged the Family to fulfill Don Giovanni's dream and relocate their vast empire on the Moon.

By this time, transnational industrials were mining the Moon for its rich mineral deposits. The Caputos catered to the miners by building a casino and brothel directly on the surface. They brought up the first headliner on the Moon— Cosmotica, direct from Berlin.

By this time, the helium-dust boom was on, and the miners began moving out of their barracks and building themselves houses out of iron manufactured from lunar ilmenite. They began to marry and start families. The Caputos built the first supermarket, library, and school. The miners were grateful for the many goods and services the mob Family provided, and treated the Caputos very, very well.

However, Topside radiation was a big problem. In search of the titanium, iron, and aluminum in the soil, the miners burrowed beneath the surface, and everyone decided they liked it better down there. The Caputos went underground with them, and started building the Lucky Star Casino.

As soon as it was apparent there was money to be made, the other mob Families wanted in. Twenty-one Families made their way to the Moon. With the disgruntled Caputos, who had no wish to share the spoils, they formed a loose cartel to build the enviro-dome and fit it with one of the new and hopefully improved Feynman Fields, and bring in the other amenities and utilities. But in those early days of jostling for position, more hits went down than power stations went up. It was a bloodbath, and at least two of the Families—the Mitchells and the Goldbergs—were completely wiped out. Other families disappeared through alliances, mergers, and marriages.

The general populace appealed to Earthside to curb the violence. They requested that the remaining fourteen Families be barred from the Moon. The League of Decency added its voice to the call for deportation.

But the Conglomerated Nations had a problem: They had had the foresight to levy hefty taxes on the Families' Moonside profits. Eventually a solution was reached: The Families would be managed. Rather than allow them to continue to run things in an atmosphere of lawlessness and chaos, their dealings would be codified and regularized. They would be overseen by a governmental watchdog organization called the Department of Fairness. Their elaborate vendettas, the various insults and dishonors and percentages of deals and house cuts and who knew what all, would be kept track of by the Betting Board. It would be reworked and called the Charter Board.

For decades, the Families fought against these measures. Finally, acknowledging defeat, they worked with the Department of Fairness, providing their own talent to assist in the retrofit of the Betting Board. As one Conglomerated Nations senator pointed out, they had cooperated in the building of the domes to assure their survival, and no one had ever tampered with them. No one had ever attempted to disable or outgun the Feynman Field. To harm one was to harm all. So it would be with the Charter Board.

In return, it was the League of Decency which was banned from the Moon. Anyone found to be a member of the League would be instantly deported.

It was also felt that fourteen Families were too many to deal with. Romantic legend has it that the Scarlatti don, tired of the carnage, suggested the survivors get together and roll a die and let the outcome determine how many Families should share the Moon. In actuality, six Families successfully colluded and bribed the new Department of Fairness to give them, and them alone, permission to carve out territories on the Moon: the Chans, the Smiths, the Van Aadamses, the Caputos, the Scarlattis, the Borgiolis. The DOF officials pointed to "studies" to make sense of this seemingly arbitrary decision, and a sufficient number of senators were paid off to vote the plan into law. The six Families' rights were protected by Charters. If anyone else wanted to build a casino on the Moon, they would have to be unanimously approved by all six Families as well as by the DOF.

Once the the monumental DOF bribe was made and accepted, the six Families dissolved their brief, secret alliance. For appearances' sake, they pretended to get along after that, and basically kept their more brutal business to themselves.

Soon after, the League of Decency, furious at having been banned from the Moon, pushed through legislation that made Earthside gambling completely illegal. It was swift and it was total. The eight other Families, having reluctantly agreed to the loss of the Moon because they assumed they would still profit from Earth gambling—dangerous though it might be—howled in protest. These eight became known as the DFs; the Disenfranchised Families, and went underground, operating all their activities secretly after that.

Respectfully submitted,
Jameson Jackson

Note: Jimmy, I appreciate the history lesson, but since I lost most of my own family during the QICs, I'm familiar with the territory. If you can gather information about their dealings since the Six Families gained control of the Moon, that would be appreciated.

H.C.

Addendum: I'm most interested in the lineage of one Deuce (Arturo) McNamara di Borgioli. See what you can dig up about his past. Thanks.

H.

MEMO: TO MR. HUNTER CASTLE, CLASSIFIED A-1
SUBJ: HISTORY OF ARTURO BORGIOLI

Hunter: As you know, the Moonside Liberation Front has influenced Moonsiders to tell strange little Moon fairy tales as a form of indirect discussion. In researching Arturo Borgioli's heritage, a wizened old woman of that Family told me the following story:

In the age before people knew how to measure time, a lonely orphan child roamed the world unloved and all alone. He had no mother, he had no father. He had no friends, and no one who met him cared to be his friend. Such was his pain that he thought he would burst from carrying so great a heartache.

Today if a young child were to suffer as this orphan had suffered, he would cry for a year and a day, and his tears, though bitter, would provide some measure of release. But this orphan lived before tears were created.

But this wandering child was not truly alone. Each night, Moon rose to the highest point in the sky and watched over

*the boy. As he watched the suffering, he pitied the child
with all the depths of his great being.*

*One night, Moon did not rise to his perch. Instead, he
walked the earth in search of the suffering boy. He found
him and urged him to let his sorrow flow out in the form
of tears. This the orphan did, and thus were shed the first
tears of world.*

*But Moon knew that these tears would contaminate the
earth. Crops would not grow. Animals would perish. And
so he caught the tears of the orphan's grief on his own
body. When the tears fell to Moon's flesh, they left dark
stains.*

*When Moon brought the boy release with his tears, he
also bestowed on him a blessing. From that day forth, the
boy was loved and admired. He was never alone or sad
again.*

*As for Moon, he bears the stains of the boy's sorrows as
a reminder of his sacrifice. For had the tears fallen, the
earth would have perished.*

Then she said this:

"Deuce McNamara was an orphan. A Moonsider born,
and the Moon loves him. But that will not spare him from
sorrows, for he is the son of Connie Lockheart."

I have found no listing for a Connie Lockheart in any
records. I will keep looking.

Respectfully submitted,
Jameson Jackson

Note: Jimmy, thanks. That's enough for now. Much appreciated.

H.C.

ONE

"Don't go in there, sir. It's not safe," Billy Jester warned Deuce. "If this is a setup, you might be next."

Ignoring the bodyguard, Deuce staggered through the smoking remains of what had been, until two hours before, the conference room aboard Hunter Castle's huge space vessel, *Gambler's Star*. The legendary room—site of deals that had both started and stopped wars, destroyed and built lives, and changed the Moon forever—lay in spectacular ruins, the panorama window shattered, the long table of real reclaimed mahogany floating in pieces somewhere out in space. Hunter's trophies from his sports victories, the photo finishes of his yachts and ponies, his holos with the rich and famous, had been sucked out as well.

So had many of the pieces of the dead.

Still, blood pooled around Deuce's gravity boots—such boots unnecessary, as gravity was obviously operational. As he walked, unavoidable, unidentifiable fleshy remains—organs, tissues, sinew—squished beneath them.

As a former Member of an Italian Casino Family—the Borgiolis—Deuce had seen his share of carnage in his twenty-six years. As a rule, ugly deaths did not faze him, unless civilians or children were involved. He wouldn't say that he was insensitive to gore and mutilation, but he had developed strong screening mechanisms to deal with those facts of the Family lifestyle. When you spent your life looking over your shoulder in case the next blaster pulse had your name on it, you couldn't devote much time to weeping or throwing up.

Today, he was close to weeping.

He had already thrown up, not a pretty thing in an enviro-suit.

He had never seen anything like this. He had missed the famous bloodbaths of a century ago, when Moonbase Vegas, his hometown, had been lasered out beneath the surface of the Moon. He'd seen the gas movies of the turf wars, of course, and the viso scans, and like all the kids of his generation, he had naively regretted the chance for such a wonderful amount of action. That is, until it came time to see an actual dead body of someone violently killed—in his case, that of the brother of his adoptive *mamma*, Maria della Caldera di Borgioli. Carmine had been his name.

Deuce remembered the scene even now: him, Deuce, four years old and sitting on Don Alberto Borgioli's knee, laughing and pretending to smoke Big Al's stinky cigar. The Godfather laughing in return as he pretended to lick one of the lollipops he had ordered from Earthside for all the Borgioli kids. His baby daughter, Beatrice, was in the next room, having a bottle. Deuce knew this because he had been assured that Baby Bea wasn't going to get a lollipop like him and Joey and the other big kids. Her loss meant more candy for them, which Deuce had very seriously explained to Don Alberto. The Godfather had roared with laughter and declared that when they were old enough, he was going to marry Beatrice to Maria's little Irish bastard. Adopted bastard, that is. It had remained Big Al's fondest hope, until Hunter Castle had landed on the Moon twenty-one years later.

Mamma Maria's short marriage to a very stupid man had yielded an older son, Giuseppe—Joey—a beautiful, soul-eyed boy who looked very Italian, very old world. The official line went that Joey's *papà* had died with honor in some er, ah, trade dispute long since settled. But when Deuce got older, he asked a few questions, did some hacking in the Family database, and was pretty sure that Big Al had stuffed him Topside in a crater and that it had been okay with Mamma. But there was no point in sharing any of that with the living. And despite the occasional temptation to sock it to Joey whenever he'd had it coming, Deuce never had shared it.

So, anyway, it had been the Feast of the Assumption, and the Borgiolis were good Catholics who celebrated all the holy days with huge parties. Mamma was with some of the other women—including Big Al's sister, Apogia, her best friend—preparing a gigantic feast. Rigatoni, spaghetti, gnocchi, cannelloni. If it ended in "i" and could be served with a sauce, it was on the menu. Deuce and Joey had been sent to spend the day with Big Al, who was supposedly conducting a meeting of his *capos* and assorted underbosses.

In reality, the meeting was more like a sort of combined pep rally and beer brawl, something that had to do with letting off steam after the use of a number of laser saws and a bathtub. Accordion music, everybody drinking and playing craps—the two young boys were wide-eyed and eager to grow up as soon as possible.

Then Donnie the Fixer had wheeled in, white-faced, carrying a cardboard box.

He said to Big Al, "Godfather, send the boys away a minute."

"What, you give the orders now?" Big Al had retorted, his eyes sad, his mouth angry. He had always had sad eyes, his whole life. As he dived into a plate of rigatoni, his eyes were sad. As he played with Bea, Deuce, and Joey, his eyes were sad. As he ordered a hit, his eyes were sad, hard marbles in his soft, pasty face. Bald head gleaming, cigar reeking. That was the Godfather even twenty-two years ago.

"Big Al," Donnie said, then blanched, because nobody called Big Al "Big Al" to his face. The Borgioli Godfather was big on respect because he got so little from the five other Casino Families. In fact, the Borgiolis were looked down upon by everybody on the Moon, a social given Deuce understood at the earliest of ages. Just as he had known that he was adopted, a fact he used to comfort himself when the insults about the degenerate Borgiolis got to be too much for him.

"Big Al?" Big Al shouted. "You dare to call me that? What've you got there, besides your own death warrant? Give me that box."

"Don Alberto, *mi dispiace*, don't, not in front of the boys—"

But it was too late. Big Al grabbed the box and ripped it open with his big hamhock hands.

The eyeless head of Uncle Carmine stared up at him.

So much for the Feast of the Assumption.

"Here he is, sir," a Lunar Forces paramedic said now, gesturing Deuce to the clear capsule settled on a gurney on the far side of the room. Then the man moved discreetly away. Everybody knew about Family dying: If you were smart, you put a lot of distance between yourself and death-bed confessions and deathbed obligations. In fact, most Family resuscitation capsules were tinted for privacy, no matter that that made it harder for the medical people to do their jobs. When you were in a Family, if you got as far as a capsule, it meant you were either so ill you were going to kick, or that someone had not fulfilled their contractual obligation to whack you, and soon would be back.

Once you were in a capsule, sooner or later you would die in it.

"Please, Mr. McNamara," Billy Jester protested, but Deuce minced his way around the mostly intact body of Kinky Caputo and of his cousin, Mario—not so intact— half-buried beneath large piles of cratermahogany and steel that must have crashed onto them once the grav field had been reestablished.

Deuce hazarded a glance directly ahead at the black sky and brittle stars, feeling queasy as only a native Moonsider can feel when faced with hundreds of thousands of miles of inky, airless space. Almost his entire life had been spent below the surface.

He swallowed hard. Hunter's much-beloved panorama window, a feat of engineering never duplicated, had been blown out during the explosion. Now that side of the room was a gaping hole. The engineers of this fabulous ship, *Gambler's Star*, had assured Deuce that the temporary shield—some energy field with electrons or something, a real bunch of *schiamazzo*—would hold for at least another two hours. By that time they would have encased the ruined midsection of the vessel in an enormous Kevlite bubble. Kevlite was the same material used for the enviro-domes, which covered the large ice-cream-cone-shaped shafts around which Moonbase Vegas was designed. It had withstood a hundred years of radiation, Moonquakes, and meteor showers without cracking.

But the Kevlite bubble wasn't in place yet—something about the transport vehicle getting held up at the airlock, probably someone had not been paid off quickly enough—and Deuce was nervous enough to consider another bout of severe nausea inside his suit.

He switched on his thinkerama chip with a double blink of his eyes and started recording and filing the mayhem. He'd replay it and sort it out later. At the moment, he had a funeral to attend.

He reached the inert form of the dying Borgioli kingpin, encased in its own man-sized bubble. There was a mask over Big Al's face for extra measure, although the capsule was providing him sufficient atmosphere and oxygen to preserve what was left of his life. Which was not much; they had prepared Deuce for that.

Deuce stood respectfully beside the suffering man. There was no hope that the Godfather would survive, although there might have been if the sick bay had not been destroyed. There was not enough time for transport. The old Family suspiciousness—some called it paranoia, some called it a survival mechanism—had briefly surfaced in Deuce: Most of the old regime lay gasping like dying fish aboard this vessel. It was awfully convenient that there was little to be done for them. You could call it an unforeseen tragedy, a clearing out of the deadwood, or proof that someone had developed a new Doomsday Machine, and they were not afraid to use it.

As Deuce placed his hands on the cylinder, Big Al's lids flickered open and his sad eyes looked sadly at Deuce. He fumbled awkwardly with the mask as Deuce shook his head and said, ''No, no, Don Alberto, don't.''

The mask came off. The big man took deep breaths as if the mask had been choking him—had it been perhaps feeding him with something other than oxygen?—and rasped, ''Find that son of a bitch my son-in-law and rip out his heart for me.''

''*Mio Padrino*,'' Deuce said, meaning, ''my Godfather,'' although Big Al was no longer his. Deuce had no Godfather. ''Hunter didn't do it.''

''Kill him. Swear to me. You owe me.'' He groaned and began gasping. ''I'm putting . . . on you a . . . deathbed obligation.''

''Big Al—''

The face ticked at the uttering of the despised name. The mouth opened, closed. Deuce leaned closer to the speaker centered in the Kevlite curved over Big Al's face.

''Stella. Bea,'' the old man gasped.

''That's why he couldn't have done it,'' Deuce insisted. ''He loves . . . loved them.''

''Vendetta,'' Big Al insisted. ''Declare yourself in Vendetta to the Charter Board. You were first . . . a Borgioli. You should have been my Heir.'' A tear trickled down his temple. It was tinged with blood. ''I loved you, Deuce. Little Irish bastard. Hunter, I admired. But you're Maria's boy.''

''Big Al, I beg you, don't obligate me in this way.''

With stupendous effort, the old, shattered man raised his fist and made the sign against the evil eye, thumb extended, fist clamped. ''If you fail, I curse you for all time,'' he said. His hand fell to his side.

And then he died.

Deuce crossed himself and lowered his head. In the scheme of things, Big Al had not been a great man. He had not been a good Godfather, if Deuce could be so worthless as to speak ill of the dead. But he had bought the children lollipops, and he had loved his daughter and his granddaughter to distraction.

There was much to mourn.

Deuce got a call on his badge, and took it.

"*Alors*, Deuce." It was Alex Van Damnation, Deuce's best friend and right-hand man. "Ah, this line is not secured?"

"I doubt it," Deuce replied hoarsely. "What you got, Moonman?"

"Something you need," Moonman said cautiously. "Joey and me, we are in the what do you say, the steering area."

"Navigation," Deuce supplied. He could almost smile. His Earthside friend had returned to the Moon a little over a year ago to resume his wrestling career. Deuce was certain he had never expected to become the *capo* of a Godfather. An untitled Godfather, but a Godfather nonetheless.

"I'm on my way." He sighed. "Put Joey on."

"Here." Joey's voice was filled was fatigue, grief, anger, and static. A lot of things on the ship were not yet working too well, including most of the internal comm system.

"*Mio fratello*, I speak to you in the language," Deuce said in Italian. He swallowed hard. "Uncle Alberto is in Paradise with God and the Virgin."

There was silence. Then Joey murmured, "*Grazie, mio Padrino.*"

Deuce shook his head, though Joey couldn't see him. "I'm not your Godfather, Joey."

Joey made no reply. None was really necessary.

Billy Jester insisted upon accompanying Deuce to the navigation dish, which was aft of the explosion, near the fantail. The bodyguard surveyed the area, which had sustained absolutely no damage, nodded to himself as he observed the busy clumps of crewmen and officers working their magic among the computers and telemetry to resume *Gambler's Star*'s orbit around the Moon, and planted himself outside the hatch, which Deuce himself closed. Beneath Jester's folded hands he held a Tycho 217, capable of firing off 217 pulses of juice a nanosecond.

As soon as the hatch was secured, Deuce turned to his two most trusted men, his brother and his best friend, and ignored the crewmen, who were saluting him like he was a freakin' admiral. The dish's air was heavily recycled and smelled of smoke, but it was preferable to the stench of vomit in Deuce's helmet.

He put his helmet on a table and regarded them both. Joey's deep-set, dark Italian eyes were red from crying. Moonman's arm was bandaged, but blood was seeping through the gauze. The Belgian looked gray.

Joey said, "Deuce, you look like hell." A tear trickled down Joey's face, matching Big Al's last gesture of humanity. Deuce's big brother had loved Big Al to the end. It was no wonder; back in the dark days, Big Al had upheld Joey's claim to their *mamma*'s entire estate when she died. Though it was clear to Deuce that she had meant to provide equally for her two boys, her will had been ambiguously worded. Joey had seized on the notion that Deuce was adopted and therefore not entitled to an equal share in order to keep almost everything for himself.

Then Joey had proceeded to blow their inheritance on booze, drugs, and broads. By the time he and Deuce had reconciled, all he had to offer Deuce was his heart, which was a cloned replica of the one he had lost due in part to a botched assassination attempt on Deuce's life. He also offered his loyalty. Which was the original article.

Deuce said, "There's a little cabin behind that sign."

Moonman and Joey turned and looked. Moonman said, "*Mais*, Deuce, she says, EXTREME BIOHAZARD. NO ADMITTANCE."

"Yeah, Alex, it's okay." Though he was tired and sad, and it felt like all the hope of resuming his former life had been drained from his bones, Deuce grinned at his earnest *paisan*. It must make for a strange journey, taking things at face value the way he did. "Not only can I read, but I put that sign there myself."

It was an old Family trick. There were signs all over the vast warrens of tunnels and miles-long, lasered-out canyons of Moonbase Vegas that said things like, ABANDONED SHAFT. DO NOT ENTER, compliments of Deuce. And others that said things like, NO ADMITTANCE. RADIATION LEAK, compliments of his counterparts in the other Casino Families. The only people who paid any attention to warning signs on Moonbase Vegas were tourists, the youngest of cops, and the most careful of the Non-Affiliateds. The rest of the Moonsiders—mainly, the Family men—removed warning signs from dangerous areas as a matter of course and put fake ones where it suited them.

Deuce, however, had stopped short of removing real warning signs. When he'd been a Borgioli, he had always felt that pulling tricks like that was deliberately putting civilians like Moonman—earnest, trusting types, "rabbits," in Casino talk—in harm's way, and he had always been strictly opposed to such a policy. Just a personal aberration, one not shared by the general Family populace. Nor shared with. You went around acting soft, you got squashed.

Deuce had grown up believing that the life of the average Moonside Joe was tough enough without the need for dodging bullets—since there weren't actually bullets on the Moon—from Family blasters. To all the Families, another word for average Joe was "Non-Affiliated," or, "N.A.," AKA the scum of the satellite, the lowest of the low, the losers in that great roll of the die that was life in this universe. Deuce's wife, Sparkle, was an N.A. Now Deuce was, too, having voluntarily opted out of the Borgioli Family after he'd realized he was no longer a committed Family man, and that he could get farther in life—and, possibly, live longer—if he owed his allegiance to no one.

The fact that Deuce had subsequently become allied with the most powerful man anyone knew about—Hunter Castle—had immediately raised the status of all the N.A.'s in the Moon. This had most royally pissed off the Families and thrown the balance of power so totally out of whack that the Earthside government buttheads in the Department of Fairness had gotten involved. Further pissing off the Families, of course, but what could they do?

Try to blow him up?

"Okay," Deuce said to his guys as they trooped into the small cabin and shut the door. He watched while Joey swept the place for bugs and assorted other surveillance equipment with a Scarlatti-built Sniffissimo. Hunter had been as careful about being watched as any other Godfather, but you never knew who was going to betray you next, and sweeps were a part of any big shot's daily life. Hunter had gone so far as to purchase and build his own line of sweepers, but even he had to admit that the Scarlatti stuff was better.

That is, if you could trust that there was truly no direct feed to the Scarlattis' own spook network. The Scarlattis swore up and down that everybody's Family system had integrity. But nobody was as technologically advanced as the Scarlattis, and despite the constant industrial espionage perpetrated upon that Family, nobody was likely to become so. So nobody knew if the Scarlattis were telling the truth, and thus, everybody assumed they were lying.

The cabin was little more than a storage closet, with a very small round table that was bolted to the floor, and four slider chairs attached to the floor by means of tracks, like the old-fashioned Earthside monorails Deuce had heard about.

"We're clean," Joey said, and mouthed, I guess.

You never knew if you could speak freely, but sooner or later you had to take a few chances or nothing would ever get done. Learn sign language, it would turn out that a hidden camera had betrayed you. Write it all down, and the tables or minis or something had stroke translators. It was always—or could be—something.

So Deuce cleared his throat, and said, "You found the ship's log?"

Joey and Moonman traded surprised glances that he had guessed. Sometimes they made Deuce feel like a freakin' genius. However, he knew that he was not—although Sparkle was—so he said, "Logical guess, *fratelli*. That's all."

"Little brother, sometimes you scare me," Joey admitted. He held up a handful of data rods. "The man was verbose."

"*Is*," Deuce insisted. "*Is* verbose. We have no evidence that Hunter Castle is dead."

"We 'ave no evidence of Hunter at all," Moonman argued, "and so one is inclined to believe that he 'as been blown to ze smithereens."

"Yeah, well." Deuce didn't like thinking like that.

"Hunter said his POS should go into effect if he's ever

absent without warning for more than six hours,'' Joey
added. He glanced at his watch. ''We got fifteen minutes
to go.''

''In fifteen minutes, we'll talk about it.'' Deuce's stomach was riding the Heinlein Catapult, the wildest ride in
the lame theme park located up Topside. You were rocketed
in this little gondola almost straight up, practically smack-
ing face first into the Kevlite dome, released, and allowed
to freefall back toward the surface wearing a ridiculous par-
achute that did nothing but look good in pictures.

The reason Deuce was so terrified of the possibility of
Hunter's demise was because he knew—as did his brother
and his best friend—that even now, the Families were holding meetings about what to do if Hunter indeed proved to
be dead.

Two options came to mind, creating a flowchart of more
detailed courses of action: *Grind Castle Enterprises into
the dust*, and, *Make as nice as possible to Castle's survivors*. Deuce was knee-deep into a novena that the Families
would would go for Door #2.

''Well, let's see what the good old boy had to say about
life on the *Star*,'' Deuce ventured, pulling a mini out of his
pocket and positioning a data rod into the correct port.

''If you don't think he's dead, we shouldn't read his
diary,'' Joey ventured reluctantly. It was pretty clear where
he stood on the issue: ze smithereens.

''This ain't his diary,'' Deuce said patiently—because
Hunter's diary was located in the safe in his cabin, which
Deuce had not been able to access as yet. Joey didn't have
a need to know that, however, and in this life, the less you
knew that you didn't need to know, the longer you lived.
The problem was, because of his high profile, Deuce had
to know a lot.

''But I thought we had found ze log,'' Moonman said,
confused. He frowned at Joey.

''A log is the diary of a ship, not a man,'' Joey answered,
but it was obvious he didn't believe it.

''Bravo,'' Deuce said ironically, and pushed the rod in.

From the Captain's Log of Gambler's Star:

We are orbiting ten miles above the lunar surface, as we have been for fourteen months.

It's the anniversary of my greatest achievement. Thirty years ago today. Hard to believe how that one thing changed my life. What I found in that crash.

But that's for my own personal log.

But how does a captain separate his exploits from those of a vessel he regards with the adoration one reserves for his mistress? Without Gambler's Star, *I'd be nothing.*

By God, I played my cards right, and the Moon is my oyster.

Darkside City will be my pearl.

It's a thrilling time to be a Moonsider. They haven't had a challenge this enormous since the founding of Moonbase Vegas over a hundred years ago. All that scrabbling for territory, all the corruption, all the killing hardened these "Casino Families," as they call themselves. They're a different people than Earthsiders. But tough as they are, not one of them had the guts or the vision to blast out a new Casino City on the dark side of the Moon. None of them dreamed it could be done. That was left up to me.

These are folks who take no prisoners.

My kind of folks.

When I first arrived last year, all they could think about was protecting their precious status quo. I know each House discussed putting a hit out on me. What they didn't realize was that despite their swagger and bravado, the innumerable hits they perpetrated on each other, the Vendettas they waged, the insults and bets they kept track of, these great-grandsons and great-great-nieces and aging, rejuved brothers and sisters of the Original Families had basically become gun-slinging accountants. I never saw so much accounting in all my life, ticking off percentages for the house, protection money for the police, and bribes so numerous that added together they amounted to more than the economies of several of the Earthside Conglomerated Nations.

When I was in the thick of it, I needed to remind myself repeatedly they had not grown soft, just unimaginative. I still can't take them for granted. Not if I want to live.

Building my great gambling paradise beneath the cratered surface of the Darkside may spark a few imaginations. I pray at night on my lucky star, the Gambler, that it will toughen them even more, and change them more radically than even I could imagine. What lies ahead needs a new breed of people. Not Earthsiders or Moonsiders, but star riders.

So I need more people like Deuce McNamara. He's the closest thing to perfect I've got. And though as unofficial leader of the Non-Affiliated, he protests his independence, he is my right-hand man. Surely he realizes by now that I find him indispensable.

And the universe needs more people like his wife, Sparkle. I mean that sincerely. Once the big plan is set in motion, we'll need more minds like hers.

I do wish things could have gone differently between the former Miss de Lune and me. She is still the most intriguing woman I've ever met. I could have had her; of that I'm certain. She never gave me any reason to assume otherwise. My dear benighted wife, Beatrice, has no idea that ours was a political liaison engineered to keep the peace among the Families and free Deuce up in order to more fully control him. I think Deuce knows that by now. Sparkle surely does. I will allow Beatrice her happiness, and play the doting husband. As the months pass, it grows easier. Her slavish devotion touches me. Her desire to please moves me. I can do no less than allow her to make me happy.

I hear that the McNamaras are planning to purchase a Family Voucher. Their child will be amazing, of that I'm sure.

As is our tiny daughter, Stella. My other lucky star. Just a baby, and yet with her soft fuzz of white-blond hair, she reminds me of the Moon as I used to gaze upon it back on Earth. Her tiny hands grip mine with unbelievable strength. And her smile? There's nothing of the Moon there. Only the Sun.

Enough of the softer things of life. As fortunate as I have been up here, getting to the Moon is just a stepping-stone. I'm here to be a player in a bigger game. I'm an adventure capitalist who gets one hundred percent on my return because of who I am.

And who I am varies with my circumstances. And never have anyone's potential circumstances loomed as large as mine. All of them—Deuce, Sparkle, Beatrice, and the tens of thousands of Moonsiders I employ—are, at present, keys to my ultimate triumph. And as my great-great-many-times-great-grandpappy used to say, the graveyards are full of indispensable people.

I'm one sorry, exploitive son of a bitch.

For Deuce and his people, Darkside City is the pot of gold at the end of the rainbow.

For me, it's simply a means to an end. No rainbow involved. None needed. None wanted.

If it all blows up in our faces, Deuce will forgive me once I tell him why it did. I'm not sure anyone else will. Which is the reason I live aboard my amazing ship, Gambler's Star, *above the danger and the bitterness, the unbridled ambition and every scheme they have. If they kill me, Stella will take up where I left off.*

That is, if I live long enough to teach her what it means to be one of us. Yet even then, God willing, I will have my backup to fall back on.

Hunter Castle
Aboard Gambler's Star, *2144.1*

The three sat in silence. Then, with a hand that shook with anger, Deuce popped the data rod out. He was so furious he could do nothing else but stare down at the rod as he wrapped his fist around it.

"*Cretino, bastardo*," Joey said, spit, making the sign of the Borgioli curse. "Pot of gold? What, does he think we're leprechauns that he talks of us with such disrespect?"

"*Mon ami*," Alex said gently, reaching for Deuce's arm. He must have realized which part had infuriated Deuce the worst. Which made sense: A few years ago, he and Deuce had trashed a Moonside bar fighting over Sparkle. Moonman had left for Earthside, resuming his wrestling career down there. Deuce had kept Sparkle.

She never gave me any reason to assume otherwise.

"What time is it?" Deuce asked his brother.

"T minus twelve," Joey said.

"Your watch just came up double sixes," Deuce ground out. He pushed his chair back on its tracks and stood up. "Hunter Castle has been missing for six hours. I declare him legally dead, and by his express orders, I implement his Plan of Succession."

He took a breath. He did not want this. He had begged Hunter not to do this to him. He had never dreamed he would ever have to play with this particular set of dice.

He said, "Anybody found Bea yet?"

Joey shook his head. "Her Family's pretty worried."

Deuce was, too. Most definitely they should have heard from her by now. She should be coming in every thirty seconds, looking for her husband and her baby.

He waved his hand over the ship's interior comm-link system. "Now hear this." He wasn't sure how many of the speakers throughout the ship were operable. But this was part of the ritual. This was what he had promised to do. "Mr. Hunter Castle has been declared legally dead. His widow, Mrs. Beatrice Castle di Borgioli is now the C.E.O. of Castle Enterprises," he said, pitying her with all his soul, praying to the Virgin and the Saints that she had wisely gone into hiding and was not lying dead somewhere pumped full of juice. "And I, Deuce McNamara, also formerly known as Arthur Borgioli, assume full responsibility and authority for the completion of Darkside City." He flicked off the switch.

"It's done," he said heavily.

Joey hung his head. "Three days, you'll be dead. Four, tops."

Moonman buried his face in his hands. "*Alors*, Deuce, don't do it. It's over with all this craziness and building. You can do what you want. Have a life for yourself. And for, ah, your wife."

Deuce glared at them, hating for a moment their pessimism and their fear. He wasn't so sure Hunter had been right about Moonsiders being so tough. It's easy to be tough when you've got a blaster in your back pocket and a Family to back you up. Not that the Borgiolis ever had backed him up much, or anybody else in the Family.

"And what do I want?" he demanded. "To put the thousands of Moonsider Independents who are building Darkside City out of work? To throw all the Family guys who declared their loyalty to Hunter to the dogs? You know their Families consider them traitors. Their Godfathers are just waiting for a chance to juice them to a pulp and bury their corpses in craters. If Bea—assuming she's alive—and I stand firm, our guys will have a little hope." He grimaced. "Not much, true. But a little."

"She cannot lead ze Family," Moonman said flatly. "She is too stupeed. If she is alive." Deuce sighed. That was so true.

"I give her one hour," Joey said. "Then . . . pffft."

Deuce felt awful. That was a good estimate.

Deuce popped the knuckle on his left ring finger, as he did for luck when a dealer shuffled or he placed bets with his bookies. When he needed Lady Luck—who, to him and most other Catholic Italian Family Members, resembled the Madonna very closely.

"Boys, you got to look upon this turn of events as the greatest of opportunities. For instance, what crash? What anniversary? Thirty years ago, something big happened.

They stared at him as if he were insane.

"I take it back," Joey said, his face etched with pain. "Her, I give an hour. You, thirty minutes."

Deuce grinned tiredly at him. "I'll have to hurry then, if I want to get everything done that I gotta do."

"*O, Mamma mia*," Joey groaned, and crossed himself.

"I say ze same," Moonman said morosely.

"Thanks for the votes, guys," Deuce said sarcastically. "Anytime I need fair odds on a new game, I'll know who to dial up to make my book." Deuce crossed to the hatch. Pulled his blaster.

Opened the door.

Killed the *assassinio* guy crouched on the other side of it: some poor *scemo* wearing Chan colors and carrying a Smith-marked headcracker. He hadn't even had time to pull the trigger.

"Vendetta," Joey hissed.

"Don't be stupid. He's just somebody's idea of a bad joke," Deuce said, studying the inert form on the floor.

He didn't tell them about the warning he'd received earlier in the day, printed across the mini of an underling but pretty much meant for him, or so the security guys figured: STOP BUILDING OR DIE.

In the nav dish they were freaking out, pressing sirens, calling for security, for paramedics. So helpful *now*. How many of them had been paid off to let this moron get so close to Deuce and his cabinet?

"Mr. McNamara, I don't know how this man got in here," said one of the navigation crewmen as they raced over in a clump and surrounded the dead guy. The crewman was a kid and had a Southern accent like Hunter's, upper class without that twang that made you think of guys marrying their sisters and running around barefoot. Deuce looked at his name badge—DE VILLEAU—and the kid goggled and swallowed hard, clearly expecting retribution from the evil wiseguy.

Sweat beading his forehead, De Villeau peeked into the small room and saw Moonman and Joey. The two had dropped behind the slider chairs for cover. Each of them had drawn a weapon, neither of which had gone off. It had happened that fast.

"Sir," De Villeau said. "Please. We didn't let him in. I didn't see him. No one did. Please. I have a family."

Deuce ignored him. He said to Joey, "Maybe someone thinks this is a funny kind of salutation to the new regime. Maybe this is a big joke, like with you and Don Andreas."

"Or someone just fulfilling some old deathbed obligation that they've slacked off on for years, maybe," Joey said. "We're all running around like chickens without our heads,"—not that Joey had ever seen a chicken—"the timing was convenient, and . . . pow."

Deuce shrugged, thinking about his new deathbed obligation to Big Al to kill Hunter if the bastard wasn't already dead.

"Sir, I am so sorry," De Villeau insisted, white-faced.

Deuce put his blaster on recharge and slowly walked through the nav room, scanning for the next *assassinio*.

Then he opened the main entrance hatch. It swung open. Billy Jester was propped against it. There was a very large hole in his chest, gushing blood and other things. The bodyguard stared at him with dead eyes as he collapsed on the floor, leaving a smear of crimson on the wall.

Deuce stared down at him as De Villeau, beside him like a shadow, lost his most recent meal.

"Deuce," Joey yelled from behind him. "The Borgiolis just commed us. They're looking for Beatrice. They want to know if we're holding her hostage."

"*O, maledetta,*" Deuce said irritably.

This sure wasn't turning out to be a very good day.

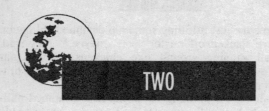

TWO

Earlier That Day

STOP BUILDING OR DIE.

Deuce scratched his head as he stared at the mini. He looked up at his informant, name of one Bucky Barnum, and said, "And you got this how?"

Tall, skinny, but otherwise nondescript, Barnum looked nervous as he stood before Deuce's desk with his hard hat in his hands. Which was good. Other employees of Deuce's had not been nervous upon receiving death threats in their work lockers, and they were now dead.

"It just showed up," Barnum said. "I went in there to get my lunch and a new pulse rod for my torch, and there it was."

Deuce frowned sternly. "Did you give out your locker code?"

"No, Mr. McNamara," the man said sincerely. That was a very serious infraction of company policy, instituted for just this reason.

"Have you got a voicer on it you maybe lent someone?" That had gotten one of Deuce's other stoolies, Little Wallace Busiek, blown to bits the previous year, when an android-and-cyborg hit team had been dispatched after Deuce. Deuce had stocked a locker with some toilet paper and other luxuries as thanks for Little Wallace's help on some things, then given Wallace a recording of his,

Deuce's, voice to get the locker open. But Club and Spade, the hit men, had been there first.

There had been just enough left of Little Wallace for a DNA scan to confirm his identity prior to cremation.

Deuce said, "I ain't going to tell you not to worry, Bucky. But I'm pretty sure they meant for you to see the message and bring it to me."

Barnum swallowed hard and tapped his fingers on the rim of the hard hat. "They, um, who?" He paled. "If it's the Scarlattis . . ."

Bucky Barnum was an okay welder, but his chief worth to Deuce was as a stoolie. His sister, Dixie, was in a liaison with one Nuncio (real name, Henry; he wasn't even Italian), a talkative and boorish Scarlatti soldier. Nuncio was an N.A. who had become Affiliated with the House, and he had never gotten used to this accomplishment. It was Bucky's job to listen to all the stuff the insufferable man bragged about and repeat it word for word to Deuce once a week. So far, in a year, he had brought nothing useful to Deuce. Not one word. But you never knew when the dice would heat up.

"The Scarlattis? That I doubt," Deuce assured him. He was sure the Scarlattis had cautioned Nuncio to watch what he said, having pieced together the fact that his girlfriend's brother worked for Castle's organization and that Deuce had probably coopted him in some way. For all Deuce knew, they were meeting with Nuncio once a week and telling him, word for word, what to say around Bucky.

"But I spy on Nuncio," Bucky said anxiously. "If he found out—"

"Forget about it. We're spending a fortune on security equipment with Nuncio's bosses. They ain't about to bite the hand that feeds them," Deuce pointed out.

But there were a lot of Scarlattis who were furious with Deuce and Hunter for building Darkside City. Just as there were factions within each of the six Casino Families—the Van Aadamses, the Borgiolis, the Smiths, the Caputos, the Scarlattis, and the Chans—who would like this project stopped.

Deuce put the mini in a drawer and folded his hands on

his desk. "Look," he said expansively, "take a week off. Get the missus and go stay in the company compound over on Moonbase Vegas. I'll stripe you some tickets to that fancy new show at the Caputos'. The jousting one with Merlin and all like that? I'll comp all your meals. With wine, also. The Van Aadamses have a great Fontodi Chianti in their cellar. I'll send a bottle to your room. You can even go swimming if you want." Barnum's eyes widened. Deuce was handing him a holiday few Moonsiders could even dream of taking.

"Mr. McNamara," he began, "I don't know how to thank—"

Deuce waved a hand. "Bucky, you've been a huge help to me over the years. I'd just like to give you a small token of my gratitude." It was one of many tokens, large and small, he had already given Barnum. Deuce tipped often and well. He was generous—to a fault, Hunter liked to tell him—to the people who helped him. Deuce figured you got what you paid for.

"Call your wife and tell her you'll be by in an hour in a company limo," Deuce went on. "They'll take you straight there. Meanwhile, I'll research this mini, okay? And we'll get you a different locker."

"Thank you, Mr. McNamara." Barnum bobbed his head. "Thank you so much."

"It's nothing. Truly," Deuce said. He smiled briefly at the man as he backed out of Deuce's trailer.

As soon as he was gone, Deuce commed Castle Enterprises security. "Got another one," he said.

Within seconds, two burly men burst into the trailer in full bomb squad gear, grabbed the mini from Deuce's outstretched hand, and dashed back out. They would check it for explosives. If it was okay, they'd hand it over to the brains, who would start piecing together the puzzle of who, what, when, where, and why.

With barely a moment's hesitation, Deuce returned to work. He punched in the coordinates for the Kevlite suspension pylons into his mini and stared at the gobbledygook that spewed onto the screen. He must have forgotten one of the freakin' variables. He knew nothing from variables.

Sparkle was the one good with this kind of stuff, not him.

He spared a glance at the holo of his wife spinning and leaping in the corner of the room. It was a commercial portrait from her days as a showgirl in *Venus on Ice*, her solo where she kickboxed in her ice skates, all the while wearing an enormous headdress made of ostrich feathers. Not that Deuce had ever seen an ostrich. You couldn't have them on the Moon. They would die of starvation. There was not enough gravity for them to swallow their food.

Anyway, there she was, his beautiful woman, her platinum hair hidden by the feathers as she executed some swan-dive thing—there was a name for it, but him, with all his newfound class, could not recall it—as cymbals crashed and a volcano exploded in the background. Next she executed a fabulous roundhouse kick, not missing a scrape of the ice on her ice skates. He marveled at her huge, blue eyes, her magnificent *poppas*, as she soared into the air.

Then his eyes drifted back to his far less impressive office—which was a portable trailer—in the left trunk cavern of Darkside City. Through the window, he could see a crew blasting the rock with lasers. Or trying to blast it. Either this was rock of a species they had never seen before, or the lasers were hinky. Deuce firmly suspected the latter. He hadn't paid the last bill for blasting equipment—thanks to His Cheapness, his boss, who didn't get rich by forgetting how much a single penny weighed—and he was getting his money's worth. The guys were standing around and scratching their heads now. They'd probably scratch for a few minutes more so they could justify overtime. Then they'd take another break.

Unions.

The ironic thing was, Deuce was the leader of these unionized goldbrickers. In his capacity as hero of the masses, he had fought for, and won, the right for most of the Independent trades and services to organize so that they could have a voice in their futures.

The Casino Families had been furious, of course. Through the years, they had spent millions of credits dividing and conquering the little people with disinformation

campaigns, threats, and trumped-up rivalries. As a result of
Deuce's interference, they had had to escalate, of course.
Result: more expensive division and conquest, but success
nonetheless. The idiots were forever going on strike and
perpetually lodging complaints against each other. They
held grudges that made the Families' Vendettas look like
pillow fights.

It was enough to make the most idealistic hero of the
people pretty darn cynical, and Deuce had not started out
this gig as the most idealistic hero of the people. That honor
belonged to Levi Shoemaker, the head of the Moonsider
Liberation Front, whose stated goal remained closing down
the Casinos and finding a ''decent'' way for the Moon to
provide for its people.

Not stated was the fact that most of the MLF members
were religious fanatics who had bought into the party line
of the League of Decency, the antigambling, antiliquor, an-
tifun organization officially banned from the Moon because
they had banned gambling, liquor, fun, and the Families
from Earth. Also not stated was Deuce's private but firm
belief that Levi's activities were funded by the Eight Disenfranchised Families. These were the mob Families who
had not shared in the spoils of the Moonside gambling syn-
dicate, and had been left to rot on Earth.

The Eight declared themselves ''in Vendetta for perpe-
tuity'' against the Six Moonside Casino Families. But over
time, with the Earth such a boring, moral place, the Eight
had lost their clout and faded into the background . . . or so
most people believed. Deuce was certain they were as
strong as ever, and that they were biding their time. Out of
sight was not out of mind, as far as he was concerned. He
knew from Vendettas. He believed in them.

And so his mind returned to the threats he'd been receiving. There were all kinds of people who might threaten
to kill off a few tens of thousands of people who were busy
building not just a casino, but an entire city founded on
wagering.

Sighing, he dragged his attention back to the freakin'
computations. Suddenly, his wine class launched in the

upper quadrant of his screen. That meant it was almost 6:00 P.M.

A babe in a tight black gown and a diamond necklace said in a very snooty accent—Earthside London Redeemed, very hoity-toity—"Hello, Mr. Deuce McNamara. Welcome to lesson number seventeen. Today we shall discuss the concept of noble rot."

She smiled like this had some sexual meaning that she would share later, if only you kept listening. After sixteen class sessions, Deuce knew better. She was a dry hustle all the way.

Now that he was a big shot, he was attempting to learn about the various classy things in life to polish his image, but so far, all wine was about was swirling and spitting, which he been brought up not to do. Also, memorizing lists of wines. He was pretty good at that.

He was also taking an art class. Perspective and placement, placement and perspective. Rubens, Tintoretto, blah-blah-blah. In the world of the Borgiolis, good art included a lot of swirling and layers of gold. He now understood that to be considered low-class and very *kitsch*.

Whatever.

Someone commed him. He said to the wine dame, "Freeze," and barked, "Yeah," at the speaker.

"*Buon giorno, mio fratello,*" Joey said. "Good news."

"Speak to me, Joey," Deuce said to his brother, as he wiped the screen clean, erasing his wine teacher. She could tell him about her rotten grapes later. "Good news I could use."

He lit a cigarette and commed for the pollution levy. The uptight people who hated gaming were the same ones who forced him to pay a pollution levy every time he lit up. Hunter kept threatening to ban "cancer sticks" on his property same as all forms of hallucinogenic and addictive drugs. It was a lot of *sciocchezza*, a lot of show for the Earthside monitoring arm of the government, the Department of Fairness. Who, let's face it, was nothing but a front for the League of Decency. Who got cancer anymore?

"What's the matter?" Joey asked.

"Nothing special. Forget about it. I'm just tired. My

mind can't stop wandering. I got so much bad news today I feel like I'm running a newspaper, not building a casino.''

''Well, you're not building a casino. You're building a freakin' city.''

Deuce shrugged. ''Rivets is rivets. I just use more of them than most people. Show me your pretty face and give us a smile.''

''Yeah, yeah.'' Joey came onto visual. Since he had gotten off the highly addictive Chan-made drug, Chantilly Lace, and had had his poisoned organs replaced, he looked much younger, much healthier. His sad Italian eyes still begged women to save him from some unnamed tragic fate, but at least now those eyes were lying, not foretelling his speedy demise.

Joey sat in his own trailer in the right trunk cavern of the Darkside Project. Dressed in a white T-shirt, he was wearing a hard hat and smoking a cigar, and he looked to Deuce how he pictured his own unknown birth relatives, blue-collar types running numbers and pounding jackhammers down in Earthside Chicago. Despite his adopted *mamma*'s official bedtime story that his people were dirty Irish Earther cops, a heritage he would have been proud to claim, he suspected construction workers was more what his particular brand of McNamara had been. If McNamara was even his real name.

''Here it is, my good news. I put a hit out on Andreas Scarlatti,'' Joey proudly announced. He leaned back in his chair and crossed his ankles on his very messy desk.

''*What?*'' Deuce nearly fell out of his own chair.

Joey laughed. ''Relax. It's just one of those joke hits. For his birthday.''

Deuce closed his eyes. Sure enough, today, October 25, flashed on his internal calendar with Don Andreas's name and age. The man was very young, only forty-two, recently promoted to the number one spot in the Scarlatti Select of Six.

Deuce used to know without checking all the stuff like when the birthdays of the *dons* were and how far you could push them with a practical joke. This time last year, he had been a mere Casino Liaison whose mission in life was to keep track of all kinds of personal data on Moonbase Family Members, big shots, little shots, and crack shots. Now he was practically a Godfather himself, and it occurred to him that he couldn't for the life of him remember when Sparkle's birthday was, much less Andreas Scarlatti's.

"You're sure he knows it's all in fun?" he asked.

"*Sì.*" Joey chomped down on his cigar. "His wife told me about how he put a hit out on her for their anniversary. She said he had such a good time watching her juice the crap out of the mechanical hit man that Andreas said he wanted one someday, too. I told her the Borgiolis would take care of it. For old times' sake. She thought that was hilarious. The old times' sake part, I mean."

Deuce sighed. It was not like the old days of Moonbase Vegas. Then, a hit was a hit that made somebody fall down and bleed to death. Not something you picked out on a terminal at a freakin' Hallmark Cards.

But these were better days, he reminded himself. Peace was better. Getting rich was better. Being Non-Affiliated was better. Making backroom deals with dozen of eager young Family men who wanted bigger action than their stodgy elders was better.

Stop building or die.

Well, basically better.

"*Va bene*, I hope he enjoys it," Deuce said. "Listen, the lasers are crapping out. We need to find out if they're broke because they don't work or if they're broke because we are."

"Sssh." Joey frowned from the mini screen. "*Mamma mia*, Deuce, keep your voice down."

Deuce snorted. "Like it's a freakin' secret that we have no fish."

Joey took off his hat and ran his fingers through his hair. He had dark Italian hair, too. Olive skin. The entire Mediterranean package. Side by side with his brother, it was very obvious that Deuce was adopted, or else that he had had a complete body makeover: white-blond hair, green eyes (chemically enhanced? he wasn't saying), pale Scandinavian skin.

"You know what people are saying, Arturo?" Joey

asked, using the first name their sainted *mamma* had put down on Deuce's birth certificate. As if to ease his suffering that he wasn't a Borgioli by blood, only legal technicalities: as the best friend of the sister of Godfather, she was entitled to adopt kids into the Family and name them anything she wanted.

"What are they saying, Giuseppe?"

"That you're lying about not having any money. That it's a scheme between you and Castle to extort everything you need because this city is going to fail and Castle knows it. People think he's dragged everyone over here to keep them busy while he puts his real plan into action, which no one can figure out but they believe includes a bloodbath. And worse, the collapse of our local economy."

"In other words, my real job is not to worry about girders and laser caverns, but to spread disinformation." Deuce smiled, cheering a little. "Which I am, in a way."

He leaned forward. "Despite the fact that I supposedly have the best-secured comm links in the satellite, on account of I have paid the Scarlattis enough credits to send all their kids to private Earthside colleges and universities, I will tell you now what no one wants to hear but will, anyway: Darkside City is going to be built, and it's going to be the best goddamn Casino City there ever was."

"Yes, Godfather," Joey said.

"Don't call me Godfather. And get some real clothes. Dress up nice."

"*You* are telling *me* how to dress?" Joey sniped, and disconnected.

Leaving Deuce bobbing around in his trailer with his gaze on his malfunctioning lasers and his irritated, lazy construction crew, and a sensation of deep contentment. He was over budget, understaffed, and more than knee-deep under the gun.

And underestimated, too.

He cracked his knuckle for luck. This was the kind of action he thrived on: chips down, card counters at the horseshoe figuring he had a mitt full of meatballs.

Because, speaking of meatballs, he himself did not know what was going on with the finances of Castle Enterprises.

Even after all this time of supposedly being in the know, Deuce wasn't sure if Hunter really was just a cheap bastard who hated striping his credit card or if he was slow to pay his bills because he was juggling and kiting from one account to the next.

Hunter talked rich, he walked rich. But you never knew. Bugsy Siegel, the con who had built the original Vegas down Earthside, had done it on stacks of markers and loans upon loans. That was one of the reasons he had been assassinated. Maybe if the wrong guy came knocking, Castle Enterprises would collapse.

Maybe not. Maybe this was some dumb game Hunter was running, see how far Deuce could stretch a dollar.

After about an hour, one of the brains commed him, and said, "Mr. McNamara, we traced the mini. It belongs to a Connie Lockheart. She got fired last week. Some kind of welder's assistant."

Deuce nodded to himself as he stared hopelessly at the numbers on the screen. "And her boss was Bucky Barnum."

"Yessir."

He punched a button and changed a value here, a value there. Not so much because he had any idea it would yield the correct result but to have something to do while he noodled on this new problem. "Have you talked to her yet?"

"No, sir."

"Let me know when she turns up." He checked his watch. He was due to close up shop soon. "If it turns out she did it to get my personal attention, schedule a meeting with her for tomorrow." Dames that smart, he wanted them on his side.

"But if she just wanted to get Barnum in trouble, give her to the cops." Dames that stupid, he wanted them out of circulation.

"Yes, Mr. McNamara."

"There'll be something nice for you and the other boys in your pay envelopes next week," Deuce added. A figure of speech, of course. Everybody got paid in credits these days. That and casino chips were the only two forms of legal tender on the Moon. Also, he would give them some Dievole Chianti. It had a nice tart cherry taste. Or so he was supposed to be able to tell. Most Borgiolis judged the goodness of wine by how much sediment settled in the bottom of the glass.

"Oh, sir, that's not necessary," the man said in a rush.

"Yeah. I know." Deuce disconnected.

He farted around for a while longer, wondering if Joey was having fun at the party, wishing he'd gone, too, knowing he couldn't have. Someone had to run the little wheel inside the cage. But that was why he was making the big bucks. On paper, anyway; he hadn't actually gotten anything dumped into his account in two months because there wasn't enough money to go around. He made sure his business colleagues got paid, then the help, and then the suppliers, and last were the big shots such as himself. If there wasn't enough to go around, the big shots suffered. So far, nobody was complaining.

Finally, Deuce gave up. He was not put on this Moon for office work.

"Aichy, front and center," he said into his comm badge.

"I am on my way, Mr. Deuce McNamara," his car replied efficiently.

Deuce said to the mini, "Let's close up shop, hon."

"Yes, Mr. Deuce McNamara." It immediately passed out to save energy, screen blanking. A year ago, Family men such as himself did not worry about batteries and BTUs and like that. But Hunter had insisted that Darkside City be as tightly controlled as possible, which meant not tying into the very large array of solar panels on the surface. And turning down the co-op deal Moonside Vegas had offered on the reactors that provided additional juice to the superconducting mesh that surrounded the city.

"If you don't own it, don't use it," Hunter was fond of saying. As inspiration for this absurd notion, Hunter had shown Deuce some old flatfilm, *Gone With the Wind*, about some brassy dame digging around in the dirt to build herself a mansion. Hunter had sat in his big stuffed chair in his private ready room in the ship sipping those awful mint juleps of his and going on about the South rising again.

Since Deuce had fallen asleep on the big stuffed couch halfway through the movie, he wasn't sure he had the vaguest notion what the hell Hunter had been going on about.

For his money, the words to live by were, "Travel light and use somebody else's." People and things were put on this satellite to be used, and woe to the joker who didn't play the game. The more deals, the more action, the more security. Hell, if you owned something, it could be taken from you in one fell swoop.

Shrugging—it had never done any good to try to explain any of this to Hunter—Deuce rose from his chair. Sending it and the desk to the ceiling—old habit—he headed for the door. His office in the trailer was enormous because his trailer was enormous. In fact, it was bigger than the apartment he and Sparkle had been sharing in the Moon Unit Two complex—in secret—when Hunter had arrived last year. Space was and always had been precious in the Moon. But one thing for sure: Hunter did not stint on ostentatious displays of wealth and power. Everything in Darkside City was going to be the biggest, tallest, deepest, widest. And Hunter had the architectural plans to prove it.

But it was up to Deuce actually to build it, even if he had to scrabble around in the dirt like that broad Scarlett.

"*O maledetta,*" Deuce swore in Italian, which actually he did not use so much since he had gone Non-Affiliated, but he reverted after being around Joey. Joey was to him the equivalent of the Old Country some of the older Italian Family Members talked about. The beauty and joy of the Mafia. The grapes, the virginal brides. That was just not Deuce anymore. Truth be told, that was just not anybody. Only no one had the heart to tell that to the geezers. And no one had the *minchia* to tell it to Joey. Since he'd cleaned up, he'd gotten a lot more aggressive.

Deuce stepped outside just as the aichy pulled up. It was a sexy, low-slung two-seater, supernova red, license plate reading DRKSIDE, which some smart-ass had once said meant "dorkside," an old Earth insult.

Deuce's cousin Angelo had offered to juice the smart-ass for being stupid at the least. Deuce had nixed that and instead, taken the smart-ass for a spin in the so-licensed vehicle. Guys like that were usually bitter because they stood nowhere near the limelight, not even the one in a bowling alley. If you gave them some attention, made them feel special, they generally were so grateful they would do anything for you.

The smart-ass had been Bucky Barnum. But maybe it was going to turn out that ol' BB was the dork, hitting on some girl employee name of Connie, who then threatened to blow them all up. Or something similar. Deuce had been wrong about people before.

"It's me, honey. Open up," Deuce told the aichy. It complied, raising its gull-wing door with a certain flirtatiousness that made Deuce grin every time. He slid in and assumed manual control as the hovercraft—"h.c.," or "aichy," for short—said, "Good afternoon, Mr. Deuce McNamara. How was your day?"

"Just super. What about yours?" he asked, as he verified the inputs on the strips of touch panels on the dash and the aichy lifted up.

"Very fine, thank you," the aichy replied smoothly, although, let's face it, the day it had had you could summarize in one word: boring. It had done absolutely nothing all day. It was like the most kept mistress there ever was, nothing to do but lie around and look pretty. Deuce suspected it watched the viso scan when it was alone. It seemed to know an awful lot about what went on on *Phases*, everybody's favorite Earthside-produced soap opera.

"Let's go slow, take a tour, hon," Deuce told the aichy.

As they ascended the main shaft, Deuce proudly surveyed his handiwork. Building foundations were being laid in the five caverns that had been successfully lasered. The casino itself would be the largest ever built anywhere, including Earthside, with forty stories (intersected, of course, with tunnels; you could not get away from tunnels in the Moon) of gaming, shows, dining, and rooms that ranked from swanky high-roller suites to broom closets for the dime trade.

Nice broom closets, however. Deuce never lost sight of the fact that their main competition lay on the bright side of the Moon, the Van Aadamses' Down Under, the plushest carpet joint in the satellite, with real wood roulette wheels and real woolen carpets. Most everybody else settled for crater materials. Not those snooty Aussies. Not Hunter and Deuce, either.

There was going to be a mall twice as big as Velvet Drive—"velvet" being slang for "winnings." Which is what tourists were supposed to spend on its three levels on Moonbase Vegas, being where the fanciest, flashiest, and most marked-up merchandise on the satellite could be and would be purchased. Darkside City's mall was going to be called the Milky Way, since Hunter wanted no references to Family life in Darkside City. No Gambino Court, no Meyer Lansky Lane, no Bugsy Siegel Way, like on Moonbase Vegas.

Anyway, their mall was one of the biggest sources of the friction between the two gambling meccas. The old regime—the aging Godfathers and their advisors—were convinced that only so many Earthside tourists could afford to come to the Moon to gamble—around 275,000, the number who came now—and that Darkside City, being the new thing (if it ever got built) would drain away all the trade from Moonbase Vegas.

Hunter contended that the ten square miles of Moonbase Vegas drew a capacity crowd and couldn't support more tourism. His studies showed that with more facilities, especially more convention facilities, more tourists would come to the Moon. More tourists would mean cheaper shuttle tickets and stuff like that, which would mean even more tourists. The greater the opportunities to spend money, the better off everyone would be. Including the N.A.'s: There would be more spring-up mom-and-pop businesses for the locals, which would make them even more dependent on the casino-based economy.

The self-satisfied old guys didn't buy it. But the restless young guys did. And they were the ones Deuce was making deals with—left, right, and center. The old guys knew that, too, and they hated Deuce for interfering with the established hierarchy of their Families. Things should happen a certain way, they figured, and in a certain time.

To Deuce's way of thinking, the geezers had a point about the new competition not being so great for business. But Hunter always talked about baking new pies, not cutting up the same old one into smaller pieces. That was the antithesis of the way most Moonsiders were brought up to think: On the satellite, all resources were limited, including raw materials and breathable air. And all Family Members and Affiliates were also brought up to consider honor the scarcest and most valuable resource, one you had to fight constantly to protect.

Which brought up the water situation.

The thing was, it was believed that while there were a few pockets of ice on the Moon—thanks to early research by the Clementine people and Lunar Prospect—all that had been claimed by Moonbase Vegas a long time before, and there wasn't enough to bother with anywhere else.

That was what was believed.

However, there are usually two sides to every story.

When Hunter Castle had declared his intentions to build his casino on the dark side of the Moon, everybody figured it was some big show about being rich and powerful and thinking he could do whatever he wanted. Deuce had thought that, too. But what no one but Hunter and some tiny handful of extremely well-connected and/or well-paid people had known was that there was lots of ice in the dark side. Lots more than the ice at the poles that Moonbase Vegas had claimed.

Hunter had suppressed the real data and substituted his own disinformation for at least two decades before coming to the Moon. When he announced his plans to build Darkside City, everyone figured he'd have to go with his hat in his hand to the Moonbase Vegas Water Authorities to purchase that most valuable commodity. His request to build his own still had been turned down once he announced that he was building his own supermesh.

Hunter found a way around them. Once a week, Castle Enterprises water transport vehicles dutifully arrived from Earth, ostensibly carrying water for the Darkside project. In fact, they were full of other supplies. So far, everybody believed the charade, but Deuce kept waiting for their cover to be blown. It was so *obvious*.

It was also one of the reasons a lot of people figured Darkside City to be in trouble and Hunter in a financial bind. That much water, for that long . . . the cost had to be astronomical.

As Deuce ascended, he mentally ticked off the millions of credits they had already spent. Like for the foundations for the very, very ritzy condos that would ring each of the three main shafts. That was the same setup on Moonbase Vegas, except there was only one shaft.

Okay. Enough dawdling. He said to his aichy, "Take me up."

He commed his boss to say he was on his way. They had a private meeting planned. Immediately on the aichy's "B" screen, a quicktime started running. Hunter must be tied up on a call. Deuce lit a cigarette and blinked twice so his thinkerama chip would file the keywords in the message.

After a swoosh of CASTLE ENTERPRISES, Hunter Castle's salt-and-pepper hair, darker beard and moustache, grin, and dark, almost black eyes, popped into the center of the screen.

"Deuce," he began, "I've changed our meeting somewhat. The Family heads and the MLF will also be attending. It's just a PR thing to tell everyone how the project is going. And of course, it's going very well, thanks to you." He smiled his confident, good-ol'-boy smile. "Then I'll be going Earthside for a couple weeks."

Deuce exhaled his cigarette smoke. No thrill there. Media displays were Hunter's specialty. Also, the trip was no big deal. Hunter made short forays back to Earth now and then, couple days here, week there. You had to get in your face time, any smart operator knew that. Maybe this visit would loosen up the purse strings, Deuce hoped. Deuce had assumed he'd accompany him soon, but so far it had not happened.

"Oh, and Deuce." Hunter paused and looked sidelong at a point beyond his recording camera. "There's a dead man sitting across from me. I have no idea who he is. When you get up here, take care of him, won't you?''

Deuce closed his eyes and nodded to himself. ''If it's Andreas Scarlatti, I'm docking Joey's salary,'' he muttered.

It would have been nice, if not so prudent, for Hunter to include a shot of the stiff in the quicktime. However, he hadn't, so Deuce started making calls. The first one was to Don Andreas himself. Deuce heard party sounds: people laughing, music, a lot of clinking that was probably Andreas's silverware.

''Don Andreas, many happy returns,'' Deuce said, scratching him off his list. ''I wanted to show my respect on your special day.''

''Don Deuce, I'm so honored,'' Andreas said. A year ago, Andreas would never have given Deuce the title of ''don.'' ''The hit was terrific.''

Andreas laughed heartily. ''When it went down, I almost whacked your brother by accident. He's fine, though. Had a good, stiff drink, and now he's dancing with Beatrice Castle. Hey, Joey, it's your brother!'' he shouted.

Deuce's thinkerama chip filed all that away. SCARLATTI, ANDREAS. JOEY. BEA. He loved the chip, the most redundant of all his redundant systems, and the most secure. You would have to pry his eyeball out of his head to get to it, as he had had it surgically implanted on the dark side of the socket. It even had some recipes programmed in, particularly his *mamma*'s recipe for spaghetti Bolognese.

A year ago, all he could afford was a cheesy lidclock, which told the time when he closed his eye. It had been embarrassingly antiquated, and, he later discovered, had lost time at the rate of about five minutes a week. However, the thinkerama was state-of-the-art. Deuce had purchased it with the dividends from his shares of Palace Industrials, the stock that Hunter had forced him to buy as a means of making initial contact with him when *Gambler's Star* had first appeared on the lunar horizon.

''Yeah, he's fine,'' Andreas informed him.

''I'm so glad,'' Deuce returned.

''The insurance on that hit must have cost a fortune,'' Andreas went on.

"It bankrupted the Castle organization," Deuce said. "We're calling off Darkside City."

Andreas laughed again. "I hope that's not true. I got a lot of fish tied up over there. I want to hear about what you're doing with it at the meeting."

"Yes, of course, Don Andreas. I'll see you there."

Andreas disconnected first. Deuce let him. The guy had to play the big shot, and Deuce was not about to do anything to piss him off.

He sighed. *I'll bet it cost a fortune to hit me.* Brag, brag, brag. Well, it was true. You paid a lot to pretend to hit a Godfather, just in case you actually did. It had happened, more then than now, when the fad had started. Some *scemo* had complained to the Department of Fairness, the branch of the Earthside Conglomerated Nations that oversaw the Families. The DOF had tried to ban the practice, but by then it was too popular.

So some tweaking was done—a few refinements added, a couple fail-safes—and only one guy had gone down since then: James Van Aadams, the new Designated Heir to the Van Aadams Family after Deuce killed his older brother, Wayne. Then James goes down in a stupid *schiamazzo* birthday hit. Those Van Aadamses were having bad luck. Most everybody suspected it had been a disguised hit, and you could bet that when the perp was discovered, he would not be brought to trial. Where he would be brought was outside the enviro-dome, and left on the surface to suffocate.

Deuce used to feel there was an elegant simplicity to that solution, it being cheaper than all that legal nonsense. The cost of bribing a jury rose every year right along with inflation.

Funny thing was though, now that he was sort of in charge of the people who were not Family Members, he no longer felt that way. In the Family system, a clever person could find lots of ways to atone for his mistakes and the dishonor he brought his House.

Look at him, last year practically facing a firing squad just for pissing off Wayne the Moongoloid, the then-current Designated Heir to the Van Aadams Family. A few quick shuffles of the deck, and less than a month later, he secretly hit Wayne as a favor to the gravoid's own uncle. If you had smarts and a little luck—*and* you were in a Family as a Member or an Affiliated—you could blaze your own path like a freakin' comet.

Trouble with being born Non-Affiliated on the Moon was, you had very little luck on your side, if any at all. From the first breath you took, your dice were shaved, your cards marked. Talk about bribing an entire jury; now he knew a lot of people who couldn't afford to buy groceries, much less a smart lawyer.

Deuce stuck his cigarette into the ashtray and tapped it. The ash would be captured; no way did you want all that crap accumulating inside your car.

He also carried an enviro-suit—a nondescript white one, he looked like an old-fashioned astronaut in it—in the air-bag compartment, the air bag being a little ball you could climb inside if for some incredible reason your car crashed on the surface outside the main dome.

This was more likely for Deuce than for most other people, because Hunter had given him this slick, retrofitted aichy in part to save time. While other people had to get over to a transport tunnel, debark, go through an airlock, then take one of Hunter's shuttle limos up to the ship, Deuce could simply fly through the airlock and up to the ship in his own vehicle. Truth be told, he had never gotten used to it. It gave him the willies to travel through airless space in nothing more than a chassis, a reactor, and a few onboard computers. But he'd be damned before he told Hunter that.

Speaking of damnation, he still needed to find out about the dead guy in Hunter's office. With the practiced skill of an old information barterer, he placed another call.

"Hey, Angelo, it's Deuce," he said.

"*Mio Padrino*," Deuce's cousin Angelo replied happily, even though it was bad for his life span to call Deuce his Godfather. Officially he was still a member of the Borgioli Family, and his allegiance belonged to Don Alberto. But he had made it very clear that when the time was right, he was switching his allegiance over to Deuce. That being when Deuce could offer real security, real protection, such as with legal Papers of Affiliation to a publicly formed and declared McNamara Family.

"Angelo, stop with that," he said, waving his hand. "Listen, anything happen to anybody today?"

"A hit, you mean?"

"Yeah, maybe. Not one of those *schiamazzo* hits, either. Or some kind of industrial accident over there?"

"Not that I heard of." Angelo sighed. "Business on our side of the Moon has been kind of slow." "Our" side being Moonbase Vegas.

"I see," Deuce said. And he did, a lot: Angelo was dying for some action. He wanted like anything to get involved in Deuce's side of the Moon.

Angelo added, "I hear there's a big meeting up there you're going to."

Apparently everybody but Deuce had heard about it. "Yeah," he hedged. "Forget about it. It's just a PR thing, a bunch of bull. What else you hear?"

"I'm sure nothing I got's news to you," Angelo said. "How does Sparkle feel about Bea moving in with you while Signor Castle goes Earthside?"

Deuce nearly choked. What, were Hunter and Beatrice de-liaising? That would rock the entire economy. Not to mention make his life more difficult, if Bea decided the torch she carried for him was still lit.

But that still wouldn't explain her staying with Signor and Signora McNamara while Hunter was out of town. Hunter had a million properties he could set her up in and forget about her. Besides, she should stay with her own Family, the Borgiolis, if she was going to move out of the protection of the Castle security forces. Not only was she Hunter's wife, but she was the Designated Heiress to the Borgioli Family.

To cover his surprise, he coughed into his fist. "You know Sparkle," he said carefully. "If I tell her Bea's staying with us, she won't make any noise about it."

Sparkle couldn't stand Beatrice Castle di Borgioli. She thought she was an airheaded bimbo with bad taste and worse breath. Which was pretty much right on the money.

O Mamma mia, what was Hunter doing, pushing Bea back into Deuce's life?

"Angelo, got an incoming," he said. He disconnected and tried a half-dozen other sources, still looking for the identity of the dead man in Hunter's office but wondering if it was linked in some way to the Beatrice affair, or to Signorina STOP BUILDING OR DIE Connie Lockheart, or a dozen other nefarious possibilities.

No one Deuce checked with had anything. His security goons couldn't even find the Lockheart broad. Like Angelo said, business was slow.

"Deuce." It was Hunter on the line, real-time.

Deuce tapped his comm badge. "Yeah."

"Y'all are on your way?" His Southern accent was a little thicker than usual. That was usually the only way you could tell if the big man was stressed.

"That's a big ten-four," Deuce said cheerily, hiding the fact that when Hunter got stressed, Deuce got much more stressed. You tie your wagon to a star, you do not want it to go supernova. "Do you have pressing business for me, boss?"

"Actually, ah now have *two* dead guys sitting on my couch. It would be good of you to show up soon, before ah have it any more."

"Jeez, Hunter, what are you doing up there, having target practice?" Deuce blurted.

Hunter actually chuckled. "I think it's natural causes, but truly, ah'm just guessing. I mean, do people often explode up here?"

"*What?*"

"I thought about having Mr. Wong remove the bits and pieces, you know, clean up the place. But I figured you'd probably want to take a look first. I mean, so you could see if you can figure out what the hell is going on."

How thoughtful. Deuce closed his eyes and wished for a good, stiff drink. His thinkerama flashed him the recipe for a Copernican Iced Tea. Then he got a few microseconds of a filed documentary on the South Sea Islands, as well as a tempting 3D scent-holo of a club sandwich.

Damn, something was off with his chip. He'd have to

get it fixed immediately. It was too valuable to—

All at once, from Hunter's end, came a jaw-rattling *ka-BLAM!* There was a shout, and then the line went dead.

"Hunter?" Deuce tapped his badge. Again. Again. "Hunter?"

"Mr. Castle's line does not respond," his badge informed him. "Shall I try another uplink?"

"Yes, yes!" Deuce shouted. "Try them all!"

He punched numbers into his comm board like an Earthside polyester princess addicted to the slots. Emergency numbers, stoolies with the news network, reporters, priests. To the aichy he said, "Death run, go faster than you ever have, all fines and levies guaranteed."

"*Gambler's Star,*" came a shaky voice on the car speaker.

"It's Deuce," he bit off in reply. "Where's Hunter?"

There was a pause. "We don't know, sir. That part of the ship is in flames."

"What do your readouts show?" Deuce shouted.

"Dead bodies, sir."

"How many? Damn you, how many?" Two. Let it be two, the two dead guys on Hunter's couch.

"At least forty, sir."

Deuce said to the aichy, "Manual," and bulleted his car up and out like no man had flown before.

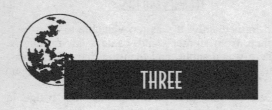

THREE

Violating what few traffic laws had been established on the relatively lawless dark side of the Moon, Deuce reached the James R. Hoffa Memorial Airlock by way of an illegal left turn on Sinatra in record time. When he got there, he had to fight every impulse he had to blast the damn thing open—a capital offense on the Moon, one of only two or three—murmuring, "Come on, come on, baby," as he cracked his knuckle and scanned the aichy readout panel.

There was a traffic jam at the lock. Emergency vehicles and media vans were practically ramming the aperture in their haste to get to *Gambler's Star*. His badge was hot to the touch, there were so many calls coming in, and he defaulted on all of them to quicktimes except those that could be traced to Sparkle, Joey, Hunter, or the ship.

Joey could offer nothing except to whisper, "Deuce, you're alive, Deuce," over and over, but Sparkle had this: "They're saying it's a new kind of Quantum Instability Circuit. They're saying Castle's dead. A lot of other people are dead, too. Family Members."

"Mamma mia, o, maledetta."

"Deuce, I downloaded one of the docking manifests. You were expected to be there half an hour ago."

"So I'm late," he quipped.

"You're alive. Hold on. I've got an incoming," she said. After about thirty seconds, she came back on. "Deuce, Levi Shoemaker is dead."

Deuce's eyes widened. Shoemaker had saved Deuce's caboose on a number of occasions, because he'd hoped to turn Deuce to the correct side of the Force—the MLF's—and use him as a figurehead. Deuce had gone along only so far. Although he agreed that the N.A.'s still deserved a far better shake than they were getting, he sure as hell didn't believe the Moon could survive without the Families and the casinos.

"What about Shoemaker's kid?" he asked.

"Alive. Angelina Rille has issued a press release stating that her father's assassins will know the fury of the MLF. Through the court system."

"Yeah, court schmort. Where's my brother?"

"Deuce?" It was Joey. "I'm in my car. Andreas left to go up to the *Star*. No one's sure when. Don Alberto was already up there for certain. No one's heard from him." He took a deep breath. "*Mio fratello*, I think our Godfather is dead."

A sharp, painful blow lodged in Deuce's abdomen. Or maybe it was in his heart. Despite all the hassles Big Al had put him through; all the mortification of having a Godfather so stupid that Deuce used to withhold information as a matter of course so Big Al wouldn't hurt himself with it; despite Deuce's opting out of the Family and going Independent, deep in Deuce's red corpuscles he was Borgioli-born, and Big Al had once been like an uncle to him. A big, scary uncle, but an uncle nonetheless.

He crossed himself and sighed. "Rest in peace."

"Amen," Joe added. On her line, Sparkle said nothing. She was not too keen on the rituals of organized religions.

"Who else ate it?" Deuce asked tiredly. He kept waiting for them to tell him something about Hunter.

"Lots of people. It's just coming in. Chairman William Atherton Van Aadams."

In that organization, they didn't have a Godfather, but a C.E.O. Chairman William had been in the process of designating a new Heir to replace James, the successor to Wayne, who had died in the *schiamazzo* birthday hit. But after all this time, the name had still not been announced. To keep everybody dangling, Deuce had figured. But had the C.E.O. actually died without a Plan of Succession in place?

"Four of the Scarlatti Select of Six." Joey grunted. "Including Andreas. Arturino, we wasted our money on that fake hit. He died anyway, on the ship."

"It's got to have been a setup. All those big shots in one location, it was too hard to resist." Deuce cracked his knuckle. "But who has the *minchia* to do such a thing?"

"You shouldn't go up there," Joey said. "They might have another bomb."

"I gotta go up there. Hunter's up there." He had another thought. "Is Bea still at the Scarlatti do?"

"No one knows," Sparkle cut in. "But I got a quicktime from Hunter today asking if she could stay with us while he went Earthside on business."

Deuce narrowed his eyes. "Cousin Angelo told me pretty much the same. That don't wash. She'd never stay with us. Her being the Borgioli Heiress, she'd stay at . . ." A beat. "Oh, my God. Big Al."

"If Don Alberto is dead, Beatrice is the Godmother of the Borgioli Family as well as the Heiress of the Castle dynasty," Sparkle finished. "She's probably the most powerful person in the known universe."

"Hunter knew something was going down," Deuce said, mentally fanning out his cards, moving them this way and that. "That's why he was sending her to us." He meant "to *me*," and he figured Sparkle would realize that, but he was trying to be delicate.

Pick a notion, any notion. "Maybe he even set this whole thing up himself. I'll bet you a million credits he ain't even on that freakin' ship."

"That occurred to me," Sparkle said.

"Then forget about it." Joey shook his head. "Even more reason not to go."

Deuce set his jaw. "Look, whoever perped this, their cover's blown, and they know it. This is probably the safest time to go. The cops will be swarming like locusts and by the time they're done, there won't be anything left." Not that Deuce had ever seen a locust. Who would bring them to the Moon?

"That also occurred to me," Sparkle said. That was her way of giving him her consent to go.

"This is nuts," Joey insisted. "Listen, I'm your older brother, and I say you better stay out of this and—"

"I have an enormous backlog of calls," Sparkle announced. "I'm going to check on them."

Deuce waited for his comm system to verify her disconnect with a little beep. Still, he lowered his voice as he continued.

"Joey, you cannot deny that it's because of me that you're alive today, correct?"

"And you cannot deny that it's because of me that *you're* alive," Joey shot back.

Each of them had a point: Deuce had saved Joey from a slow, agonizing death by poisoning. It had been a death meant for Deuce, because Wayne Van Aadams's cheap, immoral girlfriend, Diana Lunette, had fingered the wrong Borgioli as the keeper of her cheating heart, in hopes of keeping Joey alive.

On the other hand Joey had saved both Deuce and Sparkle from an ambush, also perpetrated by Wayne, during last year's historic race across the Moon.

"Hmm," Deuce said grudgingly. "Yeah, well, okay, you saved my life that one time, but—"

"So we're even."

"No," Deuce insisted. "You still owe me for not sharing our inheritance. *Scemo, cretino,* gravoid, you blew it all on drugs and broads."

There was a long pause. Then Joey hung his head and nodded. He looked at his hands as if he had written something important on his palm. He said, "Why are you bringing this up to me now?"

"Because I'm calling in my favor." Deuce paused. "I'm putting you in charge of our Family business if anything happens to me."

Sparkle would never forgive him if she knew he had selected Joey over her to run their affairs. She was more than capable of running the show. But when fans got hit with the stinky stuff, Godfathers and Godmothers got gunned down. Spouses and in-laws did not. It was the code of the craters.

Joey said, "But . . ."

"You will protect her with your life."

"But . . ."

"*But*?" Deuce asked incredulously. "You are refusing?"

"*No, no, mio Padrino. Mi dispiace*, I meant no such disrespect. It's that you've insisted over and over we aren't a Family." Joey took a breath. "Not that we aren't a family, I mean little 'f.' Since you forgave me for not only keeping your half of our inheritance, but also since you forgave me already for spending it on drugs and broads," he added pointedly. "And booze."

Deuce sighed. "Maybe we should become a Family now. Big 'F.' "

There was a long pause. Then Joey asked, "Our name?"

Deuce had second thoughts. Once he did this, there was no going back. He enjoyed—in every sense of the word—the fact that he had been a force of leadership for the Independents. Earthside Switzerland had screwed up somehow, because in the Moon, if you played your cards as a neutral party correctly, you could easily wind up with the jackpot.

Announcing the formation of a new Family would set all the Families against him, especially during a time of crisis. Even Hunter Castle might turn on him. If Hunter was still alive.

"Joey, you're Borgioli born," Deuce said slowly.

"Are we the McNamaras?" Joey pressed.

Deuce tried to inhale. Couldn't manage it. He was scared, big time.

"Forget about it," he said. "Now is not a good time to be in any Family, much less a brand new one that hasn't had time to form alliances."

"Deuce, I was drug-addicted, not brain-damaged," Joey retorted, clearly insulted. "I been a big help to you lately, yes or no?"

"Yes." Deuce found it within himself to grin. "A huge help, big as my genitals." He chuckled nervously. He was still blathering. He was too scared to control his mouth. "Who do I sound like?"

"That freakin' David statue at the Palazzo," Joey said. They both laughed.

Deuce moved on. "Listen. I got a stash hole. You know, like my old one in the apartment Sparkle and I had that got fire-bombed? It's heavily armed, emphasis on armed."

"Okay," Joey said eagerly. "What you got in it, weapons?"

"No. Well, yeah, a few. A prototype of something the Smiths are giving Hunter for his birthday. A blaster, something very blam-blam. I, ah, decided to give it a once-over, make sure it wasn't rigged."

Also, he had wanted to see if he could make more of them ah, privately. What if someone had found out about that?

"Maybe it's got something to do with whatever blew up today. I dunno."

"Maybe it's rigged to go up, too."

Deuce nodded unhappily. "*O, maledetta.* There's also a coded list of people who have either told me they would join my Family if I formed one, or people I think would do it."

"We do not want any bad guys to get that list," Joey said.

"It was stupid of me to make it in the first place. I was planning on transferring it to my thinkerama. I just didn't get around to it yet." Stupid, stupid, stupid. How could he put all those people in danger like this?

"So I'll get it and you can upload it. No problem. Forget about it."

Deuce hesitated. "Only if I give you the signal. It's too dangerous."

"Aw, Deuce, forget about it. Dangerous is my middle name."

"No, it ain't. It's Vincenzo. Don't do any acrobatics, Joey. I need you alive and kicking."

Joey huffed. "Okay, but if you do send me the signal, then what?"

Deuce cracked his knuckle. Having people to care for

slowed you down. That's why in Family life, most relationships were casual and superficial. It was safer to hedge your bets—hold on to your heart, keep your head—than it was to put it all on red, say, "What the hell, let's get married," or "Let's be blood brothers," or any other kind of entangling talk. Most people had lots of superficial relationships rather than a few deep ones. Even if you lost a few points in a number of them, you could still build the pot at another table.

"Deuce, c'mon, man. I owe you my life. Do you like to see me dangling in your debt? Is that it? A way to keep me under your thumb?"

"Jeez, Joey, you're just like me," Deuce grumbled. "You can't keep your yap shut when you're nervous."

He gave in. "Okay, the list. Guard it with your life. Try to meet each contact name where you can't be followed. They'll be scared to talk on comm links. For obvious reasons." It was highly likely that someone was listening to them right now.

"How do I get into the stash hole?"

"It's coded for Sparkle's voice and my voice," he said unhappily, not liking this subject at all. "It won't take a recording. It has to be live."

"So then she has to be there," Joey said slowly.

"No. Lemme think a minute."

"I'll be there," Sparkle cut in.

Oh, crap. Deuce was dead meat. She'd been listening in. She must have reconnected in some sneaky way he did not know about. That worried him more than the fact that she had heard what he'd said. Who knew who else could patch into his most heavily secured calls?

Sparkle's face flared onto the B screen. Her beautiful face was tight with anger. "I'd be the logical head of the McNamara Family if you die," she said without ceremony.

"Hey," Joey protested. "Gee, thanks."

Deuce sighed. Now was not the time for there to be a civil war in a Family that hadn't even had time to register its existence with the Charter Board.

"Okay, wait, stop. We definitely are not forming an official Family," Deuce announced. "It was a bad idea."

"Yes," Sparkle said, and Deuce realized that was where she had wanted to steer him: no Family, not now. As usual, she was a couple of steps ahead of him. She scared him sometimes, she was so smart.

"Okay. No Family," he capitulated. "Joey, leave the list alone."

"Well, what the hell *can* we do?" Joey asked petulantly.

"You can pray, since you believe in God," Deuce said to his brother. And to his wife, the atheist, he said, "And you can think positive. I'm going in now."

The airlock finally fwommed open. Deuce maneuvered his vehicle through, then up, still nervous after all this time at not being inside something more protective. He realized he should put on his enviro-suit, and popped the aft trunk to retrieve it, setting the vehicle on autopilot.

He hopped into the back, got the suit, and had just climbed into it when the aichy announced, "*Gambler's Star* dead ahead, Mr. McNamara."

And it must have really meant dead ahead as in dead. The enormous jet-black ship, into which you could fit 2,432 aichies the size of this one—Sparkle had done the math—had lost a huge pie-shaped wedge directly where Hunter's ready room and the larger of three meeting halls were located. Since space is a vacuum, there was no fire, but the charred superstructure showed that there had been an interior fire—one of the most dreaded situations in spaceflight and in the Moon.

Debris floated, small bundles hung as if suspended. He magnified his view and saw that the bundles were body parts. One was a blackened head. Another was a severed arm sporting a Scarlatti brand.

"*O, Madonna mia,*" he murmured, crossing himself and kissing his thumb. His mind was spinning into overdrive, weighing all the possible consequences of who knew what had happened, what was going on right now. Was Hunter in the wreckage, dead? Had he escaped to another part of the vessel? The rest of it looked to be intact.

He announced his arrival to TraffCom, which was busy with all the press and emergency vehicles, denying docking to most of them and urging Mr. McNamara to stay away because the ship was unstable.

But TraffCom couldn't enforce that suggestion, so Deuce drew closer to the vessel. Then he clicked into *Gambler's Star* comm system, and was acknowledged by a voice entirely unknown to him.

"Who're you?" he demanded.

"I'm Mike, the backup computer," the voice explained. "I'm fully functional and ready to serve you, Mr. Deuce McNamara."

"Okay. Guide me in. Make sure there's air. And no fire," he added.

"I will comply, Mr. McNamara," Mike told him.

Deuce hunched over the controls, still on autopilot, staring through his windshield at the carnage. He swallowed and said, "Mike, you got a reading for Mr. Castle?"

"Not at this time," Mike reported efficiently.

Damn. When had Deuce started to truly care for Hunter Castle? What an affliction of his good sense. Better to cover his own ass, and those of his wife and brother, than to worry about a weird rich guy who didn't meet the payroll half the time.

"Docking Port A is filled with smoke," Mike reported to Deuce. "I am diverting your vessel to Docking Port B."

That was farther away from the damaged section of the ship, and it looked like they were sending everybody over there. There was already a traffic jam.

Deuce put on his helmet and said, "Belay that. Take me to A. I have a suit. I'll carry my own air."

There was a pause. Then another voice came on the line. "Deuce, this is Jimmy." Jameson Jackson, Hunter's personal assistant. Deuce didn't care much for him. Like many of his ilk, he mistook his job title for "right hand," "best friend," and "better half." "Docking Port A is unstable, too unstable to use. Go to B. It's in much better shape."

"Mike, do you have any fires on board?" Deuce asked.

"We think they've been contained," the computer responded.

"Jimmy, what about Hunter?"

"We can't find him." There was a beat. "But Deuce, he was definitely aboard."

Deuce closed his eyes just as his comm badge went off, coded to Sparkle. Deuce said, "Hold on, Jimmy." He went blank and said to the badge, "Earphone."

"Deuce, it's Angelina Rille."

He frowned. "What are you doing on my wife's channel?" he demanded, then realized that it was a naive question: Gina was a terrorist, and terrorists were resourceful. "Go ahead," he said.

"I have word that Stella Castle's on board and she's in danger from the fire," she said. "Her nanny's with her. The nanny, uh, checks out. According to our information, this whole thing may have been engineered specifically to get to the Heiress."

She checks out. Meaning, probably, that the nanny was an underground operative for the MLF. "You're sure you guys didn't organize this yourselves?" Deuce asked pointedly.

"Positive," Angelina assured him. "We don't have any operations against Castle authorized at this time."

At this time. "Yeah, well, meaning no disrespect to the memory of your father"—he crossed himself—"and I offer my sympathies, Gina—he didn't authorize several capers that your more enthusiastic guys have run, and they still went down."

"We run a tighter ship these days," she said, meaning that she had been actually running it. Her father had once been a very commanding presence, but he had grown tired and scattered in the last year. Deuce didn't understand what was wrong with him, but it had hurt the MLF's public image. Many people who had been in favor of the Moonside Liberation Front now viewed them as little more than terrorists.

"She's in a private dining room located on the aft port side."

"I know the one. Hunter took high rollers there for yucks."

"Deuce, the Heiress, she's vital to us. We believe she

can be a symbol to the next generation of real Moonsiders, someone in a power position who's not a Family Member, and—''

''Yeah, yeah,'' he said gruffly. They'd been through this a million times. As far as the Families were concerned, Castle was a Family.

''Listen, Deuce,'' she said with asperity, ''I'm trusting you with a lot, all right?''

''All right.''

''Because I feel I can trust you. I understand why you won't take over the organization officially, but—''

''No buts. Not officially, not unofficially.'' He said, ''I'm at the ship. C'mon, what's up?''

''Okay. One of Castle's bodyguards, Billy Jester. He's a . . . he sympathizes with our cause.''

''Spy. Got it.''

''Hold on.'' She went off-line for a moment, came back. ''Deuce? I just got a call from your wife. She's very worried about you, said she couldn't get through to you.''

''Tell her I'm fine,'' he said.

Now he was scared. It was so unlike Sparkle to share her concerns about him, and most particularly was it unlike her to share them with essentially the head of another Family. She was a woman of few words, and it went without saying that people like Deuce—people involved in building new empires—were often placed in harm's way, and moreover, were difficult to reach.

But Sparkle got these *feelings*. She went, like, into a trance and *saw* things, like she had a thinkerama that could tell the future and read other people's minds.

If Sparkle was really worried about him, something was probably going to happen to him.

''What about Jimmy Jackson?'' he asked, wincing in case the line wasn't as secure as he was hoping.

''What I've got is sketchy at best,'' Angelina told him. ''But we don't trust him.''

''On account of he's too close to Castle?''

''There is that.''

''Like me?'' he asked pointedly.

''Not like you. Very different from you.''

"I've kept someone waiting too long on another line," he said. "Disconnect, Gina."

She didn't. "Deuce, you know how I feel about you."

"Baby, I do," he said gently, and hung up. Then Deuce patched back in to Jackson. "Jimmy, I got word about Stella. I know she's on the ship and in trouble."

There was a pause. "From what source?"

From what source? Deuce was stunned. "Who gives a damn? She's aboard, right?"

"Well, yes," Jackson said slowly. "But how—"

Deuce cut the crap. "I'm going in after her."

"I can't authorize that, Deuce," Jackson said.

"Jimmy, listen to me and do like I tell you." He didn't know how to run this down. Aboard the *Star*, Jackson was in charge whenever Hunter was absent. The City was Deuce's territory. If Gina had good data from her various sources, Jackson could be the dirty cog arranged this whole thing in the first place. "Patch me back into the traffic computer."

"But, Deuce—"

Deuce hit an interrupter button, and said, "Mike, acknowledge Deuce McNamara. Queen to Queen's Level Three."

Deuce had no idea what this meant, vaguely understanding only that it had something to do with chess, but it was his own personal access code to the various parts of the ship's brain that Hunter had permitted him to peruse.

He wasn't sure it would work in this instance, but somehow Mike got back on and said, "Yes, Mr. McNamara. I acknowledge you."

"Is this line secure between you and me, Mike?"

"Yes, sir."

"Tell me if there are any undetonated explosive devices aboard."

"Yes, there are."

"Specify."

"*Gambler's Star*'s weapons locker is secure. It contains explosives," Mike told him.

By accident, Deuce had stumbled onto an important fact:

no one had gotten any firepower out of the ship's stores. That was very good to know.

"No other evidence?"

"No."

"Evidence of cause of current damage?"

"No. The cause is unknown," the computer replied.

"Then take me to A," Deuce said.

There was another pause. "Very well, Mr. McNamara. I will comply."

Deuce smiled grimly, kind of wishing it had some kind of override on it that would make it so it could not put him in harm's way.

The airlock sphincter opened up in its strange, other-worldly way that never ceased to intrigue Deuce, because the airlocks on *Gambler's Star* were like no others. It was almost as if they warped the space around them, or something. As Deuce fumbled around getting into his white enviro-suit, his aichy glided into a minor inferno of roiling smoke. Perhaps this was not his best idea. If he'd gone to B, he could have taken a few minutes to get his bearings while he waited for a parking spot, checked the computer, that kind of stuff. Why did he do this kind of thing? Angelina Rille would say it was his heroic streak. She'd mean that as her biggest compliment. Sparkle would say the same thing, and mean it as a put-down.

"Mike, what is the environment where Miss Stella Castle and her nanny are located?"

"The hull was breached, Mr. Deuce McNamara. Vacuum occurred. The secondary stasis field went up, and there is some oxygen inside, sufficient to sustain two human lives for approximately five more minutes."

An eerie sense of déjà vu hit Deuce; he had almost lost Sparkle to suffocation. He hated to think of a baby girl dying that way.

"I'm going in," he told the computer as he put on his helmet. "Whatever doors you can still control, open them as I reach them, you savvy?"

"But if I open the doors, the smoke will penetrate the area."

"Suck it out."

"The fan motors are down."

Deuce thought for a moment. There was no good solution. "Open them anyway." To the aichy, he said, "Let me out."

As the doors opened, he commed Jackson. "I'm aboard," he said. "I'm going to Stella."

He told Jackson this because he would know it already, and because it would be obvious that he suspected him of something if he didn't stay in contact.

"I cannot authorize this," Jackson said again, a bit on the frantic side. "If something's happened to Hunter, you are the key man on the development, and I must ensure that—"

"Jimmy, shaddup," Deuce said. "Short of juicing me, you ain't stopping me."

And short of somebody else juicing Deuce, too.

Somewhere out there was Hunter's lucky star, the Gambler. He clenched his fists and said a quick prayer for luck and for baby Stella.

For her daddy.

For a lot of people.

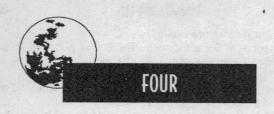

FOUR

People in white-and-silver enviro-suits swarmed all over Docking Bay A. They were spraying dampener on the smoke to dissipate it. Deuce assessed the damage as quickly as he could. The walls were blackened and charred, and part of the companionway that led from the upper level to the flight deck had been blown to bits.

Could it possibly have been a Quantum Instability Circuit?

It had been a QIC that had blown up Earthside Las Vegas over a hundred years ago, prompting the flight of the mob Families to the Moon. The nations of Earth had banded together to stop the proliferation and use of the circuits, which made matter and non-matter collide, causing cataclysmic events. Detection and dampening fields had been developed. The Moon was enveloped in such a field. However, rumors had circulated for decades that the Smith Family was prototyping a new generation of the ultimate weapon, something that could evade all detection.

But had they actually done something as stupid as blow up Hunter Castle's ship? Thinkerama on max, Deuce was going down his lists of stupid people and stupid groups, and he couldn't imagine a single one who would take on Castle. The Smiths would never overplay their hand like this.

In the docking bay, Deuce felt another twinge of déjà vu. There were these two guys wearing masks but, as always, dressed in white suits. They looked like twins, names of Billy Jester and Eddie Courvois. They were Hunter's favorite shipboard bodyguards; Deuce used to call them the Men in White before he knew their names. Then Deuce called the second guy Eddie Courvoisier, which Eddie did not find humorous in the least. Joey had made pretty good friends with them, but somehow Deuce had failed to charm them. They were waiting on the docking level, oxygen masks on, their hands folded, as they always were, while they waited for Deuce to get out of his car.

In the old days, that is to say, before Deuce agreed to help Hunter build Darkside City, these two came to fetch him every time he visited the ship. He'd tried to snoop into their pasts and had come up with nothing. Then, once he was established as a regular, they stopped sniffing around him and he gave up sniffing around them. Today they were back, and according to Gina, Billy Jester was the backup for Deuce's brave, daring, and monumentally stupid rescue raid.

Deuce didn't normally bring weapons onto the ship, which is to say, he usually left them in the aichy. Now he loaded himself up with everything he had. He wished he had a caddy to carry even more.

"Okay, let me out," he told the car.

"Good luck, Mr. Deuce McNamara," it responded. That also unnerved him a bit; how did it know to wish him luck, and why did it think it should?

"Thanks, baby."

He climbed out. Billy and Eddie took steps forward to greet him, hands still folded, masks covering their faces.

"Mr. McNamara, we'd like to assist you in your search for Miss Stella," Billy said without preamble. All Castle Enterprises masks came equipped with earphones, so Billy's Southern-accented voice came through loud and clear. Eddie inclined his head in a "me too" gesture, and Deuce figured he wasn't going to get the one he had been told to trust without the one he didn't know a thing about.

"Okay, boys. Then let's rumble," Deuce said. They began to move toward the ruined stairway. "You packing heat?"

Eddie told him, "Both of us have Kepler 98Ks and Tycho SigSauer multis."

Impressive. Multis could process more pulses per nanosecond than any other weapon in the Moon, at least that Deuce knew of. The Smiths probably had something even more amazing, but if they did, they weren't selling it to anyone else. And it wasn't in Deuce's safe, either.

The three men scrambled up the rubble. On the upper level, they checked once more with the shipboard computer about location, shield strength, etc., number of other rescue parties, and so on, while pressing on.

Gambler's Star was in chaos. Sirens wailed. People ran everywhere, shrieking, crying. Firefighters sprayed the corridors and paramedics raced into the flames with tanks of oxygen strapped to their backs.

A woman with a seven-inch gash in her head wove down the corridor, shouting to no one in particular, "Where are all the doctors?" Before Deuce could respond, she stumbled on.

Deuce commed the twins. "Any word on Hunter?"

"No one's pinpointed him," Billy told him.

"Escape pod?"

"Possibly," Billy replied. "But I can't believe he'd leave Miss Stella here."

"Did he know she was aboard?" Deuce asked.

The two men glanced at each other. Apparently that question had not occurred to them.

Suddenly, a steady pulse of juice shot down the hall. Deuce yelled, "Kiss the ground!" and the three men dropped.

Deuce rolled to the far side of the corridor. So did one of the boys. The other one lay where he had fallen, in an ever-widening pool of blood. Deuce couldn't see the face of the survivor, covered as it was by the mask and by the man's hair.

"Who've I got?" Deuce demanded, as he pulled his blaster from his pocket and returned fire. "Who's with me?"

"I'm Billy," came the reply. He was firing for all he was worth. The juice was still streaming toward them.

Deuce implemented his body shield. With the next pulse, the shield wobbled, but held. Barely.

"What is that crap?" Deuce commed Billy. "It's penetrating my shield."

"New to me," Billy responded.

"We've got to get out of here." Deuce rolled back to the inert man and checked his pulse. Eddie Courvoisier was dead. "We're leaving him."

"Roger that."

They both rose to hunched-over positions and freighted it down the hall to the next intersection, where a man blasted at them with a conventional pulper. He had good aim. Deuce had better. The man dropped like a stone.

Okay, like bits of gravel.

They jumped over him. They had to go this way to get to the main area where Stella was. Through his helmet, Deuce said to Billy, "Who can we trust?"

"Don't know. I don't even know if I can trust you," Billy answered.

The feeling was mutual, but they had to start somewhere. Deuce tried again. "I didn't get told about the meeting until I was practically on my way up here."

"It was very last-minute," Billy said.

"What was it for?"

"These men showed up from Earthside. Said they had something Mr. Castle wanted. That's, ah, all I heard."

Billy had been eavesdropping, Deuce realized. Naughty, naughty. "How many, two?"

"Yes." Billy sounded surprised that Deuce had guessed correctly.

"You happen to see them again?" As in, seated lifeless across from his boss?

"No, sir."

Dropping the subject for the moment, Deuce asked, "Does Jimmy Jackson have access to the oxygen delivery system to Miss Stella's location?"

"I don't know. I would hazard a yes, though."

"Then if you really did come to me courtesy of a friend of mine—initials of A.R.—and you're thinking she might be right about ol' J.J. setting this up himself, we gotta run faster.''

The corridor that led to the dining room was thick with smoke. Deuce's thinkerama played him a piece about fire safety as Deuce barreled toward the sealed hatch behind which little Stella and her nanny, Nina Watkins, were trapped.

He checked the hatch with his hands. Its heated surface seared his palm and he pulled back quickly.

He commed Jimmy Jackson and said, ''Goddamn it, where are the other rescue teams?''

There was no answer.

''Here's the rundown,'' Deuce began.

Through the smoke, Jester lifted his helmet polarizer and looked hard at Deuce. Then he tapped his mouthpiece and pointed at Deuce.

''Can't you hear me?'' Deuce asked. Jester squinted at him as if waiting for him to say something. ''Jester?'' he said more loudly.

Jester kept waiting. Finally Deuce shook his head. He motioned for Jester to talk to him. After a few seconds— precious seconds—it became apparent that their comm systems were no longer working. So what had happened—at the exact same moment in time, both of their helmets had failed, or had somebody deliberately cut off or jammed their linkup?

Deuce pointed to the door, then made a motion for Jester to move aside.

Jester pointed to the hatch and shook his head. Big fire on the other side; if they blew the hatch, the incoming oxygen might cause a backdraft. But if Nina the nanny and Stella were located inside a pocket of oxygen, the fire might have found them already. Maybe other guys had figured all this out and were in the midst of performing some kind of rescue from another, safer venue.

On the other hand, Deuce had no way of knowing if Jimmy Jackson had lied about the other rescue teams. What if the little Heiress was in there, burning to death, and Jackson hadn't wanted anyone to know about it because he had set the fire himself?

What if Stella wasn't in there at all, and something even worse was happening somewhere on the *Star* while Deuce was diverted over here? Who knew from Mike the Computer? Why had Deuce trusted it? Hell, who knew the voice even *belonged* to a computer?

Deuce shrugged again, gestured Jester behind him, and moved to the side of the hatch. He bent his elbow at a right angle, took a deep breath, and blasted at the hatch.

Nothing happened. Deuce's blaster wasn't strong enough to penetrate the safety door.

Jester added his own blaster to the effort, both of them firing at the same time. Still nothing. Deuce closed his eyes and checked the clock on his thinkerama. He had to assume the baby and the nanny had mere seconds of oxygen left.

Then some joker jumped from around the right corner of the nearest intersection and fired off a round of something as brilliant as moonshine but with a molten metal sheen.

Deuce pushed Jester to the ground and fell on top of him. The blaster sheared open his enviro-suit, searing Deuce's back, and he grunted low and deep from the pain. His helmet clamp held, feeding him oxygen and preventing the smoke from billowing into his lungs.

The assailant ran toward them and shot again.

The hatch exploded.

Deuce covered his head.

As he had predicted, there was a moment almost of stillness, during which time he rolled to the side of the hatch and threw himself on top of Jester. Then the fire blasted out of the room and slammed into the guy at the end of the hall, knocking him on his back.

The fire raged in the corridor. After a few seconds, a team of men in enviro-suits appeared from the same direction, loaded down with firefighting equipment. Daring to test the front of his suit against the powerful flames, Deuce ran toward them, grabbed one of their hoses and a shield, and tried to run into the room.

Then someone smacked him hard over the head. He staggered, dazed, and spun around.

It was Jester.

Furious, Deuce aimed his blaster just as Jester pointed behind him, through the hatch.

A figure in an enviro-suit walked like a soldier of death through the flames. On his breast pocket was the name JA-MESON JACKSON. He was carrying an enviro-ball in his arms. An infant-sized enviro-ball.

The figure said, in Jackson's voice, "Deuce? I've got the baby."

And it felt like there was something very wrong about the way Jackson's helmet worked, and Deuce's worked now that Jackson was here, but Billy Jester's still did not. But what could Deuce say about it at the moment? He nodded and pulled Jester to his feet.

Then, as the firefighters successfully killed the corridor fire and raced around him to battle the flames beyond the dining-room hatch, Deuce trotted after Jackson, who had started running down the hall.

Deuce caught up to him and held out his arms for the enviro-ball. Jackson shook his head.

Deuce glanced back at Jester, who was up now and on his heels. Deuce punched up his polarizer and stared hard at Jackson as he tapped him on the shoulder. Jackson kept his visor down, effectively masking himself.

Again, Deuce held out his arms. Again Jackson shook his head. Deuce tapped his helmet. Jackson did not speak.

And there was no concrete reason for Deuce to do what he did next, just a number of little indications that he ought to take care.

So he did take care. Specifically, he took aim—at Jackson's kneecaps—and shot him.

The man screamed and fell. Deuce grabbed the enviro-ball and got around the corner, where there was little smoke. The ball was featherlight in Deuce's arms, and he wondered, panicked, if baby Stella was even in there.

Jester looked dumbfounded, as did the firefighters, who turned and stared at what was going on. One of them must have commed for help, because as Deuce ran forward, he was met with a wall of security and medics. They tried to take the baby from him but he wouldn't let her go.

Then someone forcibly held him as the ball was wrenched from his grasp. One of the medics opened the ball and Deuce leaned in close, nearly fainting with relief when he saw that he had Stella after all. A very red, very unconscious, tiny infant. They closed the ball and ran with her.

Deuce pushed away the security guys and ran with them.

They fled through what looked to be a makeshift morgue filled with body parts and cadavers, into somewhere that had become what would have to pass as sick bay. A very gorgeous blonde in gore-streaked scrubs and second-skin gloves gestured to them to hand over the baby.

Even then, Deuce hesitated about forcing them to give him the baby. This was Hunter's kid. The Heiress to the largest financial empire in existence. Who to trust? He wished Sparkle with her ESP-type feelings was there. He could read situations, size up people, but sometimes she just *knew* what the deal was. She might have been able to tell him if he should trust these doctors.

Jester clapped him on the shoulder and nodded vigorously. Deuce took his helmet off, too. He realized he had no option but to trust them. If he kept the baby from them, she would probably die. She looked bad, a strange red and gray. He prayed to God and the Virgin there wasn't brain damage from lack of oxygen.

"I'm Dr. Clancy," the blonde said, as around her, people starting doing things to the baby with tubes and machines.

Deuce wanted to shout, "Hurt her, and I'll whack you and your mother and your dog," but he nodded mutely.

"I'm the senior doctor aboard," she went on. "I'll take care of her."

"She dies . . ." Deuce said threateningly.

The security guys gathered around Deuce.

Jester said, "Boys, this is Deuce McNamara."

Instantly, they backed off, but did not leave.

Doc Clancy looked unimpressed, almost contemptuous.

"Saving her life is my job," she snapped. "And my honor."

"Where's Nina Watkins?" Deuce said, looking around. "She make it?"

"No, sir. She's dead," said one of the security guys, and the others looked down at their feet. Like maybe they weren't sure if they should still speak to Hunter's *capo*.

Deuce commed his badge to the computer, and said, "Mike, is there a priest on board? A Catholic priest?" Hunter was not Catholic. In fact, he had no religion. But Deuce did.

"There are three Catholic priests," the computer informed him. "Two Scarlatti and one Borgioli."

"Sir, you'll have to come with us and answer some questions," one of the security guys said to Deuce.

Deuce shook his head. "I ain't going no place until a priest comes." He commed Mike. "Contact the Borgioli priest and send him over here."

"Father Rudolfo is gravely wounded."

"I don't care. Stick him on a stretcher and get him over here."

"Yes, Mr. Deuce McNamara," said the computer.

Deuce slumped. His back felt like it was still burning.

Dr. Clancy handed him something, a pill. He looked at her questioningly. "It'll dull the pain and give you energy," she assured him.

Who to trust, who to trust.

He looked at the security team and said, "I shot Jackson. I had a reason. Right now, we're in crisis, and I'm the highest-ranking Castle employee aboard."

The men glanced at each other uncomfortably as if conceding that Deuce had a point.

Deuce commed Mike, looked to Jester. "I need more backup security for the Heiress. Lots of it."

Jester snapped to. "Yes, sir. And might I add, you need security, too."

Deuce waved a hand. "I die, it's nothing. She dies, it's the end of a lot of somethings."

Again, Jester demurred. "I'm your man," he said.

Deuce sighed. He said, "Okay, then we wait for the backups, and you tell me man by man if they're all right."

He fingered his blaster, hoping Billy Jester got the point: Anybody Jester said wasn't all right, they would be dead before they hit the floor.

This was war.

* * *

Within five minutes, Father Rudolfo showed up and gave the baby last rites, and the nanny last rites in absentia. Such a thing was done all the time in Families, because most of the time you never found the body of the dearly departed. Deuce insisted that he baptize Stella first, just in case, because Deuce had never been invited to her baptism and Bea would have invited him if there had been one. The priest complied.

He also confessed Deuce, who knelt on the slick, bloody floor and whispered his sins in rapid-fire Italian: *I've lied, I've lusted, I've killed, I probably will again, it's the job, forgive me, amen.*

Moments later, the backup guys came. Jester gave them all the thumbs-up and Deuce had no choice but to trust him. So a bunch of security flacks lived to fight another day.

Jackson's body was brought in, and the doc told the vultures who carried in his bag to put him over there on the floor, no, wait, over there, like she was rearranging furniture in her living room. A lot of bodies were being shipped down to the Lunar Security Forces pathology lab for autopsies, but with a bit of pasta here and there, the Families would have their own coroners examine the bodies of their high-ranking dead. Taking something to the LSF was no guarantee you were going to get an impartial result on anything. Most of the honest forensics guys either ended up on Earth or in a crater.

Deuce said to the vultures, "I'm paying a vig to let the doc here dig through that guy's cadaver."

The vultures looked surprised. So did Dr. Clancy. So did the highest-ranking Lunar Security Forces detective on site, who cleared his throat and said, "We can't allow that, Mr. McNamara. Not if there's going to be an investigation."

Deuce glared at the man, name of O'Connor, and said, "Gimme a break. This body isn't going anywhere."

O'Connor flushed and was about to say something when Doc Clancy spoke up. "I'll do the autopsy, Detective," she said, "and you can watch."

The detective shrugged, but suddenly he looked a little

piqued. Or maybe he was that way naturally; he was a redhead and he had lots of freckles. "I'll send someone to stand in for me." He glanced at Deuce. "Okay with you, Mr. McNamara?"

"Sure," Deuce replied, and held out his hand. "That's fine with me, Detective O'Connor." The man deserved something for that. Some Irish whiskey. Although Deuce was not learning about such things in his wine course. He'd stick with Atherton Gold.

They all three looked down at Jackson's body bag. Deuce was surprised he was dead. He should be moaning in agony and cursing Deuce, but the blast Deuce had dealt him was definitely not mortal. Deuce knew from felony entrance wounds and misdemeanor grazes, and Jackson should probably have walked again, maybe even without replacements.

His death upset the security guys, but they put their questions on hold while Deuce took over. Jester walked Deuce out of the medical area like a proper guard. The doc gave Deuce a reassuring nod as she worked on the little baby.

Deuce put his helmet back on to keep out the smoke. And the smell. The place was swarming with Lunar Security Forces bomb squads, detectives, evidence collectors, and vultures—the guys who put the dead into the body bags. As one of the principals of Castle Enterprises, Deuce had to preside over the cleanup. He had his thinkerama keep track as they counted and sorted the dead by Family. They included all the people he'd already heard about plus many more Borgiolis and an interesting overabundance of Van Aadams. Their organization had been practically decimated, which literally meant, Sparkle had once explained to Deuce, reduced by one-tenth. The Van Aadams Family was going to be very weak in the new world disorder, unless it had a lot of very strong alliances and treaties that Deuce didn't know about.

The blast, he learned, had taken out a sort of pie slice equivalent to one-sixteenth of the mass of the ship and included mostly entertainment areas and personal spaces. Interestingly, nothing that was required to navigate the vessel had been touched, and all the fuel cores were intact.

Twenty-five percent of the crew were dead, and another twenty-five were unable to report to duty. However, they tended to be support staff, waiters, comms people, like that.

The little people. The ones whose lives had been changed the most dramatically because the great Hunter Castle had signed them up for his outfit. The guys with six kids and the girls who wanted to marry a Moonsider and have a second chance. Now they had no chance. Now they were charred, and pelleted with twisted metal, and one once-beautiful girl raised the stump of her arm to him and murmured, "Cristofore."

It was around then Deuce threw up in his helmet.

With a phalanx of Castle PR droids, he began issuing missives and making phone calls of condolence. He opened up a direct comm link to the Charter Board and blinked on his thinkerama to keep track of the number of Vendettas and less severe complaints the Families lodged against Hunter, Castle Enterprises, and Deuce himself.

There were dozens on the way to hundreds. It was like in the olden days when you sued everybody in sight, even guys you figured had done you no harm. Until the smoke cleared—literally—the Families would blame everybody in sight for their losses.

Not their potential gains, which was what Hunter had promised. Newness. The thing was, back on Moonbase Vegas, there was no growth. There was no way to climb the ladder of Family advancement except to wait for someone to die or get hit. Part of the problem was that with rejuv and organ cloning, people could live for a long, long time. Age and injury ceased to be the big problems they once were.

So maybe all Hunter's talk of baking new pies was not so nuts. Because that was what had made Darkside City so exciting for the Family turks and turkettes, and so terrifying to the Old Guard. When you're holding all the cards, it don't make you happy when they tell you the game's been switched to seven card stud instead of five card draw.

Deuce thought about the hours and hours he had taught the young people the new rules of the new games, and wondered if he had wasted his time. Somebody wasn't following any rules. But most of those young people were alive. It was mainly the old guys who had bought it. Surely he was not the only one to notice this fact.

Some of those Vendettas were going to be canceled, and still others were going to be lodged.

His sigh came out a rattled, husky breath. His blood-stream was pumping a mixture of smoke, ash, and adren-aline. His fingers were numb and his head pounded. Even his teeth hurt.

"Signora Scarlatti, *mi dispiace*," he began as he placed another call, comforting another widow who was screaming her grief somewhere safe below the surface. "If only I had known. If it could have been me . . ."

They sobbed, the widows. You're a woman in a Family, you grow up expecting to outlive your husband. But you never really believe it's going to happen. Death was an abstraction. Just like in the early days of the old Mafia, the ladies never believed their handsome Sicilian husbands were actually, ah, *hurting* anyone on their nights out "with the boys."

Meanwhile, a cursory investigation revealed that Jackson had not sent in any additional rescue crews. Also, that Deuce's and Jester's helmets' comm systems had been dis-connected via the control panel in Jackson's office.

The Lunar cops, apprised, agreed to let Deuce go about working the surrounding chaos into some semblance of or-der, but asked him to stay available for further questioning. He sincerely hoped he would be available.

After five hours that felt like five years, Deuce found himself alone with Jester in the ruins of a small galley off a freight dock. The two of them had two glasses each in front of them, one for water and one for whatever pleased their fancy. Mr. Wong, Hunter's mechanical waiter, who had survived, poured Deuce three fingers of Atherton Gold. Billy had some George Dickel, some old Earthside corn pone moonshine *schiamazzo* Deuce had no stomach for.

"Jester, excuse me," Deuce said. He spoke to the robot. "Mr. Wong, in a few minutes I gotta talk to you alone, but first get me some more Atherton Gold," Deuce said, not at all bothered that this might seem rude to some people. In a Family, it was a protective gesture to an inferior to exclude him from conversations the contents of which might get him killed.

"As you wish," said the robot, and it glided serenely away.

"Okay," Deuce said, throwing back his whiskey and letting the alcohol burn away.

He poured himself another drink. "Billy, it was Miss Rille told me to trust you."

Billy's eyes flickered. "I gathered that. At first I wasn't sure if you had had a chance to talk to her before you came aboard."

"You know I ain't MLF myself," Deuce said.

"Not officially."

"Not officially and not unofficially," Deuce said. "I'm the most independent Independent on the satellite."

Billy got that smile everyone got when he said things like that. Since Deuce carried honorary Papers of Affiliation with the Smiths, the Scarlattis, and even the Chans, each of those Families assumed his true allegiance was with them. Since he had been born into the Borgiolis, they assumed they owned him. The Moonside Liberation Front was absolutely positive that he was their unnamed leader. And the rest of the Non-Affiliateds prayed to God that he was their savior.

He sighed hard. "Anyway, I don't have time to go into that. What I need is for you to organize a meeting between me and Miss Angelina. I'm sure you realize all is not calm and bright around here, *capisce*?"

There was a comm on his badge. "Mr. McNamara, I have located Don Alberto Borgioli," a voice crackled. It was Mike the computer. "He is dying, sir. And I have given coordinates to your brother and Mr. Alex Van Damnation for landing."

"Tell them I'll meet them in a few minutes," Deuce said, as his stomach clenched. "I'm going to Don Alberto first."

"I will comply," Mike informed him.

"Don't go to Don Alberto," Billy Jester warned Deuce, but Deuce shrugged him off.

"He was my uncle," Deuce told him. "And my God-father."

Mr. Wong glided in. Deuce looked at him and said, "Signor Wong, we'll talk later."

The robot lowered its head. It appeared to be very subdued.

"Yes, Mr. McNamara," it said. "More water?"

"Yeah, load me up," he replied, toasted Jester, and threw back the precious liquid.

The Present, an Hour Later

Don Alberto seen to, the *assassinio* seen to, every damn thing seen to except whatever the heck was going on around him, Deuce knelt outside the hatch to the nav dish, closed the unseeing eyes of Billy Jester, and was very sorry this man was dead. He wondered why he was dead. A man like Jester, a trained bodyguard, he would have drawn and fired at the merest provocation. Unless he was also part of the *assassinio* equation. Or unless he had been exhausted and worried and distracted, like everybody else.

For maybe the fiftieth time, he commed baby Stella's medical team.

"Miss Stella has sustained a great deal of damage because of smoke inhalation," Dr. Clancy replied. "We're discussing the possibility of cloning her lungs for replacement."

They disconnected, beyond formalities now.

He turned to Joey and Moonman, who were bending over the dead bodyguard. "I want you to go check on the Heiress in person. Keep in contact."

He got commed again.

"Mr. McNamara, this is Dr. Clancy again. I . . . I have something here I would like to show you." She paused. "Something that does not concern the Heiress."

He hesitated for a moment, but before he could speak, she said, "I'm not currently with the Heiress. I'm in the pathology area."

As in, the corpse corral. Deuce's mind jumped to Hunter's conversation with him about the multiplying dead men in his ready room.

"On my way." He said to Alex and Joey, "Don't let them do nothing that looks hinky to you on Stellina. One strange move, give me a call, *capisce*?"

Joey put his arms around Deuce. "Godfather," he whispered, "it's like the end of the world. They might blow up the Moon. They might be that insane."

"No, Joey." Cleaned up off the drugs and booze as he was, Joey would always be the soft one. In a sense, the younger one. "Don't be a *scemo*." Deuce mock-slapped him. "We are taking over, big brother. We are not letting any bastards with fuse boxes rule us. We are going to gather our forces together, and if we have to go to war, we will win."

He gave Joey a huge, confident smile that he did not feel himself, winked at him, and caught sight of Moonman's frightened expression as he picked up his helmet and screwed it on again. The vomit smell nearly overwhelmed him.

"Go to the baby," he ordered the two of them. "I put on you an obligation to take care of her, deathbed if I don't come back."

"Deuce," Joey said in a choked voice. "Don't speak like that."

"You got to be practical, Joey. Especially if you end up leading our Family."

Joey looked sick and tired and overwhelmed. Deuce sighed, gathered up the ship's log, and left his brother and his friend. Maybe Joey was not such a great choice to lead the Family they would one day become. Maybe it was putting Sparkle more directly in harm's way to make her answerable to someone who wasn't half as smart as she was. Well, that was true of him, and she was still alive, wasn't she?

Tired and worried, he prepared to go in search of Dr. Clancy and whatever revelations she had for the hero of the people.

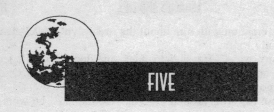

FIVE

Before Deuce left to meet Dr. Clancy, he decided to bring along a cover story. Now he walked beside the gurney supporting Billy Jester like a pallbearer. Someone called a physician's assistant jostled it along, deftly steering around the debris in the corridors like a regular ramfreight Teamster. The dead man's profile was clearly delineated by the sheet Deuce had himself placed over his body, for respect and so as not to further terrify the many terrified survivors on the ship.

After his debriefing with the doc, Deuce planned to hold a meeting with those survivors in Hunter's large conference room, the one that was not so fancy-schmancy with trophies and such.

The one Sparkle had always preferred to meet in.

Now he was wondering where else she had preferred to meet Hunter. That big-ass bed in his stateroom?

"Sir?" the physician's assistant queried.

"What?" Deuce groused at him.

The man shrugged. "I'm sorry. I thought you were speaking to me."

Deuce was even more agitated. What, was he so out of it that he was talking out loud to himself?

"Sorry," he gritted. "It's been a rough day."

"Yes, sir." The physician's assistant looked as if he had been pushed beyond his capacity. Tired, rings under the eyes, mouth drawn in pain and sorrow. Perhaps he had actually cared about his employer. It happened.

The man—name of Shiflett—gestured to the right. "We've got a makeshift ah, holding area in there."

He didn't want to say morgue. Who did? The Borgiolis always called it the makeup room, on account of some widows still wanted their dead husbands rouged and painted. A strange custom, given that you got cremated minutes after the casket was closed. If it was open to begin with. Family deaths were not usually too attractive.

Shiflett made the turn. Deuce followed behind. The gurney wheels squeaked. If you stared at a dead body long enough, you swore its chest rose and fell. You swore it was still alive.

Deuce knew better and stared at something else.

He went ahead of the gurney and opened the door.

Christ.

There were dead people everywhere. Dead arms, dead legs, dead faces. And in the middle of the slaughter, the young doc in scrubs who was coated up to her elbows in blood.

Deuce couldn't help but bob his head in respect for her calling and her courage. It took a strong stomach to cross-section and categorize damage like this and act like it was all in a day's work. Which, from her calm, steady expression and the sandwich she held with some plastic wrap—to keep off the gore, Deuce realized—she was managing to do.

"Doc Clancy," he said.

She looked up from a chest cavity and spoke into a transcriber. "Cause of death confirmed. Aortic transection. Massive inner thoracic hemorrhage."

The doctor said to the transcriber, "Shut off." She bobbed her head at Shiflett, the physician's assistant. "Thanks. You can go," she said bluntly. He obeyed without comment.

"Okay. Let's get to it." She looked around, set down the sandwich, found a towel, and rolled her arms in it. After the initial blotting, she fwapped off her gloves and dropped them into a trash bin. There was a big pile of them in there already.

She began to turn, but he stopped her with a hand on

her forearm. "Doc," he said in a low, tense voice, "are you going to show me Hunter Castle's body?"

She blinked at him in surprise, as if the idea had never even occurred to her. "No."

He nodded. "Okay, then." He was ready for whatever she had to show him. Except for the baby.

"What's that?" she asked, looking down at the fistful of data rods.

"Junk mail," he replied smoothly. "You got something I can put these in?"

She handed him a small blue plastic bag with the words ORGANIC WASTE: DISPOSE OF PROPERLY in black letters on the front. He slipped the rods in and slipped it under his arm.

In a daze, he followed her as she wound her way through the maze of death. Incredibly, she had resumed eating the sandwich. She was short, as were most Earthside women, maybe six feet. They hadn't gotten into the tall thing, them not having a lot of call for showgirls, of course. Deuce still wasn't used to Sparkle's diminished stature. He'd been surprised when she'd had her grafts removed. Gone to outpatient, hadn't even told him beforehand. Hadn't discussed it, as some wives or girlfriends did. She probably figured it was none of his business. If he didn't like it, he could leave her.

Maybe Hunter liked it. Maybe that's why she'd done it.

Deuce made it through the charnel house in one piece, cheering a little as the doc opened another door, stood back to let him pass, shut the door, and locked it.

Reflexively, Deuce reached for his blaster. Dr. Clancy must not have realized what he'd done, or maybe she was such a *paisan* that she didn't care. She kept walking toward a table on which lay a corpse covered with a sheet. So far, he saw nothing different from all the other corpses and sheets he had seen.

Then she pulled back the sheet. It was Jimmy Jackson, slit from sternum to pelvis and gutted like a fish. One eye had been removed. His nose was gone. His cranium had been sawed open, and his brain was lying beside his left ear.

This was by far not the most unsettling thing Deuce had seen today, so he kept his cool and folded his hands.

"Yes, Dr. Clancy," he urged her.

"I called Detective O'Connor about his autopsy stand-in, but he never got back to me. So I did it anyway," she said boldly. She looked at him hard. "I didn't want them to try to pin anything on you. I know how those LSF guys can be."

She coughed into her fist.

"That was very thoughtful of you, Doc," Deuce said sincerely.

She coughed again. "I've got some turkey in my throat. Hold on." From a tray, she poured herself a glass of something pink and fizzy. Girlie stuff. He liked that.

"Not thoughtful," she said in a hoarse voice. "I'm a Castle employee, too. It was my duty to protect you." She coughed again, drank again.

"This man had . . ." she began, and then she looked very startled. She made a kind of strangled noise, and then she keeled over and landed facedown on the floor. The glass in her hand tumbled beside her, then came to rest without breaking.

Deuce dropped beside her and rolled her over. She was gasping.

He tapped his badge. "Emergency, morgue!" he cried. "Dr. Clancy's choking!"

Deuce began to lift her up. She shook her head. Her eyes were bulging and her mouth worked.

"I'm going to do the Heimlich on you, Doc," Deuce explained. "Get the turkey out."

"Ja . . . Jame . . ." she managed.

He whipped her around and pushed his double fists in hard below her rib cage. Again. Her arms flailed and she batted at his hands.

"Jame . . ."

"Jackson," he said for her, squeezing her again.

She nodded. "Not . . ."

"It's okay, Doc," Deuce said with relief, as someone pounded on the door. Deuce leaped up and unlocked it, and Shiflett and three other guys burst into the room. Shiflett got there first and he took the doctor from Deuce.

"There's some turkey stuck in her throat," Deuce said.

Even though she was apparently choking to death, Dr. Clancy had the presence of mind to grab Deuce's hand. "Not huuuuu," she managed, and then they were all over her doing exactly the same things Deuce had done.

Immediately Deuce thought of Stella. If this was some kind of diversion . . .

He grabbed the toxic waste bag and flew down the hall to the makeshift sick bay, his blaster drawn. A nurse was standing with her hands in the incubator sleeves, stroking the baby and singing to her in a foreign language.

"Get away from her!" Deuce shouted.

"Attack!" the nurse cried. She positioned herself in front of the incubator, acting as a shield. "Don't you harm this child," she said with some foreign Earthside accent, bravely raising her chin.

At once, Joey and Alex burst through the doorway. A room's worth of security guys burst in after them.

Deuce looked at Alex and Joey angrily and said, "From now on, you stay in here with the Heiress. Right next to her. Not in some other room. Don't let her out of your sight."

"What's up, Deuce?" Joey asked anxiously.

The nurse was shaking. Deuce looked at her, and said, "It's okay. I'm Deuce McNamara." He glanced at her badge. DAVIDA VON FRANTIZIUS, R.N. There would be a little something extra for her in her pay envelope that week, too.

"Deuce, what's goin on?" Joey pressed.

"Later," Deuce barked at his brother. "Don't leave this room. Stick like glue to this incubator and this incubator only."

"Sure, Deuce." Joey looked at Moonman, who nodded.

To the nurse he said, "You did the right thing, calling out like that. I won't forget it." Maybe he would also give her a nice bottle of Liebfraumilch. Noble rot, and all like that.

Trembling, Nurse Von Frantizius nodded at him.

Deuce turned and ran back to the morgue.

Dr. Clancy was lying on a stretcher. Her face was a mottled purple and blue. Tubes that hadn't been in her when he'd left were being pulled back out of her and draped over silent machines like giant plastic spider legs. Two guys worked silently to deactivate everything; only one looked up when Deuce came into the room.

Shiflett, at her side, glanced up with a gray expression, and shook his head.

"She's dead." His eyes were filled with tears.

"What?" Deuce said, stunned. He walked to her side and picked up her hand. There was no pulse.

"Mr. McNamara," Shiflett murmured, "I need to talk to you."

They just looked at each other for a moment. Shiflett was about to pop.

"Clear the room," Deuce said to the other medics. "Just me and him."

The others looked disgruntled but did as they were ordered. Once they were alone, Deuce made sure Shiflett's badge was turned off, then said, "Spill."

"I'm almost positive she was poisoned." He swallowed hard. He licked his lips uneasily and glanced at her tray of girlie drink. "We had some sandwiches sent in about an hour ago."

"Yeah, she was eating it when I came in."

The man looked terrified. "Turkey on rye. Real turkey," he added. You did not get real stuff so often on the Moon, although Castle's shipboard crew got it more often than anybody else. Still, it was an occasion.

Deuce said, "Let me guess what you ate for lunch."

Shiflett took a breath. "We all did."

"Maybe it was in that pink stuff. You drink any of that?"

The man wrinkled his nose. "No way. She was the only—" He stopped talking.

"The only one who drank that shit," Deuce supplied helpfully.

Shiflett still looked scared, but he also looked a tiny bit more hopeful. Deuce prodded, "You take an antidote yet?"

Shiflett met his gaze. "If it's what I think it is, there is none."

Deuce shrugged. "Don't be too sure, Shiflett. I used to be a Family man, and we have secret fixes for a lot of things."

Shiflett's face flared with hope. "I think it was Golden 32." He turned Dr. Clancy's head to one side. There was a small trickle of bloody drool with a yellow metallic cast to it shining at the lower corner of her mouth.

Deuce looked down sadly at the dead woman. He wanted very badly to sit down.

"Or something made to look like it," Deuce said, offering the guy a little more hope. Because there was no antidote to Golden 32 that the Borgiolis knew of.

He accessed his thinkerama. Got a minidocumentary on the history of gold mining on the Moon. Cursed in Italian and shut the worthless piece of crap off with a double blink of his eyes.

To the physician's assistant, he said, "I'm sorry, but we don't have anything to take care of Golden 32, either. But get as many people working on an antidote as you can handle while you analyze both the turkey and the fizz." He tapped the pitcher. "What is it, anyway?"

"Something called a Warm Fuzzy, or something." Shiflett was busily gathering up the remains of the turkey sandwich with a pair of something that looked like pincers.

Slapping the man on the back, Deuce gave him a helpful smile. "See, chances are you didn't get any. And chances are good that with all the swell docs on board, you'll find a fix. But if you do kick, I swear to you that I'll take good care of your heirs, and I'll find out who whacked you and her."

He waited for thanks, got none, realized the guy was too petrified to remember his manners.

He gestured to Jackson. "I want you to freeze this guy ASAP, you got that? Now. You. No one else. Do it alone."

Shiflett looked surprised. Maybe even shocked. "Yes, sir, Mr. McNamara."

"And I want you to keep the freezing a secret. I'll take charge of the body."

"Of course," Shiflett said, still baffled.

Deuce had to make sure the guy understood him. His life

might depend on it. ''I know you probably want to tell all your friends about this, but you gotta keep mum. For the rest of your life, which we both pray will be very long.'' Deuce crossed himself. ''Or until I tell you you can say something. Only me, okay? Only if I tell you myself that it's all right.''

Shiflett ducked his head. *Davvero, davvero*, the poor guy was having a worse day than Deuce.

''Mr. McNamara, my loyalty lies with the Castle organization,'' he said.

Deuce patted his shoulder again. ''Signor Castle always picks the best, I know. Listen, after this is over, and you're still with us, you want to go Earthside, it's done. You can have any job you want. You want to get additional training of some sort, you have it. Now, who helped the doc with Jackson's autopsy?''

Shiflett switched to professional mode. ''She might have done it alone. Or else, Bernardo Chang might have assisted. She was impatient to do it. I don't know why.''

''With a 'G,' '' Deuce clarified. That was an important distinction on the Moon. The Chans, once a powerful Casino Family, had been severely weakened when Hunter framed them for Deuce's hit on Wayne Van Aadams. The Godmother, Yuet Chan, had been taken prisoner and sent to an Earthside pokey for the crime. She had declared herself in personal Vendetta against the two of them, but she never Registered it, which would make it sanctioned by the Charter Board.

It was not particularly ladylike of her to put an Unregistered hit on the boss of a huge conglomerate like Castle Enterprises. Not that there was another huge conglomerate like Castle Enterprises.

The thing was, hits on big shots affected everybody. So everybody deserved to know about them, via the Charter Board. And especially if you wanted to hit the guys and girls of Castle Enterprises. Her bad manners had prompted, in kind, Unregistered hits against Yuet, even by minor players, because they were pissed off that she might screw up their carefully arranged alliances with Hunter.

Which made whoever's volley against *Gambler's Star*—

with so many Godfathers and *capos* aboard—all the more heinous.

Deuce remembered the mysterious assailants on him and the Men in White. He wondered why Jackson was dead when he should be yelling to the Charter Board that Deuce had unfairly shot him. Why the doc had been poisoned.

There were enough mysteries here to last a lifetime, given that Deuce had an actual lifetime to spend solving them.

His badge went off. He tapped it.

"Deuce." It was Sparkle, who wasted no words on her relief that he was still alive. "Monsignor Alfredo just called. Beatrice is at the Borgioli compound, and she wants you to go get her."

One mystery solved. He felt a rush of gratitude to the God he was sure existed, although perhaps not on the *Gambler,* Hunter's not-so-lucky star.

"I'll comm her," he said to his baby.

There was a beat. "She's been sedated. She was pretty . . . overwhelmed by everything that's happened."

Deuce was shocked. Beatrice was the declared head of Castle Enterprises, the widow of the most important man alive . . . or formerly alive. She was also the new Godmother of the Borgioli Family. For her to remove herself from the action by taking a powder was essentially the same as a high roller staying in a plush suite, gobbling up all the expensive food, swinging with some broad, and then . . . not playing. You didn't get the goodies if you didn't place a few bets.

Not even if your husband got blown to bits.

"She's so worried about Stella," Sparkle went on.

"Yeah, so worried that she couldn't be bothered to see if she was on board. So upset that if decisions have to be made about her, she's unconscious," Deuce said angrily.

"As one of Hunter's closest men, you're legally empowered to do so as well," Sparkle pointed out.

"Well, I ain't her *mamma* or *papà.* I confess to you that I'm stunned speechless, baby. That she should do this is unforgivable."

"Deuce," she said quietly, "who knows which lines are secured anymore?"

"Yeah, yeah."

He was furious, and he realized his fury was somehow connected to the fact that everyone had always assumed him and Beatrice was a done deal. That she had failed so utterly to assume her duties reflected in some way on him, although he could not quantify exactly how.

"How is the baby?" Sparkle asked.

"How nice to know that someone cares," he said angrily. "They don't know yet. They're talking about cloning her lungs."

"Oh, she's so little," Sparkle murmured.

And in that moment, all the hideousness and the deaths and the guts and the politics floated away into cold, dark, and brittle space. For a few heartbeats, Deuce was alone with Sparkle on some Earthside tropical island, and he reveled in the heart of the woman he loved, who had always been true, just to him. And a blond-headed child toddled over and hugged their legs, and they lifted him up—a boy, what the hell, forget about it—and his skin smelled of baby lotion and kisses.

"Sparkle," he said hoarsely, but what he wanted to say must not be said on an unsecured line. Or maybe by an unsecured heart.

He did not understand this softness inside him. It was very dangerous. It could get him killed.

But somehow, in some way he could not explain because he did not fully understand it, it was also what could keep him alive.

"I'll go over there now," he said.

"Take something armored," she said, which was the closest Sparkle ever got to "be careful."

They commed off.

Deuce found himself fighting tears and had no idea why. To him they were a terrible sign of weakness, one he must never display to anyone who could hurt him.

And Sparkle could definitely hurt him.

He said to Shiflett, "I want to talk to Bernardo Chang."

Shiflett nodded and tapped his badge. "Bernardo, come in."

There was no answer.

Deuce asked Mike the computer to make a sweep of the ship for Bernardo Chang.

"He is not aboard," Mike said.

Shiflett had begun preparing Jackson's body for a freezing tank. Deuce raised a hand at him and said, "Make it a portable one."

Shiflett looked surprised, but nodded and said, "Yes, sir."

Deuce returned his attention to Mike. "Any indication Chang left recently?"

"I was not activated until after the crisis," Mike reported. "If he left before the explosion, I would not have knowledge."

"But aren't all departures logged and recorded?"

"Not always, Mr. Deuce McNamara," Mike told him. "Sometimes Mr. Castle prefers that data to be privileged."

"Well, there's got to be a record somewhere."

"Then that knowledge has not been programmed into me."

Deuce huffed. Then he shrugged and tapped his badge. "Okay, Mr. Wong," he said, "let's have our meeting." Maybe Wong would know about this.

But there was no answer.

An hours-long search of the ship revealed no presence of Mr. Chang or the robot. But during said search, Deuce pieced together a snippet of conversation here, a bit of detail there, and learned who had personally prepared Dr. Clancy's lunch, including her pink fizzy:

Mr. Wong.

He told Detective Andrew O'Connor none of this when they met up in the docking bay, and the detective said, "It's pretty interesting that both Jackson and Clancy are dead, and you were present both times. And that she proceeded with the autopsy against my orders."

Deuce sighed patiently. "No, it's not interesting. It's today's business as usual. You want to charge me with whatever, you'll have to wait. I got a bloodbath to avert."

The detective nodded in agreement. "Mr. McNamara," he said, "I wouldn't want to be you for all the tea in China."

"Since most of it is still radioactive, that ain't saying much," Deuce retorted.

Still, he was kind of wishing he wasn't himself, either.

SIX

It was with yet another feeling of déjà vu that Deuce headed back to the Moon and to Borgioli HQ, a magnificently tacky conglomeration of spires and turrets trembling with bilious colors that rose at the end of a shaft called Carlito's Way. A little over a year ago, he had been summoned to Borgioli HQ by Big Al for serious infractions against Family policy. He had not been sure he would leave the compound alive.

But he had had with him a trump card—Hunter Castle's business card—and a plot to get close to the man. He'd succeeded too well.

Now he slipped one of the ship's log data rods into the car's mini and sat back, waiting for the text to materialize on the B screen.

"This rod is damaged," the aichy announced. "It is unreadable."

"What?" He frowned. "Try again."

"Unreadable."

"Try this one." He pushed another rod in.

"Likewise. I apologize, Mr. McNamara."

He was very frustrated. He said, "Are they coded to work on the *Star* only?"

"I cannot tell. But we've reached the Borgioli Building, sir."

Since the fairy-tale joining of the lowlife Borgiolis with Hunter Castle, Big Al had spent vast sums to upgrade his headquarters. Before, it had looked like a cheesy opera set.

Now it looked like a cheesy resort villa such as would be frequented by the wives of Mafia *capos* back in Earthside Sicily before the great leap to the Moon. At least, that was Deuce's impression from the flatphotos he had seen. The Borgioli Building was just one giant curlicue after another, with the Borgioli coat of arms—three hands, one holding dice, one holding the Queen of Hearts, and one crossing its fingers intertwined with the Castle corporate logo—"CAS-TLE" in slanted, rushed letters; Deuce would have used a real castle—set in some fake stained-glasses windows. Also stamped into a concrete derivative over the main, arched entrance, surrounded by cupids and unicorns.

As Deuce's aichy approached the roof, he nodded with satisfaction at the awesome display of security. There was firepower everywhere—headcrackers, soupers, blasters. Guys toting juice superpumpers, very lethal, very illegal.

After extensively verifying that he was who he looked like and said he was, there was a lot of *sciocchezza* over protocol as to who should group around him and lead him down the escalator that diverted from the offices to the heavily fortified Family bunker. Beatrice was holed up there.

Just as Deuce was going to berate them for taking so long, the honor guard was finally picked. He knew a lot of them by name, and they tried to make small talk with him. He returned the favor, flicking on his thinkerama and keeping track of names, faces, and new tidbits they gave him— that so and so had de-liaised, that someone had seen a quicktime from Yuet Chan to one of the minor Chan *capos*, something about supporting a new Smith conspiracy against the existing Chan regime—very interesting, that—and that Andreas Scarlatti's mistress was pregnant and his wife was claiming that she should get the baby since her husband had been blown up and there was no one to carry on their family name. Except, of course, for about two thousand other sons of the Scarlatti Family.

But seeing as everyone was wearing black armbands to mourn the dead, it was not the time to do a lot of chatting. After a time, everyone sensed that and the conversation lagged. Deuce turned his attention to the changes that had taken place in the year since he had been Casino Liaison for the Family. Improvements, mostly, the kind that money could buy.

For instance, the red, white, and green carpet on the escalator ramp was new and very clean. Deuce surveyed it with pride, remembering the many times he had come down this ramp, embarrassed to death that everything was so ratty. Before Bea had married Castle, nobody wanted to work for the Borgiolis. You couldn't get anybody in the unions such as the Affiliated Fraternal Order of Maintenance and Housekeeping to lower themselves to come over, and few N.A.s would even consent to besmirch themselves with Borgioli soap deposits and carpet fuzz.

Now there was incredible cognitive dissonance among Moonsiders about the Family: On the one hand, the Borgiolis had moved uptown, allied with Hunter Castle. On the other, they were still the Borgiolis.

Deeper and deeper he glided, past bare rock and bright lights and the metallic crossbeams from the old mining days. The escalator was faster than the old days, too. At the bottom, his phalanx of security guys peeled off and Back-Line Tony, one of the most intensely enhanced musclemen of the Borgioli Family, stood with his hands folded before him.

Deuce couldn't suppress his arrogant smirk. Back-Line Tony hated him. Why, Deuce could not remember, but now Tony had no hope that Deuce would ever be taken out by the Godfather. Which, Deuce knew, had been Back-Line Tony's fondest dream.

"A sad day, Signor McNamara," Back-Line Tony said deferentially, as he coded the door behind him. The man was so enormous he filled up the entire doorway and then some. He had to keep his head bent because otherwise it would have hit the transom. The result was that it appeared as if he were giving Deuce all kinds of respect, and Deuce knew it was making him crazy.

"A very sad day, Tony," Deuce responded.

The door opened. Deuce had a moment of concern and, without realizing it, cracked his knuckle. If you were not coded to go inside, you were blown to bits right on this very spot. Given all the hits going down in the chaos, Back-Line Tony might seize this opportunity to finally, "accidentally" zap Deuce into tiny, gooshy bits.

"Please," Tony said, extending his hand like it was his joint Deuce was entering.

Just then, Deuce's cousin Angelo appeared. Deuce gave Tony a moment to shout, "Oh, whoops, I made a mistake in the code." When he didn't, Deuce figured it was okay. Tony would not risk killing him in front of Angelo, who was very highly placed in the Family organizational structure.

Deuce walked to Angelo, who embraced him and whispered very softly in his ear, *"Buona sera, Padrino."* Good evening, Godfather. More loudly, he said, "A terrible day, eh?"

"Davvero, davvero," Deuce answered, sounding like an old, angry Don. "God be with the dead."

They both crossed themselves.

Followed by Back-Line Tony and a battalion of Family muscles who joined them at every intersection of the bunker's corridors, Angelo walked him into the Family chapel. Everybody dunked their fingers in the holy water and blessed themselves. Then Tony and the muscles moved respectfully away.

Veiled in black, Beatrice was sitting in the front pew with the Family religious big-shot, Monsignor Alfredo Borgioli. There were at least a hundred candles lit at the feet of the statue of the Virgin. The joint reeked of incense.

The Monsignor saw Deuce and quietly glided toward him like he had no feet beneath his robe. They maintained a distance from Beatrice, who hadn't registered that Deuce was there. Too doped up, Deuce guessed, flaring with anger. What on earth had Hunter been thinking of, leaving her in control?

"Good evening, my son," the big-shot holy man said to Deuce. "Is it true about Don Alberto?"

"I fear so, Monsignor," Deuce said sorrowfully.

"Then this child is the Godmother of both the Borgioli and Castle Families," the Monsignor said, gazing at Beatrice.

Deuce did not correct him about Castle not being an official Family. Like him, the holy man had grown up in the life, and who cared what it was officially called, anyway? It was a Family.

"Yes, Monsignor," Deuce said.

The Monsignor sighed. "Then God have pity on her soul."

Deuce nodded and crossed himself.

"And on you," the Monsignor added. He placed a hand of blessing on the crown of Deuce's head. "God be with you, my son."

"*Grazie*," Deuce murmured, feeling a trifle comforted.

"Duchino?" Beatrice said in a small, trembling voice as she rose from her knees. As she turned toward him, she lifted her veil.

The thing was, Beatrice was not a particularly attractive woman. In fact, one must admit that she was *uno piccolino* unattractive, and she was at a loss about how to correct for her deficiencies. Her motto was, and always had been, *More is still not enough.* Though there were maybe a dozen fashion magazines in circulation throughout the base, Beatrice seemed to subscribe to her own personal edition of *Mobster Beauty*: Her black hair was curly and frizzy, her makeup thick and heavy over her hard, big features and small, narrow-set, Big Al eyes. She was chunky and she did not dress to dechunk: She favored ruffles and gold lamé. Even her mourning dress, of maroon-tinged black, featured a ruffly hem of very out-of-date sequins. Her legs looked like barrels, and her body looked like a bigger barrel.

And as usual, assessing her like this made him feel like the superficial jerk he was.

"Bea, I'm so sorry," Deuce said, and then she was in his arms, sobbing for all she was worth, which, let's face it, was a lot.

"I loved him, I loved him," she grieved. "Not the same as you, of course, oh, Deuce!" He colored, surprised, because she had not shown one tiny bit of regret over dumping him for Hunter when her engagement had been announced. For him, it had been a godsend, since he was already in love with Sparkle and had no idea how to impart this information to Beatrice—or her revenge-loving father.

"Beatrice, listen to me," he said seriously. "Our hearts are broken, and it will take forever for them to mend, but there are very important matters to discuss. Where are your *capos*?"

"My—" she began, sounding surprised. He privately despaired. Beatrice wanted to go shopping, have her nails done, and gossip at the Catholic Ladies Association meetings.

"*Sì*," he said. "Your *papà's* top guys. Your bosses. Your underbosses. All your key advisors." He ran down the list: Silver Tongue Tommy, the Family *consigliere*, Ninety-Days Nino, Johnny Canoe, Danny, Carlo, Massimo, a dozen others.

Just last year, most of them had voted in favor of whacking Deuce for the infraction of the public brawl with Wayne Van Aadams. Now they called him up to play poker and brought him fancy presents. Johnny Canoe had recently tubed over a dozen real beefsteaks, which Deuce had not told Sparkle about because she was against red meat. Danny had presented Sparkle with a very nice string of fabulous opal gemstones. Such was business. It was nothing personal, either way, and the guy who worried about it—or thought it meant these guys suddenly liked him—was a *cretino* gravoid who was needlessly risking his future.

"Bea," he said again. "These guys are *your* guys now. They need to interface with you. You need to take command."

"Oh," she said, without much enthusiasm. "Yeah, I guess. They're waiting to talk to me in my father's . . ." Her voice caught. "In my meeting room."

"You should go talk to them," he urged.

"Oh, you do it," she said, waving her hands as if to wipe the duty off them. "I just want to take care of my baby. Take me to her now, please?"

"They're preparing to shuttle her down," Deuce said, frustrated with her. If she didn't assume command soon, she would probably get hit. Didn't she realize the delicate situation she was in? Being a big shot was not about what you could and couldn't handle. It was about acting like you should. Doing what was required.

"As soon as she's stable," he added, "they'll put her in the Borgioli hospital."

"Oh, no, not our hospital," she protested, looking to him for agreement. But he was not sure he still agreed with that sentiment. Each Family had its own private hospital, because in a more public setting, who knew who had been paid off to dump stuff in your IV or stick a pillow over your face? A year ago, any doctor with a decent medical degree went just about anywhere else except the Borgiolis' sickhouse to get a job. But now, with the Castle influence, he knew there had been significant upgrades. Maybe he'd ask Shiflett if he wanted to work there.

"Bea, where else?" he asked. There was really nowhere else safe to take her. The interdenominational Darkside City Hospital was nothing but a skeleton of a building. There were as yet no docs, no nurses, not even any Band-Aids. And you did not take the Designated Heiress of one Family to the hospital of another Family. Ever. There were all kinds of diseases they could give her that would not manifest for years, and they would never be traced to their original and correct sources.

"Not there," she said. Her eyes widened as she realized there weren't many other options. "Not anywhere."

"Bea, that's not possible," Deuce said.

She began to come unglued. "If you had married me in the first place, none of this would have happened!" she wailed, grabbing his arms. Her breath was bad. "I know you married that floozy showgirl on the rebound, Duchino. I know it's me you love. I'm offering you the Godfathership of the Borgiolis and the Castles if you'll divorce her and marry me."

The Monsignor sucked in his breath. Deuce's cheeks flamed. A lesser man might have been tempted. Actually, a stupider man might have been tempted. The man who tried to divorce Sparkle de Lune would have to be a moron.

"Bea, you and I are Catholics," he reminded her gently. She looked at him as if he was crazy. After all, they were Moonsiders first. The average life span of a legal marriage on the satellite was 2.3 years.

"An annulment can easily be arranged," the Monsignor said helpfully. Deuce wanted to juice him.

"Oh." Bea looked at him with shining, hopeful eyes. "Then . . ."

"Bea," Deuce said anxiously.

The Monsignor cleared his throat and gestured for Deuce to walk apart with him. They went together past the altar and the rows of candles to the Virgin, moving behind to the Borgioli crypts. From floor to ceiling, small titanium plaques recorded the name, birth and death dates of the Borgioli departed. Each repository was two inches tall, containing the very fine powder that was the dust of the deceased. On the Moon, only one kind of burial was permitted—cremation. If you had strong feelings about being buried, you could send yourself back to Earth or get shot into space. But Moon land was too valuable to clog up with moldering corpses.

The Monsignor stopped beside the plaque of Deuce's adopted *mamma*, Maria Caldera di Borgioli, bowed his head, and murmured a little prayer in Latin. Deuce joined him in saying, "Amen," and crossing himself.

"My son," the Monsignor said, "do you recall the words of Jesus in the garden?"

"Um." Deuce had not prepared himself for a catechism quiz. "The cup thing."

The Monsignor looked pleased. "Yes. The cup thing." He paused, smiling gently. "Let me tell you a parable, my son."

"The earth, when first created, was laden with darkness. There was no light. The earth and sky lay close together, as lovers lie. People were tiny, living squeezed tightly between the two. As they moved upon the earth, they bumped their heads on the clouds.

The people were tired of living like this. A hero stepped forth. His name was Lingo, and with the help of his brothers, he raised the clouds so that people could walk upright.

Pleased with his resolution to this terrible problem,

*Lingo turned his attention to the equally bothersome prob-
lem of eternal darkness. With the help of twenty-five men,
he cut down a great tree. From this he cut two enormous
disks.*

*Then he stole from a village a newborn babe, brought
him to the place where the disks lay in darkness, and fed
the disks the child's blood. The larger disk drank freely,
and became the sun. The smaller disk drank only a little,
and became the Moon.*

*As for the villager, he grieved for his son but a short
time. He looked up at the sky and saw the bright sun and
the pale but beautiful Moon. In these, the babe lives forever."*

The Monsignor looked at Deuce. "You know that with
all these deaths, the Moon is going to be thrown into chaos.
You know that we have had problems in the past with disaffected persons complaining to Earthside about our lawlessness, our violence."

That was very true. Deuce felt his insides constrict.
"Monsignor, I have feelings for the woman I married.
We've applied for a Family Voucher. To leave her would
be a sin, would it not?"

The Monsignor looked at him sternly. "You don't have
the luxury of such theological arguments, when the fate of
your world rests on your shoulders."

"Now, just a minute," Deuce protested. "I ain't the only
single guy on the satellite." Inspiration hit. "My brother—"

"Is not the man you are, Arturo."

He tried another avenue of escape. "We don't know that
Hunter's dead."

The Monsignor just looked at him. Apparently, that route
was likewise considered blocked.

"We may have only hours, perhaps minutes, to act," the
Monsignor continued.

"How's about this," Deuce suggested. "She marries my
brother, but I tell him what to do."

"You and Beatrice were promised to each other from
birth."

"No, Monsignor, that ain't true," Deuce protested. "It

was assumed, sure, that we'd liaise, but it was never official.'' He wondered if he could come clean with the padre, confess that he had lived with, and loved, Sparkle for over a year during the time that Beatrice had assumed he was in love with her.

But he understood that he presented a desperate solution in desperate times. Even as he and the Monsignor spoke, and his entire being protested the man's proposition, he was cracking his knuckle. If he did as they asked, he would be the most powerful man not only on the Moon, but Earthside as well. It was a heady thought, to say the very least that could be said about it. His adrenaline was pumping.

The Moon was going to need a powerful man. And he owed it to Hunter to protect his little girl.

''Think on it,'' the Monsignor urged him, patting him on the back. ''God's ways are mysterious to us mere men. Many people have told me in the past that it should be you, not Hunter Castle, who is the Godfather of the Moon.''

Deuce reeled. Was that why Hunter was dead?

''Monsignor,'' he said softly.

The man smiled sadly, gently, like Jesus in the garden. The cup thing. It pained this man of the cloth to deal in such affairs. It worried him that he must intervene in politics.

Yeah, right.

Deuce trudged back toward Beatrice with absolutely no notion of what he was going to say to her. She was clasping her hands together like a hopeful virgin.

Then, just in the nick, his badge went off. Deuce tapped it and said, ''Earphone,'' to the badge. Then, ''Yeah.''

''Big meeting, the Charter Board Building. Twenty minutes,'' Joey said. ''All the survivors are leaving the ship to attend. They want you there.''

''Okay.'' That was good; that was orderly. Maybe the survivors were smart enough—or afraid enough—to know that coming together made a lot more sense than killing each other off. ''I'll go as the Independent voice,'' Deuce added.

''You want I should go as the McNamara Godfather?'' Joey asked, speaking very quietly.

"No. Sit tight."

"You heard the latest about the blast?"

Deuce's ears perked up. "No."

"For sure not a new kind of QIC. Evidence is pointing toward the Smiths and a new kind of weapon, but not a Quantum Instability Circuit."

Deuce snickered. "Who leaked that, the Chans?"

"Dunno. I heard it on the viso net." Joey hesitated. "Bea there?"

"Yeah."

"Sparkle contacted me. She says Bea should definitely stay with you guys."

Deuce was silent as he processed that. Talk about your left field.

"She says Bea ain't safe anywhere but with you."

"Is she out of her mind?" Deuce asked. "Bea is like the queen of the friggin' satellite. What, she's going to sleep on our couch?"

Then he realized that Sparkle was correct in this, and sadly so: Beatrice was no longer a person, but a pawn. If he wanted to keep control of things, he needed possession of her.

The door to the chapel opened. At least two dozen Borgioli men stood silhouetted in the light from the interior of the compound. The Monsignor walked over to them and started to speak, then paled and moved out of the way as they drew their weapons.

Deuce immediately drew his own and rushed to stand in front of Bea. Her life as a private citizen had clearly just drawn to a close, and Deuce chalked it up to typical bad Borgioli management that it had lasted this long.

"Deuce?" she asked nervously, putting her hand on his arm. "What's happening?"

"Easy, baby," he said to her. He whispered to Joey, "You still with Stella?"

"*Sì.*"

"You packing heat?"

"*Sì.*"

"Stand next to her capsule and keep your blaster where

everybody can see it. Now, put this line on as many speakers as you can."

"Signora Castle," Deuce said to Beatrice, loud enough for the guys in the chapel to hear, "speak into my badge and say where you want your daughter, Stella, to be located."

"With me. With you," Beatrice said anxiously. "Deuce?"

"My brother, Giuseppe Caldera di Borgioli, is with her now. Does he have your permission to move her and to remain with her?"

"*Sì*," she answered, her voice rising. Finally, she was beginning to grasp the situation. She stared at the crowd of armed men with huge, terrified eyes. "Duchino, we're in grave danger."

"Shut it off," Deuce said quickly to his brother.

"We're private," Joey said. "I disconnected the public speakers as soon as I heard her say 'Duchino.'"

"Good. I'll disconnect as well." Deuce did so.

"We're in terrible danger," Beatrice repeated.

He embraced her, easing her head down on his shoulder. "I know, honey."

He tapped his badge three times.

His own thirty guys—Castle employees and a few N.A.'s he had commed on the way back from the *Star*—walked quietly into the chapel behind the Borgiolis' twenty guys.

Deuce eased Beatrice along with him and faced the angry group of men, his cousin Angelo at their head. He looked as if he thought Deuce had somehow ambushed him.

"*Buona sera,*" he said. "I'm escorting Signora Castle to the Charter Board meeting."

"I can't authorize that," said his cousin Angelo.

Angelo looked nervous, and he looked like he wanted Deuce to understand that this was nothing personal, only business, and in fact only show business. Because since Angelo wanted to be in Deuce's camp, Deuce taking charge of Beatrice would be a good thing.

Deuce glared at him, also for show. "It ain't for you to authorize. Signora Castle has stated her wishes."

The guy next to Angelo aimed his blaster at Deuce.

Angelo whipped out his own blaster and said to the guy, "Lower it, Mario."

"No," Mario said. "He doesn't leave with her. She walks out of here, the Borgiolis lose their trump card."

"Let me pass," Beatrice said like a duchess. Deuce was proud of her.

Deuce's guys pointed their weapons at Angelo's guys.

Then Angelo shot Mario. As Beatrice screamed, Mario crumpled to the floor, dead.

All the other wise guys looked stunned. Even gangsters respected the sanctuary of the church.

Maybe Deuce should have shot the guy himself. He didn't consider himself a gangster anymore.

"Monsignor, some last rites, please," Deuce said as steadily as he could.

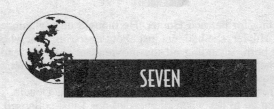

SEVEN

About fifteen minutes later, Deuce, together with Beatrice, Angelo, and an army of Castle and Borgioli bodyguards, flew over in a Borgioli stretch limo to the steps of the Charter Building. In sealed aichies, another army of bodyguards encircled Deuce, Angelo, and Beatrice's vehicle. Deuce had outfitted the three of them in Kevlite body armor.

Across the sea of men in Borgioli white, red, and green and Castle orange and black, Deuce nodded to Joey, who was standing on the steps cradling a superpumper across his arms. Other guys were milling around. Maybe nobody wanted to be the first to go inside. Maybe they were waiting to see if it blew up first.

Seated next to him, Beatrice slid her hand into Deuce's grasp and squeezed tight. She sat tall—well, as tall as she was—and straight, like she was indeed a princess. Her medication was wearing off, and so was the shock. Deuce was proud of the way she was rallying. Maybe Hunter had coached her in the event of a crisis like this. Maybe because he knew a crisis like this was going to happen.

Deuce had returned, not happily, to the notion that Hunter himself had set this up.

"I'm terrified," Beatrice whispered. "You know, on our honeymoon, Hunter told me that my life as I knew it was over. I pretended he was wrong." She sighed. "I'm so sorry I married him."

Deuce thought of the Darkside City penthouse digs he

was building for her and Hunter. He thought of how, since
marrying Hunter, she had met just about every big shot who
was ever born, including all the movie stars she had read
about in her magazines. Her real diamonds, her real furs.

"But you have Stella," he said.

Tears formed in her eyes. "I'm so ashamed, Deucie. I
didn't even go to her when she needed me. I just collapsed.
I was afraid the ship . . . the ship would . . . blow . . ."

He didn't want her to talk like this in front of Angelo.
He said, "It's all right. She's safe." But he didn't think he
would ever really forgive her.

The aichy stopped, lowered, settled. A phalanx of bodyguards got out, joining the others who were scanning the
streets, and made a dang army as they opened Deuce's
door. He got out, deliberately presenting himself as a target,
were one desired, and then helped Bea out.

Arm in arm, he and Beatrice walked in the middle of
their security forces, everybody kind of shuffling around in
close quarters. Angelo walked ahead of them to clear the
way.

Joey took a step forward. He said, "*Buona sera, Signora.*
My deepest sympathies."

White-faced, Beatrice nodded and looked down. "*Gra-
zie,*" she whispered. Then, in a rush, she said to Deuce,
"This isn't right, me being in charge. It's not at all what
Hunter said would happen if he . . . if something happened.
He said he would name you."

Deuce shook his head. "That wasn't in the Plan of Succession he gave me."

"But he told me . . ." She stopped speaking as they
started up the steps. She was shaking badly.

The sea of other surviving Family Members parted in
respect. The major players included the swaggering, handsome Rudy Caputo, youngest son of the very ancient Caputo Godfather, Giancarlo, and little brother to the dead
Kinky, who had been the Designated Heir. Doting and dod-
dering Don Giancarlo was also there, a withered mummy
in a wheelchair who looked like he was dead. He didn't
actually run the Family anymore, and everyone knew it, but
no one would ever say such a thing to his face.

Standing to one side of the Caputos were the two surviving Scarlatti Select of Six, Vito and Santo, who also went by Sandy. They were bandaged and limping. It looked like Vito would have a wicked-ugly scar running diagonally from his left temple, under his nose, over the upper right corner of his mouth.

Also, Roger and Abraham, the two co-Godfathers of the Smith Family, both alive and looking shaken but otherwise none the worse for wear. That was interesting, since there was speculation that the Smiths had perpetrated the bombing. A team of lower-ranking Smith Family Members who had been aboard the *Star* training Castle security forces in Moonsider strategy and tactics had been taken out; that might have been done to deflect suspicion. If that was their goal, it would have been better to take out someone higher up.

The Van Aadams group was looking pretty dismal, a scattering of the not-so-connected and even fewer highly ranked guys. Their big shots had not had a lot of children, and Wayne and James were the only nephews of Chairman William Atherton Van Aadams. For all that the rumor had been that Wayne Van Aadams was a clone of the Chairman gone bad, there didn't appear to be any other clones. And the way everybody in the Van Aadams party on the front steps was looking at the gawky, nervous Robin Van Aadams, Wayne and James's second cousin, either he was going to be proclaimed the new Godfather or they were going to rub him out and pick some other poor joker.

Rounding out the Family leaders was the first son of one of Yuet Chan's stepbrothers, Sying II, which meant Star. That he was the Family representative fascinated Deuce. Yuet had hit Papa Sying and Uncle Cheung when her own mother, Dai-tai, had died. No one had ever found their bodies, but everyone knew they were dead.

It was the short but brutal turf war that had followed Dai-tai's death that had inspired the Charter Board to order each Godfather, C.E.O, and Select of Six to file a Plan of Succession. It did not have to made public, and it could be rescinded. The Board claimed the creation of POS's was to help keep order by ''encouraging'' the Families to plan for the future. But Deuce agreed that it was just another instance of the Feds having too much say in how the Families ran their business.

Sying II had been put in place by the Caputos, who had been handed the keys to the front door of the Pearl of Heaven, the Chans' casino, following the arrest of Yuet for the murder of Wayne Van Aadams. And although Hunter had been the one to hand over the keys, the Charter Board had agreed with the decision, modifying it to include the "good side" of the Chan Family. Sying II was really just a puppet of the Caputos. However, as he tooled around Moonbase Vegas in his gorgeous stretch aichy, he didn't seem to mind that he was just a figurehead.

But a lot of Chans did mind. They wanted all the Chan action back in Chan hands.

Deuce had made a lot of secret deals with those particular people.

Deuce looked up, imagining that somewhere above them, *Gambler's Star* hung in the air like a fish some shark had attacked. Of course he could see nothing here but klieg lights raised above the cavernous tunnel in which the Charter Board Building was situated.

The ornate Charter Board Building was located deep within the Moon, for security and as a holdover from when no one had been too sure that the domes would keep out the lethal radiation. The reasoning went that the lower you dug in the Moon, the more likely you would not mutate or die.

Deuce wistfully remembered the first day he had come here. It was his alleged thirteenth birthday (who knew for sure?), which in Family life counted as the beginning of your adulthood. After a brief ceremony at Borgioli HQ that consisted of slashing his palm and reciting the oath of *omertà*, he and his *mamma* had come down here with Big Al, who stood in for Deuce's unknown father.

Despite the arrival of Castle as the seventh player in the Family system, and Deuce as representing the people who had no other representation, the building was the same now as it had been thirteen years ago. The six crests of the Families were lasered in stone on massive columns, three on one side of the blind statue of Justice, three on the other.

She wore Roman robes and held up a scale. On each side of the scale rested a die. Both of them showed sixes.

Deuce had half expected Castle to request a replacement with some other kind of symbol. Moonside gaming did not sanction the use of seven- or eight-sided die. Maybe a little castle should be carved somewhere. But Castle had requested no changes, and of course the Families didn't want anything changed on account of him.

The MLF, however, did want a change. They wanted the Non-Affiliateds to be artistically represented. However, like so much else in their lives, the amount of bickering this created among the various Independent factions proved that they were not a cohesive group. No group, no symbol. So for now, the Charter Board Building pretty much belonged to the Families, even though Deuce was the designated voter for the N.A.'s (an innovation that had come about last year), and Castle got a vote as the holder of a seventh Casino Charter. So Deuce was here for the N.A.'s, which he hoped everybody remembered.

The black armbands kept parting. Deuce put a staying arm in front of Beatrice, and said to her, "No way you're going in there without a security sweep."

This caused a minor rumbling through the assembled masses. This was unheard of. To the Casino Families, the Charter Board Building was more sacred than any chapel, any cathedral, any Mormon temple. No security checks were ever run because the Charter Board Building represented security; if this joint wasn't safe to be in, no joint was.

Which was Deuce's point. The rules had all changed. Life as they had all known it was over. And if Hunter had caused this, Deuce would honor Big Al's deathbed obligation and rip out the bastard's heart.

He and Beatrice waited while Joey and the bodyguards went in, totally ignoring the protests of the Charter Board employees who tended the facilities and kept the big Board happy. Since Borgioli and Castle guys went in, the other Families sent guys in, pretty much eliminating the usefulness of a security sweep in the first place.

Joey came out and waved Deuce and the others in. Deuce

thought of the old flatfilms of the First Mob, filing into various what did they call them—speakeasies and gin joints—to plan their wars against the G-men and each other. Deuce half wished he had a violin case with him; it was that tense and eerie kind of day.

Yeah, a violin case with a nuclear warhead inside it.

The big shots trooped in. The old round table was there, eight pie shapes decorated with the colors and the crests of the Families and the logo of Castle Enterprises, and a wedge stripped of whatever colors it had been before. It was bare wood now, and it was Deuce's piece of the pie. This whole thing only served to underscore the general belief that there was a limited amount of action to be had and that because of the two new players, everybody else's pieces had shrunk. They should buy a newer, bigger table.

Only Family heads were generally allowed inside at the table; usually there was one, maybe two chairs at each pie section, except for the Scarlattis, who were run by the Select of Six. Vito and Santo looked lonely as they sat down.

Don Giancarlo, wheeled in by Rudy, picked compulsively at the blanket covering his withered legs and pointed to Joey and Angelo.

"These two are not Family heads," he said. "They should not be here."

"The rules are different today, Don Giancarlo," Deuce said firmly, lowering his head to give the old Godfather respect.

"Hmmph. They should not be different. What has happened is the kind of thing we should expect with our lifestyle," Don Giancarlo grumbled.

He smacked Rudy's hand. "Where's my heart medicine? Give me my heart medicine. I need it. *O, Mamma mia*, this is all such a *stupidaggine. Mi sono proprio stufato.*"

Which the Australians and the Smiths would not probably understand to mean, "I'm sick and tired of this."

Ignoring the old man, Deuce guided Beatrice over to the Borgioli sector, then thought a moment and took her to the Castle sector. More clout there. The others had better remember exactly who they were dealing with.

That should have been whom.

A classy guy knew that.

As she sat, he pulled out his deck of cards—every Family Member carried one, and old habits died hard—and he placed them squarely inside the Borgioli pie wedge, as if to save his place.

"What is the meaning of that?" Don Giancarlo demanded.

Deuce shrugged. "Signora Beatrice Castle di Borgioli don't carry."

"Okay, right," grumbled Don Giancarlo. "She don't carry. But that's your deck, and you aren't a Borgioli no more."

"I asked him to do that," Beatrice said, "on account of I am naming him my regent. If anything should happen to me, Deuce McNamara speaks for both my Houses." She cleared her throat. "That is, the Borgioli House and the Castle organization. I also publicly name my daughter, Stella Castle di Borgioli, as my Heir." And God help the little mite, should anybody take it into their heads to further clear the decks today.

"The Charter Board calls this meeting to order," a disembodied voice said above the noise.

Everybody except Don Giancarlo rose and bowed to the scans that lined the wall behind the table. The Board had eyes; the Board could see if you did not pay it respect. It would remember. It remembered everything: every hit, Sanctioned or not, Registered or not; every Vendetta, every dishonor. Everything. It calculated everything, weighed everything, decided everything.

Or so it felt to those it controlled.

It had been installed by the Department of Fairness after all the bloodbaths. The public had wanted Moonbase Vegas shut down. Even Deuce had to admit the stats proved its effectiveness: The violence level had definitely dipped after its creation. And Earthside was pleased with the setup, because it could police the Families in a remote and impartial way. And collect its vigorish, in the form of what were politely referred to as "taxes."

Bribes, pure and simple. And as for the impartiality of the Board, each Family had an elite crew that monitored the Board and tried to covertly reprogram it to favor that Family. So far, all attempts had failed, or at least, that was the public line. Sometimes Deuce wondered if someone really had hacked into the Board. But if that was the case, it wasn't possible to tell. The Board did seem to act fairly.

"This emergency meeting has been convened to reestablish normalcy as soon as possible," the Board's voice continued. "The Board seeks to clarify the current status of the Family System, and to account for all Vendettas, dishonors, and hits, and to determine if Earthside governors should be called in."

"I die first!" Don Giancarlo shouted, raising his fist. "I blow up my casino and strangle all my children!"

"Dad," Rudy said nervously.

"What? What?" Don Giancarlo demanded. "We built this place! We, the Caputo Family. We were here first! We should have kept all the action for ourselves."

"You have two casinos," Robin Van Aadams said bluntly. "What more do you want?"

Don Giancarlo sputtered at him. "How dare you speak to me like that, you little boy!" He gestured to the Charter Board screens. "I consider that an insult! Register it as such."

The Board's lights blinked. It would remember.

"Sying, you protest as well," Don Giancarlo pushed.

The young Chinese man blinked and looked down at his hands. "Don Giancarlo, with all due respect, we should wait until another time to worry about this," Sying said. Deuce liked his approach. It had class: He stood up a little to the old man, yet he didn't indicate he was unhappy with his arrangement with the Caputos. It was a nice job of walking the line.

"Is there any other old business?" the Board inquired, and several present chuckled. The old CB had a sense of humor.

"Let's proceed," Deuce urged. "We got to have a united voice on what's going on, or there's going to be rioting in the streets."

"Like last year, which you caused yourself, with your hero *sciocchezza*," Don Giancarlo groused. "Okay, go on.

Don't listen to me. I'm old, and no one listens to me anymore.''

"Don Giancarlo, you have my respect, and you will always have my respect,'' Deuce said sincerely. Which was true. In his day, there had been no Godfather more clever or ruthless than Giancarlo. Deuce didn't know why he hadn't done another rejuve. There had to be something wrong with him that medical science could not fix.

"First agenda item,'' the voice continued. "The disaster aboard *Gambler's Star*. Preliminary Reports indicate this was an accident caused by Mr. Castle's experiments with a new power source.''

"What?'' Robin Van Aadams demanded. "Are you out of your mind? Or did he finally pay you enough to flat out lie to our faces?''

There was a collective gasp. You did not attack the Charter Board personally. You did not ask it if it was out of its mind. Ever. Not that the Charter Board was supposed to register dishonor on its own behalf. At least, that's what everybody believed. But you never knew. To attack it was to question its judgment, and one of the fundamental principles of the Casino System was that the Board was completely fair and unbiased. If you didn't go along with that, chaos would surely follow.

Kind of like right now.

"With all due respect,'' Deuce said, standing as he addressed the Board, ''what kind of evidence do you have against Signor Castle?''

"We have been replaying the quicktimes from the *Star*'s data stream. It seems that Mr. Castle was trying to develop a new type of starship engine.''

"For what?'' Don Giancarlo blinked and looked at the others. "Where did Il Grande Fusto want to go?''

Despite the gravity of the situation, Deuce almost smiled. Don Giancarlo was calling Hunter "the grand he-man.'' It was an insult, to be sure. For all his athletic competitiveness, Hunter had been a relatively small man. Trim and in good shape, but in no way a he-man.

He thought back to the log entry he had read in the presence of Moonman and Joey. *The Moon is just a stepping-stone.* From the look on his face, Joey was thinking about it, too.

"Then I lodge a protest against Mr. Castle and I demand he compensate our house for the loss of my Heir, Kinky, and my nephew, Mario," Don Giancarlo said.

He held up a hand as he tapped his comm badge. "I'm contacting my *consigliere* to give me the entire list of our dead. And I will demand blood money for each one we lost."

"Our House demands compensation as well," said Robin Van Aadams, who, let us realize, had personally benefited greatly from all the deaths.

For at least fifteen minutes, the talk turned to money. Beatrice lowered her head and began to cry. Deuce knelt beside her chair, and she whispered, "What is the price that you put on the loss of your father and husband?"

"Signora Castle?" the Charter Board asked. "Do you request monetary compensation, and from whom?"

She looked at Deuce and whispered, "Well, since they think Hunter did it . . ."

He laid a hand over hers. "You head two Families, Bea. One is a very old and proud Family with a rich heritage." She looked unimpressed, but he persisted. "Very rich heritage. The other is a conglomeration that puts out an annual report only, and has no sense of history."

She blinked. "That's not true. Castle Enterprises was in Hunter's family since before the Earthside Civil War of the 1860s."

"But he didn't think of it the way Don Alberto thought of the Borgiolis," he pressed, trying to lead her to the water. Conflict of interest though she might have, the Borgiolis would not forgive her if she didn't demand a lot of fish for their pain and suffering. The Castle shareholders would yowl, but they would not Register hits and Vendettas. That was not the Earthside corporate way.

No, as Hunter had put it, the Moonsiders were a nation of gunslinging accountants, and they would keep tabs on every single credit that exchanged hands as a result of the explosion.

Bea was silent for a moment. "That's so dumb," she said finally.

O, maledetta. She was still not thinking like a Godmother.

Deuce raised his hand. "As second to Signora Castle, I propose that Castle Enterprises make a one-million credit donation to the Borgioli Scholarship Fund for a Drug-Free Moon."

"A million?" Don Giancarlo scoffed. "Castle Enterprises is worth a million times a million."

"It's a worthy cause, though," Beatrice murmured. Deuce turned scarlet at the public display of her ignorance. There was no Borgioli Scholarship Fund for a Drug-Free Moon. The Borgiolis loved drugs, used them, and ran them. It was Hunter and Hunter alone who had been antidrug. His stance had made him tremendously unpopular. Particularly among the Chans, the Family who produced Chantilly Lace, the most potent and addictive hallucinogen in the satellite. Joey had been severely hooked on it, as was nearly every one Family Member in ten. Only Yuet Chan, the Godmother, had shared his antidrug sentiment, and he had fingered her for a murder she had not committed. And that setup of her had never made sense to Deuce. Unless Hunter had coveted the notoriety of being the only drug-free casino on the planet.

Maybe the Chans had blown up the ship.

Deuce raised a hand. "This is important, *amici*, to that I agree. But we must also work to erase our hostilities and suspicions about this tragedy from the deep friendships we have for one another. That is what my boss would have wanted."

"Why?" Don Giancarlo said scornfully. "It's over. Castle's dead. Surely his city will be abandoned."

"And why would you think that?" Beatrice asked in a loud, strong voice. "When I'm here, and Signor McNamara is here? When we have various agreements with you, and with the Independents?" She narrowed her eyes. "Don't you think we have the *minchia* to finish my husband's dream?"

"*Mi scusi, Signora*, we meant no offense," Rudy Caputo

said quickly. Don Giancarlo batted his hand.

"If anyone here wants to challenge me, do it now," Beatrice said, rising to her feet. "Be honorable and let me face my enemy. Because if I discover anybody has an Unregistered hit on me, I'll gouge their eyes out with a spoon."

Deuce forced himself not to grin. That was an old saying of Big Al's, and it was great to hear his daughter repeat it. Maybe this was going to work out after all. Maybe, with any luck—and with an emphasis on tradition—someday he would hear little Stella speak those words. If he, Deuce, lived long enough.

If any of them lived long enough.

"Who's threatening to hit you, *Signora*?" Sandy Scarlatti, also rising to his feet. "We'll hit him for you."

Vito also stood and nodded vigorously.

"No, we'll hit him for you," Robin Van Aadams offered.

Beatrice sat back down as she took all this in. Deuce didn't know whether to cheer or draw his blaster.

He also didn't know what the Smiths thought. They had remained silent since the opening of the meeting. Shrewd people, those Smiths. Perhaps he had been foolish not to cast his lot in with them. But then he would be just another *capo*, and not a leader.

There was a lot more discussion, during which Deuce kept his thinkerama going, even though it kept going off on tangents like showing him a minidoc on the mating habits of robins as well as a lecture on various types of heart disease. Judging from the nature of his medication, Don Giancarlo suffered from some kind of arrhythmia, which in these days was simple to cure. Also, you could just clone a new organic heart or install a mechanical one. Deuce wondered why he hadn't done either. Some people just had a death wish, he supposed.

After over an hour of discussing and haggling—during which the Smiths still said nothing—the Board requested the attention of the assembled gathering.

"The Charter Board has reviewed the survivor lists and balance sheets of each Family," it announced. "The Board has determined that, for the most part, the balance of power remains the same as before today's accident. With one exception: the Borgioli Family has lost more high-ranking Family Members than any of the other Houses, including the loss of the Scarlattis' majority of the Select of Six and the *capo di tutti di capi* of the Select, Andreas.'' Everyone in the room crossed themselves.

It continued, ''But the number of Borgiolis lost is partially compensated for by the fact that the Borgioli Godmother is also the C.E.O. of Castle Enterprises.''

And the most attractive widow on the satellite, Deuce thought. And he was the husband she wanted.

''Accordingly, the Charter Board tables at this time any plan to request immediate emergency oversight from the Department of Fairness, in the form of a representative from Earth. This recommendation assumes that the Families will comply with their leaders' filed Plans of Succession, and that through the Board satisfactory agreements will be reached regarding the amount of compensation each House will receive once proof of liability for the explosion aboard *Gambler's Star* is established. And finally, that no bloodbaths are contemplated, and that all hits will continue to be Registered through the Board.''

It paused, as if it half expected someone to raise a hand and say, ''Oh, no, please do call in the government *scemos,* and make everyone's life a living hell and completely undermine our economy. Because we're most definitely planning a bloodbath, time and place to be announced.''

''However, this situation will be closely monitored, and the Department of Fairness will be called in the moment the Board determines it is necessary.''

Like the others, Deuce grunted unhappily. Even though the threat might be enough to make everyone behave, the reality of significant government intervention would never be tolerated by the Casino Families. Already the Feds were too involved in their business, was the general feeling.

''This emergency meeting is adjourned,'' the Charter Board announced. ''Another meeting will be held in twenty-four hours, at 6:30 P.M. Moon Standard Time, once more information is gathered and incoming hits and Vendettas are tallied and examined.''

Slowly, everyone got up. Everybody's eyes were on everybody else. The mistrust in the air was thicker than blood.

A mechanical glided up to the group, and said deferentially, ''Ladies and gentlemen''—even though Bea was the only broad in the place—''we are now serving refreshments in the Dutch Schulz Memorial Dining Room.''

As they pushed back their chairs, every man in the room circled Beatrice like a vulture as she sashayed over to Deuce and clasped her hands around his wrist like a pair of cuffs. Her tear-stained face beamed lovingly up at him, and he cleared his throat meaningfully.

''Bea, you're a grieving widow,'' he murmured.

''Everybody knows you and I were destined.'' She made a moue and brushed a tear from her eye. ''Though of course I loved Hunter, in my way.'' She hesitated. ''And he in his.''

''He adored you, Bea,'' Deuce said firmly. Maybe if he said it enough times, she would remember it that way, or at least, act like it.

''Oh, no.'' Mournfully she shook her head. ''He adored *her*.''

He stiffened. ''Her who?'' Fully expecting—make that hoping—that she was referring to your typical Daddy-Mommy-Baby Girl kind of triangle.

''Your wife. That Sparkle woman.'' She rolled her red, smeared eyes. ''Honestly, Deuce, what did you two see in her? I mean, I know you were shocked that I went with Hunter. It was Daddy's wish. He ordered me to.''

Deuce almost laughed out loud. Imagine Big Al ordering Bea to do anything. That was rich.

He remembered Big Al's last order to him: Kill Castle. He wondered, if the big guy walked in here and confessed that he had engineered that explosion on purpose, what Bea would do if Deuce popped him on the spot. Which was, she would flop, hurtling herself to her dead husband's body and screaming at Deuce that he would pay for his terrible deed. She was that kind of emotional broad. No offense meant. It was the way she was brought up, a typical Italian Family princess. There was no reason in the world she had to be mature. Except for the reason now presented: She was the unwilling, untried, and unprepared head of two major organizations.

But it didn't matter. Hunter would never confess to such a thing as a haywire experiment. If he was still alive. Which was looking less likely with each passing hour.

Deuce said to Beatrice, "Let's go eat. It's bound to be nice stuff, this being a wake for the accumulated dead and all."

"Champagne and caviar," Bea said unenthusiastically as they walked into the dining room. The walls were decorated with holos and flat oil paintings of famous men of action—Capone, Luciano, Schulz, and earlier Godfathers of the Six Families. Deuce could now state without reservation that the paintings were not so good.

"Real caviar, though," Deuce offered, admiring the spread. The champagne was Bollinger. Good stuff, he was proud to report to himself. Not that it was good stuff, but that he knew it was. Cheese and little canapes, all kinds of real fruit. "Not anything crater in sight."

Bea looked unimpressed. "I can all have this for every meal if I want."

She looked straight at him and trailed her hand down his chest. Deuce knew everybody else was taking notes. Knew someone was sure to mention this to Sparkle, if they could figure out how to do it without her breaking their legs.

His girl did not put up with much.

But Beatrice didn't seem to care about other people. Maybe she thought she didn't have to. But nobody was that powerful, ever. That was one of the rules you learned on your Godfather's knee. Or should learn. Figuring you were invincible just made you an easier target. Maybe that's the lesson Hunter had just been taught.

"Bea," he began, taking her hand. She turned her palm inside his grasp and made as if they were holding hands.

She said, "Do you have any idea how rich I am?"

"Yeah," he said bluntly. "Do you?"

"Rich enough," she said, smiling flirtatiously at him, and handed him a glass of champagne.

Just then, there was a huge commotion in the foyer. Heads turned; blasters got pulled from jackets and pockets. So much for the rule about not packing heat in the inner sanctum.

The House animals rushed to the front door while the Heirs and Godfathers remained in the dining room. If the building was being attacked, let the Charter Board guys die in the line of fire. Maybe lightning don't strike twice in one day, but why tempt fate?

"Deuce, what's happening?" Beatrice asked, clinging to him, even though his view was just as bad as hers.

"I demand entrance!"

Deuce smiled. It was Angelina Rille, officially the head of the MLF, now that her *papà* was dead.

As the leader of the Non-Affiliateds, Deuce stepped forward and said boldly, "I move that we should let Signorina Rille come in. The MLF is a powerful special interest group and better that she talks to us face-to-face than perpetrates hits on us in secret."

"Oh, and then what, we let the Mormons in here?" Don Giancarlo asked derisively. "And then, who, our prostitutes and our taxicab drivers?"

"I will be heard," Angelina said. Deuce couldn't see her. She was surrounded by heavily modified security guards, and as she had never had her legs extended, she was actually shorter than them. But he did see one hand waving above her head. Nice manicure. Angelina went in for the girlie stuff.

"Deuce, get these thugs off me!" she yelled.

Deuce grinned and winked at the Family Members. "Just to humor her," he said in a patronizing voice. "She just lost her *papà*, she thinks she's running things. In a few days, who knows? She'll probably be dead."

He prayed not. But it would not do Angelina's cause any good to promote her to the others. They hated the MLF; it was one of the most dangerous factions on the Moon, existing as it did outside Family influence. To the Casino

Families, the MLF got all the privileges of Family life without any of the accountability.

"I say she stays out," Robin Van Aadams said, maybe because he had the Mormons in his back pocket, and he had to show that he had his special interest group under control.

"Bea?" Deuce asked.

Beatrice's eyes widened. It was clear she did not want to cast a vote either way. Also, on a personal basis, she was jealous of Angelina Rille. She had picked up the vibes between her ex-fiancé and the militant but very attractive dame.

"Gentlemen, lady," said one of the building employees, "I suggest we consult with the Charter Board."

Don Giancarlo muttered something that made Rudy turn white and murmur, "Grandfather, please, let's be careful."

"Careful. In my day, the people trembled when a Caputo walked down the street. Now we are . . ." He gestured to his wheelchair and let his hand drop to his side. "All right, all right, we'll play this out. But this game is rigged. The dice are cackled; who denies it?"

He looked around the room. Everyone else blinked back at him, not at all interested in agreeing that the Charter Board was capable of partiality.

So everyone trooped back into the meeting room. Beatrice picked up another full glass of champagne, then a second, gesturing for Deuce to carry them like some adoring *gigolo*.

On the way to the meeting table, he gulped one down and handed the other one to Beatrice. She looked mildly put out.

He said into her ear, "Honey, with all the medication you took, you shouldn't drink very much."

Her face softened. "You're right." She raised the glass to him and gulped down the contents in three big gulps. So much for savoring, tasting, enjoying.

Everybody sat down at the table while Angelina was escorted into the room by a freakin' phalanx of security guys. The Charter Board was blinking like crazy, assessing the situation, trying to decide how to rule.

The goombahs parted a little, and Deuce saw Gina. He was surprised at her appearance, having expected an MLF uniform. What she wore was a stupendous scarlet evening gown studded with silver moons. She wore silver flats, which were the fashion. Her hair was pulled up high above her head, galvanized to a burnished copper, and tumbled in curls down her back to her shoulder blades.

There was a murmur of appreciation around the table. Beatrice's cheeks were stained red. It was obvious she liked being the queen bee, even if she didn't want to act like one. Queen Bea, that was rich.

Princess Angelina, now, that could be a different story altogether . . .

"So, am I in or out?" Angelina demanded of the Board. She stood with her shoulders square and her chin jutted, but you could tell she was scared. No MLF had ever been inside the Charter Board Building in the history of the Moon. You could just see that she wanted to look around and take in her surroundings.

"What is the current membership of the MLF?" the Board asked politely.

Angelina laughed. "You've got to be kidding me. We don't post our statistics."

"Yet you insist that your organization is of sufficient size and strength to send a representative to this emergency meeting," the Board pointed out.

"Strength in numbers is not always the best indicator," she shot back. Deuce was proud of her. In another world, given a whole lot of different things, maybe him and Gina would have—

"We deny access," said the Board. "Don Giancarlo is correct in his statement that we must not initiate a policy of allowing less significant groups."

Gina was outraged. "I will be heard!" she shouted at the top of her lungs. "I will be heard, or you will regret this decision. Bitterly regret it."

Like a finger had snapped, the security guards raised blasters, headcrackers, and various other weaponry and aimed straight at Angelina's head. She whirled around and glared at them.

"Oh, just do it," she taunted. "Do it and my people will be all over this place. And your precious Board will be blown—"

"Gina," Deuce said, stepping forward. "As spokesman for the Independents, I would be glad to have a sitdown with you and discover what are your concerns. Which I promise I will bring to the table exactly as you describe them to me. I got a thinkerama and I can play it back word for word." Finally, he would get some use out of the damn thing.

She looked uncertain. Beatrice rolled her eyes, which was stupid of her, but at least she kept silent. The others nodded, impressed with King Solomon here.

"I want to talk to you now," she said. "I don't want to arrange a meeting. I want to talk this minute."

Deuce turned to the others. A few shook their heads. Others shrugged. But it really wasn't for them to say.

"Agreed," said the Board.

"But I don't want to go outside," Deuce said. "Too much is going on. For all we know, there are snipers." Since the MLF was the only group that officially had snipers, that was a bit of a dig against Gina. Which he knew. He didn't want anybody to make the leap that this babe was going to stick him in her back pocket once she got him alone.

"Agreed," the Board said again. "We will provide a small antechamber for this meeting."

"Not bugged," Angelina said. "All surveillance turned off."

There was a pause. Then the Board said, "Agreed."

"And in the meantime, we cool our heels like, what, dogs?" Don Giancarlo grumbled. "I don't allow such treatment."

Suddenly, Beatrice smiled at the old don and sidled over to him. She laid her hand on the back of his wheelchair and said in a breathy voice, "Don 'carlo, please, I just lost my *papà*, and I know you knew him from when he was very young. We don't often have time to sit down, just among friends, and remember the old days."

She turned to the Board employee and clapped her hands.

"Enough with this *schiamazzo* champagne and silly little sandwiches. We want *Chianti* and some nice *focaccia*." She looked at Sying II. "And pot stickers." And Robin Van Aadams. "And what do they eat in Earthside Australia? Grilled shrimps?"

"No, *Signora*," Robin Van Aadams replied, with a faint smile. "But I believe that you eat grilled shrimps for breakfast."

To Deuce's intense pride and relief, laughter swept the room. Maybe she wasn't a queen, not yet, but she was Family royalty, and she wasn't going to let these bums forget it.

When Beatrice glanced at him, pleased and surprised, he gave her a wink. Perhaps it was that wink that got him in so much trouble later.

"Miss Rille?" he said, gesturing as the security guys milled around.

Together they left the room, Deuce aware that he was smoky and stinky and she looked like a fashion model. She smelled great, like orchids, many of which he had seen. They were the flower of choice on the Moon, on account of they had been grown in hothouses for so many centuries. It was easy to duplicate their environment even if you were five miles below the surface of a sunless, airless satellite.

Deuce and Angelina were escorted into the marble entryway, then guided to the right into a room. It was very small and simple, reminding Deuce of many of the offices he used to go into when he was a Casino Liaison.

They sat in two overstuffed green chairs with a little table between them. Against the wall was a large couch upholstered in matching fabric. Overhead, a chandelier.

Deuce said, "Confirming that all surveillance is off."

"Confirmed," said one of the walls.

"Okay." He blinked twice. "I'm recording, but I won't tell them our personal business."

He leaned forward and took Angelina's hand. "Gina, I'm so sorry about your father," he said.

Tears welled in her eyes. "He'd been sick for a long time. I don't know what was wrong with him," she said sorrowfully. "People just don't get sick anymore."

"*Davvero, davvero,*" he commiserated. "I had wondered about that, myself."

She looked nervous. "You knew?"

He shifted and gave her a sad, lopsided grin. "You actually thought I wouldn't know?"

She sighed and glanced down at her hand. Her skin was warm. Her gown draped low, revealing cleavage he had not realized she possessed. He had never seen her dressed up before. Mostly she wore her MLF commando togs as if they were correct for any occasion.

"What do you want, honey?" he asked gently. "What do you want me to tell them for you?"

She sighed again and let go of his hand. "We demand to be heard. We have never been given a voice in the governing of the Moon. Now that things have changed, we want them to change even more." She looked hard at him. "Or we'll make them change."

"Baby, they haven't changed that much." He yawned. He was tired. Now he was sad again. Because nothing was going to change for Gina and her troops. Any fool could see that.

"Hunter's dead, it's true," he said. "And a lot of people got taken out. But Hunter was the C.E.O. of a major corporation, not a king or a god."

"Don't talk to me like I'm a fool," she snapped. "I know very well you're terrified of a turf war."

He shrugged, trying not to convey just how accurate she was. "But that's part of the lifestyle," he said. "That don't concern the regular people."

Blazing, she doubled her fists and slammed them down on the armrests of her chair.

"God, Deuce! How stupid can you be? Your turf wars do concern the regular people. Because the regular people get killed in them!"

"Not if they stay out the way," Deuce said defensively. Because he knew she was right.

"You're one of the only Family men who worries about the little guy," she said. To his astonishment, tears coursed down her cheeks. "No one else makes sure they aren't going to hit an old lady coming out of her apartment when they perp a hit. No one else gives a damn if the getaway car slams into a kid crossing the street.''

''No, Gina—''

''Deuce, you have to stand up for us,'' she said. There was desperation in her voice. ''You absolutely have to, or . . .'' She took a breath. ''We'll find someone who will.''

He was silent a moment. Was she talking about taking him out?

''What do you want me to tell these guys?'' he asked gently.

''We want representatives from the Department of Fairness to come up from Earth,'' she said in a rush. ''We want someone to monitor the situation.''

''But the Charter Board—''

She shook her head violently. ''We're not even programmed into its equations. We're a nonentity.'' She squared her shoulders, as she had done when facing the Board. ''We won't be overlooked anymore. This is our chance.''

Deuce's lips parted. He sat quietly for a moment, watching her. Her chest was heaving. He had a wild flash of image of the two of them—there was that couch—and then he suppressed it. He had a wife.

''Gina, did you blow up *Gambler's Star*?'' he asked.

She laughed harshly. ''As if we could.'' She leaned toward him, took both his hands, and squeezed them. ''But I'm telling you this, my darling, my love, if we could have, we would have. We're that desperate.''

Deuce swallowed and stood. She did not let go of his hands as she stared up at him. Their gazes locked.

He said hoarsely, ''I'll tell them, Gina.''

''Don't tell them,'' she shot back. ''Convince them.''

With as much care and tenderness as he could afford to show—which was not much, not at all—Deuce eased himself away from her and walked out of the room.

''Convince them,'' she called after him.

Deuce raised a hand.

And then he went back to the meeting.

*   *   *

The meeting did not reconvene until after Miss Angelina was escorted from the building. Deuce replayed the pertinent parts about what the MLF wanted. When he got to the part about requesting Earthside's assistance, Don Giancarlo went into defib and ended up being taken in an ambulance to the Caputo hospital.

At which point, Rudy Caputo turned to Deuce and hissed, ''If my Godfather dies because of this insanity that you wasted our time with, I will send your head home in a box.''

But the Charter Board announced that it would rule on her request later in the week. This drew the ire of the rest of the Family Members.

''I am only the messenger,'' Deuce protested, but that didn't seem to carry much weight with the angry group.

All in all, not much of an improvement in his day.

EIGHT

When you're traveling with a combination Godmother/ Heiress, it takes forever to go from place to place. The security, the precautions, are agonizing. Never mind that everyone is so mad at you they're just itching for you to have an accident on your way home.

Thus, after the meeting at the Charter Board Building broke up at 8:00 P.M., it took four hours to get from Moonbase Vegas to Darkside City. Deuce knew that when the express tunnel was completed, it should take less than an hour. Unless, of course, you were still traveling with someone who's considered the closest thing to a hand grenade your satellite's got.

And unless you were never forgiven for having the stupidity to sit down with the MLF.

However, witnessing Beatrice's reunion with Stella was worth the hassles. At Deuce's instructions, the medical team and all the security guys had been shuttled down to his apartment. A fully functional intensive care capsule and support system had been plugged into one of the several extra bedrooms, and the place was bulging with people who otherwise would not have made it through Deuce's front door without being reduced to bits of DNA.

Now, at almost 1:00 A.M., Beatrice leaned over Stella's incubator and cooed at her, tears sliding down her face. Touched, Deuce almost forgave her earlier faltering. Almost.

What he did not forgive was that *cretino* detective,

O'Connor, calling his house after midnight to talk about what had happened to Jackson and Dr. Clancy. The cop was pretty angry, having recently discovered that Jackson's body was missing.

Deuce yelled at him for disturbing him on this, everybody's night of mourning.

"And as for Jackson's cadaver," he added, "it's not my job to keep track of the dead. It's yours. And God's." He crossed himself.

He hoped Shiflett would be a stand-up guy about this and forget that Deuce had had Moonman ship Jackson down with the other medical equipment, and he was now lying frozen in a portable cryo tank in Deuce's garage.

"I want to talk to you first thing tomorrow morning, McNamara," O'Connor said, like he had any authority over a Family man. Then Deuce reminded himself that he wasn't a Family man, and Hunter had always maintained a friendly and respectful relationship with the local law-enforcement people. Or at least pretended that he respected them.

"Yeah, whatever," Deuce said. "Pencil me in for your midmorning coffee break." The first of many, he was sure, since the Lunar Security Forces were unionized.

He hung up and walked down the hall, watching his own shadow grow large on the opposite wall. He felt dizzy looking at it. He didn't feel like he was anyone he knew.

Just then, Moona Lisa, their Dachshund derivative, skittered toward him in utter delight. Pencil-thin tail wagging, crooked body wiggling, she yipped with joy at the sight of him. They had gotten her at a discount because the cloning hadn't gone precisely according to Hoyle. She looked somewhat individualistic, to put it nicely, to be kind, and because he loved her: eyes a little strange, legs rickety and uncertain.

"Go on, baby, go back to bed," Deuce told the little dog. He watched her skitter back down the hall in the direction of her soft and plush doggie bedroom.

Deuce and Sparkle shared very snazzy digs, no matter that at least two-thirds of the Independents who worked on Darkside City were still housed in trailers. They were nice trailers. Deuce's apartment had twenty rooms, upon which

Poppy Dancer, the famous Earthside decorator, had lavished loads of gold and white, with discreet touches of orange and black. Gold and white for the Moon, Poppy told him. Orange and black were Hunter's colors, and putting them in his home had given Deuce pause. It was almost like wearing them on his sleeve, which would have identified him as a Member of the Castle Family. Which he was not. He was an employee, sure, but he was his own man.

Whether or not anybody else believed that.

The thing was, the notion of big shots being employed by corporations was not a Moonlike notion. The Casino Families lived at the top of the heap, even though everybody pretended that the Mayor and the police chief and like that were just as high up. That was a load of *schiamazzo* that no one bought. Except for guys like O'Connor, who must be either new to the Moon or real straight arrow.

Before Castle came, if you wanted the good life, you got yourself born into a Casino Family and automatically inherited Membership for life. Naturally, you had no say in the matter. Only the Mormons—a very powerful interest group on the Moon—believed you literally picked your parentage before you came into the world. Oh, sure, your parents could do a lot of preprogramming. That went without saying these days. But nobody—who was Catholic, anyway, and half the Families were—believed that you sat in some heavenly waiting room with your ticket in your hand and waited for your number to come up.

The most a non-Family Member could hope for was to be made an Affiliate of a Family. This you achieved not by grace but by good works, and being an Affiliate was almost as good as being a Member. But it was not the same. It was just like in the old days of Earthside mob life, when only Italians could become "made men" in the Mafia. Non-Italians were accepted, even loved, but they were not made.

Deuce was pretty much a legend now, adopted as a child into a Family, which was very, very unusual—even if it was the lowest-class Family, the Borgiolis—then renouncing that priceless Membership to go undercover for his Family; then remaining Independent even after he could go back into his Family and had been invited to Affiliate with nearly all the other Families. Then finally, allying with Castle. No one else on the Moon had ever gone through such a Byzantine route to the big spin.

So, the fact of his fancy apartment didn't piss off many of the Joes living in trailers. It actually gave most of the N.A.'s hope that something magical would happen to them, too. Guys like Bucky Barnum, who had better explain everything there was to explain about Connie Lockheart. Deuce had sent some boys over to the Moonbase Vegas compound to pick him up.

There were also your grumblers, your union bosses and Family *capos* and underbosses, but Deuce knew their envy came from secretly fretting that they weren't as connected or as cunning as him.

So, among the gold trim and white carpets and glass-and-gold tables and crystal chandeliers, Deuce lived what most people, including him, considered a princelike lifestyle. They had a cook and a maid. They even had their own swimming pool, which on the Moon was almost unheard of.

Most of the apartment's rooms were decorated with drawings and models of the City, as well as memorabilia from Sparkle's showgirl days and her kickboxing trophies. Trophies she had tons of. Also, many gas photos of them together with lots of celebs and mucky-mucks, mugging for the cameras. And if you had a good eye, you found the Borgioli family crest tucked here and there, Deuce's gesture of honor to his fairly dishonorable heritage.

Now he and Sparkle stood in the doorway of one of the spare rooms, observing the reunion between Stellina and her *mamma*. For all her flakiness, Bea was a good mother, very tender as she leaned over the capsule with her fingers in the sleeves, caressing the tiny girl as tears rolled down her cheeks. Despite the demise of Dr. Clancy, the medical team was still performing miracles vis-à-vis the health of the Heiress: It looked like she wasn't going to have to have cloned lungs after all.

"Sweet, ain't it?" Deuce murmured.

Sparkle had a tight, funny look on her face. Deuce wondered if she were wishing they already had a baby by now, or if she was tired of his bad grammar. While he was pondering this, his thinkerama chip conjugated the verb form, "to be." He sighed and blinked twice to turn the damn thing off.

Then he took his wife's hand. She let him do it, but she didn't exactly reciprocate. That was Sparkle. Sometimes he wondered if she found him just too needy. Knew that wondering that proved just how needy he was.

Beatrice may be a frowsy dresser with bad hair and worse judgment, but she was Italian; she was out there with her feelings. Sparkle, dressed in a shimmering, straight gown of black satin with a robe belted over it that outclassed Beatrice by a mile, had been almost distant when she kissed Deuce hello.

"What happened to the nanny?" Sparkle asked quietly. Deuce was impressed. Hardly anyone else had asked.

"Died protecting the little one," he said. "Apparently she put Stella in the enviro-ball first, then tried to save herself. It was too late." Even though she could take it, Deuce spared Sparkle the gory details.

Sparkle said, "Beatrice should compensate her family and mention her by name at Big Al's funeral."

"I'll mention it to her," Deuce said, admiring Sparkle's insightful suggestion. "You, ah, foresee this?"

She thought for a moment, then shrugged. "I've had the feeling for a while that something bad was going to happen." She looked at him. "But I thought it was going to happen to you."

The hair rose on the back of his neck. "Jeez, honey, why didn't you tell me?"

She almost smiled. "It would be harder for you to take more precautions than you already do. I didn't want to add to your stress level."

His stress level. Through the roof already was his stress level.

"You got feelings about Hunter?" he asked, half-casually.

Her gaze was neutral. "As in how?"

As in, are you his freakin' mistress? Deuce wanted to ask. But he said, "As in, is he alive?"

She put her hands around his neck and kissed him. It seemed so odd for her not to have to bend down to kiss him. He had been brought up to appreciate tall women, so he hoped he kept it a good secret that he'd been disappointed that she'd had her grafts removed.

Still, no one kissed like Sparkle. And before his marriage to Sparkle, Deuce had done a sampling of the female Moonside kissing population.

He felt himself melting against her, and she against him. Her lips moved over his in that special way of hers, and he gasped. When he pulled away slightly, she was smiling at him.

He confessed, "I thought something was going wrong between us lately. I thought you didn't love me anymore."

She snickered. She was romantic that way. "Remember back in our little apartment?" she asked softly, trailing her hand down his chest. Whoa, shades of Bea. "When you were just a Casino Liaison and I danced at the Down Under?"

He sighed. The good old days when they were peons. "Being a big shot is a lot of work," he confessed.

"Being married to a big shot is a lot of work," she countered. "Do you know who Lady Macbeth is?"

"A horse?" he guessed. He hated looking ignorant in front of her.

She smiled proudly. "Exactly. I have a feeling that when she runs her next race, a lot of this tension will dissipate."

Deuce was fascinated by these premonitions Sparkle got. Neither one of them could explain them, but she seemed to be getting more of them, and they were getting more accurate and detailed.

"What color of horse?"

"The most beautiful horse you've ever seen." He heard the lilt of humor in her voice, and wondered if she was somehow making fun of him. But Sparkle was too straight-arrow for that kind of thing. She wasn't the kind of dame who teased you or put little sexy notes in your lunch pail. She was the kind of dame who oversaw your portfolio and refinanced your house if interest rates went down. Not that they really had to worry about that kind of thing anymore.

"When she has a baby, she'll change," Joey said on occasion, whenever he saw that Deuce was a little disappointed in her efficient coolness. "You just wait."

Deuce just hoped the baby she had would be his. Then he was shocked at himself for thinking such an unworthy thing, and let it go.

Or maybe he just buried it.

Maybe.

And speaking of Joey, Deuce thought as they watched Bea with Stella, and Joey and the armed guards lounged all over the house, it might be a good time to marry him to somebody. He wondered if he could actually pull off getting Bea to accept his brother as his substitute. If Deuce's current wife was pregnant, not even Beatrice would expect him to divorce her . . .

Sparkle narrowed her eyes at him. "What are you thinking about?"

He jumped guiltily. He wasn't sure if she could actually read minds. Sometimes he thought yes, sometimes no. He said, "Affairs of state."

She laughed and kissed him again, a kiss as sweet as sugar-coated almonds.

Beatrice turned toward them at the moment that Stella finally yowled, a lusty shriek that indicated her good condition. At the sound, Deuce half turned his face and saw the look of hatred and pain on Beatrice's face as she stared at him and Sparkle smooching. Through the incubator sleeves, she was clutching the baby tightly, maybe so tightly the little girl was screaming.

"Hey, hey," Deuce said, pulling away from Sparkle and crossing to the capsule. Beatrice looked stricken as he bypassed her and leaned over Stella in her incubator.

"*Mamma mia, Mamma mia, bambina, carina.* What's the matter with you, Stellinina?" Deuce whispered.

This baby should have black hair. He had thought it before. Her *papà* had salt-and-pepper hair now, but it had been dark. Bea was dark. He knew you could get those throwback genes, and that Beatrice insisted she had had auburn hair as a baby, but this was yellow-white. Someone looking at her might think she was his own child. But that was impossible. He had never, ever, slept with Bea, a fact of which he was both proud and a little apologetic, since he knew she would have liked him to.

Beatrice walked past him and snipped to Sparkle, "I'm hungry."

Sparkle kept her composure. It would have been less than classy to join the catfight, and Sparkle was nothing if not classy. Plus, she was the one who had Deuce, so she could afford to be gracious.

"I'll be happy to make you some soup," Sparkle said, maybe offering to prepare it herself in order to humble her household a little before Beatrice. After all, the cook had already made sandwiches for the medics and the security people.

"Or scrambled eggs. We have real ones," she added, with an uncharacteristic show of pride.

"No pasta?" Beatrice asked with disdain. She glanced over her shoulder at Deuce as if to say, *How could you marry a non-Family girl? How could you get married at all? You should have pined for me at least a little while. Like your whole life.*

All the daughters of Godfathers thought like that. It was just that Bea, being a Borgioli, had never been subtle about her feelings on any subject.

"We have lots of pasta," Sparkle replied evenly. "What kind would you like?"

Deuce decided to make a graceful exit. He gave Sparkle a nod that Beatrice couldn't see. Sparkle shrugged as if to say, *What ya gonna do?*

In the next room, Joey and Moonman waited for Deuce. They had minis loaded with requests for meetings. Things were beginning to heat up. In the streets, in private clubs, and in heavily secured bedrooms, they all knew that Family Members were busily offing each other, either directly or with hired help. Lots of fairly low-level guys had died within the past twenty-four hours, but a number of higher-ups had been whacked, too. It was to be expected: The ambitious underlings were taking advantage of the chaos to make a couple jumps on the checkerboard.

Any big shot got whacked right now, Deuce figured he had either underestimated the loyalty of his soldiers or hadn't paid enough for security. His own apartment was surrounded by the Earthside equivalent of an army, and every square inch was surveyed and scanned by Peekissimos, Sniffissimos, and armed with lasers that would fry anything that even so much as blinked counter to programming.

After conferring with his two key men for a few minutes, Deuce took his place in his office—his more formal at-home workplace, as opposed to his comfortable study—and prepared to receive his visitors. It was almost 2:00 A.M. now, and he was tired.

The first to creep nervously through his door was his cousin Angelo. Deuce met him in the center of the room and kissed his cheek in the old Family way, accepting Angelo's kiss in return. Then he offered him a chair in front of the desk, just as he would any other visitor.

Deuce did not consider himself a cynic, but he was a realist: Relationships would change today. Some friends would become enemies. Some enemies, bedfellows. You couldn't be sure of anyone, even after they declared themselves. It happened whenever there were shifts in power. It was no big deal. It was part of life.

Angelo sat forward slightly. He was a handsome guy, rather like Joey except he had very wavy black hair and his eyebrows were bushier. He had changed into another good suit and put on aftershave. There were no Borgioli colors on his sleeve, a very telling absence, for Angelo always wore his colors. High-up guys were expected to. Deuce was pleased that he had made this gesture, even if it was dangerous for Angelo.

"*Padrino,*" Angelo began, then waited as if he expected Deuce to stop him. But tonight Deuce did not. Tonight— this morning—Deuce wanted to hear what Angelo had to say on the subject of Deuce being his Godfather.

"*Padrino*," Angelo repeated, "I've come to pay my respects."

Deuce inclined his head. Angelo had stated the obvious.

"And to tell you that I have two hundred loyal men in the Borgioli Family who are yours. We'll do whatever you want."

Inwardly, Deuce cheered. But he said casually, "That's wonderful, Angelo."

Angelo beamed.

"In exchange for?" Deuce asked easily. From a silver carafe on his desk, he poured himself a tumbler of water and offered one to Angelo. Angelo's eyes widened slightly. Deuce and Hunter had let it be well-known that Castle Enterprises brought up real fresh water from Earth—not mere recycled Earthside water, although even that was superior to Moonside processed water—and also, that very few outsiders ever got to taste it. It was a big honor to be offered some.

So Deuce made a show of pouring it for him and handing the precious liquid to his cousin.

Even though it was really Moonside water—the virgin stuff, to be sure, the dark side ice kind.

The secret kind.

"In exchange for protection, if we're found out," Angelo said with big, wide, honest eyes. He fingered the tumbler and stared down at the water, clearly distracted by the prospect of drinking it. "If we need to come to you, that you'll give us a place."

"A place?" Deuce asked, smiling faintly. "For two hundred of you?"

"Deuce," Angelo said, maybe treading close to the edge of disrespect by still using his first name, maybe trying to remind Deuce that he, Angelo, used to be his superior in the Borgioli Family and had done him innumerable favors. "I know that by the end of this day, you're going to have thousands of guys promised to you. Soon, when you're sure you could have a decent-sized Family, you'll go public."

Angelo finally sipped the water. Looked stunned by the flavor, the bouquet. He added, "I mean, I'm thinking that, anyway."

Angelo was making his points. But it was one thing to negotiate secretly with someone, then sit back and see if he failed or succeeded. If he failed, you could pretend you'd never shaken hands with the dead man. But if you were named in his public Family book, your old Family could claim Vendetta against you. You would be labeled a traitor. You would be scum.

You could well be dead.

"Someday, I will lead a Family," Deuce said, touching his heart to show his sincerity. "It might be now, it might be in twenty years."

"It could be the Borgiolis now, if you marry Bea," Angelo said carefully. Deuce knew Angelo was praying that he, Angelo, was not making a tactical error. If Deuce was indeed planning to assume command of the Borgiolis, he might not look kindly on soldiers who were willing to leave the Family for any reason, even if he was the reason.

Deuce felt sorry for his cousin's predicament, but it was not his place to make Angelo feel better. A deal was a deal.

Deuce went on, leaning back in his chair. "What else do you want in return for your loyalty?" The abstract notion of protection at a later date was not enough to make a man look outward from his own Family for someone to deal with. Angelo had more immediate ambitions, or else he was an idiot.

"We want a piece of Darkside City," Angelo said, unembarrassed. "We want a percentage of the food concessions."

Deuce pondered that. "At the casino?"

Angelo shook his head. "We figure that'll go to your Van Aadams faction. We want a ten percent net in the concessions on the tunnel expressway."

Deuce whistled. "That's a lot. Who are you bringing me? Besides yourself, of course." That was meant as a compliment. Angelo was a high-ranker in the Borgioli Family. In some scenarios, his loyalty would be enough to secure a deal. But not for ten percent of anything to do with Darkside City.

"I'm Bea's confidant," Angelo said. Now he did look embarrassed, and well he should. He was essentially betraying Deuce's childhood sweetheart to Deuce himself. "She listens to me."

Deuce kept his face a mask and made a steeple of his fingers as he sat back in his chair. He felt bad for Bea. Real bad. She shouldn't be a pawn in this game. She shouldn't even be in this game.

Deuce said, "If you told her to marry Joey, would she do it?"

Angelo shrugged and moved his hands like an Italian. "She'd give it a lot of thought, anyway. But you know she don't love him."

"You know I don't love her," Deuce said softly.

Angelo hesitated. "*Sì.*"

Deuce waved a hand. "But Joey loves women. All women. I think he would look upon Bea as . . . raw material to focus his energy on, *capisce*? Like, he don't especially need a particular woman to love, just *a* woman. Like a gambler. It doesn't matter where the game is, as long as it's a game. And Joey will play the hand he's dealt. He'll play it well."

Angelo nodded. "Just a game." He looked unhappy, his very handsome features twisting with sadness. "I feel so sorry for her, Deuce. She doesn't really have anybody now. Her *papà*, who doted on her, God rest his soul"—they both crossed themselves—"has cashed it in. The only other man she loves is married to somebody else, and I think she knows she was just a trophy for Signor Castle."

Deuce looked curiously at Angelo. Here was a better mate for Bea than Joey. Here was someone with some depth, who would honestly care for her. Which had to have been Angelo's angle all along. This was what he really wanted.

But he was only Deuce's cousin, not his brother, and therefore, more likely to turn on him with the next blow of the wind. Not that there was any wind in the Moon. On both Moonbase Vegas and Darkside City, the temperature was kept at an even seventy-four degrees Fahrenheit and sixty percent humidity.

Deuce sighed, regretful that he couldn't satisfy his ambitious cousin.

"Joey will be good to her," he told Angelo. "Now, what can I do for you?"

In essence, *What will you take as compensation?*

Angelo lowered his head to hide either his disappointment or his anger. It would be better if it was disappointment rather than anger. Anger often resulted in revenge. With disappointment, you just took a deep breath and tried another angle.

"You know I got Moonman and Joey as my two top advisors," Deuce went on, before Angelo had a chance to speak. A mistake—Deuce should let him show his hand before he gave him any new cards, but he couldn't help himself. He didn't want to see anger on Angelo's face. When you were in the life, you thought about preemptive strikes if someone looked like they were mad at you. He, Deuce, was not in the life anymore. He would not hit someone he was related to, not even if that someone posed a threat.

Or so he told himself. So he hoped was the truth.

"Yes?" Angelo prodded.

Deuce shook himself. He was getting tired. "Joey never bothers much with Family affairs, preferring instead to concentrate on private business." The business, until last year, of living a degenerate lifestyle. "And Moonman, he just came back to the satellite last year, and he has never been a Family man. I respect their opinions, and I listen to what they tell me, but the truth is, I have no good, strong, Family perspective."

Angelo leaned forward eagerly. Deuce could read his body language like a book, and he figured Angelo meant for him to.

"Would you join my cabinet?" he asked, wondering if Joey and Alex would be offended that he hadn't checked with them first. "Would you serve me as a loyal *capo* and also help me with your advising of Beatrice?"

Angelo looked pleased. It was almost as good as marrying Beatrice. Not quite. But close.

He rose and took Deuce's hand. Deuce wore no flashy jewelry like some guys did, but Angelo kissed Deuce's wedding ring like it was the Pope's ring and bowed.

He said humbly, "*Grazie, Padrino.*"

Deuce raised a hand. "Only we'll keep this under wraps

until I announce the formation of our Family. There's no sense you going public until it will fully benefit both of us.''

Angelo nodded.

"And then you'll bring me your two hundred soldiers."

"Three hundred," Angelo promised.

Deuce smiled.

So did Angelo. He got up and inclined his head, then asked, "May I pay my respects to Bea?"

"Sure." Deuce wondered if he should get him married to her after all. First he'd have to talk to Joey.

But before that, Rudy Caputo was due in. Deuce felt a little twist in the pit of his stomach. Sure, he was used to dealing with Godfathers, but not as their equal, or close to it. Before, he had played the one singular hand Lady Luck had dealt him, parlaying his position into Hunter's lieutenant. But now Hunter was gone, and he was on his own.

He got up and moved from around the table. He would go to his front door and greet Don Rudy with respect and humility. And pray that everything went well.

As he left his office, Sparkle approached with a worried look on her face. She put her hand on his chest and urged him back inside.

"Rudy Caputo's dead," she said without preamble. "He got hit by his cousin Alphonse."

Deuce took that in. "You heard how?"

She looked at him very seriously. "I saw it."

He swallowed hard. One of her visions. "You're sure, baby?"

"I was walking across the room, when everything went black. I saw him. I saw a man with a blaster. Alphonse was there. He nodded." She shuddered. "Then I saw the top of Rudy's head sliced off."

"Do you know if Alphonse is on his way here?" he asked her.

She nodded. "He's practically at the front door."

"I'll meet with him." Deuce started to go, then stopped and looked at her. "Honey, what is it?"

"I have a bad feeling about this."

"Which part?" he asked nervously.

"All of it. Something feels very wrong." She rubbed her

arms. "Now, when I close my eyes, I see red and black."

"Roulette," he said, trying to sound cheerful, even though he was scared to death.

"Blood and death," she replied, standing aside for him to pass. She grabbed his hand.

"Mine, you mean."

There was actually a tear in the corner of her eye. Sparkle never cried. He wasn't even sure she knew how.

"Be careful," she whispered.

"Always am."

"You liar." The tear spilled down her cheek.

Thoroughly terrified, Deuce left her, making his way past a dozen armed men who jumped to as he approached. He chatted with them for a few minutes, let them see he was not nervous or tired. He was their leader, and he was worth following.

After a few minutes, he went around the corner and saw his brother standing facing him at the closed front door. He had a large box in his arms.

Deuce froze and thought of Uncle Carmine.

"It's his head," Joey confirmed, nodding slowly.

"Rudy's?" Deuce asked.

Joey sighed. "Alphonse's."

"Who brought it?"

"One of Rudy's boys," Joey told him. "He's with some of our boys right now, filling them in."

Deuce took that in. Sparkle had not read the situation entirely correctly—or had she. She'd said Alphonse was on his way over here, and that she didn't have a good feeling. That pretty much made it two for two.

But this was not good for business, all this whacking of big shots. The Department of Fairness was going to have a field day with this.

"Who's in charge over there?" he asked his brother.

Joey shrugged helplessly. "Who's left?"

Deuce thought a moment. Then he said, "Joey, get Moonman and start calling all the Casino Liaisons for a sit-down. No, I'll do it."

Joey's deep-set Italian eyes got huge. "You have meetings scheduled with Godfathers and like that."

"Maybe I do, and maybe I don't," Deuce replied.

He hustled back into his office.

Sparkle was sitting behind his desk, and when he sailed in, she looked startled and guilty, but she didn't get up.

They looked at each other for a beat. Then she said, "I was reading the *Journal*."

He pretended not to be verifying her story as he came around and leaned over her, kissing her slick, cool platinum hair. Now that they were rich, Sparkle used the very best galvanizers money could buy.

Sure enough, she was reading the early edition of the *Wall Street Journal*. It had been her daily ritual ever since he'd first met her. The other showgirls, they read some whacked-out beefcake zine called *Fabricated Beast*. Not his baby.

"You know what? Even in a crisis, you're one cool lady," he said.

"I'm Lady Macbeth," she answered, which he did not understand. Lady Macbeth being a horse and all.

He cracked his knuckle and said, "Baby, I've got to cackle my dice."

Which meant, in gambling talk, that he was going to make it look like he was shooting straight, when he wasn't. The time for making nice with ring-kissing and social calls was past.

Things were going to get rough.

He put his hand on her shoulder, then on her stomach. Nuzzled her under the jaw. "Honey," he said gently, "are you pregnant?"

She stiffened. "What?"

"Because if you are, I'm sending you Earthside."

"You know I'd never go in a million years," she said, almost angrily. Then she turned around and looked at him. "Our Voucher hasn't been approved, has it?" All this with Vouchers was new. The Charter Board had instituted a system for applying to have a kid when the Smiths lodged a complaint about the larger number of births to the Italians, pointing out that said Italians already held a majority— three casinos to everyone else's—and they didn't need to breed quite so much.

This was weird, because as obvious a move as it might seem to outsiders, the Italian Families—the Borgiolis, the Scarlattis, and the Caputos—did not have any kind of special, private alliances going. They viewed each other with the same amount of suspicion and hostility as they viewed the other Families. But in this case, when their right to reproduce was threatened, they did ally. They retorted that: So, their people were loving and fertile. What crime was that? Bigger was the crime of birth control, which His Holiness back on Earth still decreed was against the will of God.

The Mormons got in on the act, too, and through them, the Van Aadams Family. The Mormons were allied as a religious body with the Australian Family. So basically, the only two Houses who wanted the Voucher System were the Smiths and the Chans.

The Board had appealed to the Department of Fairness, which went ahead and instituted the Voucher system. The result was that you had to apply for permission to make a baby, and the application fee was stiff. In essence, all it was was a freakin' bribe. No Family Member had had a single Voucher rejected yet.

On the other hand, Non-Affiliated's were supposed to be exempt from the Voucher System, a bone thrown to keep them happy with their lot in life. But Castle employees above a certain income level were considered Members of his Family, and so they had to pay, too.

Now Deuce shrugged. "Maybe the Voucher don't matter." The worst thing that could happen to them would be a hefty fine for not applying. Before, after, what was the difference?

He pressed the door to his office shut and unbelted her robe.

Her eyes flared with excitement and she half smiled as she helped him, murmuring, "You animal."

"I'm your stallion, baby," he replied, and her smile grew.

"I figured you were putting me on," she said. "I knew you knew who Lady Macbeth was."

That almost, ah, dampened his ardor, because he wasn't

following her at all. But she lay back over his desk and held her arms out invitingly, and he didn't care if Lady Macbeth was a dog she had bought to keep Moona Lisa company.

"Deuce," she whispered. He leaned over her and she ran her fingers through his white-blond hair and kissed him over and over again. Sparkle kisses. Wonderful, wonderful kisses.

All the lines on his comm system lit up and stayed lit. He was one of the hot tickets in town.

That was for sure. Hot as the surface on a sunlit day, hot enough to boil all your blood. Passion, did it pass for love? When some rabbit was addicted to gambling, you knew they would die waiting for that one big score. You knew they would play any game because if you lost enough, you just had to win something back.

Prior to falling in love with Sparkle, Deuce had looked at love that way. You lost a little every time you rolled the dice. Each card you drew pushed you past magic twenty-one.

With Sparkle, it had started not to matter whether he won or lost. Just that he got to play.

But were they using the same rules?

Did she love him?

"Maybe tonight we'll make that baby," Sparkle breathed into his ear. His lunar surface, his lady of shadows and rilles and big dreams and bigger realities.

The only game in town, for him.

"I'll do my best, honey," he promised, as the eagle landed.

She sighed with pleasure, and that sigh warmed him like a comet. She reached for him.

"You always do." Then she whispered:

"The moon shines bright; in such a night as this,
When the sweet winds did gently kiss the trees
And they did make no noise, in such a night
Troilus methinks mounted the Troyan walls,
And sigh'd his soul toward the Grecian tents
Where Cressida lay that night."

Deuce heard the words like wind through the trees as he moved over Sparkle.

When they were finished, he murmured, "Baby, what were you before you were a showgirl?"

She took a long time to answer. Then she finally said, "Just another dumb kid." She touched his hair. "Like you."

NINE

It was like old times.

Dressed in a black-leather jacket and tight leather trousers that molded to his contours as he stood before the mirror in their bedroom, Deuce checked his blaster and took his secondary off the charger. For a moment, he was the kid again, the swaggering Liaison with a girlfriend and a future. A Borgioli with nowhere to go but up.

He missed that kid in the mirror. Man, did he miss him.

Sparkle was elsewhere, maybe even sleeping, and Moonman and Joey were busy making his apologies to the big shots for canceling their meetings. They were pleading fatigue on Deuce's account, which made sense, and could not be held against him as an insult. So if anybody was lodging complaints down at the Charter Board, they could only be said to be petty, insecure gravoids who would regret their small-mindedness later.

Plus, since everybody knew Bea was at his place, anyone with half a brain was making real nice to him until they figured out if they could get her to stay at their place.

So it was that Deuce actually sneaked out of his own house and whistled softly—well, tapped his badge, actually—for a nondescript, black aichy to pull up around the corner. No sense going incognito if he was going to use his fancy, well-known car with DRKSIDE emblazoned on the license plate.

How he got past his own security, he hoped he would live to brag about at a later date. Maybe it was stupid to dodge lasers and retinal scans that would cream you all over the wall if you did not check in with them first. Maybe he should have concocted some kind of lie about where he was going and go through his own proper channels.

But if the bosses ever discovered that he was planning to sit down with some of the little people—mere Casino Liaisons—rather than those at the top, there would be hell to pay. Not only would it be a grave dishonor to the big shots, but it would look, feel, and smell like he was encouraging disloyalty in the ranks. Families ran like armies—like the MLF—and sure, you had your side deals and your own personal business. But on matters that affected the entire Family, you reported to your boss, who reported to his boss, and it was the big boss who talked to Deuce about it.

Deuce was new to being in these top levels himself, but he wasn't new to dealing with them. If he did say so, he'd been a great Liaison. Even without his thinkerama, he'd kept track of tons of names and faces, working deals upward and downward, gathering so much information that he had to parse it out to his Godfather, Big Al, so the man would not be overwhelmed by it. And withholding what Big Al could not process or would waste . . .

He was also used to the other guys who were used to dealing with the big shots. In his heart, he was still a Casino Liaison, and he knew how to talk to Casino Liaisons, straight across the table, man to man. Maybe he was supposed to know about wines and like that, but in his heart, he would rather go bowling and slug back a Bad Moon brew.

Maybe Sparkle had realized that, too. Maybe that's why Hunter was so sure he could have had her.

Whatever. That kind of fretting was for later. For now, it was glorious to move on his own, down among the folks, working by his wits rather than the fact that he was, or used to be, Hunter Castle's lackey. He had forgotten the good feel of his Casino Liaison clothes, the sensation that anything could happen.

Of course, none of the sizzle and flash of his hometown was on display here in Darkside City. It really was pretty much dark. No huge neon signs, no holos, just a lot of skeletal buildings in caverns and tunnels standing beneath a minimal set of kliegs. Security guards were walking beats and sitting posted in trailers.

He sneaked past a makeshift casino and entertainment complex, hastily erected to keep the workers from whacking each other out of boredom. There were ten such complexes spread over the massive construction site. Most of them featured a gas movie hall, pool and gaming area, bar, fancy restaurant—by blue-collar standards—and a more reasonably priced coffee shop. Everything was offered way below cost, to get the guys to stick around rather than go off to Sin City on the other side of the Moon, AKA Moonbase Vegas.

Speaking of sin, Deuce had persuaded some of the more adventurous prostitutes to come on over here, at least part-time, and he knew the workers were grateful to him for that. The guys were grateful to the girls, too, and paid them more than double what they got on the other side of the Moon. So everybody won—which was why his union guys should not futz around with their hinky lasers and coffee breaks, and just do the job they were being overpaid to do.

Hunter didn't know about the girls, and he didn't need to know. Sparkle, he figured, did know, and just looked the other way. She must have had a lot of showgirl friends who were working girls; that was the lifestyle. Not hers, however. At least, not that she had let on about.

He zoomed around, altering his direction, keeping watch for suspicious activity while he accessed his thinkerama and sorted through a dozen different files, looking up names and matching them with faces. There was a fairly good chance about a hundred different people were out to whack him, for a hundred different reasons. Right now, everyone was riding teeter-totters and they were either looking to leap on or off.

After a time, he pulled over to make sure there were no tails on him, and that was when he saw the little girl.

She was trudging along the sidewalk, her head bowed, barely able to move her thin legs. He watched her for a while, and every now and then she would stop and look around.

He squinted his eyes suspiciously—this was the dumb kind of trap you had to look out for, someone trying to make you lose your edge worrying about a kid. Except that in the Moon, most big shots didn't even notice forlorn little kids wandering around alone in the middle of the night, much less risk your life seeing if they were okay. The way she was dressed, she had to be an N.A. He could name on one hand the Family men who would be so stupid.

Unfortunately, he was on the list.

Swearing under his breath, he told the car to land, and got out.

She was weeping loudly.

"Hey," he said.

She turned around and caught her breath. She looked like she wanted to run, only she was too exhausted.

In a blind panic, she fell to her knees and began to sob in earnest.

"Hey." He ran to her. "Hey, I ain't going to hurt you."

He took her hand. It was pitifully cold. She was lucky this area of Darkside City was domed and filled with beautiful oxygen.

She tried to pull away. "I'm not supposed to talk to strangers," she said. "Go away."

"What are you doing out?" he asked, taking her other hand. She was shivering. "Where's your *mamma*?"

She shrugged. "She's sick."

"Where's your *papà*?"

"He went away."

Deuce frowned. "Where do you live?"

She sniffled. "Darkside City."

He was taken aback. It moved him deeply that she considered this half-formed town to be her home. That she had been told that. That she believed it.

"Do you know your street?"

"Co-Copernicus," she said uncertainly.

He knew where it was. A nondescript street among the nondescript streets of the nondescript trailers of the worker bees.

"My name's Deuce," he said sincerely. "Let's comm your mother."

"Our link doesn't work." She burst into fresh tears. "Please don't hurt me, mister!"

Deuce shook his head. "No, no. I won't hurt you, *cara.* Never."

"*He* did."

Oh, God. "Your father?"

She nodded.

Deuce closed his eyes. This man, he would kill.

"What's your name, sweetheart?"

She looked very tired. "Annie," she said.

"What a lovely name."

"My mommy calls me Annie Bannany."

He made himself chuckle. "That's pretty cute. Have you ever had a banana?"

"No."

"Well, we'll get you home, and then I'll see about sending you some over." He pointed to his car. "Will you come with me?"

She pulled back. "I'm not supposed to go with strangers."

He debated about calling the authorities. The old habits of Family life died hard. You never called the authorities. Also, he figured that as he was the head of this project, he had as much authority to deal with situations like this as they did. And he'd probably do a better job of it, too. They'd go through channels, they'd do something really stupid.

All he would do is take her home.

"Annie," he said gently, squatting so that he would be at her level, "listen. It's very late, and you are lost. I'm glad that your paren—your mommy—has taught you not to go with strangers. I'm proud of you that you don't trust me. But I'm all you've got right now." Her eyes widened. "I got to be straight with you. This is not a good place to be alone. So I want you to come with me, now, and all I can do is promise you that I will take you home."

Her lip quivered. Tears ran down her face and she said, "I ran away, and now my mommy will hate me."

''Why did you run away?''

She shook her head. ''Annie, tell me. I want to help you.''

She lowered her head. ''My mommy was talking to Ellie, and she said she didn't know what to do with so many mouths to feed. She said we were going to starve to death because my daddy left. So I thought if I went away . . .''

''Oh, *Mamma mia*,'' Deuce said, enfolding her in his arms. ''Annie, I'm going to take you home, and then I'm going to buy lots and lots of food for your family. And I swear that you will never be hungry again.'' There was that flatfilm with the broad again. He couldn't get it out of his mind.

She let him hug her. He felt her bones through her dress. She sort of collapsed, and said, ''Can we have pancakes, even?''

''Every day, you want them.''

He picked her up and carried her to the car. Her little hand clutched the edge of his jacket, and he held her more tightly. He was crying. He was a schmuck and a putz, he told himself. But he couldn't stop.

He settled her gently in the passenger side. She was half-dozing.

He let her sleep until they got to Copernicus. She had trouble picking out which trailer she lived in—who wouldn't?—until she noticed a drawing in the one square window beside the door. She had drawn it herself. It was the sun shining down on some rectangles.

''Darkside City,'' she told him excitedly. ''When it's all done, we'll have sunshine.''

He blinked at her strange hope and set the car down. Before the gull-wing doors were open, a woman was at the door, screaming for Annie.

''Mommy!'' Annie shouted.

Deuce gave her a moment to stumble toward her mother, who was gaunt and sickly-looking. Deuce felt his stomach clutch. These were the N.A.'s Angelina Rille was talking about. These were the voiceless people she wanted to speak for.

He felt horribly ashamed of everything he had.

He walked over to the woman, whose eyes grew huge as he neared. She said, "Oh, my God. You're Deuce McNamara."

He shrugged. "Guilty."

"Oh, my God." She looked down at her daughter. "Annie, remember this day," she said. "You met Deuce McNamara, the man who—"

Deuce cleared his throat. "*Signora*," he said, "let's go inside and talk about a few things."

"Oh." She looked over her shoulder. "My house—"

"Don't worry."

They went inside. The place was in bad shape, dirty, the walls cracked, and there was a smell.

"Our toilet doesn't work," she said, humiliated before the great and terrible wizard.

"Where is your husband?"

She looked at her daughter, back at Deuce. "A show-girl," she said simply.

He sighed. Nodded. "Okay." He put his hands flat on the table like he was waiting for his cards. Only in this case, he was dealing from a fresh deck. "First, I'm sending you groceries. Lots of them. Then we're getting this place fixed up. Then I'm putting you to work." He grinned at her. "There's a nice concession building, they've got a coffee shop. They need a manager." They hadn't, actually, until this moment.

"Oh, but I don't have any experience," she said in a rush.

"You got how many kids?" he asked.

"Five," she said, shamefaced. "We, um, don't have to apply for vouchers."

"I know," he assured her, nevertheless thinking it had been a little on the irresponsible side to have so many kids if you couldn't take care of them. But that was neither here nor there. "My point is, I figure with five kids, you got enough management experience to run a casino. We'll get the kids in day care while you work. Annie's in school?"

"She hasn't been going," the woman admitted.

"That's okay. We'll get her started." He leaned forward. "All this I'm doing on one condition."

She looked terrified. Everybody knew Deuce McNamara was really a terrible, loathsome Family man.

"You don't tell nobody I did it," he said, winking at her. "You make up some dumb story about an inheritance. You let 'em think you got some hunky boytoy taking care of things. Whatever."

"Oh, Mr. McNamara," she breathed.

"Please, *Signora*. Don't embarrass me. It's nothing." He cocked his head. "What's your last name?"

"Bonnanio," she told him.

Annie Bannany. He chuckled for real and commed his badge. This was going to blow his cover, at least for the time it took to arrange things. Well, what was power for?

"Listen," he said to the super over at the Castle Darkside receiving docks. "It's Deuce McNamara. I got this situation . . ."

Her first name was Leslie, and she offered to bed him. She wanted to bed him. Deuce settle for a kiss on the cheek and an invitation to dinner in one week, when he would check on them. He gave her a private comm-link number in case of emergencies.

Before he left, he commed for clothes for her and the kids, furniture, and a bottle of Bollinger.

"For when you have me over for dinner," he told her.

Then he left, feeling much better than when he had arrived.

Annie, long since asleep, would wake up to pancakes.

Later, En Route to the Sitdown

Deuce got through the laborious airlock system over at Moonbase Vegas. He had all kinds of fake IDs and he used them, hoping he had resumed moving incognito. But you could never assume such a thing.

Once he was on the Base, the neon was practically blinding. He could almost hear the *ka-ching!* of the slots as he swooped down a side street near the Chans' Pearl of Heaven. The enormous Chinese facade of the casino disappeared into the darkness at the top of the cavern.

For the first time since the disaster, he was was able to relax. He was on his own turf.

Lasers had carved out the shafts and tunnels and later, a single enormous interior canyon that contained the baseline level of the Strip. The entrances to the casinos were ranged along this level. For one brief shining moment, you might imagine yourself in old Earthside Las Vegas. Everywhere you looked there was shine and gleam and hustle. Movement and noise, a constant *ching-ching-ching* of the come-on, the shakedown, the takedown, and the score.

Only this was Las Vegas II. Huge holograms—most of holo science had been developed on, by, and for the Moon, and the holo research brains also lived in fancy-schmancy quarters in the Big Shaft—and real neon signs reverberated off the lunaformed interior of the cavern. Then the casinos rose straight up like old-fashioned skyscrapers—who knew how far, since this was the land of the big con and the grand illusion?—their superstructures washed with revolving lights and signs, all of which were powered by the superconducting mesh that surrounded the city.

And they used to believe that magnetic fields were bad for you. Huh.

On Moonbase Vegas Boulevard, the casino entrances throbbed in a relatively straight line. First was the Lucky Star, decorated in the blue and white of the Caputo Family. FULL OF STARS! the sign read, which was basically true: The Lucky Star attracted the most and best headliners. Two of its top draws were the Blasts from the Past temporary clone celebrity look-alike contests and the annual Elvis Festival, due to start in a week. It was also home to the Moonbase Vegas Historical Museum, where all kinds of neat stuff was put on display, but not very many tourists visited it. Gravoids. *Cretinos.* If it didn't *bing, boop*, or promise to pay them off at less than fair odds, they weren't interested.

To the west, on Moonside Freemont Street, glittered that monument to bad taste, the Borgiolis' casino, the Palazzo di Fortuna. Deuce knew a lot about bad taste and practiced it frequently, according to his art class. But even he had known before the class that holograms of the Last Supper overlaid with sparkling mosaics of gondoliers and gas movies of men and women dressed in ancient gowns drinking wine were not the way to go.

Not to mention the enormous statue of David in the lobby that activated on the hour and the half hour and made amazingly idiotic jokes about his titanic genitalia.

And at the far eastern end of the Strip (how appropriate), almost penetrating the more mundane neighborhoods of the worker bees, stood the last casino built, that of the Chans, in salmon and jade, on Bugsy Siegel Way.

Two hundred seventy-five thousand tourists a year journeyed from Mother Earth to the fabulous Moon, to get what they could no longer get on earth: vice. Clubs and casinos and hot girls and hotter boys and all the booze you could swallow. Put on your weight belt, tank up on illicit drugs, have sex at one-sixth gravity—it was all on Moonbase Vegas.

And there would be more of it—flashier, more extravagant, more breathtaking—on Darkside City, where the sun, in some strange way, would one day shine. He made that his personal vow to Annie Bananny.

He started making his calls. Taking his proximity to the Pearl of Heaven as a sign, he commed Lee Chan, the Chan Casino Liaison to the Borgioli House. Lee Chan was pretty new to the job, but Deuce had known him for a long time. Casino Liaisons knew tons of people, up the ladder and down. Ah, yes, Deuce remembered the good old days of spending his nights gathering gossip and snippets of data and making more side deals than a bookie.

"Signor Chan," Deuce said, "this is Deuce McNamara di Borgioli. I'm the former Borgioli Casino Liaison to your house."

"Yes, Mr. McNama—Borgioli," Lee Chan said, clearly getting that Deuce wanted to emphasize his Family connections. When Deuce was a young hothead, he beat up guys who called him Mr. Borgioli. But Deuce wanted this guy to remember that Deuce was essentially a Family man who understood Family problems.

"It's a real pleasure," Lee Chan added, sounding both thrilled and wary.

"Likewise," Deuce said agreeably. "The pleasure is

mine. Let's go visual.'' He flipped on his car's internal
Peekissimo so Lee could see him in his cool proletariat
black-leather duds.

"You're too kind. Visual it is.'' Lee blipped onto the B
screen. He was dressed in a stylish sort of robe of the Chan
colors, salmon and jade green. If Deuce could have picked
out which Family to be in based on fashion sense, it would
have been the Chans. Deuce knew sometimes nuns picked
which order to belong to based on the habit they got to
wear. He had been told this from a real nun, so he figured
it was not some *sciocchezza* somebody made up to dispar-
age the Catholic religion.

Now Lee Chan inclined his head and made a very suave
bow. He was being real deferential, but not too. Deuce had
liked this guy before, and he liked him a lot more now.

"What may I do for you?'' It was clear Lee Chan was
hoping for some action with the distinguished Mr. McNamara.

"Look, I'll show you my hole card,'' Deuce said. "Your
line secured?''

"Hold on.'' There was a pause, then Lee Chan clicked
back on. "Yes. Pardon the interruption. I was just making
sure I was secured, Mr. Borgioli.''

"Okay. Listen. I come to you as a Liaison because that's
what I was in the Borgioli Family. And for all my fancy
suits and my title and like that, that's what I really have
been for Mr. Castle and what I am for his widow.''

"You are too modest,'' Lee Chan said. His eyes were
shining with excitement. Deuce remembered the feeling.
Night after night, you look for that one big score. You work
all the angles and hope and pray. And then, if Lady Luck
blows you a kiss, the brass ring lands *ka-ching!* right in the
middle of your pile of poker chips.

"I come to you as an equal, Liaison to Liaison,'' Deuce
continued. "The big shots are whacking each other, and the
soldiers are falling in the line of fire. But you and I know
that Liaisons really run the show.''

Deuce held up his hand to stem another round of you-
are-too-modest-I-am-not-worthy. "I am not trying to flatter
or patronize you, Lee Chan. It's just that the world as we

know it is falling apart, and I am appealing to all the Liaisons to help me out. I want to have a sitdown, just with Liaisons. All thirty-one of us." There were five Liaisons per House, one for each of the other Families, making thirty. Plus him. No other Castle employees would be invited. "I want to see if we can pool information and stop this war before Earth comes in and stops it for us."

Lee Chan cocked his head, clearly intrigued.

"But I can't agree to that without clearing it with my boss," he said. "Such a thing amounts to disloyalty. In our House, it's a capital offense."

"My point is that in five minutes, your boss might be dead. Then his boss next. Tell me if you don't see that coming. Tell me if it isn't happening all around us." Deuce leaned forward into the screen.

"Lee Chan, you and I both know that the Earthside *scemos* have been itching to take this place over for years. They didn't dare try while Signor Castle was alive. He was too big, and he dealt with them the Earthside way. As much as we hated and feared him when he arrived, he acted like an enviro-dome to keep those Earthsiders away from us. But now that he's dead, they may come if they can see a crack of light in the doorway. A big turf war would be all the light they needed."

Lee Chan nodded slowly. "It's true, Mr. McNama—Borgioli."

"You know what's going on in your Family," Deuce said. "You know more than you're supposed to know. I'm not trying to flatter you. It's your job. It's my job. And I will spill." Not much, but enough. Same as Chan would. Deuce had no illusions. Just hopes.

Lee Chan looked thoughtful. "Whom else of the Liaisons have you contacted?"

Wow. The guy knew when to say "whom." Deuce wondered what he knew about wine and art.

"You're my first. I called you even before I called my successor, Snake Eyes Sal." Whom Deuce detested. "But I'm sure I'll get a yes from the Caputo Liaison," he said. The guy owed Deuce a ton of money from a marathon poker tournament they had both played in. Deuce knew the guy didn't have it and was looking to loan sharks to scrape it together. Deuce would wipe the debt clean if the guy showed.

He added, "And a yes from the Smith Liaison."

"Really." Clearly, Lee Chan was impressed. Stan "the Man" Smith would just as soon drop you in your tracks as sit down and talk. But Deuce had Honorary Papers of Affiliation with the Smiths, and that carried a lot of weight over at their House.

"Scarlatti, I'm not so sure about," Deuce said honestly. "Gino, Pio's predecessor, well, you know how dirty Gino was. Pio associates me with all the bad stuff that happened over there. And I ain't called the Van Aadams guy yet. That new guy."

"Stephen," Lee Chan supplied. "We're on excellent terms." He hesitated. "If I might call him first for you?"

"Maybe I should first talk to Snake Eyes," Deuce said. "Give him a chance to show me he can do the job. But if he don't work out, I'll turn to you."

"Thank you, Mr. Borgioli," Lee Chan said. "My relationship with Pio is also very solid," he assured Deuce, boasting a little. "I'm glad I called you first," Deuce stroked him. "The sit-down is for 7:00 A.M. this morning. Beer joint I know, Trini Golden's Cues and Brews. Call Estrella, she's the owner, tell her Deuce asked for all this. Tell her *chingadero*. She'll know it's me. Let's don't get fancy. Everybody should pack their heat. We may get raided." Chan looked thoughtful a moment, then nodded.

"I'm in your corner, Mr. Borgioli," he said, sounding almost grateful.

"I know I'm asking a lot," Deuce admitted. "You have no reason to trust me. I'm honored that you do."

Lee Chan looked a little bashful, and murmured, "But Mr. McNamara, everyone calls you the new Godfather of the Moon."

"Hush, be careful," Deuce said quickly, even though they'd already said enough to get them both whacked by any number of whack-oriented guys: Chan for taking meetings without permission, Deuce for ignoring protocol and shining on the big shots, and just being who he was: the picker of tea in radioactive Mongolia.

"I will." Lee Chan looked over his shoulder as if to display his carefulness. "I'd better disconnect."

"Seven A.M.," Deuce said, and disconnected.

If he got killed this morning, he prayed that he went down in an honorable way, and that his killers had enough class to let Sparkle know what had happened to him. He had seen too many widows wait way too long before facing the fact that Mario or Gino or whoever wasn't coming home again.

Most notorious for keeping their hits a secret were the Scarlattis, who were the most notorious at anything. Their Members got branded. They implanted themselves with hallucinogenic circuitry, they experimented with strange brain programming. They pushed, pushed, pushed with the high-tech weirdness.

The Smiths were considered the most violent Family, blue-collar, union-busting thugs whose main profit center was arms dealing. The Van Aadamses, the most elegantly wicked with their old-school, old-boy network and their association with upper-crust Moonsider society. The Chans were all into that *tong*-stuff, and their drugs were lethally addictive. The Caputos were the most predictable, being old-style Mafia, but their rigidity was also their strength.

Of all the Families, it was the Scarlattis who scared Deuce the most.

So his hair stood on end as he drove like a shadow through an abandoned construction channel when he realized two or three Scarlattis were trailing him. His onboard scanners picked up their colors; they were not trying to hide from him. Or else they weren't very good at it.

"Go into standard Borgioli defense mode," Deuce told the aichy. Hunter didn't have defense modes, at least not that he shared. Hunter said that back on Earth, business was conducted in an entirely different way, not like the Families but through lawyers and lawsuits. Deuce tried very hard to believe him, but that sounded so completely foreign—not to mention inefficient—that he truly could not imagine such a world.

"Defense mode program accessed, Mr. Deuce McNamara," the car informed him.

"Designate Scarlatti vehicles left to right as A,B,C."

"A, B, C designated as requested."

Okay, the prelims were over. He cracked his knuckle and touched the St. Christopher medal around his neck. Not that he was supposed to believe in St. Christopher. The Pope had de-sainted him over two centuries before. Deuce didn't care. His *mamma* had given him this medal on his first Holy Communion.

"What weapons are they carrying?" he asked the car.

"Pulse torpedoes and chassis crackers," the aichy reported. Meaning that they were heavily armed. Not such good news.

"Okay, keep an eye on them." Could be they were just nosing around with no idea who he was, even if they were packing enough pulse power to level a city block.

"Mr. McNamara, B is preparing to fire," Deuce's car announced. "He is not yet fully charged, however."

Then it was pretty stupid of him to let Deuce know he was preparing to launch an offense. Who were these guys, just obstacles thrown in Deuce's way to slow him down for some reason?

"Time for him to make full charge?"

"Ten, nine, eight . . ." the aichy counted.

Before Deuce could even tell his car what to do, it dive-bombed toward the bottom of the tunnel, correctly assessing the oncoming debris as collapsible as it rammed a huge crate and several bags of garbage. It was a classic Borgioli maneuver.

From force of habit, Deuce craned his neck to see what he had run into. His heart skipped a beat. Ladies' dresses! An entire crate, a gross at least. What *cretino* gravoid had dropped his load in here?

Blam! The detonation of the torpedo shook the tunnel but missed Deuce. Lunar Security would be here any second. What the hell did the Scarlattis think they were doing?

Blam-blam!

"Yoo-hoo, baby, they're still firing at us!" Deuce shouted. "Do something!"

His aichy returned fire, then rose over a catwalk, then dipped back into the garbage.

"Good job, sweetheart, keep going," he told it. It was following his Borgioli programming precisely. They were old tactics, but tried and true. Using them, he had escaped attacks with more unbalanced forces than this one and lived to tell the tale.

He soared over more crates, one marked, EAU DE CO-LOGNE and another EARTHSIDE WEEKLY MAGAZINE. Such marvelous stuff! You hold up everybody's EWM, it would be worse than if you cut off the supply of Chantilly Lace. There would be rioting in the streets, that was for sure.

Deuce spared time to wonder if maybe this was a drop spot for rerouted merchandise (a Family word for "stolen," because how could you claim something was stolen from you if you stole it from someone else in the first place?). He blinked on his thinkerama and filed it away under OP-PORTUNITIES. Then he laughed softly to himself. This was really the tiniest of potatoes to a man in his position. But old habits died hard. Before linking up with Hunter, he had thought nothing of risking his life for a crate of contraband toilet paper.

The Scarlattis missed him and blew up the crate of Eau de Cologne. He saw the bottles flying and the liquid spewing, all at one-sixth grav. That gave him pause. Scarlattis as a rule were excellent shots. That they hadn't even grazed him was suspicious in the extreme.

Cracking his knuckle, he said, "Manual," and wheeled around, royally ticked. "Power up, hon. We're going to take 'em out."

The aichy hesitated, then said, "Yes, Mr. Deuce Mc-Namara." He guessed that a self-defense mechanism had just been defused, probably overriden by the Borgioli programming.

The Scarlattis saw his change of direction and pulled back, hovering just out of reach of his own pulsers and chassis bombs. He made a dead run at them, and they pulled back some more, until they were almost out of the tunnel.

Suddenly the tunnel reverberated with the *WA-wa-WA-*

wa of Lunar Forces Security. They were coming up behind Deuce.

He had two choices: talk to the cops or rush the bad guys.

He rushed.

To his surprise, the three Scarlatti cars whipped around to face the same direction he was going in and surrounded him, flying alongside him almost like an escort.

He sighed heavily.

Exactly like an escort.

He opened a channel.

"You *cretinos* trying to get my attention or whack me?"

Their channel opened up.

"Mornin', Deuce," said a voice.

It belonged to Hunter Castle.

TEN

"And why am I not surprised?'' Deuce asked sharply, as he walked with Hunter into the hidden bunker tucked into the side of a nearby supermesh shaft. The Scarlattis had been told to wait with the cars, and so far, they were obeying. Deuce vaguely recognized one of them, but all three were young kids. He was dying to know why they were with Hunter.

The entrance to the bunker was camouflaged by a black door covered with ancient pieces of PVC pipe and cables. The lower depths of the base were referred to as C&C, for "cables and coils." You had to wonder about the people who had founded Moonbase Vegas. They had had such primitive technology. They had to have been insane to fly into airless space without better stuff than they what they'd had.

Insane, or very ambitious.

Dreary, dirty, and dilapidated, there was nothing to distinguish this bunker from many a hidey hole etched into the tunnel walls by scavengers, escaped prisoners, and those little groups of Moonsider Liberation Front members called cells. The floor was filthy, and the walls were covered with grime and old posters, some of showgirls and some with slogans like, MLF MEANS MORE LOCAL FREEDOM!

Yeah, whatever.

Deuce followed Hunter, who was wearing a hooded jacket, his hand on his blaster. He half expected someone to jump out and shoot him and Hunter or just him. He had no idea what the hell Hunter was up to.

Maybe the prudent thing to do was take him hostage.

Or kill him.

Deuce sighed.

Tourists and all like that always assumed the Moon, that glowing beacon of vice and pleasure, was a safe and well-regulated place. Because Moonbase Vegas—and when it was built, Darkside City—were heavily regulated by the Department of Fairness, the rabbits believed all the games were legit and all their odds were fair.

And because the Moonside environment was a far more closed system than the Earth's—meaning that there weren't many places you could go topside unless you wanted to die—visitors also assumed it was a pretty safe place. They believed there was no way for bad guys to sneak in or hide out, ignoring—Hunter had once told him—the fact that Earthside Hawaii had been a crime-ridden location.

At any rate, the Moon was not a fair or safe place. For the clever fugitive, there were any number of warrens like this where you could hole up, many of them very large and even luxurious. And there were a handful of unscrupulous doctors who would perform body or facial makeovers for you, usually substandard, and usually without much anesthesia.

"I'm glad I can still surprise you," Hunter drawled. "I thought I had lost that ability."

Hunter stopped in the middle of the corridor and turned around. He pulled down his hood and a weak, sick light overhead cast a blue gleam over his face. Well, well, well, speaking of makeovers, Hunter Castle had had himself a bit of one. He looked extremely Asian: bronze-skinned, his eyes almond-shaped, and his hair short and solid black, as opposed to his usual salt-and-pepper.

In fact, he looked very much like Mr. Wong.

Hunter just smiled at him and led the way.

They opened another door with a poster that read, CO-MANCHE NIGHTS! AT THE SMITHS' WILD WEST! and showed a babe in an Indian thong and feathered headdress straddling a tom-tom. She was cute.

Hunter crossed a small, depressing cubicle and sat on a torn and tattered couch. He was wearing a black one-suit and he looked like a Chan *tong* leader.

"Take a load off, Deuce," Hunter invited, patting the couch.

Deuce knew he was Hunter from his voice and his eyes. Granted, both could be duplicated. But the mannerisms, the inflection, even his way of sitting with his legs crossed at the knee, assured Deuce that this was the genuine article.

His boss.

Deuce stood standing for a moment, then complied. He leaned forward and hung his hands between his knees, suddenly exhausted. He had had a very, very long day.

"If you care, your daughter is fine," Deuce said flatly.

Hunter visibly jerked.

"Deuce, I truly did not know she was aboard," Hunter said. His voice was agonized. "I was told . . . I was lied to," he said simply. "And the one who lied to me is dead."

Deuce almost went down the list of suspects—Jackson, Clancy, Wong, Jester—but he kept his mouth shut. He had no reason at this moment to trust Hunter.

"Well, speaking of dead," Deuce drawled, "we got a few more bodies lying around than whoever it was cluttering up your office."

Hunter nodded. "I'm real sorry about that." He looked tired. "The explosion was an accident. I swear that."

Deuce had never completely held by Hunter's word on anything. Look at the way the *bastardo* paid his bills.

"So, who were those two guys?" Deuce asked. "You ever find out?"

"Not sure," Hunter said. "I think they were working with Jackson."

Deuce had the feeling he was lying, but he let it go.

"Bea know you're alive?" If so, she should shuttle Earthside for the upcoming Academy Awards.

Hunter shook his head, maintaining silence as one of the Scarlatti guys brought a little round table and another Scarlatti guy carried in three glasses and a water bottle which Hunter must have brought with him.

"Someone else is joining us," Hunter added, gesturing

with his hand for that someone to come forward.

As Deuce stared in astonishment, a side door opened and Sparkle glided into the room. Dressed in a very neat and body-hugging black one-piece trimmed with platinum to match her free-falling hair, she looked like some exotic *tong* action babe. With a swish of her hair, she looked straight at Deuce and sat beside him on the couch. Deuce didn't know what to say, so he said nothing.

"Let's drink a toast, Deuce," Hunter said. "To Darkside City."

While Hunter did the honors, Deuce clenched his jaw and took deep breaths. This was the second time in their relationship Sparkle had popped up at a tense meeting between him and Hunter. There was so much he didn't understand about her. So much she would never allow him to understand. It made him feel . . . unmanly, having a wife with so many secrets.

"So," he said finally, "was it a setup? Was it a QIC?"

Hunter shook his head. Then, with an impish grin, he pulled a small flask of Atherton Gold from his jacket and pulled the cork with his teeth. He took a shot, then passed it to Deuce.

Deuce did not drink. He motioned for Hunter to keep the flask.

"No. Not a setup." Hunter took another drink. "It was an experiment of an entirely different sort."

Deuce waited a beat. Hunter just sat there.

"Hunter, I am trying to be patient," Deuce said, "but an awful lot has happened in the last twenty-four hours."

"I love that Italian understatement of yours," Hunter said, chuckling. "Okay. It was . . ." He trailed off. "I was trying a new energy source."

He was lying. Deuce's hair rose on end. He didn't know why Hunter was lying, and lying to him, but it was a very bad deal. If Hunter Castle no longer trusted him, Deuce was in big trouble.

"This source, it's for what, blowing up my home-world?" Deuce asked heatedly.

"Here's the evidence you'll need to convince the authorities," Hunter continued. He leaned over. Deuce took his blaster out of his pocket and raised it. Hunter looked shocked, then he smiled. Slowly he lifted a large black box and placed it on the little table. Showing Deuce his hands, he clicked two locks and the box fwommed open with a hydraulic sort of pulse.

He withdrew bits of wrecked circuits, a couple vials of something, a burned schematic. Hesitated, said, "Maybe the schematic's a bit much, y'all think?"

He crumpled up the schematic. He put more charred junk onto the table. Deuce watched impassively. When Hunter was finished, he sat back in his chair and looked expectantly at Deuce.

Deuce snorted. "What *schiamazzo* is this, Hunter?"

"Proof of the accident. Just show it around. It'll cool things down." He pushed one of the pieces of wreckage at Deuce, who reluctantly held it up and examined it.

"Cool things down? I got the world practically coming to an end. And it's going to make it all okay because it was an accident?" He thought a moment. "And you are not stepping forward because of why?"

Again Hunter hesitated. Probably while he tried to think up another bad lie. "I need to be out of this for now. I hate to leave you holding the bag—"

No, he didn't.

"—but that's why I pay you the big bucks," he finished, grinning.

Deuce wanted to wipe the room with that grin. He shook his head. "No freakin' way, Hunter. I'm not taking the fall."

"No, not the fall. Just the reins." He squinted at him. "Didn't they retrieve my succession plan?"

Deuce squinted back at him. "The one I had, in which Beatrice is your successor?" He wondered where Castle went to have his face modified. Somewhere on the Moon, had to be. He hadn't had time to go Earthside, get it done, and return. Another ship?

Or had he done it a few days ago, in anticipation of this event?

Hunter looked surprised, then disappointed. "I updated it. So Jackson was dirty, after all. Just as Gina Rille sus-

pected.'' Deuce was not surprised to hear him talk like this.
He and Hunter were in contact with anybody who was anybody on the Moon. Any little power broker, any big one.
Terrorists. Con artists. Some days all Deuce did was
schmooze.

He thought of his meeting with the Liaisons and wondered if he'd make it.

''Her old man's dead,'' Deuce said. ''Levi Shoemaker.''

''Yes. A pity.'' He didn't look the least bit sorry. Then
he gazed at Deuce hard. ''A lot of the hierarchy's been
cleared away, Deuce. New players will be stepping up to
the plate.''

''You son of a bitch,'' Deuce said slowly. ''You arranged this.''

''I arranged the blowing up of my own ship?'' Hunter
said derisively.

''Just a section of it. Easily repaired,'' Deuce shot back.
''What deals have you made? Who are the successors?''

''People who want to work with you.'' Hunter nodded.
''But it was an accident, Deuce. I didn't plan a bloodbath.''
A slow, grim smile spread across his face. ''But we can
certainly profit by it.''

A lesser man would pretend outrage. But Deuce, for all
of his being raised a Borgioli, believed in honesty. And so
he took Hunter's observation in and felt his own wheels
begin to turn.

''For all the wheeling and dealing I did to forge alliances
with the Families, the old regime resented the hell out of
Darkside City. Even my esteemed father-in-law, Don Alberto.'' Hunter spoke with disdain, which you had to expect
when someone with as much class as Hunter Castle talked
about Don Alberto Borgioli. The man had been an animal
in a lot of ways. Still, he had also been the closest thing to
an uncle Deuce had had. It took everything in him not to
fulfill Don Alberto's deathbed obligation and whack Hunter
right now.

But the shadows were moving. They were not alone. He,
Deuce, would be dead before he hit the floor.

''The younger generation sees the potential. They see the

action. They also see that their elders were standing in the way.''

The explosion was sounding less and less like an accident. Deuce wondered why Hunter had even put that on the table. It was an insult to Deuce's intelligence at the very least. And a badly frayed loose end that would easily unravel.

''Some of the young guys died,'' Deuce observed. ''They enemies of the big picture?''

''Like I said,'' Hunter replied, ''it was an accident. I was probably going to take them out, yes, but in a far more elegant manner.'' He sighed. ''First, I was going to try to reason with them. Believe me, Deuce. I'm not lying.''

''I'd love to believe you, Hunter, but my bullshit detector's sending off sine waves,'' Deuce retorted. He poured himself a shot of fresh water. Wow. It was the real stuff, and it packed a wallop.

''I hate to leave you in the middle of this mess,'' Hunter said. ''I've got to go do some things without being encumbered. But I will come back. I'll make things right.'' His eyes got dreamy. ''You can't imagine what's on the threshold.''

''Yeah, I can. Jail time, if I'm lucky,'' Deuce said angrily. ''Are you aware that we're putting in for a kid?''

''I also know Beatrice probably proposed to you,'' Hunter countered. ''Did you agree to divorce Sparkle?''

Who was sitting next to him on the couch.

''I did not,'' Deuce said clearly, swiveling his head toward his wife. ''But I did suggest that Bea marry Joey.''

Hunter burst out laughing. ''An excellent save!''

''Whatever. I thought it was pretty obvious.'' Deuce did not laugh. ''But it was incredibly stupid of you—pardon my disrespect—to leave your succession plan with a man you suspected might be dirty.''

''And who said that I did?'' Hunter shot back. He looked at Sparkle.

She almost flushed. Almost. But the Sparkle Deuce knew and loved was pretty much unflushable. She reached into a bag slung over her shoulder and pulled out a mini, which she started to hand to Hunter. However, he indicated that she should give it to Deuce instead. Her hand when it brushed his was cool and dry. She had balls. He had to give her that.

He showed the mini his thumbprint and his retina and said, "Open. Display Plan of Succession, Hunter Castle."

"May I have the password, please, Mr. Deuce McNamara?" the mini requested politely.

Oh, hell. Deuce was worn out, a little drunk, and tired of games. He was tired to death of Hunter's *schiamazzo* and he was getting very tired of the ways he constantly kept himself tied to Sparkle.

"Gambler's Star," he attempted.

"Thank you, Mr. Deuce McNamara," the mini responded. The screen flashed the words, PLAN OF SUCCESSION. Incredible quantities of legalese began to scroll down, whereas unto the other party . . . blah, blah, blah . . .

Sparkle de Lune . . . embryos . . .

"Embryos?" Deuce said, raising his head.

Hunter nodded. "Frozen. In a bank." He glanced at Sparkle, who turned a brilliant shade of scarlet.

Whoa.

Deuce said to the mini, "Hold on a sec." He put it down and put both his hands flat on the table. "First of all, using 'Gambler's Star' as your password is predictable and unimaginative, so I assume I am now seeing a decoy POS." He took another sip. "And secondly, what does my wife have to do with embryos?"

Hunter looked like he was holding a hand full of aces and was pretending they were meatballs.

"If something happens to Bea and me, she has agreed to assume guardianship of them."

Deuce flared. He cocked his head, looked at Sparkle, and said, "And you were going to share all this with me when? When you told me about this meeting?"

She lifted her chin, cool and composed and not bothered by the disgusting surroundings and the dirty fact that she had been holding out on her own legal husband. "I wasn't sure I would."

"*What*?" Deuce shouted, outraged.

Hunter said, "Okay, Deuce. She should have told you."

He looked unhappily at Sparkle. Deuce almost read his lips: *I thought she had.*

Deuce couldn't afford outrage. There were layers here he had not imagined, layers of deceit and double-dealing. He had to stay cool and find out everything he could.

"We're in a legal marriage," Deuce said. "Why didn't you ask me to be the guardian as well?"

"Because in the event that I am declared dead, she will have all the embryos secretly transferred into her body for safekeeping." Castle smiled faintly. "Modern science aside, my boy, that's one obligation you cannot fulfill for me."

"What a load of crap," Deuce said dully. "You could keep them in your freezer. And why not *your* wife?"

Hunter said reasonably, "They wouldn't be safe there."

Sparkle poured herself a glass of water. Deuce was so angry he wanted to bat it out of her hand. Essentially she had agreed, without consulting him, to carry someone else's babies. Was that why she had seduced him in his office, to pass them off as his own?

Was she carrying them already? Or was this all a cover for the fact that they had slept together, and she was already carrying Hunter's child?

No, he couldn't think like that. He wouldn't think like that.

"Well, what a surprise that you have been declared dead," Deuce said, "and now you two are here together." He glared at Sparkle, and for a moment, he could see them together. Easily. "You agreed to this why?"

"We owe Hunter a lot," she replied simply. She looked at Deuce hard, as if challenging him to deny her statement. Only last year, she had intensely disliked the notion of Deuce working for Hunter Castle. Had even foreseen, with her strange ESP-like ability, that doing so might cause Deuce's death.

"Embryo transference is a very minor procedure," Hunter cut in. Deuce knew that. Any idiot knew that.

"Transferring in, and transferring out at a safer time," Hunter added.

"You mean you already did it?" Deuce demanded of

Sparkle. "You're carrying his child right now?"

Hunter hesitated. Deuce glanced at Sparkle, who was watching Hunter.

"Deuce, you must understand, all this happened so fast," Hunter said. "I didn't know I was going to blow up the ship. For heaven's sake, *Gambler's Star* has been in my family for generations."

Deuce raised his chin. "The Castle Enterprises C.E.O. is who?"

"Deuce, it was just stopgap," Hunter said.

"Who?" Deuce persisted.

Hunter sighed, shrugged. "It's in the mini," he said, "but I may as well just come out and tell you."

Deuce braced himself to hear his own name. Then Hunter said, "It's Mr. Wong."

At that moment, the door shattered, and helmeted figures with blasters fired into the room. Pulses streamed everywhere as Deuce threw Sparkle to the floor and landed on top of her. Hunter dived behind the couch and threw himself to the floor.

Deuce shot at the oncoming figures, hitting the first one as it screamed, "Ai-ya!" and launched itself at Deuce and Sparkle. The attacker was wearing jade and salmon on the sleeve of his black metallic bodysuit. The first crumpled to the floor, and another one flipped into the air over the body and aimed at Deuce and Sparkle.

Deuce got that one, too, right in the chest. He was livid. Had Lee Chan double-crossed him? But for what reason?

"Give it up!" Deuce pushed Sparkle off him and stood in front of her, aiming at the next guy.

Someone shot out the lights.

There was a scream.

Deuce immediately dropped to the floor and groped for Sparkle's hand. She groaned. He was panic-stricken; she was hit.

"Honey," he whispered, clasping her around the waist. "Take it easy."

Miraculously, no pulses hit him as he dragged her inert body around the couch, where Hunter was firing off a few rounds. The Southerner had never been much for the blast-

and-shoot school of business, and from the swearing that accompanied his firing, Deuce assumed his aim hadn't improved much.

Pulses from the bad guys were burning straight through the couch. It was like standing behind a big piece of paper. Just about the only protection the couch served was visual, and that would soon be gone as they hit the hell out of it.

So Deuce got a little ballsier, skittering around the side of the couch and crouching low without shooting, so he could see if he could tell where the pulse blasts were coming from.

"Why the hell aren't you shooting?" Hunter demanded.

"Be glad I ain't shooting you," Deuce muttered. He kept watching the darkness for the occasional telltale burst you sometimes, but not often, saw when a pulser went off. As he stared, his eyes began to adjust to the blackness, which was not uniform.

He raised his weapon, watched, made himself wait. Cracked his knuckle.

There.

He got off several rounds and sweet victory was his— one of the bad guys groaned and fell to the floor. Then another, then another.

Then Deuce sprang up, ran with everything he had, and tackled one of the attackers by pure luck. He leaped into the air and got off a great snap kick, then whirled in a circle for a righteous roundhouse. A second, a third. He was a freakin' whirling dervish. A karate chop to the shoulder with his free left hand, an upward thrust to the sternum.

The man went down. Another came at him, rushing him. Still clutching his blaster, Deuce fell to the floor and the man arced over him. Springing onto his hands, Deuce executed a snap kick with both legs, catching the man in the crotch. He groaned in agony and collapsed to the floor.

Deuce jumped to his feet and shot him. Panting, he hunkered down, awaiting his next assailant. His adrenaline was pumping; he remembered the good old brawling days when fights like these were part of his daily routine. And the wonderful bouts with Sparkle at the dojo. She could knock the stuffing out of him any day of the week . . . except today.

Then someone jumped on Deuce's back. Without missing a beat, Deuce tucked into a forward roll and they sprawled together on the floor. Deuce shot him—it was a big, muscled person, had to be a guy—point-blank and yanked the blaster out of his dying hand.

He flung himself over the body and grabbed another guy around the ankles. The guy started swearing in Chinese and landed hard on his butt as Deuce popped him, too.

Suddenly the room was silent. Deuce rolled into the nearest corner and made himself a tight ball as he waited for reinforcements or for whoever was playing possum (not that Deuce had ever seen a possum) to reveal himself.

They appeared to be alone.

Deuce crawled on his belly back in the direction of the couch. Found Sparkle, who was breathing shallowly. As quietly as he could, he whispered, "Hunter?"

There was no answer. Oh, no, he couldn't be dead, too.

Casino Liaisons usually carried directional flashlights. Stupidly, Deuce had not put one in his pocket. Now he cursed himself for his forgetfulness.

"Hunter?"

From down the hall, a blue-white beam flared into the room. Deuce caught his breath and waited.

The flare light illuminated the interior. Five guys lay bleeding on the dirty floor.

Dressed like a soldier in khaki and olive green, Angelina Rille stood on the other side of the couch, looking very worried. About six guys in cammies flanked her, superpumpers ready for business.

"Deuce?" she called loudly. "Deuce, you in here?"

Deuce raised his hand, then slowly rose. "Gina, here," he said urgently. "My wife's been shot, and I think Hunter Castle's dead."

She ran over to him, bringing her light with her.

Sparkle lay sprawled, blood oozing from her abdomen. Deuce shouted, "My God!" at the same time that Angelina turned to one of her men, and said, "Paramedics, on the double."

The guy saluted and tapped his comm badge.

She dropped to Deuce's side and checked the pulse at Sparkle's wrist at the same time Deuce felt the pulse in her neck. Field first aid was part of every Family Member's childhood catechism. Deuce imagined it was the same in this girl's army.

"It's a little weak," Angelina said gently, the way you talk to a husband when his wife has been shot and it's serious, and if you're a very nice lady mixed up with a bunch of terrorists and you have a crush on said husband. "We'll need to take her to a hospital."

"The sick bay on the *Star* is out of commission, and right now I don't feel so much like ah, imposing on my old Family," Deuce said. If the Borgioli hospital wasn't good enough for Bea's child, it wasn't good enough for his wife.

"We have an excellent infirmary," she assured him.

"If we go with you, it don't mean anything," he said sternly as he gazed at Sparkle's pale face. He checked her pulse again. No weaker, but no stronger. "It doesn't mean I'm endorsing you guys or that I'm indebted in any way. I'll stripe my account for her care."

Angelina smiled at him, reached out her hand, and gave his a squeeze.

He registered the squeeze but did not squeeze back. Even if Sparkle might be a little liberal in her definition of monogamy—and the jury was still out on that—he was not. And he never wanted to hurt Angelina, ever, by giving her hope.

More importantly, he did not want to piss her off. After all, she was a freakin' terrorist.

Deuce looked up at the MLF men who were searching the bunker. One of them saluted Gina, and said, "Mr. Castle does not appear to be here."

"What?" Deuce frowned. "Did you check everywhere?"

The man looked at Deuce with great respect. "Yes, Mr. McNamara."

"Nothing? Not even a, forgive my saying it, a body part?"

The man shook his head.

Another man came up to Deuce and they found Hunter's three Scarlatti guys dead outside. Deuce's car was gone.

Just as Angelina's ambulance pulled up, and they carted Sparkle inside, one of her guys rushed up with a mini in his fist and said, "It appears these guys are mechanics."

Hired assassins.

Deuce gestured for the guy to hand him the mini. The man said, "It was damaged in the fighting, but we managed to hack in."

Deuce stared down at the officially Registered hit papers. They were from Yuet Chan, and they were for him and Hunter, either or both, dead or alive. Once upon a time, she had hailed him as a conquering hero, when she'd made her bid for the Chan Godmotherhood.

Deuce shook his head. He had to smile. "You have to admit, her timing couldn't be better," he told Angelina. "Our world's in chaos. Earthside has to figure no one's minding the store. But Yuet would do this only if she has repudiated her Family. Otherwise, it's a lousy time for any kind of loyal Moonsider to take me out."

Angelina looked at him with a curious, flat expression on her face. "Why is that?" she asked coldly.

Uh-oh.

ELEVEN

As Angelina gazed at Deuce with her cool, clear gaze, Deuce waited for the *pffft* of a headcracker, or the *bing!* of a blaster. Clearly, she did not think that this was a lousy time for loyal Moonsiders to take Deuce McNamara out.

He was a little shocked that she would actually perpetrate a hit on him, but his current and more immediate concern was that if she did, she would follow the rules that the Families had laid down, namely, to leave Sparkle out of it.

But there was no *pffft*. No *bing*. Only a dozen machines beeping out Sparkle's vitals as the paramedics monitored her. As the seconds ticked by, it appeared that no one was going to interfere with Deuce's vitals, either, at least not for the time being.

"Why is this not a good time to . . . get you out of the way?" Angelina said after Deuce had sweated out every drop of moisture in his body.

"Why are you asking?" he retorted. "Idle curiosity, or are you having second thoughts?"

She leaned back against the wall of the ambulance and sighed heavily. He knew that sigh, had been sighing all day. It said, *I don't want to be the leader anymore.*

Despite the fact that his wife was unconscious less than two feet away and maybe dying, and maybe he was mistaken and this broad was sighing about the inevitability of Deuce's own personal demise, he put his hand over Angelina's and gave it a squeeze, murmuring, "Let's just run away from home, okay?"

She sighed again, but she didn't pull away. They sat together, holding hands, amid the beeps and the murmurs of the paramedics.

"Deuce," she murmured, "sometimes all it takes to keep me going is the hope that someday you'll—"

At that exact moment, one of the paramedics looked up from the machines.

"Is your wife pregnant, sir?"

Deuce cleared his throat. He did not want to hurt this lady. Even if she was thinking of killing him.

"Possibly."

Angelina visibly jerked. Deuce would not let go of her hand. A strong rush of feeling made him wobbly; it took everything in him not to pull Angelina into his arms, not for anything dishonorable, but just for a moment of softness. It would not be fair, so he kept his impulse to himself. After another few seconds, he let her take her hand away and she crossed her arms over her chest.

"Can you verify if she is?" Deuce asked the paramedic, who might be a mechanical. The Scarlattis had brought out a new model so good you could easily be fooled. Mechanical paramedics getting terminated in an "accident" would weigh less heavily on Angelina's conscience.

"Yes, sir, I can verify it."

And, uh, whose it is? he wanted to ask. But he didn't quite have the balls. He sat for a moment, then had a flash of inspiration.

"Do a DNA scan if she is," he said authoritatively. "You know I'm adopted."

The paramedic nodded. There could be several reasons he would request a scan, not many of them having to do with diseases, since they were fairly passé these days, but a lot more having to do with trying to find his biological parents.

"Unless doing that would harm her in some way," Deuce added urgently.

To his surprise, Angelina put her hand back in his and actually gave it another squeeze. She said sadly, "Oh, Deuce."

"Gina, I am married," he said quietly, so as not to embarrass her in front of her men. "Things like this happen in a legal liaison."

"But, Deuce . . ." She trailed off, sighing.

He figured it would be better if they moved on.

"It's a bad time to take me out," he said, "because the Family that does it will be blamed for ruining everything. The Family, or the fanatical and misguided organization that thinks it's doing good for the satellite."

"Oh," she replied, and she did not sound impressed.

The MLF compound had not improved much since the first time he had been there. Sparkle had been wounded that time, too, although not as seriously. Now, as he watched over her inert form in the large Quonset hut that had been a dorm for some of the early miners, and was now the infirmary, the old memories came flooding back in. He vividly remembered going to the MLF chapel to pay his respects to Mamma Busiek, Little Wallace's grieving mom. He remembered how certain he was that he was probably going to die before the day was over.

Today, he was mildly optimistic he would make it out of there alive.

Now, at Angelina's urging that he needed some chow, they left the infirmary together and strolled through the compound to the canteen. Ugly green metal huts and unpainted storage units gleamed dully in the overhead lights. There were lights everywhere, and armed soldiers. The MLF was not only religious, it was militant, and very well armed.

Behind some storage units stood a small A-frame building with a military-looking sign over the door, dark blue letters on a field of gray. CHAPEL.

"You want to go in for a moment?" she asked.

He hesitated. His religious activities were highly private, usually centering around him, a priest, and the Act of Contrition.

He said, "Later," although he said a short, heartfelt prayer in the direction of the structure. The MLF chapel, as he recalled, was very plain and simple. No swirls and no gold. No cross, and no figure of Christ on it. No statues of the Virgin. No votive candles. No stained-glass windows. But like in a Moonsider Catholic Family church, a sign that read, PLEASE KEEP YOUR VOICE LOW. NO WAGERING.

He wondered if God was taking bets on the outcome of this visit. And if so, what odds Saint Peter was asking for.

He and Angelina reached the canteen. A few soldiers lounging around hup-to'ed when Angelina pushed open the heavy door.

"At ease, soldiers," she said, crossing to the bar.

The soldiers relaxed and sat back down. One of them blinked at Deuce and, under the table, moved his hand in a tiny salute.

Deuce's stomach did a miniature flip. Though Deuce didn't recognize him, he had to be an operative either for the Borgiolis or for the Castle organization. As a form of acknowledgment, Deuce allowed his gaze to rest an extra beat on the guy, then joined Angelina at the bar.

They climbed onto stools. She ordered two bowls of barley soup, two craterburgers, and two double shots of Atherton Gold with beer chasers on the side. Deuce was surprised by the Atherton Gold. It was expensive stuff, and the MLF hadn't taken to the vice of luxury so well. Bad soup and lousy burgers was more their roughing-it style.

Silently she acknowledged the set-downs of booze while the burgers began to sizzle on the grill. Craterburgers smelled vaguely like burning vinyl when they were cooked. Back in his world, no one ever touched them.

She tapped her fingers on the varnished craterwork. It was clear she was eager to get down to business. Also clear that her business was repugnant to her.

"Deuce, I have to tell you that you're losing the support of the MLF," she said.

"I kind of figured that out while you were trying to decide if you were kidnapping us or bringing us here willingly," he said bluntly. He shrugged, making rings of condensation on the varnished craterwood table with his shot glass. "Never try to fool me, baby. You haven't got it in you."

Her cheeks reddened. She was really pretty, even if she

had always been short the whole time he'd known her. Also, she had liaised with at least two Family men—to further the then-covert activities of the MLF, true, so she had to have something in the ah, love-connection department, or they would never have bothered with such a teeny-tiny woman. The taste of Family men generally went toward showgirls, the taller the better. In her working days, Sparkle had been nine feet tall.

On the other hand, both of Gina's Family men were dead, the second in what everybody assumed was a faked suicide.

"Okay, then, we can move on more honestly," she said. "I was—I am—kidnapping you. Your fate has been undetermined."

He cocked his head at her. "We've given your people new, good jobs. Jobs they would never get over on Vegas."

"But they're still not the best jobs," she said angrily, then lowered her voice. "They aren't the kinds of jobs you give Family Members."

"That ain't true," Deuce insisted, throwing back his whiskey. He felt the burn and was grateful for it. It distracted him from the ache in his gut. He wondered if he was getting an ulcer. All this worry about getting whacked wasn't going to help matters. "We give them top-notch jobs."

"Laser workers? Riveters?" she asked derisively. "What about accountants, engineers, and architects? This city is going to need a supermesh. Where is my people's share of those jobs?"

"Hunter already had those people."

"He imported them from Earthside," she snapped.

"Yeah, because he's Earthside-based." Deuce frowned at her. "Gina, we're trying to build a city, not hire a bunch of uneducated N.A.'s for on-the-job training."

She lifted her chin. "Why not?"

He blinked at her. "Gina, Darkside City is a business venture. We've got deals in place with all the Families that require us to give them a return on their investment. We can't afford to train people to do jobs where we've already got people who know how to do them."

"But you haven't hired *anybody* for a job that requires training. All other corporations provide skills enhancement opportunities for workers." She looked frustrated. "This is the chance Moonsiders have been dreaming of. A way to bootstrap our society and free them from the stranglehold their status has on their upward mobility. Find them another path besides gaming and trying vainly to Affiliate with a Family."

"Vainly?" he repeated.

"One in three hundred seventy-five people who tries to Affiliate with a Family makes it."

He made an apologetic face. "Those are the odds, huh."

"They're terrible odds." Her voice shook. "Deuce, they've been talking about Registering a hit on you."

He nodded, figuring as much. "So you come barreling in to see if Yuet got the job done, or if you're going to have to dirty your pretty little fingertips whacking me yourself." He arched his back, realigning his spine the way Sparkle had taught him.

"Look," he said, "we aren't perfect, but—"

"Register a hit, whack you, and throw the Moon into turmoil," she pressed on, staring hard at him. "And from those bitter ashes, build a decent society that—"

"Whoa, whoa, whoa," he cut in. " 'Decent society'? *Mi scusi, signorina*, but I find nothing indecent with the way things are now."

"Oh?" Her voice rose and she made a fist that she lightly pounded on the varnished countertop. "You find nothing indecent that young girls and boys are encouraged to enter a life of murdering, racketeering, and extortion?"

"Gina," he said patiently, for he saw how horribly uninformed she was about Family life, "it's not murder if you Register a hit or enter into Vendetta. It's murder if some N.A. gravoid knifes another N.A. gravoid in a bar fight." Which had occurred last night just off the Strip. It had been on the viso zippers this morning.

"According to your definition," she flung at him.

He blinked. "Yeah. So?" He accepted his burger from the bartender, who did not look pleased to give it to him.

If there was gonna be a last meal, he sincerely hoped this was not it.

"We want to change things."

"I'll tell you how you're going to change things." He stared down at the burger, then resolutely picked it up. "You're going to whack a big shot like me, the Earth guys will be here to shut you down so fast your big brown eyes will spin."

"We'd welcome their input—"

"Input, schminput. They think we're all degenerated up here. They won't treat your organization any differently than they'd treat a Family. Your only hope lies in letting Castle Enterprises provide a shield against Earthside interference and having a sit-down with whoever's in charge— so far it's Beatrice"—he wasn't sure about this new spin with Mr. Wong, so he kept that to himself—"and explaining this big problem with the jobs. Bea's got a good heart. She'll listen to you."

Her cheeks reddened again. He almost grinned, but he kept his reactions to himself.

"You agree with me," he said. "I'm still alive because you know it'll go down exactly as I have described if you kill me. Earth is not the benevolent big daddy some nutcase in your organization believes."

"That nutcase is your friend, Brigham," she said shortly.

He nearly fell off his stool. "My Mormon Brigham?" Brigham used to work as a stage security guard in the Van Aadams house, the Down Under, over on Moonbase Vegas.

When she nodded, he said, "You've coopted my Mormons?"

Deuce was in very thick with the Mormon people, who had spent many hours diligently trying to convert him. Even if he didn't agree with their entire religion, he still liked and respected them very much.

"A lot of them. They want to live in a moral world, just as we do. A world, for example, that's free from the constant violence we endure now." She ticked her glance toward his blaster, which she had not taken from him.

He shook his head. "Brigham wants to whack me," he said softly.

"No," she said quickly. "He wants Earth to come in, but he's not in favor of violence in any form. He spoke up for you."

Deuce studied her face. "Same as you did."

Her cheeks got redder. "Yes."

His best guess was that she was lying. She hadn't stood up for him. Maybe she was the one who volunteered to pull the trigger.

"You got compassionate mechanics?" he asked.

She snapped her fingers. "They'd take you out in a heartbeat, and you'd never even know it."

"That's comforting," he drawled.

"If you could talk to the Families," she ventured.

"And tell them what? To give up their rights and privileges thereunto appertaining?"

"To ease up. To see what the MLF has to offer."

"You mean the DOF. You want us to put our heads on the block of those Earthsider *scemos*."

"Perhaps with some talks, maybe they could arbitrate—"

He laughed and shook his head. "Do you know much mob history, Gina? Do you know who Eliot Ness was?" She shook her head. "Bugsy Siegel? Meyer Lansky? Al Capone?"

She smiled faintly. "The name of a street, a bar, and your mother's deceased Pekingese derivative."

"Mean little—"

"—son of a gun," she finished for him. Her eyes filled with tears. "Deuce, I know you. I know you're a good man. If you would repudiate this lifestyle, you would be a great man. I don't want you to die."

"Meaning no disrespect, Gina, but I don't plan to anytime soon."

She looked miserably down at her food. Broad like her, she could have real steak every night if she wanted. But she chose to give it all up because she believed in something.

She was a good person. But she was aligning herself with people who were maybe not so good.

As he regarded her he chewed the inside of his cheek

and cracked his knuckle. He was worried, but not for himself. You grow up in a Family, you learn a certain resignation about the inevitable. You figure out your time is up, you take off your watch and your wedding ring, and ask the following question:

"Do I have your word that you will not harm my wife?"

"Deuce . . ." She looked shocked.

He wasn't going to let her off the hook. She had admitted that she'd kidnapped them. She had to know that he knew it wasn't just so they could do lunch . . . at four o'clock in the morning.

He leaned forward, and he smelled her perfume. That brought him up short, like a revolutionary shouldn't wear perfume or something like that, that she shouldn't take time on her hair and makeup, although Angelina did. Once a babe, always a babe, even if your job was collecting up and redistributing the power to the people. It made him want her, and that threw him a little off his game.

Still, he leaned in closer, because he wanted her to see in his face that he knew exactly what the score was.

"Listen. In some outfits, they figure the ends justify the means. You people are fanatics. So I gotta believe you'll do whatever you thinks it takes to achieve your objective."

She raised her chin, but he saw the glint in her eyes. Miss Angelina Rille had loved him for a long time. It was not something she denied. But Deuce was not so sure what her love consisted of. For all he knew, she had loved her other Family men, even while she used them. People were more complex than red wines. Everybody had some noble rot that affected their sweetness and their bouquet.

"If we did . . . if we were so base," she said, "we'd be no better than the Families."

"*Mille grazie, signorina*," he said angrily, "for the compliment and for the fine dining experience."

Turning away from her, he climbed down off the stool. She laid a hand on his arm. "Deuce."

"If you're going to shoot me, shoot me in the back. I'm collecting my woman and getting the hell out of here."

He ticked his gaze to the soldier who'd signaled him when Deuce had first entered. Again, the man blinked once.

Deuce kept walking. Then he stopped, and said, "Gina, how well do you know Connie Lockheart?"

There was a moment's silence. Then Gina said, "Know her?"

He grinned. "Gina, you must be real tired. You ain't doing so good at lying, even for someone who is a bad liar. I'm astounded your group would do such a silly thing. STOP BUILDING OR DIE." He snickered and started to turn. "You guys watch too many flatfilms."

"Deuce, come here," she said. "I have to tell you something I don't want to. We, that I, I know that—"

There was a rustling noise. Deuce went on full alert. Grabbed his blaster and whirled around—

—only to see Angelina stare down at the hole in her chest, then over at the operative, who had shot her, before crashing to the floor like a wall of cavern rock.

At once the place exploded. Soldiers, frustrated for so long, started shooting at anything that looked even vaguely like Deuce. The operative was dead before he even looked at Deuce.

Deuce sprang behind one of the tables and returned fire from a dozen different quarters. This was it; it had been a good life, if somewhat short. However, very interesting, and you couldn't ask for better than that.

He got grazed; his left arm went numb, then it stung; no, it burned. Burned clear through, like from a Van Aadams dum-dum. As he fired at everybody in the canteen, he kept his mind off what the dum-dum was doing to his arm, even though the sane thing to do at that point was probably just let them shoot him dead.

Because it hurt so much, then it hurt more, and someone scooped him up from behind and carried him like a no-grav out the door of the canteen, chased by pulse fire.

There was an aichy waiting, a big thing, and he grunted, "My wife."

"Inside," answered someone.

The gull-wing door opened, and he got thrown in the back, and his rescuer plunged in after him. Before the door shut, the aichy took off, and the canteen blew up.

The blast rocked the car. Debris slammed against the door just as it closed.

Deuce gasped through clenched teeth at the pain in his arm but managed to force his eyes open. The first thing that registered was not a visual, but his wife's voice, saying, "Deuce, I'm here. I'm all right."

And then the visual came into focus.

"Hunter," Deuce said, almost laughing, because this was like one of those weird dreams you have where everything and nothing makes sense, and people pop up in the weirdest places.

But the figure shook its head, and said, "I'm sorry, Mr. McNamara. I'm not Mr. Castle. I'm Mr. Wong."

He leaned over Deuce and held out what looked to be a wicked Saturday-night special.

Damn, Deuce thought, and tried to punch Mr. Wong away. But the robot grabbed Deuce's ruined arm with his left hand—Deuce roared in agony—and aimed the special at it.

"Please, sir, hold still," Mr. Wong said politely.

With the precision of a surgeon, he sliced Deuce's leather jacket and the shirt beneath from the throbbing limb. He leaned forward and started doing stuff.

"I'm administering an anesthetic," he said, almost conversationally. "It will temporarily incapacitate you." The robot did something that went *pffft,* and Deuce could feel himself going.

"But I want to assure you, sir, that I am on your side. I am here to serve you. It is Mr. Castle's hope that my presence will allow you to complete Darkside City on schedule."

"Compete . . . compleee . . . ?" Deuce asked, hearing how stupid he sounded. "We ga friggin' war."

"No." Mr. Wong shook his head. "There will be no turf war. We'll figure out a way, sir. Now, as I said, you will be incapacitated for a little while. But you should revive in plenty of time."

"Puh . . . len . . . ty?" Deuce managed to say.

Mr. Wong's face blurred and went completely out of

focus, but some part of Deuce's drugged brain registered his nod.

"For the sit-down, sir. With the other Liaisons."

"Wha?" Deuce croaked.

Then everything weighed too much; it must have been like it was to go Earthside. All that weight, all that pressure. There was nowhere to go but down. Vaguely he heard Sparkle's voice, tinged with worry. And then, much more vaguely, he heard words that he was certain were part of a dream:

"Deuce, they did a scan. We're having twins, and they're all right."

TWELVE

Twins.

And something about the scan that said they were okay, but Sparkle remembered nothing else, nothing that might shed some light on the questions Deuce was working overtime never to ask.

He told himself it was for the twins that Deuce got Mr. Wong to pump him full of drugs so that he could preside like a real Godfather over the meeting, despite the fact that Mr. Wong had delivered the bad news that he was probably going to lose his arm. Even these days, you could not clone an entire arm. Organs, yes, and maybe they would clone some of his skin and veins and like that for the new one.

As the other Liaisons who had gathered around the tables in the back of Trini Golden's Cues and Brews accepted plates of *huevos rancheros* from Estrella, who knew Deuce from the let's-play-doctor days, Deuce stared down at the heavily bandaged limb. Maybe mechanical would be a better way to go. He was not so hot on that idea, but it would take a lot more than one arm to make him into a cyborg. Not that it was nice to have prejudices about any group, but Deuce agreed with the majority opinion prevalent on the Moon: cyborgs—beings pieced together from mechanical parts and whatever was left of some human—weren't real people.

Neither were androids, whose chassis were organically grown, but who still contained a lot of electronic components in place of real brains. Cyborgs were usually created after accidents, while androids were purposely grown; but in both cases, they weren't the genuine article. Maybe that was why he had survived a pair of them—Club and Spade, an android and a cyborg working together as hit men—or maybe it had been that luck of the Irish he still seemed to possess.

At any rate, both types of artificial beings were allowed on the Moon, but if you wanted to become one, you had to go Earthside to do it. On account of creating them was not allowed on the Moon.

And here he was, allowing his mind to wander, while everyone was sitting down and chowing down and staring at him to continue the meeting. It was actually going well. The twenty guys who had shown up were smart guys. They were responsible guys. They knew that if the Families didn't pull together right now—this very nanosecond— Earth was going to come in and take over. And they were willing to put their lives on the line by pledging their allegiance to each other on behalf of whoever in their Families understood this fact. And if they had to perp some hits or break off from the main Family tree or whatever, they were willing to do that, too.

"It's just like in ancient Earthside America, when the United States was formed," Lee Chan said enthusiastically.

Deuce was not sure what the Chan guy meant by that, but so many other heads were nodding that he nodded, too. Whatever, it sounded good, just like, "As God is my witness, I shall never go hungry again!" even though he still didn't understand what that had to do with digging around in the mud for a carrot.

At the Smiths' Wild West, you could actually do that. They had a fake farm, with real dirt and like that, and people could pay to water various crops and dig 'em up. Even Earthside tourists, who could visit real farms back home, anted up for the exotic experience.

Again he realized his mind was wandering. He said to the group, "Hold on a minute," and commed his wife, who was back home with the same crack medical team that was looking after Stella Castle di Borgioli.

Sparkle answered at once. It seemed that the blaster had

missed both teeny babies, their developing sacs, and her necessary plumbing, and had ripped a hole in a spot that was easily plugged. At least, that was the docs' explanation for this *scemo* gravoid worried husband and daddy-to-be.

"I'm fine," she said, summing up. "The babies are okay."

"Okay," he said. "I'm very relieved, *cara mia. Ti amo.*" Which was something he did not usually say when he was in a room of youngbloods.

He commed off and looked at the eager faces at the table. Of the thirty Liaisons who could have been invited, twenty-five actually had been. The excluded were four Scarlatti guys and one Smith guy. Deuce and Lee Chan had sensed these five would blow everybody's cover by informing their bosses about the meeting. Deuce wondered if any of the other five who had turned down the invite—two other Smith guys, a Chan, and a Van Aadams—had told their bosses about the meeting. If so, they were putting their fellow Family Liaisons in grave danger. It would be a quick and easy way to settle a personal beef to get any of the attendees whacked for treason.

Still, there were twenty—including Snake Eyes Sal, his own successor, and the four other Borgioli Liaisons—and these twenty knew the risks. They lived with risk. Liaisoning was a young, ambitious man's job. It was high-pressure, dangerous, and relentless. You had to hustle constantly. Results were what mattered. If you didn't produce after a couple-three months, six tops, you were history, of whatever sort your Family wrote for failures. The wiser course if you realized you couldn't cut it was to ask your Godfather for something less stressful. If you went that route, then you got fat and told your grandkids about your wild days packin' heat up and down the Strip.

If you didn't, you had basically one chance in eight that you would not live to have grandkids.

One in seven, if you were a Borgioli.

One in six if you were a Scarlatti.

Mr. Wong got a comm and took it on his earphone, listening for a moment, then smiled at Deuce. He was a very good robot, with a nice smile. They had decided to keep

Hunter's revised POS a secret. As far as everybody in the Moon knew, Bea was still the official Castle C.E.O.

Mr. Wong said to Deuce, "Lunar Security Forces are basically ignoring the explosion at the MLF compound. Since they were officially labeled a terrorist organization, law enforcement protection no longer extends to them."

Deuce was relieved. It was bad enough having to dance with Detective O'Connor over the happenings on *Gambler's Star*. But now that Deuce was a Castle employee, Hunter's reputation as a solid citizen extended to Deuce—for better or for worse—and he had to play by those kinds of rules. But it was hard to wipe out the tradition of generations of mistrust between cop and wise guy, and everything in him screamed in protest when he was forced to deal with those guys.

Now, these guys, he thought as he looked around the table, these guys made his insides cheer. These guys were his kind of guys.

"That's good, Mr. Wong. If you had anything to do with that, I'm even gladder to know you're sticking around to help me complete Darkside City."

There was a stir around the table as the boys took that in. Deuce made a show of accepting a cup of coffee from Estrella, who winked at him, and he slowly stirred it with a spoon even though he took it black.

He drank. It was cratercafe, and not very good even for crater. Sour and old. Trini's seemed to have fallen on hard times. Deuce was going to give Estrella a bundle for having the sit-down on her premises. The big shots could give her lots of trouble if they felt like it, even though she was N.A. and officially could have anybody here anytime she felt like it.

Yeah, a bundle of money that he did not currently possess. He was going to have to talk to Mr. Wong about that. If Deuce was really Hunter's successor, he should have the keys to the kingdom.

Almost as if he had read his mind, Mr. Wong leaned forward, and whispered in Deuce's ear, "We should stripe Miss Estrella a good reward for having us here today."

Deuce murmured, "You can do that?"

"Yes, sir, I can."

Deuce nodded. Good. From now on, Mr. Wong could pay all the bills. And make the back payments they owed all over the satellite. And square Deuce's own paycheck, too.

"There's this family," he said, "name of Bonnanio. I set up some special arrangements for them, but I want you to stay on the case. They are very important people to me." He thought a moment. "Get the names and ages of all the kids and chute them over some toys. Lots of toys. The girl, Annie, make sure she gets a doll."

"Yes, sir." Mr. Wong appeared to be making a mental note.

"You got people looking for Connie Lockheart?" he queried.

"Yes. We're bringing Bucky Barnum in for questioning," Mr. Wong added.

Feeling even better, Deuce set down his coffee, and said, "Gentlemen, do you all have your breakfasts?"

They nodded. He knew *huevos rancheros* was a novelty for these boys. So was having breakfast at 7:00 A.M. Most Liaisons got to bed at four or five. Breakfast was usually a cup of coffee and a bagel, something like that, around noon or later.

When he'd gone to work for Hunter, he started having breakfast at 6:00 A.M., at least once or twice a week with his boss. It had taken him and Sparkle a long time to adjust. Now they were like any other respectable couple, hitting the sack before midnight and rising with the dawn, which of course they did not really have, not way down below the surface like they were.

"Everybody has food, coffee? Everything they want? Beverages?" Deuce asked pleasantly.

"Yes, sir," said Carlo Scarlatti, the only Scarlatti Liaison to show up. Deuce was damned curious about the situation over at the guy's House. He was going to take a report from each Liaison on his assessment of his Family's strategy for dealing with the Castle Crisis, as the viso scans were terming it. Deuce himself was scheduled to go on the air at noon, after he met with Detective O'Connor at ten.

When he was supposed to sleep and/or lose his arm, he was not yet sure.

"I want each of you to tell me what you think is going down at your House," Deuce announced. "I want you to be as honest as possible. Please, think of everyone here as your brothers, and let's lay our cards on the table."

"Deuce, no way," said Bruce Chan, a very young Liaison at twenty raw years. "I have no assurance that these guys are not spies, pardon me to all of you, but I don't." He shrugged. "I'm risking my life coming here. The only man I trust in the least at this sit-down is you, and you'll excuse me if I tell you that while you have my deepest respect, I'm not certain how much I can trust you."

Deuce cocked his head. "How many of the rest of you feel that way?"

Exactly half of the Liaisons raised their hands. A couple more looked like they wanted to, but didn't have the nerve. Deuce ticked his gaze toward Mr. Wong.

The robot rose and gestured to the group as if he were about to dedicate a song to some newly married couple. He said, "If I may, Mr. McNamara, perhaps I can act in the capacity of *consigliere*. Each man here has his own worries and concerns, and while it must be stated that my primary concerns are the health and safety of Castle Enterprises, it is quite obvious that we must hang together or hang separately in this venture."

"What's he talking about?" Carlo Scarlatti demanded. "What, hanging?"

"I mean," Mr. Wong said, swiveling in Carlo's direction, "that we are now dependent upon each other. If one falls, the rest may fall as well."

"Wait a minute," said Termite Tommy, the Van Aadams Liaison to the Smiths. "That I know. But what's this about a *consigliere*? Don't Mr. Castle already have one?"

"Mr. Castle's *consigliere* is dead," Deuce said bluntly, thinking of Jackson. "Died in the explosion." That was an easy enough explanation. And true enough for this crowd. He was wondering if Mr. Wong planned to keep the fact of his succession a secret and let everyone assume Beatrice was still officially in charge. Deuce wanted another look at the POS on the mini Hunter had given Sparkle. Maybe it wasn't officially Registered. It wasn't like Hunter to be so slapdash. On the other hand, it was like Hunter to be extremely clever and, frankly, ruthless: Maybe he was hanging Beatrice out to dry, keeping all eyes on her while he gave Deuce the real cards to play.

Maybe Jackson had not been dirty at all. Maybe Hunter was just painting him that way.

With all that racing through his mind, he leaned forward on his good elbow. "Let me speak frankly. As of this moment, we are sharing loyalty with each other because we are trying to stop Earthside from coming in and taking over. We're taking huge personal risks because we believe that if we don't, our way of life will be over."

A few of them nodded.

"So my point is, there's not much percentage in holding back now. If this worries you, I suggest you leave, but I beg you not to take back word of this meeting to your Houses."

There was an uncertain pause. Bruce Chan looked at his elder, Lee, and shook his head. He scooted back his chair.

"We Chans have a long history of tradition and loyalty only to one another," Bruce said, with a tinge of sadness. "It goes against everything within me to speak about my Family's business in public." He bowed to Deuce. "I'm very sorry, Godfather, but I can't participate further. It grieves me deeply."

Deuce pursed his lips. He appreciated the guy's honesty, but he didn't know what to do with it.

But as Bruce turned to go, Mr. Wong cleared his throat.

"Mr. Chan," he said, "I, too, am of Asian extraction, despite the fact that I'm a mechanical. I was programmed in that way. I understand your dilemma, but I also sense that you wish to remain with us in some fashion."

Bruce nodded. "That's true."

Mr. Wong addressed the group. "I suggest that those Members who are comfortable discussing their Family situations remain in this room. I invite the others to follow me into the main room for some pool."

Bruce Chan smiled broadly. "That I can do." He bobbed

his head at Deuce. "You done good, Mr. McNamara. I can work with this organization."

Deuce hid his grin as a few of the younger Liaisons brightened and followed Bruce and Mr. Wong out of the room. It was a very classy move. It took the pressure off the guys, yet made them feel like part of the same team.

However, the day might come sooner than they expected that they would have to choose their loyalties. Deuce hoped there would be a lot of pool games before that time arrived.

Carrying enough medications to give him Honorary Papers of Affiliation in the Chan Family, Mr. Wong accompanied Deuce in his aichy as Deuce reported for his interrogation—correction, interview—with Detective O'Connor. It turned out that the versatile Mr. Wong had actually passed the Conglomerated Nations Bar Exam and was licensed to practice law, both Earthside and on the Moon.

As they neared the Lunar Security Forces HQ, he said to Deuce, "Sir, I suggest you decline to answer everything unless I nod. Then you may answer the question posed to you after conferring with me."

"That'll make me look guilty," Deuce grumbled.

Mr. Wong shook his head. "If I may venture an opinion, Mr. McNamara, that doesn't matter. It only matters if they can prove it."

"They'll dog me."

Mr. Wong considered. "I suspect they realize how important you are to the stability of this transition period. I don't think they'll dog you for long, if they dog you at all."

It was Deuce's turn to think. Then he cocked his head at Mr. Wong, and said, "Do you know where Bernardo Chang is?"

"No." Mr. Wong looked mildly frustrated. "I, too, have been searching for him. It is my opinion that he has valuable information."

"About?" Deuce pressed.

Mr. Wong said smoothly, "The resistance."

"As in MLF?"

"As in those parties who would thwart our plan."

"As in Darkside City."

"As you say, sir," Mr. Wong replied. "Darkside City."

"Mr. Wong, did you whack the doc?"

"No, sir."

"Do you know who the two guys were in Mr. Castle's office and why they exploded?"

"I was under the assumption that they were trying to sell Mr. Castle some components for his new propulsion system," Mr. Wong replied.

Deuce was surprised. "Looks like they gave him some bad stuff."

"It would appear so, sir," said Mr. Wong.

"But sometimes appearances can be deceiving, eh, Mr. Wong?"

"Indeed, sir," Mr. Wong replied.

Detective O'Connor worked in a tiny cubicle overloaded with minis and scanners and all manner of stuff, including a poster for a gas movie called *Capone On Mars*. Deuce hid a smile. Many lawmen had a thing for the exciting lifestyle of mobsters. You had your danger, your thrills and excitement. And you had your payoff.

Cops lacked payoff in spades. They put their lives on the line for very low pay and not much more psychic satisfaction, because usually the Families bought whatever kind of justice they needed. Within a few months of their assignment, most of the LSF either got dirty and/or scared. The others—the white knights—didn't last long. The smart ones asked for reassignment back to Earth, and the dumb ones washed out or disappeared.

What was Detective O'Connor—smart, dumb, or virtuous? Deuce would have to wait and see.

"Please, Mr. McNamara," the detective said to Deuce, half-rising as he came into the office. "Have a seat."

Deuce was pleasantly surprised by the show of respect. The LSF lackey had not seemed half so respectful back on the *Star*. Maybe he'd made a few calls . . . or maybe a few people had called him.

Deuce had changed into a nice black business suit and a

white shirt with a black-and-orange handkerchief in his breast pocket. His sling was as black as an eye patch.

When he'd first signed on with Hunter, his impulse had been to wear orange shirts with the black, but Sparkle had taken him aside and explained that bright shirts like that made him out to be a mobster, not a business executive. So for Deuce, such shirts went the way of the flashy watch and the pinkie ring, neither of which he had ever fancied. He was not a jewelry kind of guy. Joey wore a couple of gold chains, which Sparkle disapproved of, but hey, you had to enjoy life.

Detective O'Connor said, "Coffee, Mr. McNamara? It's only crater, I'm afraid."

Deuce nodded graciously. "Thanks so much, Detective. I take it with milk." To cut the wretched taste. Once you got used to the real stuff, it was hard to drink the fake. Deuce was seized with the inspiration that he would send O'Connor some real coffee instead of a bottle of Irish whiskey.

The detective left the room, giving Deuce a moment to scan around and see what kind of man he was. He blinked on his thinkerama and started filing away all the commendations and letters from big shots—there was one from Chairman William Atherton Van Aadams, the dead C.E.O. of the Van Aadams Family, who had lost two Designated Heirs, Wayne and James, thanking him for his work with the Van Aadams AntiDrug Campaign. A joke. All drugs were legal on the Moon. Including Chantilly Lace, which Hunter had been lobbying to ban.

Whew. Talk about your potential turf war. The Chans would descend like heat-seeking missiles if such a ban ever came to pass. Although their Casino had basically been handed over to the Caputos, nobody had touched their drug activities. That had seemed to be the deal, despite the fact that Hunter had made it, and he had declared himself antidrug.

The detective came back in the room carrying two cups of coffee in real cups, emblazoned with the LSF logo—a crescent moon against a field of six stars for the Families, a smattering of comets for the N.A.'s, and in the upper right corner, a purple star for Hunter Castle, newly added. TO PROTECT AND SERVE, read the curved banner beneath the crescent. Yeah, to squeeze and harass would be more accurate.

"Oh, that's right, we'll need one more," Detective O'Connor said pleasantly, as he set down the two cups. He bustled on out.

Deuce was mildly curious about who the third party would be but not surprised that there would be one. The detective didn't know about Mr. Wong. Or rather, Deuce hadn't informed him that he had brought contingency counsel. No, this was the typical kind of junk cops pulled to try to throw you off your game. It happened all the time, and it didn't mean a thing. It didn't meant they had plans to charge him over Jackson.

It didn't mean it was time to call in Mr. Wong, who was seated in a six-sided waiting room, dutifully sipping tea even though he didn't really eat or drink. The People for Ethical Treatment of Artificial Intelligence had taken that up as their big cause for a while—decrying that programming in taste and hunger would enhance the lives of all mechanicals everywhere. But Deuce had quizzed a few robots on the subject, and, to a circuit, they told him they didn't miss the necessity of grabbing a bite at all. So much for the presumptuousness of do-gooders.

"Here we are. Did you hurt your arm, sir?"

Deuce shrugged. "Yeah. It's just a sprain."

O'Connor gave him a look. Deuce shrugged. "Well, a sprain and some other injuries."

"Then I'm so glad you could join us, Dr. Shiflett," Detective O'Connor said, as the man walked into the room. Deuce looked straight at him, and the man looked straight back, betraying no fear or nervousness. "Perhaps you can take a look at Mr. McNamara's injuries."

Shiflett said, "It's just Mr. Shiflett. I'm a physician's assistant, not a physician."

"Oh?" Detective O'Connor looked surprised. "But you signed Dr. Clancy's death certificate."

Deuce pretended that none of this bothered him. It didn't

yet, actually, but he wanted to get in the groove of pretending for when it did.

Shiflett shrugged. ''I couldn't find a physician at the time. It was pretty chaotic aboard the ship.'' He gestured to the cop. ''You were there. You saw how it was.''

''I didn't see everything, though,'' O'Connor said. He opened his hand expansively, indicating the chair beside Deuce's. ''Please, sit down.''

Shiflett acknowledged Deuce as he sat.

''Mr. McNamara,'' he said, ''it's a pleasure to see you again. Do you need help with your arm?''

Deuce sat a little easier. That was a nice show of respect, and in front of the lawman, too.

''Mr. Shiflett, my pleasure as well,'' he said. ''Thanks, but I have someone working on my arm. You staying on the *Star* or in town?''

''We evacuated the ship,'' O'Connor informed Deuce. ''Everyone's been relocated until the vessel can be certified safe.''

Deuce was alarmed. He should have known about this. Should have been informed. Those guys were probably pulling the *Star* apart, searching for Hunter's secrets, ferreting out information they could use against the big man— or Deuce himself—later, if they could and if they needed to.

Hunter's personal log was still aboard. Deuce wondered again about the ship's logs—if they were coded to work only aboard the *Star*. If maybe you had to have a special password.

''We received permission from Mrs. Castle to evacuate,'' O'Connor added in an offhand manner. ''Since Mr. Castle designated her to run things in his, ah, absence.''

Deuce almost blinked in surprise, but he kept his cool. First, he noted that Bea was not keeping him in the loop. Secondly, he noted that O'Connor was hinting that he knew that Hunter was not dead.

''Mrs. Castle would know best,'' he said, ''although I have to admit that it makes me nervous to think that anybody has free rein among Mr. Castle's belongings and private affairs. He is''—he lowered his head—''*was* a very famous man, and of course he had a lot of enemies."

"Really?" O'Connor made a show of leaning forward with interest. Probably he had taken some *schiamazzo* police seminar on interviewing witnesses, complete with a training film. The certificate for said seminar was probably amongst all the clutter on his wall.

"Yeah." Deuce shrugged. "Any powerful man has enemies." No news there.

"For example?" O'Connor invited.

"For example, any schmo who lost to him in a business negotiation. Which is just about anybody he ever did business with," Deuce added, a little irritated. "Detective, not to be rude to you—I would never dream of such a thing—but I am very tired. And my arm is sore. I'm more than happy to talk to you, but I would appreciate that we get to the point."

O'Connor thought that over. He sat back in his chair. He made a steeple of his hands.

He said, "My understanding is that you come from a long line of crooked Irish Earthside cops."

Deuce sighed. "So I'm told. Only, I have never located any of my supposed relatives."

"I'm a descendant of William O'Connor," the detective said proudly. "Chicago Chief of Detectives. In 1927, he formed an elite unit of armored car forces to put an end to the mob wars that were terrorizing the city."

Mob wars. The guy had a history-textbook delivery, but nevertheless, there was his angle. Deuce nodded, "I'm working on that problem myself, Detective. It's keeping me pretty busy." He made a show of looking at the wall clock below some plaque about Little League sponsorship. "And I've got a lot of meetings today."

"And a press conference at noon, if I'm not mistaken," O'Connor drawled.

"So if you got a beef with me," Deuce continued in an easy, pleasant tone—beefs were rarely personal, and business was business—"I would appreciate that we get down to it."

"No, no beef," the detective assured him. "Just maybe

more questions than you will have the patience to sit through.''

Deuce held up a hand. "Sir, I am ready and willing to answer all the questions you have. You just fire away." He waited a beat. "But if for some reason—which I cannot fathom—I need to have an attorney present, Castle Enterprises has employed Mr. Wong on my behalf."

The detective looked amused. "And who suggested he become your attorney?"

"I believe that's privileged," Deuce retorted.

O'Connor shrugged. Then suddenly he swiveled his entire body toward Shiflett, and said, "Where's Jameson Jackson's body?"

Shiflett didn't bat an eye. He looked at Deuce, then at the detective, and shrugged. "I'm sorry, sir. I really don't know."

"Did you jettison the corpse on orders from Mr. McNamara?"

Shiflett looked very surprised. "No, sir."

"Would you be willing to swear that under oath?"

"Sure."

Deuce held up a hand. "Why are you attacking my subordinate?" he demanded. "If you'd like answers to these questions, ask the right people."

Detective O'Connor pursed his lips. "All right, then. Where is it, Mr. McNamara?"

Deuce held out his hands in a gesture of helplessness. "*Davvero, davvero*, Mr. O'Connor, I have no idea."

O'Connor looked mildly annoyed. Deuce wondered if his blurting out an Italian phrase had anything to do with it; as if the cop was thinking that Deuce was a lying Family man who, despite his stated allegiance to the Non-Affiliateds of the satellite, would never be able to wipe the spaghetti sauce off his hands.

"You have no idea?"

"Why would I care where his body is? Why would I order Shiflett to jettison it?" Deuce asked.

"To cover up the evidence that would convict you of murder," O'Connor shot back.

"Whoa. Excuse me. Time out." Deuce tapped his comm badge. "Mr. Wong, I need you, sir."

O'Connor huffed, clearly frustrated. "Listen, McNamara. I know you aren't used to dealing with the LSF. We leave the Families alone. We stay out of your beefs and your hits and your Vendettas."

Deuce wagged his finger at the man. "First of all, that's not by your choice. It's by law. And secondly, I am very used to dealing with the LSF. I've been dealing with you people all my life. Mr. Castle worked very hard to establish his excellent relationship with the local authorities, and I have worked no less hard to maintain it." Deuce couldn't help but scowl, and add, "No matter my personal opinion of you all."

O'Connor stared hard at Shiflett. "If we find out later that you helped Mr. McNamara dispose of Jackson's body, we'll charge you as an accessory to murder."

"Mr. McNamara, say nothing," said a voice from the doorway. It was Mr. Wong. He glided in silently, his face inscrutable not because his features were Asian but because he was a mechanical and they turn those kinds of things on and off. "Detective, unless you plan to charge Mr. McNamara this instant, I insist we be allowed to leave. The special circumstances under which everyone is laboring—namely, the confusion caused by the demise of Mr. Castle—require that you act reasonably."

"Which I am," O'Connor said, but the wind clearly had gone out of his sails.

His assertion was met with silence from the other side of the desk. Deuce found the maturity not to flash him a smug smile. Plus his pain medication was beginning to wear off.

O'Connor pushed away from his desk, and said, "All right, McNamara. You're free to go."

"No hard feelings," Deuce replied. He held out his hand. "I know you're only doing your job."

O'Connor looked surprised. "Mr. McNamara, you're not at all the man I was led to believe you were."

"And who led you there?" Deuce asked. "Connie Lockheart?"

The detective frowned. "Never heard of her."

Deuce moved his shoulders. "That's okay. No one else has."

O'Connor scratched his cheek. He looked tired. His red hair was a little greasy, and there was red stubble on his reddening, red cheeks. He reminded Deuce a little bit of a strawberry. Which he had seen.

The man said, "Should I get to know her?"

"Naw." Deuce cocked his head. "But here's a thought, Detective O'Connor. We want the same thing: peace and justice on the Moon. I would appreciate joining forces with you as I move forward with building Darkside City."

O'Connor was caught off guard. "Me? Or the LSF?"

"Whichever you think is the best way to go." Deuce waved a hand. "In the old days, if there were problems, what did the big shots do? Band the people together, maybe by starting a war. I'm thinking we can band our people together to stop a war. We have a rare opportunity here: Except for the lunatic fringe, no one wants Earthside to come in and take things over. We want to show them we can conduct ourselves like decent human beings."

"I'm not so sure it's just the lunatic fringe," O'Connor said slowly. However, Deuce could see he liked Deuce's notion.

"Whatever. The majority of Moonsiders, it's not." Or so Deuce hoped. "Building Darkside City is also like fighting a war. It's that big. We can rally people to that cause, keep their thoughts off carving the littler pie that is the status quo, like with the Families and Moonbase Vegas."

He leaned forward sincerely, hoping O'Connor was not so jaded that he had lost all belief in sincerity and therefore could not detect the genuine article.

"I can use your help, either with you on the LSF or if you want to go private, I can guarantee you secure employment." He glanced at Mr. Wong. "Can I not?"

"You can," Mr. Wong assured them both.

O'Connor scratched his other cheek and looked slightly uncomfortable. It probably made him antsy to discuss such matters in police HQ. "Let me think about it," he said. "In the meantime, I am conducting a murder investigation, and you are involved. I would feel less than honorable if I didn't remind you of that."

"Fair enough." Deuce nodded and held out his hand. "Let's talk soon." He gestured to the outer door. "Maybe over a nice dinner. Somewhere a little more private."

O'Connor gave him a short, quick smile. It was a nice smile. Deuce liked this guy.

"Until then," he said. He turned to go.

Shiflett and Mr. Wong followed.

In the hallway, Deuce collapsed.

THIRTEEN

It was not a bad arm, as fake arms go. In fact, it was the best that money could buy.

Since the doctors knocked Deuce out to amputate the bad one and install the mechanical, there was always a sense of unreality attached to his new arm for Deuce. When he stared at it and flexed his muscles, it seemed like nothing had changed. It was like when you met an old friend who had had a body makeover; you knew it was your pal inside, but their outsides were different.

Sparkle swore she could not tell the difference in Deuce's arm. Whatever; it didn't seem to bother her in the least. Maybe dames were like that; they got their legs extended and their hips replaced as a matter of course, the way Earthsiders had their hair reseeded. Hell, get a full rejuv, and there was officially not that much left of your original equipment.

Still, for the next couple of months, whenever Deuce touched Sparkle with his artificial limb, his first impulse was to apologize.

He got his thinkerama removed, too, somewhat regretfully. It was one of those rich man's toys you eventually figured out were not for you.

The strange and wonderful Darkside City continued to grow. With each lasered cavern, each completed structure, came new enemies, new friends, new problems, new responsibilities. Some renegade Caputos and Scarlattis formed an alliance to block Deuce's water-supply ships, with the intention of blaming the intended raids on "pirates."

With the permission of Vito and Sandy Scarlatti and Don Giancarlo Caputo (fronting for a new Caputo Designated Heir, Rudy's cousin—Giuliano—Julie) Deuce mercilessly rubbed out everyone involved in the scheme—including Bucky Barnum's sister's boyfriend, poor old Nuncio, the N.A. putz formerly known as Henry.

The sister—one Dixie—he gave a one-way ticket to Earthside. She was glad to take it.

Bucky could shed no light on the mysterious Connie Lockheart, who seemed to have disappeared into thin air. She had been caught stealing company supplies, and Barnum had fired her. Barnum offered that apparently she had left for Earth the same day—or gotten whacked—because she was never seen or heard from again.

Or melted into the MLF, Deuce figured, and let it go.

After Deuce's retaliation for the water scheme, any pretext that Deuce was just some good ol' N.A. who'd struck it rich was dropped: Whether he accepted the title or not, he was Don McNamara, and notice had been given—when he had to be as ruthless as any Family Godfather, he would be.

The Moonsider Liberation Front recovered from the blast that had killed Angelina Rille, and installed his old Mormon buddy, Brigham, as their leader. That was both a plus and a minus. Brigham liked Deuce, but Brigham also had to prove that good Mormons could not be bought or influenced. Deuce was curious to see how it all worked out . . . especially if it meant dodging the bullets from Brigham's own gun.

But the factionalizing within the MLF extended to the Families and the Non-Affiliateds. The closer Darkside City came to completion, the more everybody realized this was the big ticket, either to new riches or to total oblivion. The jockeying for position heated up. The young, the ambitious, and the disaffected Members of the Families waged Family battles, making all kinds of alliances, betraying all kinds of promises.

Yet the Moon as a whole continued to prosper. With

Sparkle's assistance, Deuce steered the finances of the satellite with the finesse of a starship captain. His sound investment advice, his mutually beneficial Family strategies, and the jobs he provided were good for most of the people most of the time. The Families were growing in strength and power, the N.A.'s as well, and revenue was pouring onto the lunar landscape from Earth. Earthside holdings filled the Families' portfolios.

It should have been a good thing.

Up above the world so high, *Gambler's Star* hung in darkest space surrounded by a high-beam Tinkertoy array, blurring in the brilliant lights like a spectacular sunken ship. Repairs were slow and desultory, because there wasn't any need for the fancy-schmancy ship, and it only served to remind people that the great Hunter Castle was not among them. Better to concentrate on Darkside City, which was a more upbeat project by half . . . as well as more likely to be profitable.

Deuce had gone up to the *Star* a number of times to search for the rest of Hunter's personal logs, but he had come up with nothing. This was intensely surprising to him. Hunter's personal quarters were curiously devoid of his personal effects. Deuce asked Mr. Wong about the diaries, but the robot assured him that he did not possess them, either. Who knew if the robot was lying? Who knew if they had been crammed down Jackson's throat, and the rods had crystallized inside the cryo tank?

The *Star* was nothing but a memorial to the dead, that once-fabulous ship. In its previous majesty, its ghost still soared across the viso screen of the channels Castle Enterprises owned or controlled—the vast majority of channels—as it had for decades. But in reality, the charred walls stank of death. Deuce figured sooner or later they would have to do something about the ship, which was drifting. All that movie stuff about decaying orbits and subsequent crashes was pretty much meaningless and inaccurate.

Unless you were talking about hopes and dreams. There was a big difference between being cynical and being disillusioned. Try telling a twenty-five-year-old kid that. Instead tell the twenty-seven-year-old he will become.

Robin Van Aadams got rubbed out, as Deuce expected, and the Van Aadamses had a hell of a time picking a successor. Such a time, in fact, that they left an entire generation of second cousins dead in the artificial Australian rain forest in the Moonbase Vegas compound. The official explanation for the purge was food poisoning, which the cops pretended to believe. Detective O'Connor was not on the case, having conveniently managed to pull some other duty on the night in question, as they used to say in the old gangster movies.

In the end, the Van Aadamses settled on some broad name of Alitji, which means Alice in Aborigine, and which made Deuce queasy, on account of a poor, drug-addicted Van Aadams dame named Alitji had died in his aichy just after Hunter had landed on the Moon. It had been a bad death, made worse by the necessity of Deuce killing her father in an effort to save her life . . . a wasted effort.

Meanwhile, there was more noise from Yuet Chan, who, it was rumored, was working with the Eight Disenfranchised Families from her lavish cell in Earthside New York. According to well-substantiated rumors, their plan was to "influence" the Department of Fairness to nationalize the casinos and put in the Eight as a block in charge of them. Yuet, of course, would return in glory . . . and probably a very short blaze of it, but that was her deal, not Deuce's.

To take care of the problem, Deuce contributed heavily to the fund to hire the best assassins money could buy. But no one could locate Yuet. Some of the Eight Family heads, yes. There was a lot of bloodshed, and more than one terrified widow appealed to the DOF for justice. So it may have been that that plan was actually backfiring on the Moonsiders.

One of the casualties of all this was Moonman, who decided all this stuff was too wild for his blood and went home. To be honest, while sorry, Deuce was also relieved, on account of Sparkle. It was clear to him there was a ghost of a sizzle between them, no matter how much time had gone by, and he never forgot that many years before, on a bachelor bender, Moonman had confessed to him that he thought pregnant women were the sexiest things in the universe.

And of the fact that Sparkle was pregnant, there was no doubt. Going on eight months, and she was one pregnant lady. In such good shape that she did not get that bloated look some women did; she was statuesque (for someone with regular legs) and thin except for her bulging, twin-filled belly. Deuce got what Moonman had meant about the sexy factor, and he agreed with it.

Problem was, her doctor had told Sparkle that because of the ways the babies were positioned, she had a bit of a high-risk pregnancy going on, and it would be better for her to refrain from, ah, relations. So there were no relations going on. And Beatrice, knowing this, was playing her little come-hither games, which made Deuce extremely uncomfortable. Not so much because he doubted his ability to withstand them, but because it made her seem kind of, well, desperate.

Here she was, the richest woman alive, and she was lonely and she was eager for that certain kind of company only men could give her. But she couldn't exactly contact a dating service. Despite the fact that a lot of people—including Angelo and the other Borgioli *capos*—had applied their energies to building her ''dead'' husband's city, there were still plenty of Vendettas and various takeover plans that included rubbing her out.

On top of that, she was a celebrity, and celebrities were always ripe for stalking and/or hostage activity. So Beatrice rattled around, a bird in a gilded cage, who took delight only in her little baby and making Deuce say, as politely and kindly as possible:

''No.''

As she stood in the doorway of the kitchen in yet another gossamer gown and sipped a glass of good old-fashioned Chianti, he wondered if there was another way to say it. She was as persistent as O'Connor once had been, trying to finger Deuce for the murder of Jameson Jackson.

The murder case was closed but not cleared. The body was still hidden in Deuce's freezer, and there were no suspects, no answers, and still no Connie Lockheart or Ber-

nardo Chang, who, for all intents and purposes, seemed also
to have vanished into thin air, which was the nice way you
said on the Moon that someone had probably been thrown
outside the domes and died on the surface. With the backup
of the key witnesses, who now insisted to the detective that
Jackson had acted in a menacing way toward Deuce (having been persuaded to that point of view with positive, not
negative, reinforcement), and the fact that Deuce was personally providing the beat cops with so many moonlight
jobs as security guards, O'Connor gave him a bye.

Every once in a while, Deuce went into the garage all
alone and opened the freezer, assuring himself that Jackson
was still in there. He was cryogenically frozen, arresting all
decay at the moment of immersion. With the press of a
beam, the faceplate on his capsule flicked open, revealing
the dead man's weird blue face in the ice like some ancient
caveman's. It surprised Deuce a little that O'Connor had
not produced a search warrant to go over Deuce's premises—but so far, either O'Connor was too intimidated,
didn't have enough evidence, or he was still planning to
ask Deuce for a private-sector job.

Shiflett was most assuredly in Deuce's camp, but Deuce
didn't know if he should ask the guy to check out Dr.
Clancy's autopsy results or let the dead rest. But there had
been something about Jackson, maybe something about the
way he had died, that had been worth killing Clancy over.
Or maybe that was a strange coincidence. Who knew? Who
to trust?

But now Beatrice was sashaying toward him while he
was on the comm line with a contractor who was saying,
in that nice Family way, that his bribe hadn't been delivered. And that, as a result, his crew would not be showing
up tomorrow to work on the supermesh matrix.

"Why not?" Beatrice cooed in a whisper. She glided
toward him, sipping her wine, smiling her smile, flexing
her fingers. She had big hips and matching *poppas*. She
had always been a, er, healthy girl. Where she had gotten
this outfit, he had no idea, maybe the newly restored Donna
MaDonna's, the flashy lingerie store over on Moonbase Vegas. They wanted to build a bigger, better, and flashier store

in Darkside City. Hunter had not been so sure that he wanted to give a license to such a trashy place.

The guy yammering into Deuce's ear was not done with his rant, and Beatrice, having grown up in a Family, knew that you did not have to pay attention to this part. You just had to let the injured party do a little venting.

"Duchino, why fight it?" she continued, trailing her nails down his chest. "You know you want me."

She slid her hand around his waist and lowered it at an angle toward his behind, thank the Virgin that she was not completely without shame. Deuce gently caught her hand at the wrist and moved slightly away, making a playful "tsk-tsk" wag with his other hand.

Beatrice pouted in her sexy-doll outfit. He could see everything she wanted him to, and that, besides her crude behavior, embarrassed him, so he turned his shoulder to her as he said to the angry contractor, "I know, T.J., I know. It pains me to my heart. I am so sorry. My people failed you, and believe me, I'll take care of this personally." Which translated to mean that he would increase the size of the bribe and send somebody more important than previously to deliver it.

Finally T.J. said the magic words, which were, "*Grazie,* Don McNamara," and disconnected.

"I heard that," Beatrice breathed in his other ear. "They call you a Don but they use your last name. Because you're the only Godfather your family could possibly have."

He had to acknowledge that yes, it was a form of a compliment. In the Families, everyone having the same last name and all, you called the Godfathers by their first names. He was the only one singled out in this way.

On the other hand, it was dangerous for people to consider him a Don. Dons got targeted as the guy to hit if you wanted to take over the action. Castle Enterprises was a corporation, not a Family, and killing Deuce was not the way to go about applying for the position of C.E.O. of Darkside City. But the reflex was there—even among N.A.'s—to whack guys in high places and ask questions later.

"Bea," he said now, dropping his voice, "honey, you

know that I adore you. I think the world of you. But I am in a legal marriage and—''

Beatrice's mouth quivered. He thought she was going to cry, but instead she burst out in a guffaw, and said, ''And you think *she's* faithful to *you*?''

Deuce swallowed. Then he said, ''That don't matter one way or the other, Bea. I'm faithful to her.''

''Good evening,'' Sparkle said from the same doorway Beatrice had swept through. She didn't look upset or angry in any way. She looked like Sparkle, maybe a little too serene, maybe awfully private. All this time, Deuce didn't really know how to read her.

''Hi.'' Beatrice put her glass to her lips and threw back some more wine. She leaned against the kitchen counter and raised her chin. Put down the glass, and said to Deuce, ''You got anything to help me wash that down with?''

''How about some water?'' Deuce asked.

Bea snorted. Then she pushed off from the counter and walked uncertainly toward Sparkle.

''You don't deserve him,'' Bea flung at her. ''You cheated on him with my husband the whole time we were married.''

Sparkle stayed calm. Sparkle stayed collected. She said, ''No.'' That was the sum total of her denial.

''I *saw* you,'' Beatrice said triumphantly.

O, Mamma mia. Deuce wanted to tell her to shut up at the same time he wanted her to go on. It was a perverse thing, wanting to know, not wanting to know.

''No,'' Sparkle said simply.

''I saw you in his arms, and I saw him kiss you.''

''No.''

''Yes!'' Beatrice raised her voice to new decibel levels. She had once studied opera. She had the lungs. ''Yes, I saw you. *Strega! Puttana!*''

She launched into a string of invective in Family dialect that made Deuce blush. Sparkle merely watched her with the idle curiosity one reserved for the insane. This was more than too much for Beatrice, who, after all, believed herself cheated not only of married love, but of the adoration she assumed Deuce harbored all their lives—and on both accounts, cheated by the same woman. Deuce was faintly surprised—but very relieved—that she had not by now grabbed a kitchen knife and hurtled herself at Sparkle. A lot of Italian Family women would have done so by now.

"You saw me in your husband's arms," Sparkle said calmly.

"*Sì!*"

"You saw him kiss me."

"*Sì!*"

"With passion?"

Beatrice sputtered. "Wha-*what*?"

Sparkle shrugged. "I've seen you kiss my husband. I've seen my husband kiss his brother. It's not the same thing." She paused meaningfully. "And you know that, Beatrice."

Beatrice pointed to Sparkle's belly. "You carry his children with passion."

Maybe without realizing it, Sparkle put a protective hand over her abdomen. She said, "These are not his children."

Deuce looked hard at first one woman, then the other. They seemed to be communicating perfectly, but he was lost. Or maybe just too nervous to figure out which "his" they were talking about.

Tears slid down Beatrice's face. She ran her hands through her hair, and said, "I'm begging you, *Signora*. You don't love him, and I do. Please, stand aside. If it's the money, I'll give you all the money you could want. If it's the power, I'll give you power."

"Bea," Deuce said, shocked.

He was further shocked when Sparkle raised a hand as if to tell him to be quiet. As if she wanted to hear the rest of Beatrice's proposition.

He was dumbfounded. He found himself wondering when Beatrice had seen Sparkle kissing Hunter.

"Please. I love him," Beatrice said, bursting into tears. "It's killing me, seeing how much he adores you and knowing that it's wasted on you! You . . . you icy bitch! When I . . . when we . . ."

Sparkle stayed where she was, her hand on her belly. She looked completely unaffected by Beatrice's break-down. Her face was smooth and young and unmoved.

Deuce couldn't stand it. He left the room and went into his office, where he poured himself a good, stiff belt of Atherton Gold. Then he commed Mr. Wong, who glided in.

"We got some business to discuss," Deuce said, yawning. He was very tired. "Touchy stuff. About Mr. Castle's wife and who to put with her in a, let's say, contingency liaison. No one else knows he's alive, and I'm sorry, but she's a loose cannon, if you get my meaning. She needs a man. Bad."

Mr. Wong regarded Deuce for a moment. Then he said, "Mr. McNamara, we need to go to *Gambler's Star*."

Deuce blinked. "Come again?"

"We need to go aboard," Mr. Wong repeated. "There are things Mr. Castle left for you there."

"Oh, yeah?" Deuce asked, intrigued, alarmed. "Of what nature?"

Mr. Wong said nothing.

Irritated, Deuce crossed his arms. "Mr. Wong, I know you won't own up to it, but I still believe that you killed Dr. Clancy. Why should I go up there alone with you?"

"Mr. McNamara," Mr. Wong said patiently, and with a touch of humor, "you've certainly been up there alone with me before. I have had dozens of opportunities to kill you with total assurance of the crime never being traced to me. I cannot show you what I must show you with another human being present. You must trust me. Or, if you prefer another perspective, you must trust Hunter Castle."

"Rock and a hard place," Deuce drawled.

Mr. Wong shook his head. "No, sir. Not really." He gestured to the clock on the wall. It was 11:00 P.M., Moon Standard Time.

"We can wait until tomorrow," Mr. Wong suggested.

Deuce sighed. "Why? Tomorrow there will be more new things to deal with."

"I'll inform our security forces," Mr. Wong said. "We'll take an armored vehicle."

"Very good," Deuce said. He checked his watch. "Meet you in the garage in fifteen minutes."

Mr. Wong inclined his head and glided away in that interesting way some mechanicals had.

Deuce went into his bedroom to change, and found Sparkle lying on her side in a very pretty metallic blue nightgown. Her tummy protruded in a way that would have made Moonman swoon. She was reading something off a mini. Probably an article about finance. Sparkle was the shrewdest businessperson he had ever met, not counting Hunter, because you weren't sure if Hunter was shrewd or impossible to bring down.

She looked up from the mini and laid it on the nightstand. He approached, sitting down beside her, and tenderly took her hand.

"Sparkle, you and me," he began, then said nothing. She looked at him placidly, almost kindly. He tried again. "How are you feeling?"

"Like we're going to have two kickboxers," she answered with a soft smile.

He liked the "we." He knew it was meant for him. For them.

"Sweetheart, I'm so sorry about Beatrice," he said. "I'm trying to do something about her."

Sparkle shrugged. "You're a very sexy man."

He smiled, absurdly flattered. "I'm thinking about a contingency for her."

She nodded. "That might help. Give her the right man, and she'll settle, but it's you she wants."

"She ain't going to get me."

Sparkle said nothing. She put her hand on his thigh, and murmured, "I'm sorry we can't do anything."

"It's nothing, baby," he said, placing his hand over hers. "I can wait."

"I'm not sure I could," she replied, maybe realizing she was shattering the moment. Maybe not. "For someone like you," she added.

Maybe. Maybe not.

He cleared his throat, wishing he felt more relaxed and trusting. But he had to admit that they had never really been that type of couple. In their life before Hunter, that uncertainty had been exciting. And excitement had made up for a lot of what he was afraid they were missing now.

"Listen, I got business."

She nodded and picked up the mini.

"High finance?" he asked.

"Breast-feeding," she replied, and got back to reading.

He turned to go.

"Deuce," she called suddenly.

"Yes, baby?"

Her face was blank. Her eyes were wide. Her mouth opened, but no sound came out.

"Sparkle?"

She shook herself. Blinked. "Take care," she said. "Take very good care."

He nodded, fear washing over him like a cold shower.

"Sure, baby. Thanks." He smiled at her.

She didn't smile back.

FOURTEEN

Mr. Wong was telling Deuce a very interesting story:

The source of all creation was the Sun. He created the Moon and took her to wife. Together they made seven sons, which are the stars of the Big Dipper.

The Sun also gave life to serpents upon the Earth. These creatures were so fertile that the land was soon overrun with their kind. The Sun requested of them to mate less often, so that the Earth could sustain them.

The serpents refused, and in anger, the Creator Sun destroyed them all . . . save one female snake who was about to give birth. Filled with compassion for her in her travail, he allowed her to survive.

One of this serpent's descendants, upon reaching adulthood, decided to seek revenge upon the Sun for the destruction of his kind. He determined to make the Sun suffer a loss as terrible as his own race had suffered.

To carry out his plan, he assumed a most pleasing human shape, known to all as Snakeman. The Moon saw him, and was moved. She fell in love with Snakeman; and true to his plan, he seduced her.

The Sun discovered her betrayal and killed her lover. Then he gathered their seven sons together and they fled her presence. But the Moon, who had fallen deeply in love with Snakeman, chased after the Sun with the intention of destroying him as he had destroyed her lover.

When the Sun created the Moon, he made her strong so

that she would always be safe. Now he realized he must arm his sons against the wrath of their mother. He gave one son a stick that could turn into a forest. To his second son, he gave a rock that could turn into a mountain. He gave his third son a waterskin that could become a rainstorm, and his fourth son a waterskin that could transform into a sea. To his fifth son, he gave a beautiful bird that could change into thunder, lightning, and rain. His sixth son received an air bladder that could whip up a mighty windstorm. And to his last son, the Sun gave the power to gouge deep canyons with the tip of his finger.

As the grief-enraged Moon closed in on her estranged family, each son fought her, seemingly to no avail. But at last, with the creation of a sea between them, the Sun and the Moon's children fled into the sky. The Moon followed and resumed the chase.

So that he and his children could rest, the Sun divided the night from the day. Through the day, they can gather their strength. But at the rise of nightfall, she is once again after them, and they seek refuge in the west.

So has it been since the beginning of the first moment. The Sun races across the sky, seeking to put distance between himself and his angered wife. When the sky turns ebony, the Moon pursues him, never failing to track his direction.

Should this eternal chase ever end, it will signify the ending of life itself.

"Well, that was a cheerful story," Deuce said, as Mr. Wong fell silent. They were traveling up to the *Star*, and somehow, just in the middle of the ride, Mr. Wong had told Deuce he was going to tell him this little ditty.

Deuce added, "Is this some kind of life lesson cooked up just for me?"

"I find it curious," Mr. Wong replied, "that the Moon, who is angry with her husband for murdering her duplicitous lover, attacks also her children, who were surely innocent of any crime."

Deuce slid a glance toward Mr. Wong. "And you are telling me this why?"

"There are parallels in actual history of betrayed lovers destroying their children. Medea, for one."

"Medea," Deuce repeated harshly, embarrassed that he didn't know the reference, irritated and worried by the whole tone of this unwelcome conversation about adulterous affairs and angry broads. "A horse, right?"

"Indeed not, sir." Mr. Wong turned to him. "A woman of ancient Earthside Greece."

Deuce felt a prickle of alarm. "Are you telling me Sparkle's going to do something to the babies?"

"I have no ability to know that," Mr. Wong said. "I am not a fortune-teller."

Deuce's alarm grew as he began to play the cards, fanning them, examining them. He cracked his knuckle. "Or Beatrice?"

"Again, I am not prescient, Mr. McNamara."

"So why you are warning me about them?"

Mr. Wong shook his head. "I'm not, sir. I apologize. I didn't mean to alarm you. However, that doesn't mean one should not keep on one's guard."

"One thanks you," Deuce muttered. "One, however, would like to know why the other one felt the need to tell this story at this particular time."

Mr. Wong shrugged. "It just came up." He gestured with one hand as if to say, "I don't get it, either."

Deuce said sarcastically. "It was just in the neighborhood."

"It was embedded deep in my programming. I did not consciously decide to tell it to you, just as I would not consciously decide to grab a cup that was falling off a table."

Deuce narrowed his eyes at the robot. "You're saying you're not consciously aware of all your actions. Then it would be possible to program you to do things that you wouldn't remember doing. You might not even know you did them, at any level. Ever."

Mr. Wong processed that. His eyes blanked for a moment; Deuce wondered if he had set off some kind of internal alarm. Or if he, Deuce, was up here so that Mr. Wong could execute some of that programming that was so deep that he would never know he'd executed it. Such as executing Deuce.

"I believe that may be true," Mr. Wong finally said.

Deuce felt in his pocket for his blaster. There was another one under the dash. Mr. Wong probably knew about that one. The aichy knew, and the aichy was a machine. Probably these guys interfaced all the time. Probably the aichy was telling Mr. Wong all the gossip about who rode in it where and when.

"Look," Mr. Wong said, pointing.

Deuce looked. There was the ship, with the hull breach repaired. The matte blacks did not match, and where the brilliant lights shone just so, you could see that it was a patch job. Hunter would not have stood for it. Deuce would not have, either. But thankfully, he was not in charge of it. Some guy named Colvin Pines had that honor.

Maybe he was up here because Mr. Wong thought Mr. Pines should marry Beatrice.

Mr. Wong voiced in their ID and got permission from Traffcom to dock. Deuce frowned slightly; Traffcom had not requested much in the area of credentials. He assumed he was expected, but still, security should remain tight at all times. He'd have to talk to Pines about that.

The iris airlock unfurled, and the aichy floated in. Deuce waited for the establishment of atmosphere and gravity with folded hands, allowing Mr. Wong to continue with docking protocol. Automatically, his eyes strayed to the overhang, where his friends in white used to wait for him. They were both dead now.

Deuce was beginning to feel melancholy.

The gull-wing door opened, and he climbed out, keeping his hand on his blaster. Mr. Wong, if he knew, showed no concern, only gestured politely for Deuce to lead the way.

"No, you first," Deuce replied, not polite at all.

Mr. Wong complied. Deuce kept his finger on the trigger as they entered the ruined ship.

Mr. Wong hesitated, then turned around and looked at the streaks of soot on the walls, the ruined carpet. In his mind's eye, Deuce saw pieces of bodies and heard screams.

He hefted the blaster in his pocket, not eager to join the ghosts of this vessel.

"It will never be as beautiful as it once was," Mr. Wong said, and to Deuce's shock, a tear slid down the robot's cheek.

"Will he come back?" Deuce asked.

Mr. Wong shook his head. "I don't know."

Deuce didn't know what to make of Mr. Wong. Tears you could program if you wanted to bother, but the robot also seemed nervous. Like tears, robots had nerves if they were programmed to be nervous. It was kind of like that sound in the forest thing: You had to conclude the robot was exhibiting these emotions in order for Deuce to notice them.

"Mr. Wong, are you really a mechanical?" Deuce asked, just in case.

"Indeed, sir," Mr. Wong said, still sounding edgy and unsure.

Deuce chewed the inside of his cheek. "Why are you acting like a person?"

"I'm going to die," Mr. Wong said flatly.

"Um, okay. How?" Deuce pressed, on full alert. "Is the ship going to blow again?"

Mr. Wong silently shook his head. That proved nothing; if you could program a bolthead to cry, you could program him to lie.

"Why are we here?" Deuce said. "Is this *assassinio*?"

"No, sir, but there's no way I can prove that to you," Mr. Wong replied. "You must simply go forward on faith."

"Faith in?"

"Hunter Castle."

Oh, fabulous. That was the best news Deuce had had all year.

"After you, Brutus," Deuce said. He pulled out his blaster and trained it on Mr. Wong. "You know I'll use it."

Mr. Wong said nothing, just inclined his head and led on.

They were met in the next passageway by none other

than Colvin Pines, who reached forward a hearty hand. Colvin was a pudgy man in an age—and above a satellite—where no one had to be pudgy. In fact, you almost had to work to be pudgy. And bald, as Colvin was. It had to be some retro look Deuce was not aware of. Maybe he would ask Beatrice about it. With all her fashion magazines, she would know what passed for fashion these days.

"Pines," Deuce said.

"Please, Mr. McNamara, just Colvin." He rubbed his hands together. "She's coming along nicely, don't you think?"

Who was he kidding? Deuce said, "It's amazing what they can do these days." Which was true. They just weren't doing any of it here.

Pines smiled sadly. "We're working on the small conference room at the moment. We're recreating the interior with holos. Each trophy, each plaque. They gleam just like the real ones did."

"Fabulous," Deuce said.

"Well," Mr. Pines said, clearly not certain why Deuce and Mr. Wong were there. That made two of them.

"We'll be in Mr. Castle's quarters," Mr. Wong said.

"Very good, sir. We'll have a light lunch sent in," Pines went in, with his oily smile and his ingratiating air.

"No lunch," Deuce said quickly. "We'll come out when we're ready."

Poor Pines. He was goggled-eyed with curiosity. "As you wish, sir." He hesitated, then smiled again and said, "I'll be in navigation if you need anything."

"Thank you," Deuce said.

The other man turned on his heel. Mr. Wong gestured for the two of them to continue on their way.

They moved more deeply into the ship, decoding security locks, reading Deuce's iris and thumbprint over and over, until they finally reached the holy of holies and the last door opened:

Hunter's quarters. The bulkheads that had been blown away had been replaced. The tattered holo wallpaper of magnolia trees and Spanish moss had been turned off. Hunter's big-ass bed, of which only a fragment remained, was encased in a plastic security cube as if it were some relic of a saint. His bureau, which had been reduced to a heap of wooden fragments, was missing. Deuce assumed someone had thrown it out.

In the far corner sat Hunter's black Kevlite safe, which Deuce had opened several times. To his surprise and delight, there had been a large stack of paper money among Hunter's various boring and uninteresting data rods and notes. No one had used paper money as legal tender in over a hundred years. Deuce loved real paper and collected it whenever he could. Dutifully he had handed the stack over to Beatrice, who had told him to keep it "as a souvenir." Mr. Wong had agreed that Deuce should have the money.

Thinking of Beatrice reminded Deuce of his original conversation with Mr. Wong, the trigger that had sent them all the way up here.

"Mr. Wong," he began, then was startled as Mr. Wong pressed against the top of the safe. The square block of Kevlite popped open like a waffle iron. Not that Deuce had ever seen a waffle iron.

A holo wafted above the top of the safe. It was Hunter's head.

"Hello, Deuce. I hope all is going well in my absence. I wonder how long it's taken you to get to this stage, but it's time I gave you a bigger set of blocks."

Mr. Wong waved his hand, turning off the lights in the cabin.

"Deuce, decades ago, I found something that changed the course of history. It was a crashed alien spaceship."

Holo of pieces of matte black material whirled in the holo beam. Deuce stared.

"I know it doesn't look like much," Hunter went on. "But it's the real thing, Deuce."

Deuce was as shocked as he was skeptical. The thing looked pretty much like a regular orbiter, nothing scary or fancy about it. He wondered if this was the beginning of some elaborate practical joke. If Hunter was going to step from the shadows, clap him on the shoulder, and offer him a stiff drink.

The drink would be nice.

"I built the actual wreck into the *Star*. Unfortunately, that's the part that blew up. I was trying to replicate its propulsion system."

Uh-huh. Yeah. Maybe. And how convenient that the only proof of alien existence known to man had been destroyed.

"However, I did save its brains, and I've passed along some of that to you. Mr. Wong isn't just a robot, Deuce. He's a data terminal, and he's coded only to work for you, Beatrice, and Jameson Jackson. Since Jackson is dead, you and Bea are the only living people on the Earth or in the Moon who can access it."

At this point, the top of Mr. Wong's head popped open and a strange sort of cylinder adorned with a sloping triangle on one end and a sphere on the other slid upward.

"You can take the terminal out of the casing—that is to say, Mr. Wong—but I have found Mr. Wong to be an excellent companion. You see, Deuce—"

Now Hunter's face popped back into the shimmering holo field.

"Mr. Wong has been helping you ever since I left by using a filtered version of the data terminal. He really is just a butler robot, but with this little accessory, he's the smartest thing our side's got."

"Our side," Deuce said slowly. Part of him was reeling, and part of him was wondering if Hunter was trying to reel him in. And yet another part was wondering which side their side was.

"The fact that you've accessed the terminal indicates that you have requested an answer to a question it can't process with its filters on. You see, its basic conceptual base is different from the stuff we're used to, but it's been filtered so that it responds as much like Mr. Wong as possible. To deflect any kind of notice, like from that detective."

Deuce looked at Mr. Wong. "When was this holo installed?" he demanded.

Mr. Wong shook his head.

Hunter's holo image continued. "When the filters come off, its data will have to be deciphered, let's say. But it'll provide you with more sophisticated information than in Mr. Wong's current state."

"Great," Deuce drawled.

"I can't be contacted right now, Deuce. I'm beyond the reach of standard communications. So you have to go it alone a while longer. I have faith in you, boy. I'll be back soon."

The holo of Hunter winked at him. "Give my regards to your pretty little wife. And try to take care of Beatrice as best you can. I know she can be a handful."

The holo clicked off.

Then it clicked back on. Hunter looked very earnest.

"Deuce, *Gambler's Star*. It's time to rebuild her. Time to put her to use. Things are going to happen, Deuce. Things you can only imagine."

The holo ended. Deuce waited a moment, then stood staring at the empty space.

"Well." Deuce shifted his gaze and stared hard at Mr. Wong. An alien data terminal? "Weren't you just busting to tell me all this before now?"

"I assume that's a rhetorical question, sir."

How much of this was he supposed to believe? "Beyond the reach of standard communications," his butt. Hunter was taking a powder, pure and simple. Assuaging his guilt by sending Deuce some new supercomputer. Or dangling a carrot to keep his donkey tied to its cart.

"Okay, big shot. Take off your filters."

Mr. Wong actually swallowed hard. He said, "Remember when I told you that I was going to die?"

Then he shuddered once, hard. His head bobbed forward, and he slumped to the deck.

"Uh," Deuce said.

The robot didn't move. Deuce knelt beside him and touched the side of his neck as if checking for a pulse.

Mr. Wong shuddered again. A low-pitched whine filled the room. Deuce jumped back from him and straightened, moving toward the door. The noise was like a blaster gearing up to blow on overload.

He pressed open the door and crossed the threshold, watching the inert form on the floor.

It sat up. Then it turned its head toward Deuce. Whatever had been programmed in to make Mr. Wong Mr. Wong had been changed; his features were different somehow. More intense, sharper. Almost sinister.

"Deuce McNamara." The voice was synthetic, flat, monotonal. "Greetings, Deuce McNamara."

"Greetings. What do I call you?"

"Terminal A is the name."

"How about I keep calling you Mr. Wong," Deuce suggested.

"Accepted."

Mmm.

Deuce hung in the doorway, pulling back slightly as the robot got to its feet. Mr. Wong's faint smile was gone. His face held no expression whatsoever. No humor, no curiosity, and none of the sadness Mr. Wong had so recently displayed. No tears, not a one for its "casing."

"Okay, Mr. Wong. Let's cut to the chase, shall we? What alien ship is Hunter talking about?"

The robot's eyes darted left, right, left, right, as it seemed to process this request for information. Finally it said, "Terminal A provided remote access."

"To the ship?"

"Correct."

"And the ship, it was from beyond this space?" This had to be a joke, like the fake hit Joey had perped on Andreas.

"Correct," Mr. Wong said.

"And it belonged to a race of aliens?"

"Correct."

"And so the aliens are here?"

The robot paused. Left, right, left, right. "Cannot enter this space at present time."

"Why not?"

"Incompatible."

"So they died when they entered our, um, galaxy?"

"Died."

"All of them?"

"Single pilot."

"And where do these aliens usually live?"

"Beyond."

Well, Deuce could see why Hunter had left this little

baby with him. It certainly was helpful. He decided to try another tack.

"Why did you kill Dr. Clancy?"

"That information useless."

Oh-ho. That was tantamount to an admission of guilt. "Why not?"

"Will not aid progression."

"Of?"

"The project." Mr. Wong blinked.

"Project?"

"Darkside City."

Deuce pondered a moment. He wasn't sure he liked the new and improved Mr. Wong. Deuce was good at games, all kinds of games. Keno and poker and mind games. But he didn't exactly relish the idea of playing twenty questions with Mr. Wong every time he wanted to know something.

"Do you have Hunter's diary inside you?" Deuce asked.

"No, Deuce McNamara."

"Is it aboard *Gambler's Star*?"

"Unknown, sir."

Suddenly the room filled with static.

"Mr. Wong, Mr. McNamara, Pines here. Mrs. McNamara is on the line. Detective O'Connor is at the McNamara home with a search warrant. He wishes to search the premises."

Deuce frowned down at his badge. The call should have come into him personally. He tapped it. Nothing happened. It had been deactivated.

"Hold on a sec, Pines," Deuce said.

"Yes, sir."

Deuce waited for the disconnect sound before he turned to the robot. "These filters that have been taken off. Do they include Mr. Wong's personality?"

"Correct, Deuce McNamara," said the flat voice.

"Can you reinstall them on a temporary basis?"

"Yes, stored in memory. Upload possible at any time."

"Okay," Deuce said. "Do it. Be as Mr. Wong as you can be, then get on the horn with me."

The robot blanked. Left, right, left right.

Mr. Wong smiled.

"Thank you, sir," he said. "It's good to be back."

"Hoo, boy," Deuce muttered. "Listen, O'Connor's on my porch with a search warrant. I, uh—"

"Jackson's body is in the garage," Mr. Wong said.

Deuce was a little startled. He didn't know Mr. Wong knew about it. "Yeah. I know I should have moved it. I just didn't know where, and I figured the heat was off."

"If the search warrant is legitimate, there's not much you can do on such short notice."

Deuce said, "Why doesn't my comm badge work?"

Mr. Wong said, "The installation of Terminal A caused a mesh-field interference. Since Terminal A has been temporarily pushed down, it should work now."

"Okay." Deuce commed his badge. "Sparkle?" he queried.

"Yes." Her voice was calm.

"Is it a legit warrant?"

"Yes."

He thought for a moment. "Put O'Connor on."

There was a pause, then, "O'Connor here."

"What are you doing, harassing my pregnant wife?"

"Mr. McNama—"

"Do you realize she's having a risky pregnancy? If she should get overly stressed, she might lose our babies."

"God forbid," O'Connor said angrily. "Mrs. McNamara, shall we come back another time?"

"That might be better, yes," Sparkle said.

Deuce could hear the frustration in O'Connor's voice when next he spoke. "All right, Mr. McNamara, we'll return at a more . . . convenient time."

"Thank you," Deuce said politely. "My opinion of you grows daily, Detective."

"As does mine, of you," O'Connor said dryly.

Communication was severed. Then Pines commed again.

"If I may have a few moments of Mr. Wong's time before you leave?" he requested. "I need to go over some billings for work on the ship."

"I'm on my way," Wong said, disconnecting. He glanced at Deuce. "If I may?"

Deuce shrugged. "Can you keep up your Wong act?"

"Yes, sir, indeed. The filters have been reloaded. They will be removed at your express request, and only then."

"Or Bea's."

"Yes, sir."

"Does she know about this?"

Mr. Wong shook his head. "No. And I have no instructions to so inform her."

"Only me."

There was a hesitation, just a blip, but enough of one for Deuce to notice.

"Yes, sir," came the reply.

"Do you have Hunter's personal log?" Deuce asked.

Mr. Wong shook his head. "I don't know where it is," he said. Deuce had no idea if he should believe him.

The robot gestured to the door. "I should meet with Mr. Pines. Shall we?"

"You go ahead," Deuce said. "I need a few minutes. All this has been such a shock."

"I should imagine." Mr. Wong smiled at him. "Thank you for bringing me back. I had assumed I would cease to exist."

Deuce shrugged. "My pleasure."

Mr. Wong pressed the door, stepped across the threshold, and pressed it shut.

Deuce made a face. He sure was glad he wasn't a robot.

For the next ten minutes or so, he reexamined every square inch of Hunter's safe, opening it, feeling places he'd felt a hundred times before. He had no idea how Wong had caused the holo field to beam. There was no trigger pad that he could detect.

He spent another few minutes examining the cabin. There were no surprises, at least none for him.

Maybe there was something in the corridor walls, or on the deck. He'd checked everywhere a million times, but you never knew . . .

He pressed open the door.

A hairy, hulking figure like something from a nightmare rushed him, pushing him back into the cabin. The door shut. The figure rushed at him.

"Hey!" Deuce cried, grabbing his blaster.

"Oh, my God." The figure sank to its knees and threw its arms around Deuce's knees. It was a man, a dirty, filthy man with a beard and ratty, long hair. But just a man nonetheless.

Deuce's badge vibrated. He tapped it. "Yeah."

"My business is concluded," said Mr. Wong. "Shall we meet at the docking bay?"

"Give me a couple more seconds," Deuce said, staring down at the man. "I gotta, ah, use the can."

"Yes, sir."

Deuce turned off his badge. He showed the man the business end of his blaster.

"Who the hell are you?" he demanded.

The man swallowed. "I'm Bernardo Chang."

FIFTEEN

Deuce sat on the floor beside Bernardo Chang. The man was nothing but skin and bones. His clothes were rags. He stank. Chang's hands shook, and when he tried to speak again, he burst into tears.

"I've been living aboard the *Star* ever since the day of the explosion," he said, finally pulling himself together. "They've been looking for me everywhere."

As if to underscore his words, he glanced over his shoulder, then scrabbled around and sat closer, facing the same way as Deuce. His stench was overpowering.

Deuce said, "How come nobody's found you? I tried looking for you that same day, and the computer said you weren't on board."

"As soon as Dr. Clancy and I realized what was going on during the autopsy, I reprogrammed our finder stats," Chang said. "The *Star*'s computer system couldn't find me because it was looking for the incorrect set of coordinates. The same would have happened with her, if she'd lived."

Deuce nodded. A simple enough thing to do. And clever.

"Okay. I'll go along with that for now. Talk to me, Chang," Deuce said. "Fast. What did you and Clancy realize?"

Chang nodded. "Okay, okay. Listen." He grabbed Deuce's sleeve, leaving a grimy handprint. "There was this box. We found it inside Jackson's chest when we did his autopsy."

"It was not a pacemaker?" Deuce asked, even though

that was an absurd question. They did not use pacemakers in this day and age. If your heart was gimpy, they grew you a new one.

"No. It was a separate and distinct object. Maybe a safe, some kind of contraband. We didn't know."

Maybe a data terminal. Deuce said nothing, just waited. He had learned through the years that the one who could wait the longest tended to find out what he wanted to know.

"I think it was that robot, Mr. Wong, who took it while she was comming you. I think Mr. Wong has it." Chang clutched at Deuce's sleeve again. "Has he told you about it? Shown it to you?"

Deuce shook his head, lying because he saw no benefit to telling this man the truth. He would come clean when and if it made sense to.

"What about you? You could have taken it."

"I panicked," he admitted. "I ran."

"Because she was going to give me the box?"

Chang said, "The box was strange, but that's not why she commed you. His structures were not quite right."

"Mr. Wong's?" Deuce asked, confused.

"Jackson's." Chang looked at him as if he were an idiot. "His biology."

"You mean, he was a robot?"

"No. And not a man, exactly."

"Cyborg," Deuce tried. "An android."

"No. And not a clone." Chang ran his hands through his hair. He looked half-crazy. And very desperate. "Mr. Jackson's physical body chemistry had somehow been altered. He was not completely human."

Whoa. Deuce was afraid to say the word. "Uh, no?"

Chang pursed his lips. "That's what Dr. Clancy commed you about. I begged her not to. As soon as she tapped her badge to call you down, I figured her for dead."

"How so?"

Chang shook his head. "That's the kind of secret no one wants told by some innocent bystander. That's the kind of thing that gets revealed in its own time and its own place." He added, "I think Castle's behind it all."

"Some other guys were trying to whack us that day,"

Deuce told him. "While I was trying to save Stella. I doubt Signor Castle would whack someone who was trying to save his little girl." Then Deuce remembered that Hunter had sworn he hadn't realized she was aboard.

"Jackson was different, not quite human," Chang repeated, as if he couldn't believe that Deuce hadn't grasped what he was saying. "We thought maybe the box did it to him. Someone killed Dr. Clancy when she found out the truth, and took the terminal out of Jackson's chest cavity. It's got to contain the information about what the hell is going on."

"So whoever killed Jackson killed her, too?"

"I would think. Whoever has it is the murderer, I would guess." Chang looked at him. "Do you have it?"

"No."

Chang sagged. "Then sooner or later, I'm dead, too."

Deuce raised his eyebrows. "Why do you come to me now, if you're in fear of your life? If I had it, I would have to kill you, too."

Chang moved his shoulders. "I had to trust someone. Everybody's always spoken well of you, Mr. McNamara. They said you are different."

"But why haven't you gotten in contact with me before?"

Chang held out his hands. "The *Star* has been both my refuge and my prison. I didn't dare leave. But I never knew when you were aboard. I live down in the hold, and the comm system wasn't fully operational down there until a couple of days ago. I heard Wong request permission to dock, then I heard Pines comm you for that call from O'Connor."

"Do you know what O'Connor's looking for?" Deuce asked, as pieces began falling into new and different places. He was also trying to decide how many of them Chang was right about. "Do you think it's this box?"

He shook his head. "I doubt he knows about it. No one knows about it."

Deuce's badge vibrated. Mr. Chang anxiously gestured for him to leave.

"I know Mr. Wong is waiting for you." He grabbed

Deuce again. Deuce was going to have to invent some reason why he was so dirty all of a sudden. "Don't trust him, Mr. McNamara. Trust only yourself."

Deuce nodded slowly. Then he patted the man's hand.

"I'll get you out of here somehow," he said.

Chang looked down at the floor. "Not now."

"Not now," Deuce echoed, and left the room.

Mr. Wong waited politely in the cargo bay. He was chatting with Pines. Below them, the gull-wing doors of the aichy were open and two guys in orange-and-black Castle one-pieces were giving it a nice, thorough cleaning.

"Mr. Pines thoughtfully had your car detailed while we were here," Mr. Wong told Deuce.

"Nice of you," Deuce said, giving Pines's hand a friendly shake, even though the guy bugged him. He reminded him for some reason of Back-Line Tony, the Borgioli who had always wanted to see him whacked. He hoped Pines was not equally eager, such that he had planted a bomb in Deuce's car, anything like that.

The men finished up, stuffing rags in their back pockets and sauntering away from the sparkling car. Deuce gave them a wave, and said to Mr. Wong, "We'll stripe 'em a nice tip."

"I wouldn't hear of it," Pines protested.

Deuce looked at him hard. Deuce hoped his reputation for generously rewarding his help preceded him. Apparently it did, as Pines stammered, "I, that is, I mean, I'll tip them myself."

"*Va bene,*" Deuce said. He clapped the *scemo* on the shoulder.

He and Mr. Wong got in. Mr. Wong said quietly, "I've done a scan, sir. I could detect the presence of no explosives."

"Are you Wong now or Terminal A?"

"Wong. As Mr. Castle's butler, one of my functions was to search for explosives."

"I see." And to commit murder at his direction?

"Also, to see that Mr. Castle's wardrobe was in perfect

order." He pointed to Deuce's sleeve. "You appear to have leaned against something oily."

"Damn," Deuce said. "Can't take me anywhere."

He put the aichy on autopilot and leaned back. Mr. Wong also settled in. They lifted from the deck, and Pines gave them a wave.

"Unfortunately, Mr. Wong, I need to talk to Terminal A some more. Please store yourself."

Wong looked sad. "Yes, sir."

The operation took less than ten seconds. Terminal A stared blankly at Deuce as they exited via the iris airlock and started their descent. Deuce decided it was a dishonor to call it Mr. Wong.

"Terminal A, are you really a remote terminal for a data system that Hunter found in a crashed alien ship?" Deuce asked.

"Yes."

"Was Jackson one of the crewmen?"

Terminal A stared at him. "Beings cannot travel here."

"Was Jackson an alien?"

"No data available."

"What is your mission?"

Before Terminal A could answer, Deuce's badge vibrated.

"Yeah?"

"It's Joey," said his brother. "Deuce, I just got word. Fifteen representatives of the Department of Fairness are scheduled to arrive in three hours."

"What?" Deuce would have fallen out of his seat if he hadn't been strapped in.

"Can you believe it? The Charter Board didn't inform us. They didn't inform anybody. They just freakin' did it!"

"They can't do that. They can't just waltz in here without following procedures. There are votes and like that—"

"No kidding," Joey said. "The Families are talking about putting together a greeting party." Joey added meaningfully, "Like, with blasters."

"This is outrageous." Deuce was livid. He was so angry

he could barely speak. "Mr. Wong," he began, then realized Terminal A was still on-line.

"And that gravoid detective, do you think he might have mentioned it while he was trying to break into our home and carry out his illegal search?" Joey went on. "Do you think he was trying to stick his nose in our business just in case he could find something to shut you down before those *cretini* got here?"

"And to think that I offered him a job," Deuce said bitterly. "I should have known better. Once a cop, always a cop."

"What do you want I should do?"

Deuce thought for a moment. Then he said, "I'm going straight to Moonbase Vegas, Joey. Take care of Sparkle. Tell Bea to get dressed and have someone very big get her over to Moonbase Vegas." They still hadn't talked about what to do with her. Which had been the trigger for the activation of Terminal A.

"Angelo came by a little while ago," Joey said. "To visit her."

"What, in the middle of the night?" Deuce said. "Whatever. Fine. Wake him up and—"

"Uh, he ain't sleeping. Bea ain't either."

Deuce couldn't help his grin. "Okay, there's the bridegroom, okay with you, Joey?"

"*Sì*. I'll alert them both."

"Okay. Put Sparkle on."

"She's resting. Asleep," Joey said.

"Okay. Leave her alone. I'll check in in a while."

He commed off. His badge immediately vibrated again. Everyone was calling him: his informants, his runners, his *capos* and lieutenants, the other Godfathers. The Casino Liaisons. Everyone was in a blind panic. Deuce remembered when news of Hunter Castle's imminent arrival had made them go crazy, just like this.

Deuce played everyone like an orchestra. He agreed to meet the Godfathers and the Van Aadams C.E.O. as soon as he touched down, comming back his own people to make sure Bea knew about the sit-down.

He took a breather and turned to Terminal A.

"Okay, so you're going to help me with great new insights or something. I got DOFs on my tail. What should I do?"

"Analysis of the situation proceeds," the Terminal announced. "The Families have been growing in strength and power. Revenue is pouring into the Moon economy from Earth. When the Conglomerated Nations approved the creation of Moonbase Vegas, it was assumed that the situation would be reversed. The Moon was viewed as a colony, not a separate governmental body."

Deuce listened hard. "Keep going."

"Earthside is threatened by the power of the Moon. The best thing that could have happened, in the opinion of anti-Moon interests, is the blowing up of *Gambler's Star*. It provides a convenient excuse for intervention."

Deuce's badge vibrated again.

"Mio fratello!" Joey shouted. "They've frozen our accounts!"

"What?" Deuce shouted.

"We can't touch our own money!"

Deuce stared at Terminal A. It nodded. "A predictable step. Assumption: All the Families are equally affected."

"Check with the others," Deuce said, but his badge was vibrating so much it was hot to the touch.

Joey said, "No need to check. My lines are burning up here. Everyone's going berserk. Those DOFers are dead."

"No," Deuce said.

"Not yet, I mean, but they will be," Joey said. "You know it, I know it."

"They're just representatives. We take them out, *we* are dead," Deuce protested.

"We can't stop it, Arturino. No one can."

Deuce looked at Terminal A.

"It's what they want, isn't it. Earthside. For us to lynch their scapegoats, so they can land on us with both feet."

"Assumption is correct," Terminal A said.

"War," Deuce whispered.

"Assumption is correct."

"Joey," Deuce said, "try to keep everyone together. Don't let Bea out of the house. Don't let nobody out of the house. Mount maximum security. Implement the Turf War scenario.''

"Turf war? Deuce, this ain't no turf war.''

"No,'' Deuce said, "this is worse.'' He wiped his face. "God, what the hell should I do?''

"Request for input?'' Terminal A queried politely.

"Yeah.'' Deuce swiveled in his chair and leaned forward. "Yeah, Mr. Great Machine, it is.''

"Interface provides data for alien technology. Weaponry.''

Deuce nodded slowly. Weapons. Such as had been fired at him aboard the *Star*. "Are you among us, you aliens?'' he asked.

"Terminal A is a data terminal. Terminal A is not a being,'' Mr. Wong replied.

"What about Mr. Jackson?''

"Experiment,'' Terminal A replied. "Failure.''

Deuce took that in. His mind was racing in a million different directions, but that one, as startling as it was, was not the most important one at the moment. "These weapons. We'll have to manufacture them.''

"Equipment is available,'' the Terminal assured him. "Production facilities available.''

"Where?'' Deuce asked, but he didn't need Terminal A for the answer:

"*Gambler's Star*.''

SIXTEEN

For the sit-down over on Moonbase Vegas, Deuce selected the Stellaluna, a known joint midway between the Scarlattis' Inferno and the Caputos' Lucky Star casinos. Now, as they headed for the roof, Deuce saw that the streets were crammed with people. He couldn't tell if they were rioting or having your standard good time on vacation. Most of the Families had all kinds of reserve credit sources that it would take a while for Earthside to discover and, therefore, freeze, so it might just be that your average Joe and your average Giuseppe as well did not yet know what *schiamazzo* the Earth had pulled.

The longer it took for them to find out, the better.

Thanks to his informant at the Stellaluna, Deuce was kept apprised of the arrivals of the other Dons. Deuce figured Alitji Van Aadams for a temporary player—he was sorry for her, but business was business and facts were facts, which were that she was new, weak, and friendless, and warriors needed generals—and Sying II would do whatever the Caputos wanted him to. Sandy and Vito Scarlatti had to be given respect, them and the new four added to their Select of Six. Those four were Nico the Greek (who was not a Greek), Georgie, Frankie, and Little Gino, so named because there were a ton of Ginos in the Scarlatti Family, not to mention the trash Deuce had once had to deal with.

Nico he knew well, from many quiet and very profitable deals, and he liked him immensely. Frankie was a hothead, not much of a team player. Georgie had been a very minor *capo*, didn't even have his own crew, so he was a bit of a surprise in the new mix. And Little Gino was an angelic-looking young man who would sooner slit open your belly than say "*Buon giorno*" to you like a civilized human being.

The aichy landed on top of the Stellaluna. Deuce said to Terminal A, "Give me Mr. Wong."

After a few seconds of rebooting, the robot flashed him a faint smile, and said, "Thank you, Mr. McNamara."

Deuce regarded him for an instant. "What's it like where you go when you are not being you?"

Mr. Wong shook his head. "Nothing. Absolutely nothing. Oblivion."

"I worry about that sometimes," Deuce muttered. "All this effort, these tears, we die, and then, *pffft.*" He shrugged. "My *mamma* would wash my mouth out with soap if she could hear me. God rest her soul in heaven with the angels, where I hope to go also," he added, crossing himself.

Mr. Wong did not cross himself. Deuce figured if the robot had a religion, most likely he would be Buddhist.

Deuce cracked his knuckle, trying to remind himself that chaos equaled disaster only for the faint of heart, and said to the aichy, "Okay. Open the door, hon." He gestured to Mr. Wong. "You go on ahead." Deuce wanted to code in a new security shield, naturally in private.

Mr. Wong complied. Deuce said to his car, "Okay, honey. Voice my new password. It's—"

"Mr. McNamara, are you aware that someone left a package on my back seat?" the car asked him.

Deuce's eyes widened. "What? Open my door!" Instinctively he slammed against the door, half-falling out as it slowly began to open.

"There is no evidence of explosives," the car went on.

Catching himself in mid-fall, Deuce hazarded a look-see over his shoulder.

Plain as day, a little metallic satchel sat gleaming against the leather. It looked a little bit like a kid's lunch box.

"Analyze contents, if possible," he said to the aichy.

"They appear to be data rods," the car informed him.

Deuce looked out the window. Mr. Wong was almost to the entrance of Stellaluna. In a few seconds, he would probably turn around to see if Deuce was coming.

"Hold on." Deuce reached through the open doorway, leaned forward, and fetched up the satchel. He swung back onto his seat and started trying to open it. It was shut with an old-fashioned codelock. After a few false starts, he easily spun the digits correctly and the satchel popped open.

Sure enough, there were three data rods, two of which looked to be rather old. And a mini.

"You're sure this thing isn't armed?" he asked the ai-chy.

"There is no indication," it replied.

"Nothing ventured," Deuce said, and picked up the mini. He gave it his thumbprint and iris, just in case it had been coded for him.

Instantly a shadowy face appeared in the small screen. It became three-dimensional, popping from the frame and twirling like a ghost. For the features had been deliberately smeared, and the skin was very pale, even by Moonsider standards.

"Hello, Deuce," said the distorted voice. "Let's just say my name is Connie Lockheart. Let's just say I'm on *Gambler's Star*."

Whoa. Deuce squinted, trying his damnedest to bring her features into focus.

"Before she died, Angelina Rille asked me to give these to you at the first opportunity. This is my first opportunity."

As Deuce had predicted, just then Mr. Wong glanced over at him. Deuce pressed the STOP function on the mini.

The holo head disappeared.

He dithered a moment about whether he should leave the satchel in the car or take it with him. Finally, he decided to keep it close by, even if he could pretty much guarantee that the car wouldn't give it up to a stranger. Deuce's security shields were always the best, but if someone blew up the car, the rods might go up, too.

If those were rioters he had seen, explosions might not be far behind.

He gave Mr. Wong a wave, picked up the satchel, and

carried it as if it contained nothing more important than a peanut butter sandwich.

Mr. Wong regarded the satchel and gave Deuce a curious expression, but Deuce ignored it. He gestured to the door, and said, "You get any bad vibes, such as bombs, that kind of thing?"

Mr. Wong shook his head. "My sensors detect no immediate danger."

"Okay." That was probably what he told the doc before he whacked her. Deuce opened the door and went in first. A lot of guys would hide behind a robot, but he was not one of those guys.

The Stellaluna looked like a Family hangout, with all your standard Italian motifs—candles in Chianti bottles, red-and-white-checked tablecloths, naked statues of nymphs and cupids. Lots of gold and curlicues, very bad art. Beatrice liked to eat here. Their tiramisu, she said, was to die for.

Deuce knew some people who had.

The owner, Donatello "Donny" Donati, hurried up to Deuce and held out his hands in a beseeching gesture.

"Padrino," he breathed. "God help us! What is happening?"

Deuce fished in his pocket and brought out a reserve credit strip. He wasn't sure if it would work, but he handed it to Donny, and said, "Put everything on this, and run it through now. Charge whatever you think is fair. Just do it quick."

"But, Godfather—"

Deuce smiled at him. "I ain't your Godfather."

Donny wiped his face. "Tonight, you are everyone's Godfather."

"Stripe it," Deuce said.

"They're in the room," Donny told him, dashing away.

Mr. Wong led the way through the empty restaurant toward the noisy back room where the Families held their private meetings. As Deuce passed various chairs, old ghosts popped into his mind. This place had seen a lot of action. Hunter had hated for Deuce to eat here once he'd officially joined the Castle organization. Deuce thought it was obvious that he needed to stay as connected to the Families as possible, and had continued his practice of coming down once, twice a month.

There was a string of goons standing in front of the meeting-room door, so severely enhanced they didn't look real; their muscles looked like overstretched balloons.

As one, they inclined their heads at Deuce and moved aside. Mr. Wong trailed behind him, although legally, he was Deuce's senior partner. Everybody had pretty much given up on that nicety, though, treating Deuce like the big shot and Mr. Wong like his *consigliere.*

The room was packed and hot. It smelled of cigarette smoke and spaghetti sauce. Deuce noted the players he had expected to see, and was shocked by the sight of the ones he had not expected: Detective O'Connor, who was standing off to one side, and none other than Yuet Chan, the deposed dragon lady.

She was dressed in the Chan colors of salmon and jade, and she wore a really snazzy pagoda-shaped headdress with bits of gold and fringes and all kinds of stuff. It set off her ebony hair and flashing, angry eyes to very good advantage. She really was one hot dame, and, seeing how thin she was from her incarceration, Deuce was even sorrier that she had gotten fingered for Wayne Van Aadams's death.

Deuce said to her, *"Buona sera,"* as if they had just met up yesterday.

"Good evening," she replied haughtily, then smiled at the detective and held out her hand as if to say, Be my guest.

"Deuce McNamara, I charge you in the murder of Mr. Wayne Van Aadams," O'Connor said. He was blushing furiously, and he looked very uncomfortable. "A murder for which this woman was blamed—"

"Tried, and found guilty," Deuce finished, then shook his head and came into the room. Someone pushed forward an empty chair and Deuce sat in it. "Please, is this the time for such nonsense?"

"I have been reinstated as Godmother of the Chan Family," Yuet declared. "My sentence has been overturned as a result of new evidence."

"Evidence," Deuce stated flatly.

"The deathbed confession of Wayne Van Aadams's great-aunt Constance, who said she watched you kill her nephew in their swimming pool. Said she gave you permission."

Deuce wanted to argue that permission from someone so senior in the Van Aadams Family pushed the death into the realm of a Sanctioned hit, but one look from Mr. Wong and he kept his mouth shut.

"Look," Deuce said, "I don't know about all that. But now is not the time."

He glanced over at Don Giancarlo Caputo and another of his nephews, Michael, apparently the current Heir. They looked angry enough to spit nails. And no wonder: Their figurehead, Sying Chan II, was nowhere to be seen. And never would be seen again, Deuce guessed. Unless someone went Topside and started digging through craters.

"Now is not the time," Deuce said again, more loudly. He stood. "This was excellent timing on your part, Madame Chan. I don't know how you pulled it off, but this was the moment for you to get back into business. But it is not the time for Vendetta, for hits, for anything but concentrating on our problem. And we have a big problem."

"It is an outrage that she is back," Don Giancarlo said, raising a shaking hand in Yuet Chan's direction. "An affront!"

"Don Giancarlo, you have nothing but my greatest respect," Deuce said, touching his heart. "But surely you must see that they are attempting to throw us into turmoil. To divide us and conquer us. Listen to me." His look took in the entire room. "All of you. We stand at the brink of war."

O'Connor blinked. "Mr. McNamara, it's not as serious as that. The Department of Fairness only wants to sit down with the major players and discuss ways to better govern—"

"I consider the freezing of our assets an act of war," Deuce said to him in a loud, angry voice. "Tell them that when you go back to them."

"Deuce, he's here as a Moonsider," Vito Scarlatti said to Deuce.

Deuce shook his head. "As a spy. He came to my house with a search warrant just hours ago."

O'Connor glanced at Yuet Chan. "I was told there was some incriminating evidence in your home that would prove her claim. A mini from Wayne Van Aadams's aunt to you congratulating you on your hit."

Deuce stared at him. Then he began to laugh. "You actually think I would keep such a thing around?"

O'Connor colored.

Then Yuet Chan dropped the bombshell: "Beatrice Castle di Borgioli told him that. She played it over the comm link for him and told him that if he came over while you were not there, she would give it to him."

Deuce was thunderstruck. He had no words for this act of betrayal. This lie, like an angry teenage girl, this stupidity was not worthy of Bea.

Just then, the door opened again and Joey hurried in. He looked disheveled and upset, and when he saw Deuce, he gestured for him to come to one side.

"Joey," Deuce said in a whisper, "tell me what's going on."

"Sparkle fell down the stairs. She's not saying nothing, but we think Bea did it. She went into labor."

"Oh, God." Deuce turned white. "Oh, my God."

"Shiflett got the medical team together. They wanted me to assure you they're doing all they can and for you not to comm them because they're too busy."

"Why do you suspect Beatrice?" Deuce asked, his mind outracing his heart, at least for the moment.

Joey sighed heavily. "I told Angelo in private that he was going to be her contingency bridegroom. He told her, thinking it would make her happy because she was so angry that you forbid her to leave the house to come to the sit-down. She went completely out of her mind."

"She thought I would divorce Sparkle," Deuce said slowly. Joey nodded.

"Excuse me, but earlier you were speaking of our crisis?" Don Giancarlo shouted. "Would you therefore discuss your private business at some other time?''

Deuce turned and faced the others. For a moment all he saw was a sea of blank faces. Then he began to fall forward, and realized he was about to black out.

''Mr. Wong,'' he murmured under his breath. The robot stepped forward smoothly and gripped Deuce's artificial arm. Deuce steadied himself, took a deep breath, and let it out.

''Madame Chan, I would like you to know that my wife has gone into premature labor with twins,'' he said. Yuet and Sparkle had had some kind of thing—what thing, how much of a thing, he didn't know—but the look of distress on Yuet's face told him that he had just bought himself some time.

He looked at O'Connor. ''O'Connor, surely you see this is not the time for turf wars and internal squabbles such as indicting me with false evidence on a murder charge. We are being invaded.''

''Again, I protest,'' O'Connor said. ''They simply want to talk.''

Deuce spread open his arms. ''Before today, it did not even occur to me that the Department of Fairness had the ability to freeze our assets, much less the right.''

The other Family heads nodded in agreement.

''It pains me to admit that I never prepared for such a thing, because I never dreamed they would do it.''

There were more nods.

''If they just want to 'talk,' as you say, tell them to unfreeze our assets. As soon as they do that, we'll talk. Eh?'' He looked to the others. Even Yuet—who had to be a DOF puppet, the first of many to come, he had to assume—nodded and folded her arms across her chest. After all, it was a most reasonable request.

''If they don't do it, we'll take it as an act of war,'' Deuce said. He pointed to the door. ''Go now, and tell them. We have to talk among ourselves.''

O'Connor rose. He looked like he wanted to say something. Maybe apologize. But Deuce was incredibly disappointed in the man. Such potential, yet so misguided.

That was a cop for you.

O'Connor left the room.

Immediately Alitji Van Aadams got to her feet. She was beautifully dark-skinned, the way the Smiths were, and she wore the burgundy and navy blue tailored suit of the Van Aadams Family with flair.

She said, "I don't understand you, Mr. McNamara. I think they have a right to discuss the situation with us."

There was a collective gasp. Roger Smith looked at Deuce and smiled faintly at Alitji's moronic pronouncement. Deuce held up three fingers, betting Roger that she had three hours to live. Roger made a covert gesture of pulling a trigger: If no one else took her out, the Smiths would.

"We're not some branch office of their department," Deuce said to her, in case anyone else shared her opinion but was too afraid to state it.

"But they already have control over us through the Charter Board," Alitji went on, truly perplexed. "We are subject to their rulings and—"

"No and no!" Don Giancarlo shouted. "We let them shove that down our throat, and it was a horrible mistake. We should never have allowed that to happen!" He pounded the side of his wheelchair. "In fact, I say that not only do we demand they unfreeze our assets, but that they destroy the Charter Board. Or it is war, as Don McNamara says!"

There was a collective gasp. Deuce raised his hands to quiet everyone.

"Don Giancarlo, with my respect, I say that now is not the time to make such a demand," Deuce protested.

"And when is the time? When they land here with their soldiers? When they break down our doors and drag our children away? *O maledetta*, where is my heart medicine? Rudy always had my medicine ready for me." He smacked Michael. "You are trying to kill me!"

"Don Giancarlo," Michael said, "please, listen to Don McNamara. We must be very careful."

"Careful? Were we careful when we came to the Moon, running for our lives from those who would wipe us out if we remained on the Earth? And now, they hunt us down here, eager to take what we have built, as they did down there? And where does it end? When we are all dead?"

Deuce could see that the Don's words had stirred the others, including Yuet.

"What the hell do you think we should do, declare war?" Joey burst out.

"Yes, exactly!" Don Giancarlo shouted back at him. "Now! This minute!" He gestured to the others. "Who knows? When we each leave here, we may be charged falsely of some *cretino* offense against their laws. We may never meet again under one roof. Thanks to certain traitors." He glared at Yuet Chan.

"Now, one moment, Don Giancarlo," Yuet said angrily.

"Oh, you!" Don Giancarlo said dismissively. "You, with your antidrug policies. Did you really think you would survive in the world of men with such a belief?"

"Hunter Castle was also antidrug," she said regally.

"And he also is dead," Don Giancarlo flung at her.

She paled. Deuce was surprised. Surely this angle had likewise occurred to her, that Hunter had been taken out because of his opposition to the lucrative drug trade. Not that it was the correct angle, but when you stood behind the eight ball, you had to look at all the possible shots there were.

Abraham Smith had been silent until now, but he looked at Deuce, and said, "If it comes to an armed confrontation, we have weapons we have not unveiled to the general assembly that may assist with the odds." His brother and co-Godfather, Roger, nodded slowly.

Deuce didn't know if he should show his hand as well. He ticked a glance toward Mr. Wong, who gave his head an imperceptible shake. Not now. Wise counsel.

"We also have some . . . private technology," Vito Scarlatti allowed, to the obvious unease of the rest of the Select of Six.

"I appreciate you coming forward," Deuce said sincerely. "My brothers and sisters in commerce, we need to formulate a plan. We need to decide where our line is that they cannot cross. We need to know what our demands are, and we need to figure out how to live until tomorrow. It would be a simple thing to bomb this place and take us all out."

"We have Heirs," Abraham said placidly.

"All of us do," Yuet Chan huffed.

"The Godmother of the Borgiolis is not here," Don Giancarlo said suddenly, as if he had just noticed Beatrice's absence.

"That's true," Deuce said. "I cannot speak for her. But this is a war council. We cannot wait to carry decisions to others. We must act. It may be our only chance to get together."

Joey touched his badge. He said, "Earphone," listened, looked grave. He gestured for Deuce to come to him.

"Something's wrong," he murmured. "They want you to come home."

Yuet stood up. "Is it Sparkle?" she demanded.

Deuce looked at her. He said nothing, but she must have read his answer in his eyes.

Her own eyes glittered. "You bastard, for giving her twins," she hissed. "You go to her *now*." She glanced at Joey. "Name him your spokesman. We'll deal with him."

Mr. Wong murmured, "Mr. McNamara, don't leave here alone. It would be suicide."

"Grab some of Donny's muscle," Joey said. "Go on. I'll be okay by myself."

Deuce hesitated. He knew it was a betrayal of everyone who trusted him to leave. Including Sparkle. But everything within him screamed for him to go.

Then suddenly the room exploded. Deuce was hurled to the ground. Joey soared into the air, then fell heavily on top of him.

Deuce shouted, "Joey!" His brother did not respond. He lay over Deuce's shoulders and head, pinning him to the floor. Deuce heard screams. He felt things falling on his brother, on his own feet and arms.

First he smelled smoke, and then he felt the flames.

Mr. Wong said into his ear, "Hold on to my hand."

Deuce flexed his fingers, or thought he did.

"Your artificial arm has come off," Mr. Wong announced. "I'll have to move your brother in order to find your shoulder."

"Be careful!" Deuce shouted. "Be careful with him."

There was a pause. Then Mr. Wong said, "Sir, your brother is dead."

SEVENTEEN

Surrounded by flames, Mr. Wong carried Deuce toward the aichy. The explosion must have occurred inside the building, because amazingly enough, portions of the roof were still intact. Some other vehicles had slid into cantilevered sections which had buckled with the force of the detonation, but miraculously, Deuce's aichy had not been touched.

"Open, please," Mr. Wong said to the car.

The gull-wing doors opened as the aichy replied, "The voice of Mr. Wong is recognized."

Mr. Wong gently placed Deuce onto the backseat, followed by his mechanical arm. Belatedly, Deuce realized he didn't have the satchel, and was about to get up to retrieve it when Mr. Wong handed it to him.

Deuce clasped it as if it were a living creature. Tears spilled down his face.

"Joey," he whispered.

"My sympathies," the robot said sorrowfully.

Mr. Wong climbed into the front seat and gave the aichy the coordinates for *Gambler's Star*.

"No. Darkside City. My home," Deuce said.

"It's not safe," Mr. Wong protested. "We have to assume there will be other attacks."

"I have to go home. To my wife."

"I must override—"

Deuce lurched upright and pressed his blaster against the

base of Mr. Wong's skull. "Do it, or Terminal A is history, and so are you."

Mr. Wong sat very still. For a moment Deuce thought he was going to ignore Deuce's threats and make for the *Star* anyway.

After a moment, Mr. Wong changed the aichy's instructions.

"Very good," Deuce said.

"This is suicide," Mr. Wong replied.

Deuce couldn't agree more.

But he couldn't do anything else.

As the vessel lifted off, Deuce commed his apartment and demanded to speak to Shiflett or better yet, one of Sparkle's doctors. A harried voice came on and spouted some nonsense about bleeding and placental something and all Deuce could think of was this didn't make sense, none of it; it wasn't the kind of thing you worried about in this day and age.

"I'm sorry, sir, I really need to get back," the doctor said.

Then Angelo came on, very apologetic, and told him that they'd locked Beatrice in one of the spare bedrooms and she had completely trashed the place.

"Guess she don't love me," Angelo said sadly.

"Guess that's the least of her problems," Deuce said through clenched teeth.

"*Davvero, davvero*, Godfather," Angelo said. "I'm to blame, Deuce. She found something out. She said something about Stella and you and something Lockheart—ain't you still looking for some broad?—and she went crazy. Then she attacked Sparkle."

Deuce's heart skipped a beat. "She said something about Connie Lockheart?"

"Yeah, but I couldn't figure it out. Something about stealing. Something about your father. Wait. Hold on."

Angelo said something to someone, then came back on. "Deuce? Beatrice, she, she's found a blaster or something. I got to go."

"I'll be there soon," Deuce assured him.

As soon as they disconnected, he opened the satchel and looked at the data rods. Wondered if they would work or if, like the ship's log, they would prove to be useless off the *Star*.

He picked one at random and put it on TEXT ONLY. Began to read:

This evening, I was a witness to a horror I will carry to my grave.

Two hours ago, a man came to visit my father. I was sitting in my cabin across the hall, reading an article about buying on margin. It was very dull; I was reading it only to please my father.

My father and the man began chatting. Dad poured each of them a couple of fingers of bourbon. I kept reading, although upon occasion I would glance through the open doorway to see if I could recognize who the man was. We have visitors of note aboard the Star *all the time, but I'm always eager to meet someone famous. As my father has explained to me, someday I will be the one drinking the bourbon with them.*

He didn't appear to be anyone famous, so I focused on my article. My father always quizzes me at dinner to be sure I've done my reading, and it's bad news when I disappoint him.

But I digress, primarily because I do not want to move forward. If I write it down, it will be with me forever. I will be more than a witness. I will be an archivist.

The man laughed and held out his hand. My father stared at him, his lips parting. Daddy turned white. For one terrifying moment, I thought he was having a heart attack.

I could see everything from an angle, such that when my father pressed open the side drawer in his desk, I saw it but the laughing man could not.

Daddy pulled out a blaster.

The laughing man did not notice.

My father rose.

Advanced.

He put the blaster into the man's mouth.

The man started choking. He dropped his bourbon onto

the carpet and clutched at the blaster. Dad held it in place, grabbing the man by the back of the neck. The man began to cry, tears streaming down his face, making a moaning sound that both revolted and paralyzed me. I sat speechless, watching.

The man started retching. His body was doubling up, but the blaster was in his way. My father held his head so that he couldn't pull away. And then he said something I can make no sense of:

"Don't you mention that name again. If you do, I will kill you."

The man nodded. He let go of the blaster with both hands and raised them in defeat.

My father let go of the back of his head. The man jerked backward, falling on his elbows, gasping for breath.

As I write this, it seems to me that this scene went on for hours. The man, gasping. My father looming over him, the blaster slowly lowering to his side.

Then the man murmured, "All right. Then just give me something for my trouble and—"

And my father shot him. He pressed the trigger on the blaster and a laser cut the man in two. It was so horrible that I couldn't convince myself that it was really happening. That it was real. The blood, the organs, the bone—it was too absurd to be real.

The man had been sliced into two halves, and they both flopped wetly on the carpet, as if he were still alive.

There was blood everywhere. My father was drenched with blood.

He crossed to the desk, put the blaster into the same drawer, and commed someone.

"Mr. Wong," he said, "will you come in here?"

At that moment, I realized that even if my father hadn't noticed me, his robot butler was more likely to. I darted into the dark recesses of my cabin and pressed both my hands over my mouth. I began to hyperventilate. Over and over I saw the image of the man being sliced in two, playing behind my eyes, before my eyes.

At some point my knees buckled, and I slid to the deck, but I still had the wherewithal to keep silent. Castle men have spines of iron; that's what my grandpappy always said.

Mr. Wong walked down the hall. I wished I had shut my door. From my position, I saw him pass, and then I saw nothing but the empty hall. That unnerved me most of all: The passageway seemed unbelievably normal. It was as if everything should be different, because my father had murdered a man in cold blood.

And then I heard him speaking to my father, and Daddy answering. And then, distinctly, two words: "Connie Lockheart."

I don't know who she is. I have no idea what's going on.

But I will find out.

Deuce looked up at the robot.

"Tell me why Hunter's father shot a man for talking about Connie Lockheart."

Mr. Wong said nothing for a moment. Then he said to Deuce, "Might I suggest some Atherton Gold, sir."

Deuce started to say something rude to Mr. Wong, then thought the better of it and nodded. There was a small bottle in the glove compartment, kept there for emergencies, and Deuce supposed this was one.

He watched the robot pour him a drink, waved a hand, said, "Join me, Mr. Wong. To the memory of my brother."

Liquor did not affect robots. They could be programmed to act drunk, but it was a sham.

Deuce threw back his alcohol and held out his glass. Mr. Wong deftly poured him another. "All right. Who is she?"

Mr. Wong calmly replied, "I'm not sure."

Deuce frowned, and said, "Not sure. Are you sure about why she was attempting to contact me?"

Mr. Wong said, "I'm unclear, sir. You have been successfully contacted. You have been given those data rods." Deuce noted that Mr. Wong didn't seem real thrilled about that fact.

"No. I mean the first time. By planting an explosive minipad in Bucky Barnum's locker."

"She did?" Mr. Wong said, surprised.

"She worked for Hunter. On our payroll. Didn't he know that?"

Mr. Wong hesitated. "I believe we are talking at cross purposes, sir. Don't you know about the Generational Protection League?"

Deuce blinked. "Excuse me? The what?"

"The GPL."

"Is it part of the League of Decency?" Hadn't Gina Rille acted like she knew who Connie Lockheart was?

"Not to my knowledge, sir." Mr. Wong gestured to the data rods and poured himself another drink. He sipped it with such appreciation that Deuce wondered if Hunter had given him some kind of special chip, like the ones the People for Ethical Treatment of Artificial Intelligence used to chain themselves to airlocks over.

"The Generational Protection League was created back during the Quantum Instability Wars," Mr. Wong began. "The leaders of the mob Families became convinced that the government was trying to wipe them out."

"Which they were." That was standard Family catechism.

"Be that as it may, sir. The Families devised a scheme whereby they could spread the risk of having their entire lineage wiped out. Certain of their children—in embryonic form—were secretly given to the GPL, who then assigned one of their members to carry the child. As a vessel. A surrogate."

The hair on the back of Deuce's neck began to rise. This was sounding a little too familiar.

"The identity of the member was held in strict secrecy, as was the identity of the child she carried, even from the Families themselves. The children were not reunited with their Families until their eighteenth birthdays. In this way, the Families hoped to preserve their bloodlines."

"This is crazy. I've never heard of this."

"It is highly classified, a secret known only to the upper echelons, and not practiced very often these days. If at all," Mr. Wong said. "Perhaps since you didn't become an actual Godfather in the traditional sense, you weren't informed."

"But it's a stupid plan. The opportunities for bribery—" Deuce began.

"And blackmail," Mr. Wong finished.

Deuce got it. A little. The man who had been sliced in half had been trying to put the squeeze on Papa Castle.

"But if Hunter had already been born, and he lived with his father, why the need for secrecy? The kid was there, his father had possession of him—" Deuce stopped. "There's some question about his parentage."

Mr. Wong inclined his head.

Deuce said, "But all Papa Castle had to do was run a DNA scan—" He fell silent. "Which he did."

He himself had asked for a scan. He had never gotten the results. The MLF infirmary and its database had been blown up along with the canteen.

"The scan showed that Hunter couldn't be his kid," Deuce finished.

"Perhaps," Mr. Wong said evasively.

"You sat in that office with O'Connor, Shiflett, and me. You heard me ask who Connie Lockheart was. Why the hell didn't you say something in private to me?"

"I assumed Mr. Castle had told you whatever he wanted you to know. I don't pry by nature."

"Oh, give me a break." Deuce narrowed his eyes at him. "There's something you're not telling me."

Mr. Wong inclined his head. "Connie Lockheart is not precisely a person, sir. It's a code name. All GPL surrogates are referred to as 'Connie Lockheart.' "

"Then why leave me a minipad from Connie Lockheart? Was it—"

He caught his breath. "I'm sorry," Gina had said, when they discovered that Sparkle was pregnant.

Sparkle was a Connie Lockheart.

Hunter's Connie Lockheart. It had said so right there in his Plan of Succession.

Deuce hung his head. The pain was intense.

So was the anger. And the knowledge that he had been right all along to mistrust her.

His brother, dead. His wife, a liar. He couldn't remember when he'd felt so alone.

But that didn't matter right now, did it. Nothing about him mattered.

"Take me home," he said dully.

As they proceeded, Deuce looked out the window, numb to the core of his being. They were in a narrow transport tunnel, and for perhaps the third time in his life, he felt a sense of claustrophobia, of being trapped. Like most Moonsiders, the idea of living in close quarters miles beneath the surface of an airless satellite bothered him not in the least. Vast space was what terrified him.

What used to terrify him.

His hand was shaking. He stared at his detached mechanical arm and wondered vaguely, giddily, if that hand would have shaken, too, had it been attached.

For a moment he was certain he was going to vomit, but the wave of nausea passed, and he fought to hold onto his self-control.

He got commed. Took it.

"Deuce, Angelo," his cousin said without formality. "The kids are born. They're okay. Boy and a girl. Sparkle's recovering. She'll be okay."

Deuce closed his eyes and slumped against the seat. *"Grazie,"* he said hoarsely. He was glad. Truly. But the moment was intensely bittersweet.

"Deuce," Angelo continued, coming onto visual on the screen located in the center of the backseat. "We know about Joey. I'm so sorry. May he rest with your sainted *mamma.*" He crossed himself.

Deuce put himself on visual and nodded mutely.

Angelo looked as if he had been in a prizefight. Deuce stared at him, and Angelo sighed.

"Bea did this. I tried, Deuce, but, well, she's dead."

Deuce leaned forward. *"What?"*

"The blaster. She killed herself."

Deuce began to shut down. It was too much for one day. Way too much.

Then Mr. Wong said, "Vessel on approach. Hailing us." Staring at Angelo's face, Deuce grunted.

"I've got to go," Angelo said.

"Go with God," Deuce said quietly.

They hung up.

Deuce looked out the front windshield and groaned. A large, boxy vehicle painted a drab olive gray faced his car. By the number and amount of exterior-mounted superpumpers and torpedo chutes pointed directly at him, it looked to be heavily armed.

"This is the Moonside Liberation Front," said a familiar voice. It was Deuce's old friend, Brigham the Mormon. "Stop or we will fire."

"In a shaft, and risk harming innocent bystanders?" Deuce snapped. "I doubt that."

"Deuce." Brigham's voice was soft. His features were sorrowful as he came onto visual. Short dark hair, hazel eyes, no marks distinguishing him as a lying, murdering bastard. "We're claiming responsibility for the Stellaluna bombing. All of you were scheduled for execution."

"So why give me a heads-up now?" Deuce demanded.

Brigham frowned. "This is a coup, Deuce. It's nothing personal. You and I are friends, and I thank God my Heavenly Father that you're alive."

"Yeah, well, I guess I just wasn't ready for paradise." Deuce held out his hands. "Just tell me why, Brig."

"We want to deal directly with the DOF. We want to overthrow the Family system once and for all."

"You're so stupid. They have Heirs and *they* have Heirs. And—"

"And right now, the DOF is nationalizing the casinos, Deuce. This very moment, as you were warned over and over they were going to do." He added, "They're rounding up the Family survivors."

"And me? Are you rounding me up or blowing me up?"

"Come with me, and we'll see."

Deuce frowned. "Brigham, have some pity for me. A few minutes ago, my wife nearly died bringing my ... twins into the world. Let me go to her. Let me hold them. You can follow me over there. We can sit. Talk."

Brigham shook his head. "I can't do that, Deuce. The time for talk is over."

"I was good to you in the old days. We were friends."

Brigham's face slackened. He looked old and tired. Like
the leader of a terrorist organization . . . not so much.

"We still are friends," Brigham said. "As I said, it's
nothing personal."

"Let me see my wife. The kids." It occurred to him that
Stella was essentially alone and defenseless, now that her
mother was dead and her father was who knows where.

Brigham bowed his head. "I can't. And if you raise your
weapons, I will have no recourse but to destroy you immediately."

Mr. Wong murmured, "I might suggest accessing Terminal A."

"Okay, do it," Deuce said.

"What?" Brigham demanded sharply.

"Nothing." Deuce wiped his forehead and glanced into
the rearview mirror. Mr. Wong's features were wiped clean.
Terminal A was on-line.

Out of Brigham's visual range, he prayed—he and
Brigham were beaming head shots to each other, just heads
and necks, and the front window of Brigham's vehicle was
armored over—he held his artificial arm in his good hand
and tapped Terminal A on the shoulder with it. As soon as
he had its attention, he let go of the arm and gestured with
his good hand to the Terminal in an old Family sign language system, having no idea if Terminal A would be able
to read it. So, just in case, Deuce made a pantomime of
pretending to shoot a blaster.

Terminal A turned its head around. It opened its mouth.

A small round object dropped toward Deuce. Deuce
palmed it quickly.

The Terminal looked into the rearview mirror at Deuce.
Began to blink. It took Deuce a moment to realize it was
an old binary code they used to use in the days of the First
Mob back Earthside. Morse code. He was amazed the Terminal knew it. He was more amazed that he remembered
it himself.

Set the timer, the Terminal told him. *One minute.*

Deuce glanced down at the round object. It had to be a grenade of some kind. Out of visual range, he turned it

over. Saw the miniature display and felt the button. He set it for one minute.

Push the pin.

Pushed the pin.

Reached for the window to lob it out.

Terminal A continued in code, *Do not throw it. Seen as hostile act.*

"Now you tell me," Deuce said, staring down at the grenade. In his car. In his grasp.

With forty-five seconds left.

"What am I supposed to do?"

"*Wait,*" the Terminal said.

"*Mi scusi*? Are you insane?"

It had been a trick. All a stupid trick to get him out of the way. Sparkle had Hunter's babies, and Deuce was in the way.

Thirty seconds.

He opened the window.

Brigham fired.

It was not a killshot, however, but a warning shot. It slammed the car to one side of the narrow tunnel, throwing Deuce against the inner door. As Deuce's vehicle's stabilizers fought to regain balance, Deuce sat back up, rubbing his head.

And realized he had dropped the object.

"Damn it!" he shouted, unbuckling his seat belt and leaning forward. He searched wildly. "Turn it off. Defuse it!"

"Cannot," said the Terminal.

He found the object and fumbled as he tried to hit the button. *Three*, said the display. *Two . . . one . . .*

Grimacing, Deuce braced himself.

Brigham said, "What are you . . . ?"

And then there was utter silence.

The object disappeared.

Deuce looked out the front window.

So had Brigham's vehicle. It had simply disappeared.

Deuce blinked.

He said, "What happened?"

"Dangerous object removed," Terminal A announced.

To the aichy, it said, "Proceed to Darkside City."

"Wait, wait, wait." Deuce sat forward. "Removed how? And to where?"

"Removed as a hazard. Object now exists in another space. Technology is available for weaponry," he added matter-of-factly.

"Another space such as . . . ?"

"Beyond the reaches of your technology."

"*Mamma mia.*"

The robot formerly known as Mr. Wong looked at him. "Weaponry available for warfare."

"Man, you're not exactly a peacenik, are you?"

"Define."

"Never mind." Deuce exhaled. "Where did the little bomb-thing go?"

"Consumed in transport."

Transport. Consumed. Deuce thought back a moment to Hunter's claim that he had blown up the *Star* working on a new kind of propulsion system.

"So, this is some kind of fueling device that sends things where no Italian has gone before? To, ah, a new space?"

"Correct. Return is impossible. Eventually, life ceases."

Deuce got the shivers. "We could transport the bad guys beyond the hope of rescue."

"Correct."

Dumbfounded, he sat back against the seat. Interstellar travel? Something even more advanced? What had Hunter given him?

"We currently laser out caverns to build Darkside City," Deuce said. "Could you simply transport the material like you did my friend Brigham?"

"Correct."

"Are there all kinds of things you can do to help me build Darkside City?"

"Correct."

Deuce whistled. He cracked his knuckle. "Okay," he said with a grim smile, looking into the space Brigham had formerly occupied. "First we'll declare war on the DOF and any of its allies here on the Moon. If they put up a fight, we'll send them to hell or what passes for it in outer space. Then we'll resume building the city.''

''Message sent,'' the Terminal said.

''After that, we'll—'' Deuce ticked his gaze to the robot. ''Come again?''

''War has been declared.''

Deuce went numb. ''What? I was just thinking out loud!''

''Message sent,'' Terminal A insisted. ''War has been declared.''

EIGHTEEN

For a moment, Deuce went wherever Mr. Wong went when the Terminal came on-line.

War has been declared.

Against Earth.

"Give me back Mr. Wong," Deuce said, panicked. *"Presto!"*

"Not available," said the Terminal. It stared at Deuce. "That data port has terminated."

"What?" Deuce stared at the smooth features, the blank face. "What are you saying? Give me Mr. Wong. Access him. Boot him up."

"No data available."

It smiled. Deuce swore it smiled.

Near tears, Deuce cradled his forehead in one hand. He took a shaky breath and let it out, whispered, "I'm sorry."

He composed himself as best he could. Which was not all that well. Then, to Terminal A, he said, "You're here to stay." It was not a question.

"Terminal A is completely functional." Was that a note of triumph in its voice?

"Take me home," Deuce said firmly.

"Rerouting to *Gambler's Star*."

"Darkside City is my home."

"Darkside City. As requested." Terminal A looked over at the aichy's readouts. "Currently en route," it informed him.

*   *   *

Deuce's building was in flames. Deuce stared at the crackling penthouse in horror as fire crews fought to put out the blaze.

This was what came of declaring war, he supposed.

"My wife?" he asked, grabbing the captain of the Castle Fire Department. Each Family had its own crew. In this, Castle Enterprises was no different.

"She's safe. So are your children. All three of them." The man jerked his thumb upward. "They're on their way to the ship."

Deuce figured he was including Stella Castle in the count, and that was fine with him. But there was a lot of territory to cover on the journey between Darkside City and *Gambler's Star*. Deuce prayed to God that whoever had escorted them knew about the strange device Terminal A had given him. More to the point, that they had a case of them in their vehicle.

"Anybody claimed responsibility for this?" Deuce asked.

The fire chief shook his head. "We think it was an accident, Mr. McNamara. It started in the garage."

"My cousin, Angelo. My people," Deuce said.

"Your cousin's around here somewhere," the man said. "Paramedics are with him. Smoke inhalation." He grimaced. "Mr. McNamara, I have to be honest with you. I don't think we can save your apartment with anything but a shield. I'd like to lower it over the building and pump out all the oxygen."

"It'll kill anybody's who's left in there," Deuce said.

"Mr. McNamara, trust me. There's no one left alive in there."

"My dog."

The man looked at Deuce as if he were completely insane.

Deuce nodded. "All right. Go." Then he turned to look for Angelo.

Beside him, Terminal A said, "Conflagration can be eliminated more efficiently."

"Let's just keep that between ourselves," Deuce snapped.

He located Angelo, who was lying on a gurney with an oxygen mask over his nose. When Angelo saw him, he gave him a thumbs-up.

Angelo took off his mask and gestured for him to come over. He said, "Deuce, where's your arm?"

Deuce shrugged. "It's in the car, I think. That don't matter right now. What happened?" He swallowed. "What about the dog?"

"Sparkle got her. She's okay."

Deuce was amazed at how relieved he was. Mutely, he nodded and waited for Angelo to continue.

"It started in the freezer," Angelo said. "I don't know how. When the alarms went off, I ran into the garage, and the whole freezer was on fire."

Angelo frowned apologetically. "We had been talking about getting rid of it after O'Connor showed up. We figured he'd gotten a lead on the body. That maybe Shiflett had told him."

Deuce was troubled. "I didn't know you knew about it, even."

"Not the best-kept secret," Angelo ventured. "I didn't know I wasn't supposed to know." He sighed. "So I'm wondering if some punk kid security guard who was also not supposed to know took it upon himself to help you out."

Deuce groaned. "So the body's all burned up?"

"I'd assume that, yes." Angelo looked carefully around. "Jeez, *Padrino*, is it true you declared war against Earth?"

Deuce closed his eyes. "Is that how it got broadcast?"

"Yeah." Angelo nodded. "That you personally declared war."

"Me, myself, and I."

"Sì."

"That's a novel form of suicide, eh, Angelino?" Deuce stood and held out his hand. "I guess we'd better head on up to the ship. *Davvero, davvero,* there ain't gonna be anyplace on the surface safe enough for us."

Angelo hesitated. Deuce looked at him questioningly.

"I'm not sure I want to declare war on Earth." His face was scarlet, maybe not from the fire.

Deuce flared with anger, then saw it from Angelo's point of view. Angelo's career-making contingency bride, Beatrice, was dead by her own hand, rather than marry him. The Borgiolis, of which he was currently a high-ranking *capo*, had not declared war on Earth. None of the Families had, although it might eventually come to that. What was a secret pledge of loyalty against all that?

"On the other hand," Angelo continued, "you are my Godfather, and I have promised to serve you."

Deuce was moved. He said, "Angelo, I release you from your oath of loyalty. This is more than you bargained for. Of that I am certain. It's sure the hell more than I bargained for."

Angelo reached for Deuce's hand. He took his oxygen mask from his face again and kissed the back of Deuce's hand.

"Mio Padrino," he said. *"Il Padrino della Luna."*

The Godfather of the Moon.

"Angelo, I'm touched. But think about this. Who else is going to stand with me?"

"The real Moonsiders," Angelo answered fervently.

And maybe he was right. For as Deuce, Angelo, and the Terminal dodged torpedoes and assorted laser blasts from many quarters on their way to *Gambler's Star*—Deuce assuming they came from anybody who didn't want to declare war—dozens of messages of support came in.

The Families, reeling in disarray from this second assault in less than a year, checked in piecemeal, more as isolated interest groups: Abraham Smith was in, while Roger Smith sided with Earth. The Borgiolis were, typically, arguing among themselves, the majority looking possibly to Angelo to serve as their new Godfather.

Deuce suspected that the intervention of his warm little bundle of alien technology was the only thing that kept them alive as they made it through the bombardment of hostile fire. And of hostile fire, there was plenty. One of the beefs the MLF had always had with the Families was the sheer amount of firepower they had stashed beneath the surface.

Then miraculously, they were in a docking bay of the *Star*, and Deuce laid aside all caution and raced down the corridors in search of Sparkle and the children.

"Where is she? Where's my wife?" he demanded of each panicked crew person he encountered.

Then finally, he put on the brakes at the threshold of Stateroom C. Sparkle was lying in a hastily made-up bed. Shiflett the physician's assistant was bustling around with a tray full of vials and assorted hypos, also a bowl of what looked to be minestrone.

"Mr. McNamara," he said, beaming as he saw Deuce. "Congratulations."

"Grazie," Deuce muttered, skirting around him. Shiflett bobbed his head and left the room.

The twins were bundled in pastel baby blankets at Sparkle's right side, and on the other side of the bed, Stella Castle di Borgioli slept in a pair of cream-colored baby pajamas. Sparkle had her arms around all of them.

Her eyes were open, but she stared at nothing. For one awful moment, he thought she was dead.

Then she said, in a voice he did not recognize, "Jump. Gate."

"Sparkle?" He did not touch her. He did not touch the sweet little *bambini*. He was apart from her. Alone.

"Jump. Gate. We." It was a gravelly voice, hoarse and slurring, as if unused to speaking.

Her eyes flickered, and she stirred. She looked up at him, looking pale and wan.

"Hi," she said.

He let her ESP thing go for the moment. There were more pressing things to discuss. "My God, Sparkle, the way they talked while I was over on Moonbase Vegas, I thought you were dying."

She shrugged. "Who dies in childbirth these days? I'm all right," she said. "It was harder than we expected, is all."

We. "So much for Lamaze." It was a feeble joke, and it fell flat.

"Moona's being checked over," she added.

"Good." He shifted his attention to the two pink newborns. They each wore a knit cap, both yellow, and tiny wisps of soft white-blond hair escaped from them.

"They're Hunter's," she said flatly.

There. It had been said. He was surprised it hurt as much as it did; he had certainly known about it long enough to prepare himself for it.

"You already knew that, didn't you," she went on. Was there any gentleness to her voice?

"I . . ." His voice caught. He had *suspected*. He had not *known*.

"Sparkle, can you not be kinder?" someone asked from the doorway.

Deuce turned. A beautiful, if slightly older, woman with a shock of ebony hair and flashing, dark eyes stood in a long purple robe. At the sight of her, Sparkle sat up a little.

The woman said, "Have some compassion, for God's sake. You're breaking his heart."

Sparkle flushed but remained silent.

The woman sighed and turned to Deuce. She held out her hand to shake with him. "Deuce, I'm your missing mystery woman. Gina's confederate."

She stepped toward him with a huge, brilliant smile and opened her arms. "And I quite possibly am your birth mother."

Deuce stared stupidly at whoever. Connie Lockheart. When she embraced him, he tensed and stood rigid. It was too much. All way too much.

She continued to hold him. "What happened to your arm?"

"It's in the car," he said slowly, stepping away from her, staring at her. Tears sprang to his eyes. He was terribly disoriented. A war and a mother, all in one day. And the wrenching loss of his own children, or what he had thought were his children.

Muzzily, he heard Sparkle say, "I think he's going to faint."

Connie Lockheart retorted, angrily, "Can you blame him?"

Then someone put a glass of Atherton Gold into his fist

and pushed it toward his mouth. He drank greedily, fighting to stay conscious.

"Don't you have any sense of what you've done to him?" Connie Lockheart said to Sparkle. "What were you thinking?"

Sparkle replied, "I sent in my resignation."

"It was never received."

Sparkle's pained expression was directed at both of them. "Then Hunter approached me after the explosion. He said he knew I was GPL, and he also suspected I was designated for him. We had met five years ago by accident. I gave him a stock tip at a party. There were some exploratory discussions back on Earth.

"He was convincing about being sure. All I knew was that I had been told to set up my life on the Moon. He told me to search my feelings . . . I have these visions—"

Her voice trailed off. In an agony, Deuce stared down at the bundles on the bed. Not his. Never his.

"Deuce, then I met you. I wanted to have a normal life with you. I didn't want to be a GPL surrogate. I resigned," she said firmly to Connie Lockheart.

"But then Hunter came to me a few months before the explosion. He told me that if I did this, he would give Deuce whatever he wanted. Deuce would be the king of this satellite. We could raise the children as our own, and he would never claim them, because he had Stella. He didn't want Beatrice to raise them, because these twins came from a different genetic mother. So I agreed."

Deuce looked at her, and she at him. He was dying.

"Then the explosion occurred. Everything had to happen fast. He wanted to leave. I don't know why. He promised to honor our original agreement."

"You wanted me to think I was their father, so you came onto me. You seduced me so you could lie to me for the rest of my life," he said bitterly.

She reddened. "We all lie all the time. It's part of the game."

"Who is their genetic mother?" Connie Lockheart asked.

Sparkle shook her head. "He said it was someone he had loved and lost."

There was a long silence. "Who are my genetic parents?" Deuce managed.

Connie shook her head. "It was all very hush-hush. I'm sorry. I always thought it might have been Maria Caldera and a lover; maybe they had a pact to create you and bring you into the world even though she was married to someone else. I'm sorry, but I have no information. It's just speculation on my part."

She smiled at him. "But I'm almost certain I carried you. I held a newborn baby with that white-blond hair of yours. He had a strawberry birthmark on his shoulder. Do you, Deuce?"

"*Sí*," he said hoarsely.

"Ah." She embraced him again. "I thought so."

He didn't know what to say. As he tried to find words, one of the twins stirred. Sparkle picked the infant up and bared her breast. She said, "If this is too painful to watch, maybe you should leave."

He regarded the baby with awe. "He said we could raise them," he said slowly.

Her gaze met his, and she gave him a tiny nod. He added, "He said I could have anything I wanted."

She nodded again.

At that moment, the *Star* rocked violently, shaking the bed, sending Deuce sprawling. Connie Lockheart grabbed Stella and the other baby and landed heavily on her back.

Deuce's badge went off.

"Colvin Pines here. We're under attack! Lunar Security Forces ships are surrounding us. And Earthside ships as well." He started to break up.

"Pines!" Deuce shouted.

"And . . . and, oh, my God, Mr. McNamara. I've just gotten word that Earthside forces are attacking the Moon."

NINETEEN

Changing Woman, who is the Moon, was born of the union of Dawn, the father, and Darkness, who was the Moon's mother.

Changing Woman did not know her true parentage. She believed in her innocence that First Man and First Woman were her father and her mother, and so she loved them dearly.

But she was very different from all the other children alive at that time. Her voice was the voice of the Wind. She could not eat the food of the tribe, but must consume only sacred pollen.

Then one day, the Wind told Changing Woman who her parents were. For a time, she kept the knowledge to herself. But then she became a woman, ritually united with the Sun during her Ceremony of Puberty. Once this had occurred, she became discontented with dwelling upon the Earth.

She said to her foster mother, "You are not my mother." She said to her foster father, "You are not my father."

She left them, journeying to the west and building there a dwelling place. It was similar to the dwelling place of the Sun, which was in the east. After she was settled, she bore twin sons from her union with the Sun. These boys became great warriors and heroes.

Then Changing Woman gave life to the Holy People. She taught them how to control the Wind and the Tempest, and to keep nature's forces in balance. In turn, the Holy People used what she had taught them to create the universe, the

Earth, and the Surface People, whom we know as humans.
So it is that but for Changing Woman, the People would
not exist.

On the bridge, Deuce stared at the viso screens with disbelief. A cluster of white ships with the black crescents of
Lunar Security hurtled toward the *Star* at ramming speed.
They were backed by an equally large contingent of blue
ships with white spheres: the fleet of the Conglomerated
Nations. As they swooped down on the hapless ship, they
fired volleys of pulse cannon and attack lasers.

Earth was attacking *Gambler's Star*.

Deuce was livid. "*Bastardi!* They were on their way here
before I declared war."

Colvin Pines stared at him in horror.

"You did *what*?"

"By accident."

"*O maledetta.*" Angelo, who had waited for him on the
bridge, shook his head head in disbelief. "We're in such
trouble, Deuce."

"They were already on their way," Deuce repeated, infuriated. "They were going to take over no matter what we
said to the DOF representatives. Sit-down, schmit-down.
We were like little veal calves walking into the slaughter-
house."

Terminal A glided up smoothly beside him.

"I know," Deuce said. "You're hot to produce weapons.
Okay, let's do it."

To Angelo and Pines, Deuce said, "There's a machine
inside Mr. Wong that Hunter left me for use on special
occasions. Such as this."

The *Star* shuddered. Pines clasped his hands together,
and said, "Oh, my God, we're all going to die."

Deuce looked expectantly at Terminal A. The robot
stared placidly, and said, "Please come with me, sir."

"I'm going, too," Angelo announced. "The Don don't
go nowhere by himself."

"Look!" Pines cried.

Deuce looked at the main screen. At two o'clock on the
starboard side, a hulking Earthside frigate fired a barrage

of laser torpedoes toward the Moon's surface.

"If they hit one of the domes, it'll probably go," Angelo breathed. "No one's ever tested them against freakin' *weapons*."

"That was stupid," Deuce said. "We shoulda."

"Are there backup systems down there?" Pines asked anxiously. He was bugging Deuce with his high-pitched scaredy-cat voice and the way sweat was beading on his forehead. Deuce wanted to slap him and tell him to act like a man and concentrate on what was happening.

"Backup? Sort of," Deuce replied. "Like, shutting down various tunnels with people in them so other people in other tunnels can survive."

"This is unbelievable," Pines said, wringing his hands. "What about channels? Isn't there some diplomatic protocol to follow?"

Angelo said to Deuce, "You'll be blamed."

"And I care," Deuce said, clenching his fists. He thought about all the friends he had down there. All the people who trusted him. Hell, he even thought about his enemies. No one should have to die like this.

He thought of little Annie Bannany, with whom he had an upcoming dinner date.

"I'm going with Mr. Wong now," he said to Angelo. "We're gonna load some pistols. I want that you should stay and help defend the ship. Use Borgioli tactics with whatever's up and running." He smiled grimly. "Shake 'em and bake 'em, cousin."

"*Sì, Padrino,*" Angelo said.

Deuce cupped his cheek and patted it, then kissed Angelo hard. "If I die, take care of Sparkle and all those babies. Hell, marry her if she'll let you. Unless she scares you too bad."

"She don't scare me," Angelo said, then both men burst into laughter.

"Yeah, well, she'd shoot you instead of herself. You can take that to the bank."

They both laughed harder, exchanged bear hugs, and parted, clapping each other on the back. Then Angelo turned and joined Pines at the window, giving orders to the harried crew regarding defensive strategy of the sitting-duck ship.

The Terminal led Deuce through a maze of passageways, into an elevator, down some stairs. Deuce wondered if anybody would ever be able to find him again.

He wondered if Bernardo Chang was still alive.

Then the Terminal paused before a plain, nondescript door, and said, "Ship located."

The door slid open, and Deuce gawked.

A curved shape approximately the size of his entire apartment rippled into view, then momentarily disappeared. It was very silvery, like hair galvanizer. A bad holo, Deuce decided.

Terminal A walked toward it. It bent away from the robot's body, as if making room for it.

Deuce followed. As the material contracted away from him, he reached out and touched it. The cold burned his fingers.

The rippling continued, then increased, and suddenly, with a strange, melodic hum, it split straight down the middle.

Deuce stared at some kind of matte black chair, and in it, the vague shape of a figure coated with something waxy and gray. The elongated head was enormous. There were no features to speak of.

There was no body to speak of. The waxy, gray stuff had solidified into a flat, saggy shape like a deflated balloon.

"Pilot," said the Terminal.

"Hey, you guys said this blew up. That the ship was destroyed during the explosion."

"Partially destroyed. Much retrieved," the Terminal told him.

"Hunter, you freakin' liar," Deuce muttered.

Then Terminal A started making some *clicks* and *pops* around the chair. Black matte shapes like enormous bullets rose from the deck and fell, rose and fell. Unnerved, Deuce took a step backwards.

Then the bullets stretched and soared into the air, meeting with a rippling band of the galvanizer as it arced across the top of the area like a lightning-fast rainbow.

A hundred round objects clattered to the floor.

"Weaponry," said the Terminal. "More in process."

Deuce bent and picked one up. It was like the object that had made Brigham go away.

"What kind of damage can this do?"

"Transport Earthside freighter, Lazarus Class," the Terminal said.

Deuce whistled.

The Terminal regarded him. It added almost proudly, "More advanced weaponry is being processed."

"Jeez. And what can *it* take out?"

"Sectors of Earthside," it replied. "Large sectors."

Deuce swallowed. Cold fingers tiptoed up his spine as he watched the black things bobble up and down. The galvanizer shot across the top. Larger objects otherwise identical in appearance to the first batch rained down.

He didn't step forward. Didn't touch them.

He wasn't sure he was ready to take out large sectors of Earthside.

The *Star* rocked again.

That is, unless *they* were ready to take out large sectors of the Moon.

Deuce picked one up and examined it. He thought about Jesus and the cup thing.

Then someone thundered behind him, "What the hell is going on here?"

"Hunter," Deuce said, whirling around.

The man looked awful. His face—his own once more—was cut and bleeding. His clothes hung off him.

He staggered forward, and fell.

Deuce ran to him. "I can ask the same thing," he shot back.

"Damn it, boy," Hunter rasped. "I'm gone a few months and this is what happens?"

"How did you get here?" Deuce asked him.

"What? Maybe your first question should be, do I need a doctor?" Hunter gasped as Deuce began a one-handed field examination of his injuries. "Leave me alone."

"How did you get here?" Deuce asked again. "How did you get across enemy lines?"

"Enemy . . . oh, my God, then it's true." Hunter winced. "You did declare war. You *idiot*."

Deuce pressed down on a gaping wound across Hunter's chest, watched Hunter writhe.

"How come you aren't dead?" Deuce demanded. "All those ships, if they wanted to get you, they would have. You led them here, didn't you, Hunter?" Deuce shook him. "Those Earthside ships. Didn't you!"

"Ouch! Damn it, let go of me! Don't be a fool. Do I look like I led them here? Where's a doctor? Where's Shiflett? I need medical attention." He gestured for Terminal A. "Mr. Wong, get over here."

Terminal A glided toward them.

Then suddenly, the ship was hit hard. It rocked to the right. As hundreds of the little round grenades skittered across the deck, Deuce lunged for the black matte chair of the dead pilot. Having only one arm, he thrust out a foot and yelled to Hunter, "Hold on to me."

Hunter did so. His grip was strong for someone so badly injured.

The ship was hit again. Perhaps losing its footing among the grenades, the Terminal skidded across the floor and slammed into the bulkhead. It collapsed in a heap, dozens of grenades landing on top of it, practically covering it.

As soon as the rocking stopped, Deuce hurried over to move the grenades off it and check for damage. Mr. Wong's features were blank and unfocused.

Deuce said, "Terminal A, please respond."

It lay inert.

"What's with this?" Deuce demanded, frantic. "This mechanical shouldn't be this messed up from a hit like that."

"I don't know," Hunter said, groaning. "Is Shiflett aboard?"

"Shiflett's with my wife. And your children," Deuce gritted. "You bastard."

Hunter bit off a chuckle. "Yes, I think I may be a bastard. I'm not sure what I am." He turned his head to look up at Deuce. "And I'm not sure what you are, either."

Deuce looked at him hard. "What's that supposed to mean?"

"You read the Bible, son? Ever heard of Genesis 6:4?"

Deuce said dryly, "*Mi scusi*, I'm Catholic." He didn't have the slightest notion what Genesis 6:4 said.

Gasping, Hunter murmured:

"*There were giants in the earth in those days; and also after that, when the sons of God came in unto the daughters of men, and they bare* children *to them, the same* became *mighty men which* were *of old, men of renown.*"

"Yeah, so?" Deuce said. "What's that, the special Bible verse for the GPL?"

Hunter grabbed Deuce's arm. He said, "It's the special Bible verse for *us*, Deuce."

Deuce stared at him. Hunter's grip slackened. Deuce said, "Could you just speak English for once?"

Hunter groaned, shook his head, and closed his eyes. "Someone carried my children for me before." He opened them. "Carried my son, specifically."

They looked at each other for a long time. Deuce's stomach dropped. His heart was in his throat. "What are you saying to me?" he asked as steadily as he could. "That you . . . that your kid is somewhere and you want . . ."

"I want . . ."

"Me to find him," Deuce said in a rush. He looked away. "You want to say good-bye to him because you're dying, you lying son of a bitch."

There was a long silence. "Yes. I want you to find him so I can say good-bye. If I die." Hunter managed one of his legendary smiles. "Which I won't."

"I've got a onechip says you will," Deuce said cruelly. "Odds are against you."

"Odds are for ordinary men, Deuce. Not for you or me. Not for *us*."

Deuce swallowed hard. There was no resemblance between him and this man. None. But these days, you could look like anyone you wanted to.

"The Moon," Hunter went on. "Right idea, wrong distance. Deuce, I have much bigger plans. And I want you with me.''

Deuce felt as if he were falling into a black hole. What was he saying to him? Why didn't he just say it?

"Because I'm your . . . right-hand man.''

"Exactly.'' Hunter closed his eyes. ''My right-hand man.''

Hunter started coughing up blood. He curled into a fetal position, groaning. Then he began to convulse.

Deuce tapped his comm badge. ''I need a doctor down in—'' He realized he had no idea where he was. ''Trace me!'' he shouted.

Hunter flopped onto his back. His lips were moving. Deuce bent down to listen.

"Main data terminal here,'' Hunter rasped. ''Carry me over to it.''

Carefully, Deuce gathered Hunter up with his one arm, Hunter trying to aid him. Deuce carried him fireman style. The man weighed less than Deuce would have guessed. He was bleeding badly, the blood soaking Deuce's clothes.

"You'd better not die,'' Deuce muttered at him. ''You're going to owe me a fortune in cleaning bills.''

Hunter chuckled. Then he broke into a fit of coughing. He fought the harsh contractions of his body as Deuce staggered forward.

Then Hunter murmured, ''Press the disk by pilot's hand.''

"Hand,'' Deuce said, staring down at the deflated sack of gray waxy stuff. ''You've got a hell of an imagination if you can see a hand, Hunter.''

He scanned it, noticing finally a couple of protrusions on either side of the sack. Hmm, maybe these guys came with more than your standard pair.

He dipped down, trying to keep a grip on Hunter while he looked around for a disk.

There. That had to be it: a small, copper-colored circle protruding from the console before the dead pilot.

Deuce dithered a moment, then tried to press it with his knee. Failed.

"Hunter, I have to put you down,'' he said.

Awkwardly, he draped Hunter across the body of the dead pilot, making a face as the waxy stuff adhered to the back of Hunter's head and body.

He pressed the disk.

Immediately the galvanizer arced overhead. Then some of it detached, whirling around in a circle, going faster, and cascaded into rivulets that pelted Deuce's back and Hunter's upturned face.

"Yeow!" Deuce shouted, startled. He tried to get out of the way, but the stuff was warm and sticky. Within seconds, it coated him from head to toe.

Then he was in . . . a place.

He heard the strangest music; his mouth was full of the taste of . . . berries? Something was kneading the tension out of his muscles, caressing his face; something was moving over him, as if it were searching for things to . . . cure.

Deuce cried. He cried like a little boy from whom everything had been taken: mother, father, lover, children. Hope.

His life.

He heard a voice:

"Deuce McNamara was an orphan. A Moonsider born, and the Moon loves him. But that will not spare him from sorrows."

The warm, sticky stuff washed over him again, then it was gone in an instant, completely gone.

He felt . . . new. He felt different.

He looked down to check on Hunter and lost his balance because he was so astonished: His own left arm was back. The mechanical, replaced?

He felt for the telltale knobby protrusions at his shoulder. There were none.

He flexed his fingers. This was a *real* arm.

Hunter opened his eyes, sat up, and made a face.

"Did you have to lay me on top of a dead man?" he asked.

Deuce only looked at him. Then he said, "It grew back my arm."

"Pretty nifty, eh?" Hunter actually grinned at him. "And that's just the beginning, Deuce. But I'll tell y'all about that later. We've got to get out of here."

He walked toward the doorway. Deuce grabbed his arm.

"This is the crashed alien ship you told me about. You really did build it into the *Star*. But it did not explode."

"I've always appreciated your unwillingness simply to believe me," Hunter drawled. "I mean that sincerely. My guess is it's . . . genetic."

Deuce's throat went dry. "Hunter . . ."

"We'll have time later," Hunter said. He continued walking. "We've got to get out of here, Deuce. I don't want to unleash the weapons we have at our disposal, but I will if I have to. It seems the wiser course is a full retreat."

Deuce stopped. "Hunter, what about the war?"

Hunter waved his arm. "Let the dead bury the dead, Deuce. We have so much to see. To do."

Perhaps he realized Deuce had stopped walking. He turned around, and said, "Deuce, I'm talking about the stars. You have no idea what we can do with this technology."

"Darkside City."

"A means to an end." Hunter shrugged. "I'd hoped to unite these people to help us with the Project, but it's hopeless. They're just people." He clapped Deuce on the shoulder. "Not like us."

"Not like . . . what are you talking about?" Deuce shouted. "I just started a war!"

"It's time to move on," Hunter said. He gazed at Deuce and held out his hand. "You have no idea what we're about to do, Deuce. It's bigger than anything you can possibly imagine."

And for one moment, Deuce felt himself agreeing, felt himself detaching from everything and everybody, and joining Hunter on whatever journey he was about to undertake. Anywhere was better. Anything was better.

But what Hunter was proposing had to be unbelievably wonderful.

And yet, Deuce said, "No."

Hunter blinked.

"We can't leave these people."

"We can't stop a war, Deuce. Believe me, I've tried. My family's tried. It can't be done."

He pointed to the console. "We're going to meet the people who built that, Deuce. In their space. In their universe."

Deuce's heart thundered. Every fiber of his being shouted, *Yes!*

But he shook his head.

Hunter crossed his arms. "I'm taking Sparkle. And all the kids."

Deuce swallowed down the pain. He would be alone. Left behind.

"Can you shuttle me down?" he asked.

Hunter looked shocked. "You really do think you're the Godfather of the Moon."

Deuce was silent.

Hunter sighed, slumped. Looked at the floor.

The silence between them could have lasted a light-year.

"All right," he said finally. "I'll shuttle you down. I'll arm you and you'll make it."

Deuce said, "Bernardo Chang's aboard. He's afraid for his life. I want you to comm him and promise him safe passage, either with you or with me."

"In fear . . ." Hunter nodded. "Because of Clancy. Deuce, I swear I don't know who killed her."

Deuce didn't buy it. "Promise him safe passage."

"Agreed."

"And I want to take Terminal A with me if he can be repaired."

"Drag him over and turn on the disc."

Deuce complied. The platinum sticky stuff coated Mr. Wong's chassis. Terminal A awoke. Deuce was satisfied.

Hunter was clearly dissatisfied. "I was wrong about you, boy," he said. "You're not ruthless enough for space."

The words did not hurt.

They did not.

But it hurt to say good-bye to Sparkle, who walked to him and kissed him long and hard, melting against him.

Hurt to the ends of his hair and his fingernails and his toes. The ache was almost unbearable.

It would never stop.

"If it weren't for the children, I would stay," she whispered. "I swear I would."

He shrugged. Maybe, maybe not. Hunter had wanted her. Now he had her.

Fighting back the hurt, he kissed the foreheads of the babies who were not his. The boy was Daniel, the girl, Star. And there was Stella, nearly two now, with her white-blond hair and her father and mother so dark.

He kissed her, too, breathing in her baby scent.

Hunter stood with his new family as Deuce climbed into the shuttle with Angelo—whose loyalty he could never repay—Moona Lisa, and the Terminal, eerily silent but functioning.

Chang, though summoned, had not shown himself. Deuce hoped he was still alive. Hunter promised to keep looking for him, and to honor his promise not to harm him.

And then, at the last, the woman who called herself Connie Lockheart joined Deuce in the shuttle. She embraced him, and said, "I'm here."

The others watched from the docking bay as Deuce's shuttle pulled away.

Only Hunter waved.

TWENTY

The fighting around *Gambler's Star* was intense. Destroyers and missile frigates threw everything they had at her. Some kind of field protected her as she roared to life, disintegrating the Tinkertoy array as she began to move.

Furiously, the combined forces of the Moon and Earth gave chase, all but ignoring Deuce's little vessel, which was also protected by the same kind of shield as the *Star*.

Alien technology.

Deuce took a breath as the *Star* flashed like a nova, then was nothing more than a shadow that passed between brittle tears.

The dog yipped on Connie Lockheart's lap. The four passengers, three human and one robot, sat abreast in a row, strapped in tight for what would no doubt be a wild ride. On the far left, beside the Kevlite window Deuce looked down at the erupting lunar surface like a stranger in his own land. On the far right, Angelo's head was bowed, as if in prayer.

Then Connie Lockheart, seated beside Deuce, turned to him and said, in a gentle voice, "Let me tell you boys a story."

A beautiful white snow fell upon the tiny village where Kay and Gerda lived as friends. Like all the other children, they would attach themselves to the carts of the people as they glided through the snow, sliding merrily along.

So when a very grand sleigh came into view, Kay tried

*his hardest to grab on to it. Perhaps the passenger—a
mysterious figure dressed from head to toe in white fur—
noticed Kay's mischievous grin and adventurous ways. At
any rate, the figure guided the sleigh in such a way that
Kay, and Kay alone, was able to grab onto it.*

*Snow began to fall, blinding Kay. He tried to let go of
the sleigh, but his hands were frozen in place. He tried to
call for help, but the roar of the snowstorm drowned out
his cries.*

*Then the sleigh sped away from the village, faster and
faster, until Kay found himself flying through the air. They
passed over huge snowdrifts, across frozen lakes, and
above the treetops. Kay thought that he would surely die.*

*At last, the sled slowed to a stop. The driver put down
the reins and stepped from the carriage. The figure was a
beautiful lady, and her clothes were not made of fur, but
of the purest snow. She was the Snow Queen.*

*The Snow Queen imprisoned Kay in a strange land of
howling wolves and screaming black crows. The snow spar-
kled in the daylight, as he slept at the feet of the Snow
Queen.*

*But at night, the Moon rose above him, keeping watch
over him. The sight of the Moon at the end of each frozen
day became for Kay the light of hope.*

*After a long time, Gerda, Kay's best friend, undertook a
perilous journey to save him. Though many times she was
almost defeated, at last she rescued Kay. Until then, the
Moon watched over Kay, willing him to survive another
day so that he might bathe in Her light.*

*To this day, children still look to the Moon to watch over
them through the long, dark night. As Kay was comforted
through the endless winter of his imprisonment, so are children sustained by the Moon's light through the blackness.*

Deuce nodded, sighed, patted her hand. He said, "*Grazie,* eh? It's very beautiful."

He leaned forward to address the Terminal. "Did you
understand that? Did it make any sense to you?"

Mr. Wong—the thing inside him—did not respond.

Angelo frowned and said, "I think it's crashed."

Deuce stared at the blank eyes. *"O, maledetta."*

He glanced back where *Gambler's Star* had last been. It was gone. So no help there.

"Hey, look, here's something. Maybe a RESET button," Angelo observed, tapping something at the base of the robot's head. He pressed it.

"Or the detonator," Deuce muttered.

The three stared at the body of Mr. Wong. It shuddered. The eyes blinked. It slowly looked around.

It said, "Identify comm port."

Deuce said, "Terminal A? Is that you?"

"Identify comm port," it said again.

"Uh." Deuce glanced at Angelo, who shrugged. Connie Lockheart stroked the dog, comforting her, and gave her head a shake.

Deuce said, "Specify."

"The following are comm links for this terminal," the robot said. It went down a list:

"A equals J23, B equals D'inn, C equals !kth, D equals—"

"Stop," Deuce said. "What are these? J23, D'inn?"

The terminal was silent for a moment. Then it replied, "As with Earth. As with Moon."

Angelo stared at Deuce. Deuce stared back.

Connie said, "Corporations?"

"Please specify comm port for access to corporation of choice," the Terminal said.

Deuce brightened. "Good guess. So pick one."

Connie thought a moment. "B."

"B selected," the Terminal said. "D'inn protocol is . . . x, xy, y, x2, x2y, x2y2, y2. Begin."

"Uhhh." Deuce frowned, and said to Angelo, "You got a mini?"

Wordlessly, Angelo fished in his pocket and reached around the terminal, handing the mini to Connie, who gave it to Deuce. He began running the numbers. Shook his head.

Suddenly, the robot said, "Moon. Moon of Earth. We are D'inn."

"Hello," Deuce said, clearing his throat. "I am Deuce."

"Deuce of Moon."

"Yes. And you are?"

"We are D'inn."

"The D'inn Corporation?" Connie asked uncertainly, frowning in confusion at Deuce.

"D'inn. Species."

"You're a species?" she echoed. "That was a list of species?"

"Warning," the Terminal said. "Jumpgate."

"What—"

Deuce touched Connie on the arm and gestured for her to be silent. Jumpgate. That was what Sparkle had been talking about in her trance.

"Okay," Deuce said. "We copy jumpgate. Specify."

"Jumpgate by Earth. By being of Earth. And !kth."

"The Earth declared war on us because of a jumpgate?" Deuce tried.

"Being of Earth. Plus !kth." The robot shook once, hard. Then it said: "Deuce, being of Moon. Being of Earth."

Deuce guessed. "Castle?"

"Correct. Castle of Earth and !kth. !kth deadly species. Invasion. Jumpgate."

"Invading us?" Deuce asked, trading looks with Connie. "Invade Moon?"

"They are invading the Moon right now," Connie said to the robot. "All around us. What do we do?"

The robot droned, "Deadly species. Castle and !kth. Jumpgate."

"Castle's helping some bad species invade us with a jumpgate. Using a jumpgate," Deuce supplied.

"Correct." The robot extended its arm. "Join. D'inn and Deuce of Moon. Halt invasion."

"*O Mamma mia*," Angelo blurted. "This has to be some practical joke of Hunter's."

Deuce shook his head. "He don't joke like this." He extended his arm across Connie to the robot. "Okay, we're joining. So how do we halt the invasion?" He gestured to the raging battle. "You got some special little pebbles like before?"

"Not invasion. Invasion after jumpgate completion."

"Huh?" Deuce peered at the robot.

"This not invasion. This Earth, Moon conflict only. Invasion of !kth after jumpgate."

"What the hell do you mean, this isn't the invasion?" Angelo shouted. "It sure as hell looks like an invasion from where I'm sitting!"

Moona Lisa yipped in response to the shouting, and Connie shushed her. As she petted the dog her hand was shaking.

"This Earth, Moon conflict only," the robot said.

"There's more around the corner," Deuce said slowly. His throat tightened. "It's not even bothering about this freakin' war."

"*O, Mamma mia,*" Angelo breathed, crossing himself.

At that moment, a hulking Earthside carrier appeared on their starboard side. It could have fit two or three *Star*s inside it. Why the Earth, supposedly at peace with itself, had required such enormous battleships had always piqued Deuce's curiosity. Maybe they had always planned to take over the poor little Moon. Talk about your overkill.

He looked at Angelo. "You wishing you'd stayed aboard the *Star*?"

Angelo actually smiled. He moved his shoulders and said, "Hell, no, *Padrino*. I've been waiting for some real action all my life."

"I'm sorry about this," Deuce said to Connie.

She smiled and kissed his cheek. "I'm so proud of you," she said. "I know Maria loved you very much. I can see why."

The carrier picked up speed.

"Uh, Terminal of D'inn? You got something can help us out here?" Deuce asked nervously.

The robot smiled. "Personal name Iniya. Female. Affirmative."

Something pulsed like a rainbow around their tiny vessel as the carrier bore down.

"Oh, how nice. Ah, to meet you," Deuce said distractedly.

The carrier fired; the juice was deflected, but the vessel rocked and and skittered like the ball in a roulette wheel.

Deuce managed to grab the dog as she sailed by, and clasped her against his chest as she struggled frantically.

"Nice to meet you?" Angelo shouted.

The two men began to laugh while the dog barked for all she was worth. Connie just shook her head.

Iniya did not laugh, but her smile grew.

"Shield will not hold," she announced pleasantly. "Destruction of vessel is probable."

"Wanna bet?" Deuce said to her.

They bulleted toward the Moon.

EPILOGUE

From the Captain's Log of Gambler's Star:

We are on our way, and Deuce has no idea of what he has let go: Stella and the twins are indeed his children.

I have become sterile, yet I have every reason to believe that Deuce McNamara is my son.

He, in essence, is my ultimate Connie Lockheart. His seed—my seed—is being carried to a new world, a new universe. He has no idea that scrapings from his fingernails and pieces of hair from his hairbrush yielded sufficient material from which to extract the twenty-three chromosomes that make him, him. But what we are, he and I, I am not sure. I'm not positive we're fully human. My scan was very strange. As was his.

The other twenty-three chromosomes of these three are Sparkle's, and I cannot believe she doesn't know it. There is nothing of Beatrice Borgioli here, although she believes only that Sparkle is the genetic mother of the twins. I'm not sure precisely how she found out, but she knew. Sparkle's mind is so keen, her intuition so honed, that I'm sure eventually she'll feel the truth.

Together, the !kth and I will build the jumpgate. I had hoped Deuce would be there, too, but I saw at the very last—when he refused—that it will be better this way. If something happens to this ship, Deuce can have more children. And the dream will live again.

If he himself survives, and that remains in doubt.

Oh, Deuce, I so wanted to tell you. But I think that in your heart, you do know.

But sacrifice is necessary in these wild times. These !kth are wondrous beings who can offer humanity so much. My name will go down in history as the one who brought them through the gate.

We had attempted to create hybrid beings, watered-down versions of !kth, if you will, using the facilities on their crashed ship. We had hoped that in a few generations they might fully adapt to conditions here sans gate. Jimmy Jackson was a willing participant, but he turned against us. He was colluding with someone to steal the remote terminal by hiding it in his chest. I believe he was planning to hold Stella hostage—in return for what, I do not know.

Nor do I know who he was working with, and that worries me. Someone else knew about the project and was trying to block us. The same person poisoned Dr. Clancy and would have stolen the terminal, except that Mr. Wong took it while she was distracted with her other duties.

I don't know who—or what—those men were who exploded in my office. They told me they were representatives of the Eight Disenfranchised Families, and they were trying to sell me water. At exorbitant prices, I might add.

The jumpgate must succeed. If there are enemies aboard this vessel, we must locate them and exterminate them.

Even if one of them is Bernardo Chang.

We are passing my lucky star, the Gambler, in serene, peaceful space, while my son—if he survives—faces hell.

On this star, the Gambler, I pray for the success of our mission. I pray for the children. I pray for the crew. I pray that Sparkle's mind continues to develop, so that we will have no need of computer interfaces. Through her, we will have a direct link to the !kth.

But most of all, I pray for my boy. My moonchild. I don't know how that old Borgioli woman knew about the Connie Lockheart—Maria must have told her—but she was right:

he is a child of sorrows. May he also be a child of hope.
A beacon for the war-torn Moon.
   God be with you, Deuce McNamara, until we meet again.

Hunter Castle
Aboard ship,
2144.10

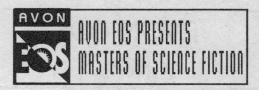

AVON EOS

RISING STARS

Meet great new talents
in hardcover at a special price!

$14.00 U.S./$19.00 Can.

Deepdrive
by Alexander Jablokov
0-380-97636-6

Full Tide of Night
by J. R. Dunn
0-380-97434-7